FIRST

Sound asleep against Claire's shoulder, Daisy let out a sound that was half gurgle, half sigh. Claire gently rubbed the baby's back in small circular motions.

Cole smiled down at the little girl. "I'm afraid Daisy has literally attached herself," he said, referring to the fistful of Claire's hair still twined in one small hand.

"She likes to grab something soft to hold before she goes to sleep. Usually it's the ribbon trim on her baby blanket. . . ."

"Here," Cole said, moving closer. "Let me help get you untangled."

Without waiting for a reply, he carefully began to unwind strands of hair woven through tiny fingers. Claire's breath caught. He was so close she could see individual threads of his jacket, smell the tangy scent of his cologne, feel her pulse hammer. Feel heat radiate from his body. If she moved a fraction of an inch, she would brush against him.

Temptation crooked its evil finger.

What would it be like to lean into him, or be held in his embrace? To savor his hard, masculine strength against her softer, feminine curves? What would it be like, she wondered, to be possessed, totally and completely, by a man such as Cole Garrett?

And what would it be like to be loved?

Glancing upward, her eyes locked with those the color of woodsmoke. Cole now held the rebellious tendril that Daisy had once claimed. Gently he rubbed the shiny, ash-blond strand between his strong, work-roughened fingers. . . .

"Now I understand why Daisy was holding on so tightly."

BOOK YOUR PLACE ON OUR WEBSITE AND MAKE THE READING CONNECTION!

We've created a customized website just for our very special readers, where you can get the inside scoop on everything that's going on with Zebra, Pinnacle and Kensington books.

When you come online, you'll have the exciting opportunity to:

- View covers of upcoming books
- Read sample chapters
- Learn about our future publishing schedule (listed by publication month *and author*)
- Find out when your favorite authors will be visiting a city near you
- Search for and order backlist books from our online catalog
- Check out author bios and background information
- Send e-mail to your favorite authors
- Meet the Kensington staff online
- Join us in weekly chats with authors, readers and other guests
- Get writing guidelines
- AND MUCH MORE!

**Visit our website at
http://www.kensingtonbooks.com**

JUST BEFORE DAYBREAK

ELIZABETH TURNER

ZEBRA BOOKS
Kensington Publishing Corp.
http://www.kensingtonbooks.com

ZEBRA BOOKS are published by

Kensington Publishing Corp.
850 Third Avenue
New York, NY 10022

Copyright © 2002 by Gail Oust
Cover art copyright © Jayne Hinds Bidaut/Grapistock

All rights reserved. No part of this book may be reproduced in any form or by any means without the prior written consent of the Publisher, excepting brief quotes used in reviews.

If you purchased this book without a cover you should be aware that this book is stolen property. It was reported as "unsold and destroyed" to the Publisher and neither the Author nor the Publisher has received any payment for this "stripped book."

All Kensington titles, imprints and distributed lines are available at special quantity discounts for bulk purchases for sales promotion, premiums, fund-raising, educational or institutional use.

Special book excerpts or customized printings can also be created to fit specific needs. For details, write or phone the office of the Kensington Special Sales Manager: Kensington Publishing Corp., 850 Third Avenue, New York, NY 10022. Attn. Special Sales Department. Phone: 1-800-221-2647.

Zebra and the Z logo Reg. U.S. Pat. & TM Off.

First Printing: December 2002
10 9 8 7 6 5 4 3 2 1

Printed in the United States of America

*For Linda Lang Bartell:
a fellow writer,
a valued friend.
Here's to white zin
and chicken quesadillas.
Here's to the good times.*

ONE

Brockton, Michigan
March 1880

"Surely, ma'am, you ain't serious?"

"I see no other choice."

"But, Mrs. Garrett, she ain't fit."

"For goodness sake, Alma! Stop fussing. You're making entirely too much of this," Priscilla Brock Garrett said. "How difficult can it be to care for a five-month-old baby? It's only for a few hours."

Not fit? Claire Sorenson shrank against the nursery wall. Humiliation branded her cheeks a fiery pink. Did Alma Dobbs, the Garretts' housekeeper, really think her incapable of caring for one small infant? Did she honestly believe Claire shouldn't be responsible for anything other than scrubbing floors and washing windows?

Through the partially opened door of Priscilla's bedroom, Claire saw Alma wring her hands in distress. "What will the mister say?"

"I couldn't care less." Priscilla fastened a jet earring in one lobe, then held up a mirror to inspect the effect before inserting the second. "Cole Garrett may be my husband, but he doesn't own me. I can come and go as I please, and I can do what I want without asking his permission. You're forgetting, I'm a Brock—my family founded this town.

He, on the other hand, is nothing more than a lumberjack who happened to get lucky."

Claire wished she could block out the conversation between the two women. It made her uncomfortable. The disdain in Priscilla Garrett's voice whenever she referred to her husband was vicious.

"But, ma'am," Alma Dobbs tried again, her round face worried but determined.

"Enough!" Priscilla snapped "My mind is made up. I've been looking forward to the Howards' party all week. I'm not going to miss it simply because *he* prefers to spend his time in some musty old office." She patted a glossy, brown curl. "Besides, it isn't my fault that the baby nurse picked today of all days to leave in a huff."

"You know I'd stay myself if I could." A defensive note crept into the housekeeper's voice. "It's just that my Harold expects his dinner on the table soon's I get home. He gets downright testy if he has to wait."

"Not another word, Alma. Surely if that girl can scrub floors she can change a diaper. Now if I don't hurry, I'll be late."

Claire heard the clasp of an evening bag snap shut, followed by the swish of silk. She peeked from the nursery and glimpsed Priscilla Garrett attired in a sapphire blue gown that left a generous portion of bare skin exposed. She watched as Priscilla regally descended the staircase, one gloved hand lightly touching the mahogany banister. Alma Dobbs, in her plain gray worsted and starched white apron, followed close at her heels.

Whether Priscilla admitted it or not, Mrs. Dobbs had raised a valid point. Claire couldn't help but worry that Cole Garrett wouldn't be pleased when he returned home to find his precious baby girl cared for by the daughter of the town drunk. The sound of the door opening, then closing, drew her across the room. Pulling aside the frilly curtain, she watched the Garretts' carriage—with Tim O'Brien, their coachman and caretaker, at the reins—roll down the drive and turn onto Elm Street. Moments later, Alma Dobbs, bundled to her chin against the biting March wind until she resembled a pouter pigeon, scurried down the drive and turned in the opposite direction. No doubt the woman was anxious to start supper for Harold, who, from her description, sounded like a tyrant.

But then, Alma had never met Lud Sorenson, Claire's father.

At a gurgling sound, Claire let the curtain drop back into place and went to the crib. She couldn't help smiling at the infant who stared up at her with big, blue eyes. Wide awake after her nap, the baby flailed her tiny arms and legs like miniature windmills.

"Hello, Daisy girl." Claire extended her hand into the crib, pleased when the baby grasped her finger. "Looks like it's just the two of us tonight."

Daisy cooed at the sight of Claire's smiling face above the rail of her crib.

Reaching down, Claire picked the baby up. For a long moment, they regarded each other in solemn silence. A perfect baby, Claire mused. A lump of longing rose in her throat until it threatened to choke her. A perfect baby, a perfect family. A charmed life.

Or was it?

At least she used to think so. Now she wasn't so sure. For a long time she had admired the Garretts from afar. She would use any excuse she could to wander down Elm Street so she could view the progress of the fine new palace belonging to lumber baron Cole Garrett. Square and sturdy, it was a grand house, fit for royalty. Its three stories were crowned with a mansard roof studded with dormer windows. A fanciful tower rose yet another story above the front entrance with windows facing to each of the four directions. Gossips claimed that the lofty perch afforded a magnificent view of Lake Michigan.

The house had been barely completed when Cole surprised everyone in town by eloping with Priscilla Brock.

Both tall and brunette, they made a striking couple, a fairy-tale king and his queen. Their child, Daisy, completed the picture. It wasn't until Claire came into the household to help with the heavy cleaning that she learned that this supposedly ideal family was seriously flawed. Underneath the surface perfection, there was light without warmth. Fire without heat.

Daisy raised a small fist to her rosebud mouth and sucked vigorously. "What's the matter, baby girl? Time for a bottle?" Claire asked.

The time passed quickly. For the remainder of the evening, Claire indulged in a game of make-believe. What harm could there be, she rationalized, in pretending she was the mistress of this magnificent house and that Daisy belonged to her? It was bitter knowledge, knowing she'd probably never have a child of her own. Her father's volatile temper discouraged suitors from calling. Her brother, Nils, also had a reputation for being quick to use his fists to settle a dispute. Men she had met thus far tended to avoid women with troublesome families. The prospect of an adoring husband, children, a decent home—respectability—always seemed just beyond her grasp.

But even so, the dream persisted.

Long after Daisy had been fed, diapered, and put to bed for the night, Claire kept her vigil from a rocking chair in a darkened corner of the nursery. The tall case clock in the foyer struck the hour of eleven, and neither of the Garretts had yet returned home. Surely, she thought, Cole Garrett couldn't still be at his office this late. She wondered if he had surprised his wife by joining her at the dinner party.

Some time later, the baby whimpered and stirred restlessly in her sleep. Immediately, Claire rose and went to the crib. Bending over the rail, she gently rubbed Daisy's back until the baby let out a small hiccup, then sighed and quieted.

"Bad dream, sweetie?" Claire murmured. "Or did you have a tummy ache?"

She started to tuck the hand-embroidered flannel shawl over the baby's shoulders when a door quietly opened downstairs, then closed. Next she heard the muted sound of footsteps on the carpeted steps. She listened, her head to one side, trying to decide if there was one set of footsteps or two. Whoever it was paused just outside the partially opened nursery door.

"Who are you?" a low male voice demanded. "And what the devil are you doing here?"

The barely suppressed fury in the man's voice drove every thought from Claire's mind. She stood frozen in place at the crib side, her hand still clutching the baby's blanket.

"Well . . . ?"

For long seconds, coherent speech deserted her. Then, slowly, she gathered her scattered wits and hazarded a glance over her shoulder. Cole Garrett glared back at her from the nursery doorway. A single gaslight burned in the hallway behind him. Its glow formed a golden halo around his tall, powerful figure. His shoulders seemed to stretch the breadth of the door frame. But it was his anger, more than his sheer physical presence, that caused her mind to stumble over an explanation.

His angry mood shouldn't have intimidated her, but somehow it did. She had grown accustomed to fits of temper in men, had even developed some skill at deflecting them. Garrett's arrogant tone, his peremptory manner, reminded her she didn't belong here. Made her feel guilty for pretending she did. Even though it had just been for a few hours, she felt like an intruder in his fine house. Or, as Mrs. Dobbs had so succinctly stated, she wasn't "fit."

"Speak up, girl," he growled. "Tell me what you're doing here before I summon the police."

"The p-police . . . ?" she stammered. Dear Lord, did he think she was a burglar? And then another, a more alarming, thought occurred to her: did he think she meant to harm the baby? "I'm Claire," she managed to say, hearing and despising the tremor in her voice. "Claire Sorenson."

As he advanced into the room, the nursery seemed to shrink. He was tall, an inch or two over six feet, Claire estimated, and brawny from his days as a logger. He seemed almost overwhelmingly masculine against the backdrop of the dainty, feminine nursery.

He glanced down at the sleeping infant as though needing to see for himself that she was unharmed. Then, reassured, he turned his attention back to Claire. He opened his mouth to speak, but she held a finger to her lips.

"Shh," she whispered.

Cole's dark brows drew together as though silently challenging her authority to issue orders. For a moment he looked as though he might argue the point; then his frown eased as he reconsidered awakening his daughter.

Claire smoothed the shawl over the tiny form, then turned and left the room. At the doorway, she looked back, expecting to find Cole Garrett close behind, but the man remained at the crib side. Though it might have been a trick of the lighting, his expression seemed to soften as he gazed down at the baby. As she watched, he reached out and with infinite tenderness, stroked the infant's rounded cheek. The love and gentleness of that simple gesture brought an ache to her chest.

Cole, his expression now as hard as it had been soft only moments ago, crossed the room and carefully closed the nursery door. "Come with me." Taking Claire by the arm, he half-steered, half-dragged her down the upstairs hallway away from the baby's room. "Now for the last time, kindly explain who you are and what brings you here."

She tugged her arm free. "It isn't necessary to manhandle me, Mr. Garrett."

"Sorenson . . . ?" He studied her long and hard, then his scowl eased. "Now I recognize you. You're Nils Sorenson's little sister."

"That's right." Claire surreptitiously wiped her damp palms on her simple cotton skirt. "You were one of the men who brought Nils home the day of his accident."

"Which your brother blames me for. He's hated my guts ever since." His eyes narrowed with sudden suspicion. "Did Nils put you up to something?"

It was no secret. Everyone in town was aware that Nils blamed Cole for the logging accident that had left him crippled. From Cole's question, she also knew neither Alma Dobbs nor his wife had informed him that she had been hired to help with the heavy cleaning chores. No wonder the housekeeper had been opposed to the idea of Claire caring for Daisy. "My brother has nothing to do with my being here."

Cole rubbed the back of his neck and closed his eyes briefly. "It's been a long day, Miss Sorenson. Just tell me why you're taking care of Daisy in place of her nurse."

"Miss Bartlesby left . . . unexpectedly."

"Damn," he swore softly. "Not another one. That marks the third to leave in five months."

She sensed his weariness, his frustration. "Your wife wanted to attend the Howards' party, and Mrs. Dobbs needed to get home, so they asked me to stay instead."

"Why you, of all people?"

"Mrs. Dobbs hired me to help with the heavy cleaning, floors and such. I . . . um . . . work here two days a week."

He pinned her with a steely gaze. "Then why haven't I seen you here before?"

Nervous under his intense scrutiny, she tucked a strand of ash-blond hair into the loose knot at the back of her head. "Usually you've left for the office before I start in the mornings, and I'm gone before you come home at night."

"What qualifies you as a baby nurse?"

"There was no one else on such short notice." She gave a small shrug.

"The last port in the storm, eh?" he grunted. "God forbid Priscilla should have to miss a social gathering to take care of her own child."

Unsure of how to respond, Claire remained silent. She used the opportunity instead to study him as intently as he had studied her minutes ago. His hair was dark brown, almost black, cut short and parted on one side. An unruly shock fell across his brow. His eyes were a compelling gray, the same soft shade as a dove's. His features reflected his personality. A square jaw revealed determination; the slight bump in his nose attested to a willingness to fight for what he wanted; his beautifully molded mouth could be firm or stubborn. Or sensual. The thought was both unexpected and unnerving. In spite of his well-tailored jacket, his shoulders strained the seams to the point of bursting. Though too big, too muscular, to be considered handsome by conventional standards, he was nevertheless an imposing figure.

And a very attractive one.

"Does your brother know you work for me?" he asked abruptly.

"No," she said. Her gaze wavered.

"He won't be happy if he finds out."

"As long as I give Nils money for drink, he doesn't question where it comes from."

"Your brother has no right to earnings you've worked hard for. Nils has a shrewd mind and a way with figures. Let him earn his own money for booze."

Her head came up with a snap. "What I choose to do with my wages is no concern of yours, Mr. Garrett."

"If anything, Nils should compensate you," Cole continued, ignoring her rebuke. "According to Doc Wetherbury, your brother would have lost his leg to infection if it hadn't been for your vigilance."

All too well, Claire remembered the endless days when she had feared Nils's leg would have to be amputated. The long nights she had spent at his bedside, hoping, praying. The days, weeks, months when he seemed to lose his will to live. Followed by a slow, painful recovery. She cleared her throat, banishing the memories. "Since you won't be needing me anymore, I'll say good night."

"As I recall, you live miles from town. How are you planning on getting home?"

Halfway down the stairs, she paused. "Why, walk, of course. I have two feet."

Shoving his hands in his pockets, he sauntered toward her. "It's nearly midnight. Much too late for a woman unescorted."

"It's kind of you to worry, Mr. Garrett, but I'm perfectly capable of taking care of myself."

"'Kind' isn't a word usually used to describe me." His mouth quirked in a rueful smile. "I'd feel responsible if you didn't reach home safely."

"I'll be fine." She gave him a fleeting smile. "Nothing ever happens here. Brockton is safe as a church."

"Humor me, Miss Sorenson." He dug in his pocket and produced a silver dollar, which he offered to her. "Tim O'Brien, my coachman, should be along soon with Mrs. Garrett. Give him this and tell him I said to take you home."

Claire debated with herself, but the thought of riding home in comfort won over the prospect of a three-mile walk on a cold night. "Very well," she agreed, pocketing the coin, "since you insist."

"I insist. You can wait for Tim in the kitchen."

The first rays of dawn seeped into the kitchen, filling the room with a murky half-light. Claire rubbed eyes that felt gritty from lack of sleep. Her mind felt fuzzy, her throat dry. She shifted in the hard-backed chair and tried to get her bearings. The house was silent except for the distant tick of a clock. She dimly distinguished the outlines of a cast iron cookstove, an oak icebox, sink, and bank of cupboards. She had fought to stay awake while patiently awaiting Tim's arrival with Mrs. Garrett. She had thought she had succeeded. Now she wasn't so certain. She distinctly remembered the hall clock chiming the hour of two. Afterwards she feared she might have dozed off at a crucial moment and missed their return.

Soon Alma Dobbs would be arriving to start her day. Claire would feel like an idiot, having to explain why she sat at the kitchen table. It would be even more embarrassing if Cole Garrett turned out to be an early riser and found her still in his kitchen. The thought mobilized her into action. The chair scraped the pine floor as she hastily scrambled to her feet. Grabbing her jacket, she slipped out the back door and began the long trek home.

Pulling her collar higher against the raw March morning, Claire trudged on, her chin tucked close to her chest. The cold, damp air penetrated the weave of her jacket, chilling her to the bone. Soon she left the town behind. Oak, maple, and sycamore trees lined both sides of the winding dirt road. The wind whipped their branches into a frenzy until they resembled skeletal arms waving at a pearly gray sky. Mounds of snow still lingered on the ground. For Claire, spring still seemed a long way off.

Thoughts of Cole Garrett invaded her mind. She was positive she had made a complete fool of herself last night. Surely, he must think her slow-witted. He, on the other hand, seemed to exert a strange affect over her. She had felt as bashful as a schoolgirl in the throes of her first crush. Standing next to him had caused her tongue to stammer and her knees to knock. Even his scent had been hypnotic. She could still remember the way he had smelled of bay rum, leather, and an indefinable essence uniquely his. But most appealing of all had been the way he had tenderly caressed the cheek of his infant daughter.

Distracted, she nearly stumbled over a rut in the road, but caught herself just in time to prevent an undignified fall. The near-miss forced her to pay closer attention to the ground beneath her feet. She was so tired her footsteps seemed to move independently of her brain. Fool, she berated herself. Idiot! It would serve you right if you had fallen flat on your face. That's what she deserved for mooning over a man. And a married one at that. She quickened her pace, anxious to be home.

At last, she turned off the main road onto a narrow country lane leading to the rented farmhouse she shared with her father and brother. A quarter-mile farther, a frame story-and-a-half house with weathered siding came into view. She headed for the back porch, then noticed her brother, his figure half-hidden behind a small storage shed. She paused, frowning. What was Nils up to at such an early hour?

She approached the shed slowly, taking care not to alert him of her presence. But she needn't have taken precautions. Nils was too intent on his task to notice he was no longer alone. More curious than ever, she studied him in silence. In spite of the cold, Nils was in shirtsleeves. He wielded a shovel in both hands as he industriously transferred a pile of dirt into a hole in front of him. It was obvious that he was burying something. But what?

"Nils . . . ?"

Startled, he nearly dropped the shovel as he spun around to face her. "W-what . . . ?"

Claire knew her brother well enough to recognize guilt when she saw it. Her curiosity evaporated into concern when she noticed his unusual pallor. In spite of the bite of the wind, she saw rings of sweat under his arms. "Nils, are you all right? Are you ill?"

"I'm fine," he snarled. "Get back inside."

Ignoring the order, she went to him. "It's barely dawn. What are you doing out here?"

"None of your damn business." He resumed filling the hole. "You've no right sneaking up on me."

All her instincts screamed that something was wrong, terribly wrong. "Nils, if you're in trouble of any sort . . ."

"Go away!" Using the flat of the shovel, he tamped

down the loose earth with more force than the task called for.

She reached out to touch him, then recoiled, staring in horror at the blood-encrusted sleeve of her brother's plaid shirt.

His expression fierce, Nils refused to look at her.

"I love you, Nils," she said, her voice scarcely a whisper. "You're my brother. You know I'd do anything to help you."

His face set in a murderous scowl, he turned and limped away, leaving Claire to watch in dismay.

TWO

Cole woke early, brimming with purpose and anticipation. He had a busy season ahead of him. Not only was it the busiest, but the most dangerous. The time he loved best. As soon as the last of the ice melted from the rivers and streams, it would be time for the river drive to begin. All winter long, lumberjacks in a half-dozen camps had been cutting hardwood and stacking it on rollaways piled higher than a man could see. Soon men armed with peavey hooks and pike poles would release the logs down the teamsters' rollaways and into the water, and the drive would be in full swing.

But first he planned to visit the camps himself. He wanted to review the scaler's estimates personally and see to it that the logs, as decreed by the federal government, carried his own special stamp. They would be sorted at the end of the drive and sent to the appropriate sawmill.

He already dreaded telling Priscilla of his plan. She wouldn't be pleased at the prospect of his being away. Not that she'd miss him, he knew, but she viewed these chores unbefitting for a man who had attained the status of "lumber baron." Particularly if the lumber baron in question happened to be her husband.

He was slipping the gold links into the starched cuffs of his white shirt when he heard a plaintive wail from the nursery. Damn, he swore softly. Where the hell was Miss Bartlesby, the child's nurse? Then he remembered that the

Sorenson woman had told him the baby nurse had left after a tiff with Priscilla—just like the others before her. What the hell did Priscilla do to send these women packing without so much as a by-your-leave?

Daisy continued to wail, her cries growing lustier by the minute. Cole let out a frustrated sigh. And where the hell was Priscilla? Couldn't the woman attend to the needs of her own child just once? Granted, Cole didn't know much about babies, and even less about motherhood, but it seemed unnatural for a woman to be so disinterested in her own offspring.

No doubt Priscilla had returned late from the Howards' party and intended to sleep until noon. The fact that Miss Bartlesby was no longer in their employ seemed to have escaped her memory. And the housekeeper—he flicked open his pocket watch and groaned—wasn't due for another twenty or thirty minutes. His faint hope that Daisy's crying would awaken her mother failed to materialize. His mouth set in a tight line, Cole abandoned his attempt at dressing.

Annoyed and more than a little frustrated, he pushed open the door to his wife's adjoining bedroom—a door he had opened only once before, shortly after their marriage when he had been foolishly optimistic that they could make things work. He was surprised to find the door unlocked. Not that a simple lock would have kept him out if he'd been determined to enter. Harsh words formed as effective a deterrent as a stout lock. Harsh words and strained silences. God knew, he and Priscilla suffered more than their share of both. And that, suffice it to say, had been the sum total of all they shared during their miserable year together.

Cole paused on the threshold of Priscilla's room and allowed his eyes to adjust to the dimness. A pale spear of light shone through the narrow crack in the heavy brocade draperies. Without even glancing toward the bed, he strode across the room and yanked open the drapes. He turned, braced for the inevitable angry volley from Priscilla.

Silence greeted him.

And an empty bed.

His brows drew together in a scowl. The bed hadn't been slept in. The heavy satin coverlet had been neatly turned down; the linen sheets remained crisp and unwrinkled. His scowl deepened. "What the hell . . . ?"

Had she made good her threat to leave? How like Priscilla to think only of herself and abandon her child. She had made no attempt to disguise the fact she was unhappy. That she loathed the sight of him. He possessed none of the traits she admired in a man. She considered him brash, uncultured, a ruffian. Their marriage had been a disaster from the beginning. And he had no one to blame but himself.

Blind ambition had lured him into a loveless union. He suffered from a driving need to prove himself. Since boyhood he had scrambled to rise above his humble origins. To show the world he was smart, resourceful, and ultimately successful. No hours were too long, no task too difficult. No risk too great. He had accepted jobs no one else dared to do. Marrying the daughter of Leonard Brock, the town's mayor and its most upstanding citizen, cemented his social standing. The match between himself and Priscilla polished his lackluster reputation and added a gloss of respectability. Thanks to Leonard Brock's generosity, the liaison with Priscilla also brought with it deeds to prized tracts of timber and the financial backing to expand his mill.

Curiously, or maybe not so curiously after all, Priscilla's desertion brought no sense of loss. Instead, Cole experienced a strange sense of freedom, as though a heavy burden had been lifted. Daisy's shrill cry, interspersed with little hiccuping sounds, brought him back to the present. He would have to deal with Priscilla's absence later. Right now there were more pressing problems.

Immediately upon entering the nursery, he caught a strong whiff of ammonia. His nose wrinkled automatically at the smell. A feeling of dread washed over him. How was it, he wondered, that he could face a log jam with less trepidation than one tiny baby? He advanced into the room, feeling like a marauding giant amid the dainty trappings.

At the sight of his face above her crib, Daisy stopped crying at once. Cole found himself responding to her smile. It was impossible to remain indifferent to such an enthusiastic greeting.

"How can one sweet baby girl cause such a stench?" he pondered aloud.

Daisy let out a loud squeal in reply. She kicked her legs with glee, the movement stirring the air and emphasizing her need for a dry diaper.

Cole looked around helplessly. Now what the hell was he supposed to do? He consulted his pocket watch again, but its hands hadn't progressed significantly since the last time he had looked. Surely the unpleasant task could wait until Mrs. Dobbs's arrival. The woman wouldn't refuse. Or would she? He dismissed the possibility with a shrug. If she raised any objections, he'd simply offer her a substantial increase in salary. Why, she'd probably be delighted to take over the job of baby nurse until another could be found. In the meantime, he'd have his secretary contact employment agencies in Detroit and Chicago. Feeling proud of himself for having the situation under control, he half-turned from the crib.

Daisy signaled her displeasure with a scream that echoed throughout the house.

With a sigh of resignation, Cole leaned over the crib. "All right, all right," he muttered under his breath. "You don't have to be a tyrant."

Daisy sniffed, once, twice, then quieted, gazing up at him with trusting blue eyes.

He ran a hand through his hair. "How hard can it be to change a diaper? Women do it all the time."

Ignoring Daisy's howls of protests, he began searching the nursery, rummaging through drawers. He let out a grunt of satisfaction when he came upon a pile of neatly folded flannel rectangles. His satisfaction was short-lived. Snatching one from the top, he eyed it with growing uncertainty. "Fine," he muttered crossly. "Simple as rolling off a log."

Alongside the crib once more, he gritted his teeth and shoved the infant's flannel wrapper up above her waist, then frowned in confusion. The lower portion of the baby's torso was encased in what appeared to be some sort of rubber drawers. But not even the waterproof contraption could contain the amount of moisture Daisy had managed to produce overnight. In addition to the wrapper, the crib sheet underneath was soaked. Both would have to be changed, but hopefully Mrs. Dobbs could handle that hurdle later.

Forcing himself to breathe through his mouth, he unfastened the rubber drawers and tossed it aside. Next, he gamely unpinned the sodden cloth diaper. "No offense, Peanut, but at the moment you're anything but fresh and sweet like your namesake."

Apparently not the least bit insulted, Daisy sent him a beatific smile that warmed his heart. Cole found himself grinning back at her. Lifting her up, he held her against her chest so that he could place the clean diaper in the dry part of the crib. His smile quickly faded as he realized his tactical error. He swore silently as he felt dampness from the baby's wrapper saturate his freshly laundered shirt.

Gingerly, he laid the baby on the folded cloth rectangle. All that remained was to fasten the diaper, and the venture could be tallied a success. His confidence gained momentum as he reached for a safety pin. He bunched two ends of the diaper together and was about to insert a pin when Daisy wriggled, twisted, and flipped over.

"Hold still, you little worm," Cole warned, turning her onto her back again. He aligned the edges of the diaper once more, but an uncooperative Daisy rolled in the opposite direction. The sharp point of the pin jabbed into Cole's thumb.

"Damn!"

His loud oath startled them both. Daisy stopped wriggling and stared up at him, her blue eyes filled with reproach.

"Sorry, kid," he murmured, wondering how well infants understood a grown-up's language. He made a mental note that in the future he'd watch what he said around her. He hated the notion of a dainty little girl spewing the vocabulary of a lumberjack.

His jaw clenched with renewed determination, Cole struggled to conquer the diaper dilemma. Changing a diaper was definitely not a job for dawdlers. Or the faint of heart. By the time it was fastened to his satisfaction, he was ready to concede that the task called for a certain finesse. His respect grew for the baby nurses who devoted their lives to caring for these tiny, wiggling scraps of life.

Not bad for his first time, he congratulated himself as he stepped back to admire his handiwork. Not as precisely fitted as before, but all in all, not bad.

Daisy started to fuss anew. Making loud smacking noises, she tried to cram her entire little fist into her mouth.

Cole groaned and rolled his eyes toward the ceiling. It wasn't enough that she was dry—now the kid was hungry? He didn't have the faintest notion what toothless babies ate for breakfast. Didn't Daisy know he had a business to run?

From downstairs, he heard the back door open and close and offered a prayer of thanksgiving. Finally! Alma Dobbs had arrived. He had already faced enough challenges for one morning. He'd gladly let the housekeeper cope with the demands of one small child. Picking Daisy up, he hurried downstairs.

Alma Dobbs had removed her heavy coat and was busy feeding scraps of kindling into the wood-burning stove. Her eyes widened in surprise when she looked over her shoulder and found Cole behind her with Daisy on one hip. "Why, Mr. Garrett," she exclaimed. "Is anything wrong?"

"I need you to take care of Daisy," he said without preamble.

"B-but, Mr. Garrett," she sputtered. "I ain't no baby nurse. I don't even like kids."

"I'll gladly pay whatever you ask for your services. Just take care of her until I get home." Before she could offer further objections, he thrust the baby into her arms.

In the process of transferring the baby into Alma's care, the loosely fastened diaper slid off and landed with a soft *plop* on the kitchen floor.

Cole took one last look at the offending piece of flannel, then turned and fled upstairs to change his damp shirt.

"What the hell do you mean, boy, she didn't come home last night?" Leonard Brock thundered. The two men glared at each other across an expanse of polished mahogany.

Cole clamped his jaw so tightly it ached. He had made the visit to his father-in-law his first order of business. It would have been cowardly not to. Even so, under Brock's accusing stare, he felt as fidgety as a five-month-old baby during a diaper change.

"If she's not home, where the devil is she?" The rising color in the older man's face was a reliable indicator of his displeasure.

Cole crossed one leg over the other. "Priscilla never returned from the Howards' dinner party. Her bed hadn't been slept in when I checked this morning."

"If she's run off, boy, it's all your fault."

Cole bit back a sharp reply. Naturally, Brock would blame him for Priscilla's disappearance.

"Should have known better than to assume you'd know how to treat a lady. Priscilla tried to warn me you were no better than a common 'jack. I should have listened." Brock slammed his meaty fist down on his desk with such force that a pen dropped out of its holder and rolled across the blotter. Picking it up, he hurled it across the room.

"I thought perhaps, sir," Cole kept his tone even with effort, "you might know where she is."

"As you well know, Priscilla is not in the habit of confiding in me. She's headstrong, always has been, even as a girl. Takes after me in that regard." His voice carried an unmistakable note of pride.

"The fact remains, sir, that Priscilla has disappeared. People are bound to find out, start asking questions. I just thought you might like to make a few discreet inquiries as to her whereabouts."

Brock heaved his ponderous girth out from behind his desk. Hands clasped behind his back, head bent in thought, he circled the room. "We've got to come up with a plan, boy, or we'll both be laughingstocks."

"Yes, sir." For once he and his father-in-law were in total accord. "I wanted to see how you preferred to handle the situation."

"For the time being, just keep your damn mouth shut. Don't say a word to anybody about your wife's disappearance. You know, don't you, this entire affair will reflect poorly on you."

His expression stony, Cole brushed a fleck of lint from his trousers. He was tempted to remind the man that his daughter had disappeared, probably with another man. This entire situation was *her* doing, not his.

"Word is bound to leak out." Brock continued to prowl the perimeter of the room. "Who knows of this besides you and me?"

"I haven't spoken to a soul, but Alma Dobbs, the housekeeper, is sure to set tongues wagging when there's no sign of Priscilla."

"Tell her anything, but keep her quiet. While you're at it, you'd better make it convincing. The woman's worked for the family for the past ten years. Tell 'er Priscilla's off visiting a friend. That she decided on the spur of the moment. If all else fails, offer to buy her silence."

Cole grunted. "Money seems to be your favorite way of handling problems."

"Worked with you, didn't it, boy?" Brock pinned Cole with his glacier-green eyes. "Didn't hear you complain none when I upheld my part of our bargain."

At the reminder, Cole felt an angry burn spread across his cheekbones. *A bargain with the devil. And the biggest mistake of my life.* The thoughts flitted through Cole's mind, but he kept his face carefully schooled. "If you recall, I also upheld my end of the agreement." Cole rose to his feet.

Brock returned to his desk. The burgundy leather chair creaked in protest when he lowered his massive frame into its seat. "I'll ask around, see what I can find out. In the meantime, don't say or do anything until you hear from me. Keep your mouth shut if you know what's good for you. Understand, boy? No better fodder for gossip than a cuckolded husband."

Once in his office at the sawmill, Cole busied himself with work. It was dusk when he finished totaling a column of figures in a ledger. He trusted his timber cruisers to give an accurate estimate of board feet, but liked to check the sums personally. Leaning back in his chair, he rubbed his eyes with a weary hand. He was looking forward to riding out to the lumber camps. At times he actually missed the physical labor that lumbering entailed. The bunch and release of muscle when wielding a crosscut saw. The tired ache after a day loading logging sleighs for their trips to the riverbank. Visiting the camps also served another purpose: they reminded him how far he had come. As a lad he had started out as a cook's helper, a "cookee," as they were commonly called. Today he was among the breed known as lumber barons.

Snapping the ledger shut, he replaced it in a locked cabinet, extinguished the light, shrugged into his coat, and left the building. Snowflakes drifted from a sullen sky as he mounted his horse, a handsome bay, and headed toward home. For the better part of the day, he had managed to keep his mind off Priscilla and her disappearance. Now, however, she returned to plague his thoughts. It was odd, he mused, that he had received no word from her father. But perhaps if Priscilla disappeared with a lover, she didn't want to be found.

Then he brought himself up short. Priscilla might have already returned. This very moment she could be at home dressing for dinner. How would she explain or justify her absence? And what would he say to her? That he was happy to see her? If he was honest, he'd tell her he was sorry she had bothered to return.

That a secret part of him hoped she had left forever.

Glancing up at the dark sky, he realized it was later than he thought. Once again, the hours had gotten away from him, a habit he had fallen into. The more time spent at the mill, the less time spent enduring Priscilla's litany of complaints. He turned up Elm Street and saw the windows of his house ablaze with light. His gut tightened with dread.

"Evenin', Mr. Garrett." Tim O'Brien stepped out of the carriage house at the rear of the property to take the reins.

"Evening, Tim." Cole absently returned the greeting.

"Looks like we're headin' for a coupla inches afore mornin'."

"Typical Michigan weather." Not in the mood for idle chatter, Cole swung down from the saddle, headed toward the house, then turned back with a half-formed question lurking at the back of his mind.

"Somethin' wrong, Mr. Garrett?"

It occurred to Cole that Tim had driven Priscilla to the Howards' last night. Had he really taken her there? Or had he taken her to meet a lover instead? If so, Cole wasn't sure he really wanted to know the sordid details. "No," he muttered, aware of the coachman's veiled scrutiny. "No, nothing's wrong."

Leaving the bay in his coachman's capable hands, he jogged up the back steps of the house and pushed open the kitchen door, prepared to find Alma Dobbs. He stopped dead in his tracks when he found Claire Sorenson instead.

"You? Again? Where the blazes is Mrs. Dobbs?"

Claire stopped shoveling pabulum into Daisy's open mouth long enough to glance over her shoulder. "You're letting in cold air."

And so he was. Cole realized that he was standing like the village idiot with the door wide open. He closed the door with more force than necessary and saw Claire flinch at the sharp sound. He supposed he should apologize, but didn't. He was in ill humor, and didn't feel inclined to pretend otherwise. This was his house, after all, and he could do as he pleased.

Claire resumed feeding the baby, her face carefully composed.

He tugged off his gloves and tossed them on the table, where they landed with a loud smack. Next he unwound the wool muffler from his neck and stuffed it into his pocket. "Finding you in my house is a bit unsettling. At the risk of repeating our conversation of last night, what are you doing here?"

"I'm feeding Daisy." As if to demonstrate the obvious, she spooned pabulum into the child's tiny mouth, which opened like a hungry bird's.

Cole clung to his control by a thread. "I specifically requested that Mrs. Dobbs stay and care for the baby until more suitable arrangements can be made."

"Mrs. Dobbs was unable to stay." Claire wiped cereal from the baby's chin with a cloth. "She said her husband, Harold, demands a hot dinner on the table promptly at six o'clock. Knowing you often work until quite late, she sent Mr. O'Brien to fetch me to watch Daisy until your return."

He shrugged out of his coat and threw it over the back

of a chair. "Alma Dobbs had no right to do any such thing without first asking my permission."

"Perhaps Mrs. Dobbs assumed you wouldn't mind. At any rate, she's aware how fond I am of Daisy." Her gaze averted, she scraped cereal from the edge of the bowl. "I, ah, I'd be happy to care for her—at least until you can find someone else."

"That won't be necessary," he said curtly. "I've already wired agencies in Chicago and Detroit for an experienced baby nurse. Mrs. Dobbs can fill in until Miss Bartleby's replacement can be found."

She turned around to look at him, her face alight and eager. "I've had a lot of experience around babies and small children."

"Really," he said, his tone skeptical. He noticed for the first time that she was quite pretty, especially when animated, as she was now.

She nodded. "When we lived in Saginaw, I looked after the children of the mill foreman when his wife took sick. I'm sure Mr. Johnson would gladly give me a good reference if I asked."

"It's not that I don't think you're capable . . ."

"But . . . ?"

Dammit, he swore under his breath. Did the girl need him to spell it out? "Look, Miss Sorenson, a professional baby nurse must meet certain requirements."

"I see." She very carefully spooned cereal into the baby's awaiting mouth. "Exactly what qualifications are you looking for?"

Cole ran a finger around the collar of his shirt. Was it hot in this kitchen, or was it just him? "Besides experience, a candidate must possess a high school education."

"I finished at the top of my class. You can see my diploma if you don't believe me."

The hopeful tenor of her voice tugged at his conscience. He reminded himself he had no personal grudge against the girl. She seemed decent, hardworking, but that didn't erase the type of family she came from. He wanted Daisy surrounded by only the best. Clearing his throat, he forged ahead. "In addition to experience and education, the woman hired must be of sound moral character. She must come from an upstanding family with strong values and principles."

She slowly rose to her feet, her face pale, her chin raised and determined. "Thank you for the explanation. I can see now that I'm not the sort you want."

"I'm sorry, too, but you forced me to be blunt."

"Yes, perhaps I did. How foolish of me." Crossing the kitchen, she removed a worn woolen jacket with frayed cuffs and patched elbows from a peg near the door. "No one can fault you for wanting to provide the best for your child."

Cole watched her prepare to leave with a heavy sensation in his chest. At the moment, he didn't like himself very much. When had he turned into the worst sort of snob? he wondered. He felt even more miserable when he glimpsed the sheen of tears in her silver-blue eyes. He shoved his hands into his pockets. "Miss Sorenson . . . Claire," he began hesitantly.

"No need to apologize, Mr. Garrett. I realize I overstepped my bounds, but," she gave a small shrug, "what can you expect from the ignorant daughter of the town drunk?"

Cole studied the floor. He had handled the situation poorly. He viewed himself as straightforward, even brusque at times, but never intentionally cruel. Still, he could hardly offer a woman of her background an important position right here inside his home. He thought of Tim O'Brien and ignored the twinge of conscience at his hypocrisy.

It was one thing to employ people like the Sorensons in his sawmill, or in his household to help with the heavy chores, but dammit, he refused to lower his standard because a slip of a girl looked at him with reproach in her shimmering-blue gaze.

Daisy had observed the exchange between the two adults from her high chair with a look of bewildered innocence. No longer happy that her dinner had been interrupted, her cherub's face puckered and she started to wail.

"You might want to give her a little applesauce after you finishing feeding her the cereal," Claire suggested as she buttoned her jacket.

Daisy still needed feeding? Cole's startled glance swung from Claire to the baby just as the child rubbed a tiny fist over her mouth, smearing cereal over her face and into her wispy gold curls.

Claire's hand was on the doorknob when she paused to look at him over her shoulder. Cole steeled himself against an angry backlash, or worse yet, teary recriminations. He could hardly blame her if she wanted to heap abuse on his already battered conscience. "Is there something more you wish to say?"

She met his look steadily. "When you've finished feeding Daisy, she'll need her diaper changed."

His expression blank, he swiveled to look at the unhappy, cereal-smeared infant. A distinctly pungent odor emanated from the direction of the high chair. With a groan, he realized his mistake. But it was too late. Claire Sorenson had already left.

THREE

The snow began to accumulate in earnest as Claire made her way down the county road leading out of town. Wind gusted out of the north, cold and biting. Turning up her collar, she burrowed her chin into the knit scarf wound around her neck and quickened her pace. If she walked fast enough, maybe by the time she got home she would forget her humiliating conversation with Cole Garrett. A cauldron of emotions—anger, hurt, embarrassment, shame—simmered inside of her. Remembering the way he had arbitrarily dismissed her offer to act as nursemaid brought a rush of blood to her cheeks.

She had been foolish to offer her services, even on a temporary basis. She should have guessed Cole would refuse, should have been prepared for the sharp sting of rejection. It shouldn't have come as a surprise, shouldn't hurt. But it did. All her life she had been made to feel that she was never quite as good as others. Respectability always eluded her. No matter how hard she tried, how hard she worked, it never seemed to be enough. People tended to judge her by her father's, and occasionally her brother's, actions. Cole, it seemed, was no exception.

Her family had constantly moved from town to town. Ludvig "Lud" Sorenson would find work in one of the many lumber camps throughout the state. The rest of the family would find a place to rent on the outskirts of the nearest town. Trouble would soon follow, usually in the form of drunken brawls. Then, they'd pack up and repeat the cycle elsewhere. Claire had gone to a half-dozen different schools, and by sheer perseverance finally managed to graduate. The Sorensons never remained in one town long enough to become part of it, to make friends or be accepted. Her mother was dead now, but the die had been cast, the pattern set.

Until Cole had turned down her offer, she hadn't realized how much she wanted his approval. Ever since coming to Brockton, she had admired him from afar. Like her, he, too, had come from humble origins, yet he had made something of his life. He was prosperous, successful, well-respected in the community. He wasn't the type of man who relied on good fortune. Cole Garrett made his own luck. She had placed him on a pedestal only to discover he was only too human.

She halted abruptly alongside the road and blew out an angry breath. In a heartbeat, Cole Garrett had swept away her usual calm. She rarely lost her temper. Over the years she had learned not to become upset about things over which she had no control. Yet right now, she wanted to scream in sheer frustration. What gave that man the right to make her feel subservient? To insult her? And even more galling, she had allowed him to do it. She had sat meek as a lamb while he informed her she wasn't good enough to take care of one small baby girl. He had politely but firmly called her ignorant, low-class, and incompetent. Well, he was wrong. She was every bit as good as some baby nurse from a fancy agency in Chicago or Detroit. If Cole Garrett got down on his knees and pleaded with her to take care of Daisy, she'd throw the request back in his handsome face. Drawing in a calming breath of cold night air, she proceeded on her way.

Upon reaching the farmhouse, she was surprised to find a light burning in the kitchen. Since it was Friday, she had expected both her father and brother to be frequenting the saloons near the riverfront. Nerves coiled in the pit of her stomach. If Pa was home, he'd be unhappy dinner wasn't ready. After brushing the snow from her jacket and stomping the snow from her feet, she cautiously pushed open the kitchen door and stepped inside.

Nils sat at the kitchen table, hunched over an almost-empty glass. A whiskey bottle stood nearby. He didn't look up when he heard her enter.

Claire eyed him warily. She hadn't forgotten the last time she had seen him. Or the blood-stained shirt. Pulling off her gloves and scarf, she stuffed them into her jacket pocket. "I didn't expect to find anyone home."

Nils grunted a reply, drained his glass, then refilled it.

Claire gave her brother a sidelong glance as she unfastened her jacket. An icy trickle of unease slithered down her spine, making her shiver. Nils preferred to do his drinking in the company of others, not at the kitchen table of a farmhouse miles from town. "Are you hungry?" she asked to break the taut silence.

"No," he snapped.

"Let me fix you supper." She hung her jacket from a coatrack beside the door. "There's some ham left over, and I could fry up some potatoes."

"No! How many times do I have to tell you I'm not hungry?" Raising his glass, he took a long swallow. "This, here, is the only supper I need."

Claire sank down next to him at the scarred pine table. Worried, she caught her lower lip between her teeth. The pale glow of a wall-mounted kerosene lamp made his complexion appear waxy, sallow. Nils had always been considered the more striking of the two siblings. His Nordic heritage was clearly evident in his flaxen-blond hair and vivid blue eyes. She, on the other hand, favored her English mother. Her hair, though also blond, was ash-toned, her eyes a somber blue-gray. When it came to personality, they differed as well. Nils, at least before his accident, had been confident, outgoing, while she tended to be quiet and reserved. Even with their differences, they had once been close. Now, they were more like strangers.

"Nils," Claire began tentatively, trying to bridge the gap. She couldn't ignore the feeling that something was wrong, terribly wrong.

"What . . . ?" Raising his head, he regarded her through bloodshot eyes.

"You look terrible," she blurted. Before the logging accident a year ago, he had turned female heads every time he strutted past. His once-jaunty grin had been replaced by a sullen downturn of his mouth.

"Thanks, Sis." He raised his glass in a mock toast. "Just what I needed to hear."

"Nils, it's obvious that something is bothering you." Uneasiness gnawed at her. He still hadn't explained what he had been doing when she had returned from the Garretts' that morning. "Does it have anything to do with what you were burying behind the shed?"

"Quit worrying. I can take care of myself."

He went for the bottle, but she moved it just beyond his reach. "There was blood on your shirtsleeve. And don't try to tell me any different."

Avoiding her gaze, Nils rolled the tumbler between his palms. "Was there? I hadn't noticed."

"Don't lie to me. I know dried blood when I see it."

"Why are you making such a fuss over nothing?"

"Why are you avoiding my questions?" she countered.

Before she could stop him, he lunged for the whiskey bottle and poured himself another drink with hands that visibly trembled. "My friends and I shot a deer last night. I buried the entrails so the wild animals couldn't get at them. There," he sneered, "are you satisfied?"

Claire sighed. The explanation sounded plausible. Deer were plentiful in Michigan. People often used them to stock their larder. Yet, her unease persisted. "Good," she said at last. "Nothing Pa likes better than roast venison. Where did you put the meat?"

Nil's expression turned mulish. "There isn't any."

"I see . . ." Claire kept her voice steady. "And why not?"

He lurched to his feet so abruptly that his chair nearly toppled over. "Why all the goddamn questions?"

"Because you're my brother. I care about you."

Her answer seemed to knock some of the wind from his sails. He shoved an impatient hand through his hair, then rolled his eyes toward the ceiling. "I owed my friends some money, so I let them take the whole damn deer. Now, Sis, is the inquisition over?"

"Nils, I never meant . . ."

He didn't give her a chance to finish her sentence. Snatching the half-empty bottle of whiskey from the table, he grabbed his coat and limped out of the house, slamming the door behind him with enough force to rattle the dishes in the cupboard.

Claire sat where he had left her for a very long time. She couldn't get rid of the feeling that he wasn't being honest with her. But what was he hiding?

Claire peered through a frosty windowpane. Last evening's snowfall had created a winter wonderland. Every branch and bough was iced with a fluffy confection of white. The sun sparkled from a bright blue sky, making the countryside shimmer with a brilliance that was almost blinding. Sipping her cup of coffee, she immersed herself in the beauty and serenity of a new day.

"Are you just goin' to spend the whole day standin' around, or are you goin' to fix a man his breakfast?" Yawning, Lud Sorenson ambled into the kitchen.

Her solitude shattered, Claire turned away from the window to pour her father's coffee. "Morning, Pa."

Lud sank heavily into a chair at his customary place at the table, a thick mug cradled between hands callused and scarred by a lifetime spent in lumbering. In his younger days, Lud Sorenson had been a strapping figure of a man, but years of heavy drinking had whittled away his once-sturdy build until flesh hung loosely on his large frame. A spidery network of purple veins across the bridge of his nose also attested to his fondness for liquor.

Claire cracked eggs into a skillet, careful not to break the yolks. Gravy bubbled in another pan on a nearby burner. Using a dishtowel folded into a thick pad, she removed a pan of biscuits from the oven. Every day of the week, with the exception of Sunday, Lud Sorenson insisted on a hearty breakfast. The habit undoubtedly was a holdover from his days in a lumber camp where a good cook was considered king. She suspected breakfast was often his only decent meal.

"Breakfast's almost ready," she said, refilling her father's coffee cup before he could ask.

Nils appeared moments later, his shirt buttoned haphazardly, his blond hair sticking out around his head like tufts of straw. "Dammit, Claire," he grumbled, "do you have to clang pots and pans? My head's about to split in two."

"Sorry," Claire murmured.

Nils helped himself to coffee, then sat down next to his father and propped his head in his hands.

"Hangover, eh?" Lud slurped his coffee, then grinned slyly when Nils winced. "Serves you right for drinkin' the whole damn bottle and not sharin' with yer old man."

Nils closed his eyes briefly. "I needed it more than you did."

As Claire piled generous slices of ham on a platter, she wondered why Nils had needed an entire bottle of whiskey to dull his senses. What sort of trouble was he in? Or was he still brooding over the accident that had left him a cripple? That's when he had first started to drink, but lately the problem seemed to be worsening.

"Hurry it up, girl. I'm near to starvin'."

"Sorry, Pa."

She set the food on the table, and the men dug in without waiting for her to join them. She took a biscuit and added a small piece of ham to her plate. The only sound in the room was the clink of cutlery and the scraping of plates.

Silence at mealtime was yet another carryover from logging camps, where meals were consumed in strict silence. Her father insisted upon the same practice at his own table, a lesson Claire learned at a young age. As a small child, she had often forgotten and been sent from the table hungry.

His breakfast finished, Lud pushed his plate away and signaled for Claire to refill his empty cup. "There was quite a bit of commotion in town last night. Quiet little Brockton will never be the same. Too bad you missed it."

Claire looked at her father expectantly. Something in his voice snared her full attention. "What kind of commotion?"

"Yes, sirree, it was quite a show." Lud slouched back in his chair and picked his teeth with a thumbnail.

Claire cast a glance at her brother, but Nils seemed to be concentrating on the worn checked tablecloth. "Are you going to tell us, Pa, or keep us in suspense?"

Lud took his time answering, relishing his news like a dog does a juicy bone. "Wouldn'ta believed it if I didn't see it with my own two eyes."

Claire leaned forward. "What did you see, Pa?"

"Wasn't just me, girl. Half the town saw Mr. Cole Garrett paraded down Main Street in handcuffs."

Handcuffs? Claire felt as though she had been turned into an ice statue. Even her heart seemed to freeze inside her chest. Thinking was difficult, speech impossible.

Nils raised his head. "What the hell happened?" he asked in a strangled voice.

"Takes a lot out of a man to be marched through the center of town like a common criminal. Somethin' like that's a blow to a man's pride," Lud smirked, scratching his chest. "And that ain't the half of it."

A day that had started peaceful and serene suddenly seethed with turmoil. Claire cleared her throat, already dreading the answer to her question. "Why was Mr. Garrett under arrest? What did he do?"

"Murder." Lud grinned at his offspring over the rim of his speckled enamel cup. His faded blue eyes held a malicious gleam.

"Murder . . . ?" Claire repeated, unable to keep the horror from her voice. She feared she would be violently ill. The food she had just consumed threatened to rise in her gullet. Cole Garrett might be a ruthless businessman, and insist on only the best when it came to his wife and child, but she didn't believe for one minute he was a vicious killer.

Nils got to his feet, his movements stiff and jerky. He limped to the window, hands clasped behind his back, gazing out across the snow-whitened landscape. "Who are they saying he murdered?"

Lud rocked back in his chair. "His wife."

"Priscilla Garrett . . . ?" Claire's eyes widened in shock. "Murdered?"

Nodding, Lud folded his arms across his chest. "How's that for somethin'? Heard Leonard Brock near went crazy at the news. Threatened to kill Garrett hisself less'n Chief Tanner put him behind bars."

Claire wanted to hide how deeply shaken she was. "Do you know what happened?" she asked, keeping her voice neutral with effort.

"Don't know all the details, but you can bet the gossips are buzzin' like bees around a hive. Heard one man claim she'd been shot. Another swears she was strangled."

Claire sat quietly digesting the horrible tragedy. She hadn't given it a second thought yesterday when she had been summoned to watch the Garretts' baby. She had merely assumed Mrs. Garrett had a pressing social engagement and needed someone to look after her child until she returned. Had Mrs. Garrett come home after she left and the couple argued? Even so, Cole struck her as someone too controlled to fly into a rage and kill anyone.

"Why is everyone so sure Garrett killed his wife?" Nils voiced the question Claire had been about to ask.

"Hell, who else could it be? Ain't anyone who don't know he and the missus were none too fond of each other." Lud drained the rest of his coffee, set down his cup, and belched. "One of the men who helped take her body to Doc's said she was wearin' a fancy blue party dress. Guess the only party she's goin' to now is her own funeral."

From the corner of her eye, Claire saw Nils clench his fist, then let it fall to his side. Making a strange noise deep in his throat, he left the kitchen without another word.

Lud pushed back his chair and climbed to his feet. "Looks like Mr. High 'n Mighty Garrett's been brought down a peg or two. Can't say I'm sorry to see it."

With the men gone, Claire remained at the kitchen table, staring blankly at a water-stained wall. She couldn't summon the energy to clear the breakfast dishes. *Cole accused of murdering his wife, the mother of his child? Impossible!* Her mind refused to accept the likelihood of that happening. Surely there must be some mistake. Maybe the authorities had already realized their error and had released him.

Something nagged at her consciousness, some small detail. She frowned, trying to remember her father's exact words. What was it he had said? She replayed their conversation over and over in her mind. Then her heart slammed against her ribcage.

. . . fancy blue party dress.

Pa had mentioned Priscilla had been wearing a fancy blue party dress when her body was discovered. *Oh my God!* Claire sat ramrod straight, one hand pressed against her chest. She vividly recalled the swish of silk, seeing Priscilla regally descend the staircase. Remembered the daring cut of her sapphire blue gown. In that instant, Claire knew with blinding clarity that Priscilla Garrett hadn't died last night, but the night before.

The night of the Howards' party.

Claire had spent that entire night at the Garrett house. Unless Cole killed Priscilla before coming home, he couldn't possibly have committed the crime. Nothing in his appearance or demeanor gave any hint of a violent encounter. She needed to find out the time the murder had occurred. If it happened anytime after eleven o'clock, she was the only one who could prove his innocence.

At City Hall, policeman Homer Bailey led Claire up the stairs and down a long corridor. When he stopped to exchange information with a fellow officer, she had an opportunity to look around. This was her first visit to the imposing sandstone building, home of Brockton's municipal offices. A series of small rooms opened off a main hallway. Trying not to eavesdrop on the men's conversation, she peered through a partially opened doorway to her right.

She smothered a small gasp. Cole sat on a hard wooden bench along one wall, his wrist manacled to one of the arms. A burly guard hovered nearby in the rare event Cole might break free from his shackles and attempt an escape. She was appalled at his appearance. He bore little resemblance to the perfectly groomed, arrogant man she knew. One cheek was bruised and bloody, bearded stubble covered his jaw. His hair was tousled with a dark shock falling over his brow. But it was his demeanor more than his physical appearance that had changed the most radically. He seemed to wear an invisible yoke of defeat, a mantle of hopelessness.

His conversation concluded, Homer Bailey motioned for her to follow him. With a lingering glance in Cole's direction, she trailed behind the policeman. He rapped on a frosted glass door at the end of the hall with the words Chief of Police stenciled in black letters.

"Better be important," a gruff voice warned from inside.

Bailey poked his head inside the door. "Got a woman here, Chief, who says she needs to talk to you. Won't tell me what for, but claims it's about the Garrett case."

"Send 'er in."

Claire felt her palms grow moist as she stepped into the room. Edward Tanner was seated behind an oak desk in front of a bank of windows overlooking Main Street. He was whip-cord lean with austere features, his eyes deep-set and intense under their bony shelf. While the hair atop his head was thinning and liberally streaked with gray, the drooping mustache that covered his upper lip was dark and thick. He answered to only one man in town—its mayor, Leonard Brock.

"Come in. Sit down," he ordered without looking up from a sheaf of papers.

Claire perched on the edge of the chair opposite him. She laced her fingers together to keep herself from fidgeting and waited for him to break the heavy silence.

After what seemed a small eternity, he pinned her with a look of steel. "I'm telling you right now, this had better not be a waste of my time. What do you know about the Garrett killing?"

She swallowed convulsively, then blurted, "Cole Garrett didn't kill his wife."

FOUR

"Didn't kill his wife, eh? You know that for a fact, do you?"

She nodded. "Yes, sir, I do."

Chief Tanner steepled his fingertips together and regarded her with a cold stare. "You're Lud Sorenson's girl, aren't you?"

"Yes, I am, but what has that to do with Mr. Garrett's innocence?"

"I'll ask the questions, Miss, if you don't mind. How long have you and your family lived in Brockton?"

"Nearly two years. Why?"

"You're living in the old Johnson place out on Beck Road."

Since it was more statement than question, Claire merely nodded. She wasn't sure where this line of questioning was going, and sensed she wouldn't like it.

"Your father's earned quite a reputation since you've been here." He toyed with a polished stone paperweight on his desk. "Your brother, too. Seems like he's a chip off the old block. He likes his liquor nearly as much as his old man."

"My father and brother have nothing to do with why I'm here," she said stiffly.

"Neither of them holds a steady job. Whiskey gets expensive night after night." Tanner's gaze never wavered

JUST BEFORE DAYBREAK

from her face. "When the tab gets too high, the bartenders cut them off."

"What are you implying?" She despised the hectic color that flooded her face, aware it could be interpreted as embarrassment—or guilt.

Tanner meticulously replaced the paperweight on the desk blotter. "Maybe Lud or Nils put you up to coming here this morning. Garrett's a wealthy man. He'd be plenty grateful to get out of this mess. You could name your own price."

Claire shot to her feet. White-hot fury burned away her normal reserve. "You bastard!" she cried. Tanner looked as surprised by the epithet as she did. The word, one she had often heard her father use, wasn't part of her normal vocabulary. Tanner had made her so angry, however, it just slipped out. "I should have known better," she continued, "than to expect you to listen. You don't want to know the truth. I should have remembered that Leonard Brock, Priscilla Garrett's father, appointed you chief of police. It wouldn't be wise to bite the hand that feeds you, would it?"

Tanner's mouth tightened into a thin line at the accusation.

"Perhaps, the editor of the *Gazette* will be a little more receptive." She turned on her heel and marched toward the door.

"Wait!"

She halted, her hand on the knob. From behind her, she heard the police chief utter an expletive under his breath.

"Come back here this instant, young lady," he ordered.

Chin in the air, spine erect, eyes shooting cool blue flames, Claire turned to face the lawman, unaware of the imperious picture she presented in spite of her shabby attire.

For a split second, Edward Tanner looked almost shamefaced. "Sit down . . . please." He indicated the chair she had just vacated. "I want to know why you're so certain Garrett didn't kill his wife."

She sat down and primly folded her hands in her lap. "Is it true what people are saying? That Mrs. Garrett was killed sometime after midnight?"

"Yes," he admitted. "We have every reason to believe Priscilla Garrett died at twelve-fifteen a.m. following a dinner party she attended."

"Then Mr. Garrett couldn't possibly have killed his wife, Chief Tanner." Claire sagged with relief. Until she actually heard Chief Tanner confirm the rumor, she had been afraid her trip to his office would be in vain. And Cole would spend the rest of his life in prison for a crime she was confident he didn't commit.

"And what makes you so certain?"

Claire leaned forward in her eagerness. "I spent the night—the entire night—of the murder at the Garrett house. Mr. Garrett returned home before midnight and didn't leave the house again that evening."

"Why should I believe you?"

"Because it's the truth."

For what seemed like hours, Claire endured Police Chief Tanner's interrogation. He regarded her story with open skepticism, but, as she reminded herself, at least he listened. He was clearly not happy that she could supply the prime suspect with an alibi. And from everything she knew about the man, Leonard Brock would be even less pleased.

"Can anyone corroborate your story?" he asked at length.

The question caught her off guard. Dismay washed over her at her own foolishness. She had never paused to consider that her account of that night might be challenged. "I—I don't know."

Tanner's mouth twitched in a small smile of triumph. "You realize, of course, I can't release a man—a suspected murderer—without first checking the veracity of your story."

Claire refused to be rattled. If he expected her to recant her story, he was mistaken. She clung to her outward composure, even though inwardly her nerves were strung taut. "It was barely daylight when I started for home, and I don't remember passing anyone on the way. Mrs. Dobbs, however, can verify I was asked to care for the Garretts' baby, Daisy, after the nursemaid departed unexpectedly. My brother, Nils, knows I didn't arrive home until the following morning."

"Stay here until I return," Tanner instructed, rising to his feet. He paused in the doorway to give Claire a hard look. "And Miss Sorenson, if I find out you've lied to me, there will be dire consequences to face."

Cole slouched on a wooden bench in a small room near the office of Chief Edward Tanner. After spending the night in the jail in the basement of City Hall, he had been escorted upstairs. Tanner, he had been told, wanted a written confession that he had murdered Priscilla.

Murder? God, had the whole miserable year of their marriage led up to this moment? With Priscilla dead and him in prison? He still couldn't believe she was dead. He wouldn't lie to himself—or others—that he'd lost the love of his life. Truth was, he hadn't even liked her very much. Yet he mourned her passing. Grieved for the daughter who would grow to adulthood never knowing her mother. Priscilla was a young, vibrant woman, her whole life ahead of her. For her to meet such a violent end was unthinkable. He shuddered at the images it conjured. Who could have committed such a vicious act?

He attempted to run his hand through his hair, but the handcuff and chain that secured his left wrist to the bench stopped him in mid-motion. With a sigh, he lowered his arm, inwardly cringing at the rattle of metal. His head felt like an anvil being pounded by a sledgehammer. It was impossible to know if the throbbing was caused by a sleepless night on a hard bunk or the blow Leonard Brock had landed before Tanner restrained him. Christ! Brock's fist had nearly knocked his head clear off his shoulders. And, worst of all, he had been helpless to protect himself with his hands fastened behind his back.

Just as he was helpless now.

Not even James Lamont, his lawyer and trusted friend, could offer much hope. James had advised him to cooperate with Tanner. *Don't make things even more difficult for yourself,* he had counseled. Cole wasn't sure whether or not James believed him innocent. At best, James had doubts. Both James and his wife Sophie knew he and Priscilla were not well suited. Unless a miracle happened, and happened soon, Cole was destined to spend the remainder of his life behind bars for a crime he didn't commit. Everything, every single thing, he had struggled for his entire life was about to be lost. He squeezed his eyes shut. He prided himself on being a man of action, but with a feeling akin to despair, he admitted in this crucial moment there was little he could do.

He didn't bother opening his eyes when he heard the door open and footsteps approach.

"You're a lucky bastard, Garrett," Tanner said. "Looks like you'll leave here this morning a free man."

Cole's head came up with a snap. He blinked in disbelief, afraid he had misunderstood the police chief's words.

Tanner reached into his uniform pocket and produced a key that he used to unlock the handcuff attached to Cole's wrist. "Don't plan to leave town any time soon. I need you around to answer any questions that come up regarding your late wife."

Cole slowly got to his feet, absently rubbing his wrist where it was chafed and raw. "I don't understand. Did you find the person responsible?"

"Not yet, but I will," Tanner returned, his face grim. "You have that young woman standing in the hallway to thank for your freedom."

Picking up his jacket, Cole tried to brush out some of the wrinkles. The garment was a sorry sight after having been rolled into a ball and used as a pillow.

Tanner started to leave, but turned back. "I'd watch it if I were you, Garrett. Brock's got the notion into his head that you're responsible for killing his baby girl. Knowing him, he won't let the matter rest until he sees you rot in jail."

And what would happen to Daisy if he were sent to prison? Cole wondered as he slipped into his jacket. Brock had never expressed an interest in his only grandchild. He had been even more indifferent to the little tyke than he had been to Priscilla while she was alive. "Thanks for the warning, Chief. I'll keep that in mind."

Tanner gave him a brusque nod, then headed for his office.

Cole couldn't wait to get home and wash the stink of a night in jail from his body. Smoothing his tousled hair, he stepped into the hallway and froze.

Claire Sorenson, looking anxious and uncertain, waited just outside the door. Belatedly, he remembered Tanner had said something about him having a young woman to thank for his release. "You . . . ?" he asked, frowning.

Shifting her weight from one foot to the other, Claire gave a small shrug. "I only told them the truth."

"Forgive me if I'm a little confused, but what is the 'truth'?"

"That you couldn't possibly have killed your wife."

He tried to smile, but all he could summon was a humorless twist of his mouth. "I don't know how to thank someone who has just saved my life."

"I don't want your gratitude."

"Then what *do* you want?" The question sprang out before he could stop it. The instant the words were said he wished he could call them back. Hurt flickered across Claire Sorenson's expressive features like a shadow. Silently, he cursed himself as a fool. Where this young woman was concerned, he seemed to have a God-given talent for saying the wrong thing. He sighed deeply. "I'm sorry, Claire."

"I want neither your apology nor gratitude, Mr. Garrett,"

she returned with quiet dignity. "Though you may find this hard to believe, I want nothing from you. Nothing at all."

He watched her walk away with rapid steps, her head held high, her back ramrod straight, and felt ashamed of himself. He had handled the situation poorly, and they both knew it. He had slept only an hour or two in the last twenty-four, his jacket as a pillow. His head felt like it would split in two. And the thought of being accused of murder terrified him. Still, there was no excuse to lash out at the one person who had come to his rescue.

"Miss Sorenson . . . Claire . . . wait." He hurried after her, but she didn't slow her pace. He caught up with her in the rear stairwell landing between the first and second floors. He grabbed hold of her sleeve before she could descend to the street below.

She glanced pointedly at his hand on her arm, then back up at his face. He released her at once. She had beautiful skin, he noticed absently, satiny smooth and pale as fresh cream. Then he brought himself up short. What the devil was he thinking?

Angry with himself, he rammed both hands into the pockets of his jacket. "Whether you want an apology or not, you deserve one. I had no call to say what I did."

"No, you didn't," she agreed equably.

He closed his eyes briefly. When he opened them again, he found her still watching him with the same infuriating calm. He fumbled for a way to explain his brash outburst. "Over the years, I've learned most people expect something in exchange for a favor. Invariably every good deed exacts a price. The greater the deed, the higher the reward. I admit I was suspicious of your motives."

"I'm not 'most' people, Mr. Garrett." She tilted her head to one side, studied him. "Have you always been a cynic?"

"Yes . . . er, no, not always." Her question caught him off guard. "Some lessons, Miss Sorenson, are best learned the hard way. In time one learns to protect oneself."

"Yes," she said, "I suppose you're right."

From other parts of the building, doors opened and closed, voices rose and fell in conversation, but the stairwell provided a small measure of shelter from the curious. "If you'd care to explain, I'd like to know how you managed to convince Chief Tanner that I didn't kill Priscilla."

"I provided your alibi."

Alibi? She had descended several more stairs when he caught up with her again. "But how is that possible?"

Digging into the pocket of her worn jacket, she produced a silver dollar and held it out, palm up. "You gave this to me the night your wife was killed. You said to give it to Tim O'Brien as payment for a ride home. I waited and waited, but I never heard him return with Mrs. Garrett. Even if I dozed off, I'm a light sleeper. It was nearly dawn when I finally let myself out and walked home. There was no way you could have left the house without my knowledge."

"But, what if I'd killed Priscilla *before* I came home?"

"Chief Tanner is quite certain that Mrs. Garrett died after midnight. You were home well before that time."

Cole tried to assimilate all she was telling him, but it was hard to think logically when he was near exhaustion, both mentally and physically. "What makes the chief so sure about the time?" He voiced the question for his benefit, not really expecting her to know the answer.

She shook her head. "I'm afraid you'll have to ask him."

Cole ran a weary hand over his face and winced when his fingers encountered the cut on his cheek.

"Who struck you?"

He grimaced at the memory. "Leonard Brock came down to City Hall after my arrest. His signet ring gouged my cheek when he took a swing at me."

"But you were handcuffed!" Claire looked outraged. "Didn't Chief Tanner try to keep him from assaulting you?"

"I think Tanner hoped Brock would beat the daylights out of me."

"Cole! There you are." A tall, slender man with sandy-brown hair bounded up the steps toward them. "I just heard you'd been released."

"James!" The two men exchanged handshakes. "Thanks to Miss Sorenson, I won't be needing the services of a lawyer, after all." Turning to Claire, he quickly dispatched the introductions between her and his friend and lawyer, James Lamont.

James Lamont flicked a cursory gaze over Claire, then, dismissing her as of no consequence, turned his attention back to Cole. "You know, of course, I never believed you guilty for a minute."

"You sure had me fooled last night when you advised me to confess."

James smiled, revealing a dimple in one cheek. "I was only looking out for your best interests."

Cole raised a brow askance. "My *best interests* did not include admitting to a crime I didn't commit."

"Touché, my friend. Regardless of how it might have seemed, I acted out of genuine concern for your well-being. Tanner has a reputation for ruthlessness." He slapped Cole on the shoulder. "How about coming to my office? You look like you could use a stiff drink. I've got some aged brandy locked away."

"Some other time, perhaps. All I want right now is a hot bath and a soft bed."

"Fine," James said. "Just remember, my offer stands."

Cole glanced around, expecting to find Claire waiting, but there was no sign of her in the stairwell. Leaving James staring after him, Cole ran down the remaining stairs, then pushed open the frosted glass door leading out of City Hall. He stood for a moment on the portico, letting his eyes adjust to the bright sunlight, then searched the street for any sign of her.

But Claire Sorenson had disappeared.

He wasn't sure what he would say if he did catch up with her. Apologize all over again? What did one say to

JUST BEFORE DAYBREAK 53

someone who's just rescued you from life in prison? Words were woefully inadequate to express the gratitude he felt. If she hadn't come forward, he most likely would have spent the rest of his years in the penitentiary.

Disregarding the curious glances of onlookers, he started for home. How odd that Claire, a virtual stranger, was the only person who expressed any real concern for his welfare. James had professed a certain regard, but when the chips were down, he had been no better than the rest of the vultures waiting for a confession. Cole almost smiled, remembering how indignant Claire had looked when he told her Leonard Brock had punched him. The thought of Brock sobered him. As soon as he got cleaned up and grabbed a couple hours sleep, he needed to pay Brock a visit. There were funeral arrangements to prepare.

After leaving Cole at City Hall, Claire decided that as long as she was in town she'd stop at Cavanaugh's Food Emporium for a few necessary items before beginning the long walk home. Cavanaugh's was the only place in town that allowed her to purchase on credit. She suspected it was because she scrupulously paid on their account.

As she rounded the corner onto Main Street, she couldn't help but notice that the thoroughfare teemed with activity. Saturdays always brought people into town for their weekly shopping, but today Brockton seemed unusually busy. Buggies and wagons lined both sides of the street. People congregated in small groups along the boardwalk, more intent on gossip than patronizing the many stores and shops. The air fairly hummed with rumor and speculation. Claire caught bits of conversation as she wove her way toward Cavanaugh's.

"Such a shock!"

"I could hardly believe my ears."

"Imagine! Killing his wife, the mother of his child."

"They should lock him up and throw away the key."

"Jail's too good for the likes of 'im. He oughta be hanged."

The comments made Claire secretly rejoice that Chief Tanner had been able to find not one, but two, witnesses who could verify her story. Both Tim O'Brien, the Garretts' coachman, and Karl Detmeijer, a milkman who had been making his morning rounds, reported seeing her leave the Garrett home. She was just about to skirt another cluster of Brockton's citizens when what she heard made her stumble to a halt.

"Garrett should be made to feel what it's like to have a peavey hook driven through the middle of his back," a red-faced man stated with conviction.

A peavey hook? Bile burned at the back of her throat. Was that what had killed Priscilla? Claire reacted physically to the idea of the pole with its long, pointed steel tip being driven into a human body.

"That poor woman," the man's female companion murmured.

"You'd think he'd have more sense than to leave the body right there where anyone could find it."

Pretending an interest in the farm implements in the display window of Horvath's Hardware, Claire eavesdropped shamelessly. Though appalled by her own behavior, she was as hungry for details as the next person.

"My butcher said the baker told him that Mrs. Garrett's body had been stuffed in a cabinet in a shed behind the sawmill and covered with a tarp," a heavyset woman volunteered.

"I heard 'er body was found half-buried in snow up near the dam," her companion volunteered.

The ruddy-faced man spoke again. "Mebbe someone came along and scared the killer off. Mebbe he planned to come back later and dispose of it properlike, where it weren't likely to be found."

Claire shuddered. The thought of a vicious murderer among the residents of this thriving little town frightened her. While she was certain Cole hadn't killed Priscilla, someone had. Was her murderer one of the many men who wandered from lumber camp to lumber camp, from one sawmill to the next? Or was it someone who lived in Brockton? Someone who at this very minute might be standing along Main Street partaking in this same conversation?

She jumped, nearly coming out of her skin, when she felt a tap on her shoulder. She whirled around and found her brother behind her. "Nils . . . what brings you to town?"

He leaned heavily on his cane. "I could ask you the same question."

Knowing how much Nils disliked Cole Garrett, she dissembled. "We were out of flour and . . ."

"Cut the crap, Claire," he snapped. "You're here for the same reason I am. Admit it—you're as curious as everyone else."

She couldn't deny it.

Seeing her expression, Nils gave a harsh laugh. "Hell, Sis, don't look as if it's a crime to be human. You try so hard to be perfect, to show everyone you're not like the old man, and what does it get you? Nothing," he said before she could reply. "That's a lesson I learned a long time ago."

Claire smelled liquor on Nils's breath. "Isn't it early in the day to be drinking?"

He ignored the question, the censure. "I hate Garrett's guts. Wish they'd hang the bastard. I'd be in the front row. Hell, I'd volunteer to be the hangman."

"Nils! You've got to stop blaming him for your accident. It was just that . . . an accident. You know better than I do that lumbering is a dangerous business. Every year hundreds are hurt, some even killed."

His expression twisted and bitter, he asked, "Did anyone say who found Priscilla's body?"

"No, they haven't. Some say she was found in a shed behind the Garrett sawmill."

"Son of a bitch!"

She opened her mouth to berate her brother for his foul language when she realized his attention was focused elsewhere. Following the direction of his scowl, she saw Cole Garrett making his way up the street. The crowd parted like the Red Sea in the biblical tale of Moses. Silence smothered the lively chatter; tension hung, heavy and oppressive.

One look at his battered, weary face caused her heart to wrench with sympathy. Dark smudges beneath his eyes attested to a sleepless night. Instead of being impeccably groomed, his cheeks were covered in dark bristle, his clothing hopelessly wrinkled. Yet, Claire couldn't help but feel admiration as she watched him. With shoulders squared and head high, he braved a gauntlet of citizens armed with condemnation, suspicion, and loathing.

No one spoke as he continued up the street. Claire held her breath, watching, waiting, feeling tempers about to erupt.

Cole slowed when he reached the spot where Claire stood with Nils. For a fraction of a second their eyes met in silent acknowledgment. He started to move past when Nils shattered the taut silence.

"You bastard," he snarled, his face pinched with rage. "Since when are they letting murderers prowl the streets? Or did you bribe your way out?"

Claire clutched her brother's arm. "Nils, don't, please . . ."

He shook her hand from his sleeve. "Are you happy now that your wife's dead?"

Other than a muscle that ticked in his jaw, Cole showed no sign of temper. "At least, Sorenson, you're not afraid to speak your mind. I'll grant you that much."

Claire tensed as an audience of onlookers formed a loose semi-circle to observe the drama being enacted in front of the hardware store.

Nils's fingers tightened around the head of his cane until

the knuckles whitened. "What the hell are you doing out of jail, Garrett?"

"Maybe you'd better ask your sister," Cole answered quietly.

Nils swung toward Claire, his eyes flame-blue in his pale face. "Care to explain, Sis? What the devil does Garrett mean by that remark?"

Claire drew in a shaky breath. Gossip traveled through Brockton like lightning. Sooner or later, the fact that she had supplied Cole with an alibi would become public knowledge in this small town. She would, however, have preferred *later*. "Mr. Garrett couldn't possibly have killed his wife."

"What?" Nils fairly bellowed. "How do you know?"

"Because I was at the Garrett house the entire night."

Excited whispers rippled through the people gathered to watch. Ignoring them, she kept a wary eye on her brother.

"You . . . ?" Nils bunched a fist and took a halting step closer.

Cole insinuated his body between the siblings, effectively blocking Nils's advance. "If I ever learn that you've raised your hand against your sister, trust me, Sorenson, you'll regret it."

"You son of a bitch," Nils hissed. He sent Claire and Cole a blistering look of helpless fury, then whirled and limped down the boardwalk, his cane beating an angry staccato on the wood planks.

The dark scowl on Cole's face caused the crowd to disperse quickly.

Lowering his voice, Cole addressed Claire, his gaze intent on her face. "I meant what I said. If your brother as much as harms a hair on your head, he'll answer to me."

She nodded, alternately pleased to have a champion and dismayed that he thought her in need of one. "Thank you, Mr. Garrett, but I'm sure that won't be necessary. Nils has a temper, but he's never raised a hand to me."

"My offer stands."

With this, he resumed his walk up Main Street toward home. Once again, the citizens in his path silently parted in front of him, then closed ranks in his wake. When Cole disappeared around a corner, they collectively turned their attention to Claire. Only by then she, too, had vanished down a side street and away from their inquisitive stares.

FIVE

Claire stood on a small rise a short distance from the main body of mourners. She was flanked by Alma Dobbs on one side and Tim O'Brien on the other. Fleecy white clouds drifted across a sky the pure blue of a robin's egg. Here and there, tufts of withered grass poked holes through the light blanket of snow covering the ground. It was one of those rare, mild March days, a prelude to spring.

A morning much too beautiful for a burial.

She had debated whether or not to attend Priscilla Brock's funeral. The woman had been little more than a stranger. Claire had scrubbed her floors and ironed her sheets, and on two occasions had tended her child. Now she was here to pay her final respects. Next to her, Alma wept softly into a crumpled handkerchief. Tim wore a solemn expression, his eyes downcast. Claire pretended not to notice the covert glances in her direction. People, she knew, continued to gossip about her role in setting Cole Garrett free.

"A young woman in the prime of life, taken before her time . . ." The Reverend Calvin Anderson's voice rang across Oak Lawn Cemetery.

A lump of guilt lodged in Claire's throat. She had always envied Priscilla Brock. To her, it seemed as if Priscilla had everything a woman could possibly want. Beauty, wealth, a lovely home, a handsome husband, an adorable child. Yet all those generous gifts hadn't been enough to make her happy. Hadn't been enough to guarantee a long life.

"A loving mother," the minister extolled.

Poor Daisy. Claire couldn't help but worry about the little girl. True, Priscilla always seemed anxious to leave her baby's care in another's hands, yet good, bad, or indifferent, a child needed its mother.

". . . and a devoted daughter."

Claire's gaze rested on Leonard Brock. He stood at the gravesite with his head bowed, his massive shoulders slumped, looking truly bereft. She felt deeply sorry for the man. Neither his power nor fortune had been able to protect his most prized asset—his daughter. Priscilla, Alma had told her, had been an only child, born after years of marriage. As a child, Brock had doted on her. Father and daughter were said to be much alike. If Priscilla had been born male, she would have undoubtedly taken over the reins of her father's expanding empire.

She noticed that the Reverend Anderson didn't refer to Priscilla as a beloved wife and wondered if others had also noted the omission. This might have been an oversight on the clergyman's part, but she doubted it. She stole a look at Cole. He stood, somber and dry-eyed, a good arm's length from his father-in-law. In spite of the crowd around him, he presented an isolated, solitary figure.

"Earth to earth. Ashes to ashes."

Uncontrollable sobbing punctuated the minister's words. Craning her neck, Claire saw Cole's lawyer, James Lamont, comfort a woman whom she assumed was his wife. When the woman turned to bury her face in his shoulder, Claire noticed her complexion was splotchy from weeping, the eyes swollen and red-rimmed.

"Dust to dust."

Reverend Anderson picked up a handful of dirt and let it trickle on the casket as it was slowly lowered into the ground. Leonard Brock followed suit. Bending down, Cole scooped dirt into his palm, stared at it for a long moment,

JUST BEFORE DAYBREAK

then dropped it into the yawning hole at his feet. The sound of dirt dropping onto gleaming rosewood echoed hollow and empty.

"In sure and certain hope of the Resurrection unto eternal life, we commend Priscilla Brock Garrett to Your care." Reverend Anderson closed his Book of Prayer and left the graveside. One by one, mourners filed after him.

"My poor, poor Priscilla," Alma Dobbs sniffled loudly. "So young and all . . ."

"Shame, all right," Tim muttered. Mumbling an excuse under his breath, he loped off across the cemetery to where the carriages stood.

The man posed an enigma, Claire thought to herself as she watched him go. She knew no more about Tim O'Brien now than she had the day she started at the Garrett household. He preferred his own company to that of others, but he had a way with horses. The carriage house was kept spotless, the equipment in good repair.

She was about to fall into step beside Alma when she spied a familiar figure standing alone near a cluster of evergreens. *Nils?* What had prompted her brother to attend the funeral of a woman he hadn't known? He stood with his hat in his hand, the morning sun glinting on his pale blond hair. She didn't remember ever seeing him look quite so serious . . . or so sad. Before she could move toward him, he hurried away as fast as his gait allowed.

Sniffing back tears, Alma stuffed her sodden handkerchief into her pocketbook. "Friends and family are invited to Mr. Brock's for refreshments after the service. Guess that don't include the hired help."

"No," Claire murmured. "Somehow I don't think we'd be welcome to mingle among the guests." Now that the burial service was over, she felt drained. She hated funerals, hated them ever since, at age twelve, she had buried her mother. Life went on, but nothing was ever quite the same. "What do you suppose he'll do now?"

"He, meaning Mr. Garrett?" Alma gave her a sidelong look.

Claire nodded, embarrassed. She hoped her interest in the man wasn't too blatant. Something about Cole drew her like a magnet. Whenever she was near him, or when he entered her thoughts, all her senses seemed to spring to life. Colors glowed brighter; sounds and smells were more acute. Enough! she berated herself silently. The man was a newly bereaved widower. Even though she knew it was foolish, she couldn't contain the sudden warmth she felt every time he was near.

Ducking her head lest somehow Alma fathom her secret, she carefully skirted puddles of melting snow. "Has he hired a nursemaid to care for the baby?" she asked, hoping her inquiry sounded casual.

"That agency in Chicago is sending out two women. I heard Mr. Garrett tell Tim to meet the noon train Wednesday. One of 'em ought to fill the bill. Can't be soon enough to suit me."

"You don't like children very much, do you?"

"Truth be known, I can't stand the little buggers. I hired on as housekeeper, not nursemaid, and that's the way I intend to keep it."

"You never wanted children of your own?"

"Me and my Harold are happy as two clams without any brats underfoot."

"How is Mr. Garrett managing?"

Alma shrugged indifferently. "That's no worry of mine. I agreed to care for the child during the day until he finds a replacement for Miss Bartlesby, but come quitting time, I'm gone. Harold wants me home, his supper on the table."

"I thought maybe the baby's grandfather would take her in," Claire remarked as they passed through the wrought iron gates guarding the entrance to the cemetery.

Alma sniffed. "From what I've seen, the old man wants nothing to do with the child."

The two women kept to the side of the road. Carriages

filled with mourners rolled past, their wheels spitting clumps of mud. A handful of stragglers followed on foot. Strange, Claire mused, that Leonard Brock would shirk responsibility for his only grandchild. But maybe she was doing the man a disservice. Perhaps Cole refused to relinquish custody of his child. If that were true, she admired him all the more. She had learned firsthand how protective he was when it came to his offspring. He wanted her surrounded with only the best. Unfortunately, that excluded her. In his estimation, the daughter of the town drunk wasn't a suitable baby nurse.

They reached a fork in the road where they would part company, Alma turning toward town, Claire in the opposite direction. "I'll send Tim for you the end of the week," Alma said.

Claire tucked a wisp of ash-blond hair behind her ear. "That isn't necessary. I can walk."

"Nonsense." Alma dismissed the notion with a wave of her hand. "You'll need all your strength for the work I've got in mind. The house needs a thorough cleaning, top to bottom. What with messy diapers and a fussing infant, I haven't had time for much else."

"Maybe Daisy's teething." Claire stuffed both hands into the pockets of her jacket. "Or maybe she senses her mother is gone."

That drew a laugh from Alma. "Don't like to speak ill of the dead, but you and I both know Priscilla Garrett didn't care for kids any more than me. Her own included."

With a final wave, Alma joined a small group of women headed in the same direction as herself.

Oblivious to a robin's song, Claire slowly walked home. Her thoughts were mired in the tragedy that had befallen what she had once regarded as the perfect family. Priscilla brutally slain, Daisy a motherless waif, and Cole struggling to cope with a suspicious town and being the single parent of a small child.

Hopes turned to ashes. Dreams into dust.

* * *

Except for the hiss of a gas jet and the crackle of flames, Leonard Brock's sumptuous library was quiet. Not even the muted glow from a wall sconce could dispel the gloom which draped the room like cobwebs. The two men seated across from each other shared an uneasy silence.

Brock stared dully at the tumbler of brandy on the desk in front of him. This morning he had buried his only child. He had floundered through the afternoon in a haze of grief and loss. Tonight he wanted—demanded—vengeance. He wouldn't rest until Priscilla's murderer rotted behind bars. His movements slow and ponderous, he raised the heavy crystal glass and drained its contents, then refilled it from the cut-glass decanter resting on a silver tray.

"Ready for another?" he asked.

Edward Tanner shook his head, his own drink barely touched. "What was it you wanted to discuss?"

Brock raised the lid of a carved teak humidor and offered his guest a cigar, then took one for himself as well. After snipping off one end, he struck a match and puffed the cigar to life. "Shouldn't come as no big surprise why I asked you here tonight."

Before answering, Tanner took his time lighting his cigar, then blew out a stream of smoke. "I'd wager a guess it has to do with Cole Garrett."

"Damn right. That murdering son of a bitch killed my little girl. Meanwhile, he's walking around scot-free. I want him to pay for what he's done." Brock's hand tightened around the heavy crystal. "Jail's too good for the bastard. I'd like to see him drawn and quartered."

Tanner crossed one leg over the other. "Now, Leonard, I understand how you feel, but the man's got an iron-clad alibi. No court in the land would convict him."

"Garrett did it!" Brock felt an angry flush start at his starched collar and creep up his neck. "He killed my girl."

"We have no proof he committed a crime. The Sorenson

woman swears she was at Garrett's home the whole time. Both Detmeijer and O'Brien saw her leave the place at dawn. And," he continued, "we know for a fact Priscilla died at 12:15 a.m. That little gold watch she always wore pinned to her dress broke from the force of the blow she received."

At the reminder of his daughter's violent demise, Brock took a long swallow of brandy. His hand visibly shook. "I don't give a tinker's damn what that Sorenson bitch says, Cole Garrett's guilty as sin."

"Have you paused to consider that you might be wrong?"

"I'm never wrong."

"But if you are . . . ?"

Brock's pale green eyes narrowed. "What the hell are you getting at?"

Tanner studied the glowing tip of his cigar. "That would mean the real killer is walking around town, probably laughing his fool head off knowing he literally got away with murder."

"Dammit, Tanner, you and I both know I'm not wrong."

"Why would Garrett kill his own wife? What did he stand to gain?"

"I didn't ask you here for a boatload of maybes and what-ifs." Brock's heavy features gelled into an obstinate mask. "Don't forget I'm mayor of this town. If it weren't for me, you'd be patrolling the streets on foot instead of sitting in some big, fancy office in City Hall."

Tanner reached for his brandy, downed half of it. "What is it you want me to do?"

"I want you to put an end to mealy-mouthed excuses," Brock growled. "Garrett killed my Priscilla. I want him ruined. I won't rest until he's behind bars. In the meantime, I want to watch him lose every dime, nickel, and penny he's ever earned."

"But Leonard . . ."

"Keep investigating Garrett. Don't give him a minute's

rest. And don't let up until you turn up something." Brock jabbed the air with the lit end of his cigar for emphasis. "Remember, if you don't have the balls for this, I'll find someone who does."

Winter shriveled into spring, each day slightly longer than the one before. Claire stared idly out the kitchen window as she waited for the kettle to boil. The weather had turned gray and gloomy in the days since Priscilla Garrett's funeral. "Gloomy" also described the mood of those around her. Nils had spoken only a handful of words to her since learning she had been responsible for Cole's release from prison. She worried about him. More and more of his time was spent frequenting bars, usually in the company of their father. Pa had also made it known to Claire in no uncertain terms that he wasn't happy she had rushed to Garrett's defense. He irrationally blamed Cole for Nils's accident. He also resented—and envied—Cole's success.

Her gaze sharpened at the crunch of wheels on the gravel drive. Leaning forward for a closer look, she glimpsed a bottle-green lacquered carriage as it rolled to a halt. She instantly recognized the vehicle as belonging to the Garretts. Alma had mentioned after the funeral that she would send Tim to fetch her to help with the cleaning. Odd, she thought, that he would come this late in the day. Unless, of course, he came with the message that her help was no longer required. She hoped that wasn't the case. The money she earned helped put food on the Sorenson table. Removing her apron, she smoothed her hair and went to answer the knock at the door.

She opened the front door and her jaw dropped in surprise. Instead of Tim O'Brien, she found Cole Garrett. Hatless and wearing an overcoat of dark charcoal gray, he looked heart-stoppingly handsome. She was so stunned to see him standing on her doorstep, she could only gape at him.

JUST BEFORE DAYBREAK 67

"I see my visit comes somewhat as a shock." A tiny smile flickered across his mouth. "Sorry to be calling this late. I hope I'm not interrupting anything."

"No . . . I . . . ah, I recognized the carriage. I expected to find Mr. O'Brien with a message from Mrs. Dobbs."

He peered over her shoulder. "Are you alone?"

"Yes," she said, hating the breathlessness in her voice that betrayed her attack of nerves. "Pa and Nils are out. I'm not sure when they'll be home."

"May I come in?" he inquired.

"Of course," she said, but continued to stand where she was and block the doorway.

"I'm afraid if you want to let me in, you'll have to move aside."

There it was again, she thought. That tiny flicker of a smile that made him seem less formidable. Then his words sank into her consciousness, and she blushed furiously. "Sorry," she muttered, stepping back.

He came inside and swept a glance around the small room that served as a parlor. Claire closed the door, then leaned against it, watching him. His large frame dwarfed the room. And his elegant appearance made it appear appallingly shabby in comparison. She watched his steel-gray eyes catalog the threadbare settee, the cheap rocking chair with its frayed cushion, and a table and chair of indeterminate style. If he was comparing her simple home with his grander one, hers must seem like a pauper's shack.

He motioned to a series of three embroidered samplers on the wall. "The beatitudes. If memory serves, Matthew, Chapter 5, Verses 3-11," he said. "Your handiwork?"

"No, my mother's," she replied, surprised by his familiarity with the Bible. His silent inventory had given her brain time to start functioning again. "I was just about to have tea. Would you care to join me?"

"Yes, thank you. If it isn't too much trouble."

"May I take your coat, Mr. Garrett?" she asked, hoping

she sounded like a proper hostess. It was a role she had never been called upon to play, but one she had witnessed many times in the upper-class homes where she cleaned.

At her tone, his brow arched quizzically, but he refrained from comment. He unbuttoned his coat, slipped it off, and handed it to her. Claire felt his gaze rest on her as she carefully hung it from a rack near the door.

She gestured toward the settee. "Please have a seat, Mr. Garrett. I'll just be a moment."

Excusing herself, she escaped into the kitchen. Once there, she blew out an unsteady breath. What had lured Cole Garrett to her parlor? Had he changed his mind about wanting her to take care of Daisy? The prospect was too much to hope for. And if her guess was wrong, the disappointment would be bitter. She made up her mind then and there not to broach the subject. She would wait for him to bring up the reason for his call. No matter how difficult, she would keep the lid on her curiosity. This decided upon, she set to work.

Steam escaped from the spout of the kettle she had put on to boil just before Cole arrived. She poured some of the hot water into a china teapot adorned with forget-me-nots. While the pot warmed, she set out a sugar bowl. She frowned, remembering she had no cream to offer her guest. Cream was a luxury in the Sorenson household. She would have to make do.

She emptied the water used to warm the teapot into a basin in the sink. Next, she carefully measured tea just as her mother had taught her, one for each person and one over, before refilling the little teapot with boiling water. While the tea steeped, she rose on tiptoe and reached into the cupboard for the Sunday dishes on the top shelf.

"Here, let me help." Cole came up behind her, and gently nudging her aside, took down the cups and saucers. "I assume these are what you were trying to reach."

"Yes, thank you."

Cole placed them on the table alongside the teapot. "You should keep these where they're easier to reach."

"I would, except they'd soon be broken." She opened a tin and arranged cookies on a small plate. Then she set everything on a cheap metal tray. "Pa and Nils have little regard for delicate china. The tea set was Mother's prized possession. She brought it with her from England."

"It isn't necessary to use your mother's best china. You don't have to fuss on my account."

"I'm not." The denial popped out before she could stop it. A stricken look swept across her face. "Sorry, I didn't mean to be so blunt."

He shrugged off her apology. "It's refreshing to meet someone so honest."

She gave him a rueful smile. "It's a fault that tends to get me in trouble. Not everyone appreciates bluntness."

"Blessed are the painfully honest," he intoned, his expression bland, "for they shall be . . . friendless."

She stared at him. Amazing. A sense of humor lurked beneath Cole Garrett's stern facade. "Strange," she mused. "I don't recall that being listed among the Beatitudes."

"An oversight on Matthew's part."

She laughed and was rewarded by seeing his lips quirk in amusement before he turned serious again.

Cole dragged a hand through his hair, then massaged the back of his neck. "It's been a long while since I've heard a woman's laughter. Can't even remember the last time."

She felt more at ease with him now, but sensed his discomfort with the situation. "According to Mother," she said, adding two worn but crisply starched linen napkins to the tray, "the best place for afternoon tea is the parlor."

"Then the parlor it is." Before she could divine his intent, he picked up the tray, carried it into the parlor, and placed it on a small table which he pulled in front of the settee.

Claire sat on a straight-backed chair, her posture perfect. "Sugar?"

Cole settled himself on the settee. "Yes, please."

"I'm sorry that I can't offer cream or lemon." She handed him a cup and saucer along with a napkin.

He studied her over the rim of his cup. "You preside over a tea table as though you've done this before."

"My mother insisted we observe a tradition she brought with her from England." Her voice took on a wistful quality. "Each afternoon, while Pa and Nils were away, we'd pretend we were ladies of the manor. Sometimes Mother served hot scones and jam with our tea. In the summertime, she'd make dainty cucumber sandwiches, and in the winter, my favorite, thin slices of bread rolled with toasted cheese."

"She sounds like a wonderful mother."

"She was more than just my mother, she was my friend." Claire sipped her tea, hoping it would slide past the lump in her throat. "Mother died when I was twelve, but I still miss her."

Cole accepted a cookie from the plate she offered and took a bite. "Umm, delicious," he said as he polished it off.

Claire couldn't stand the suspense any longer. Resolutions be damned, she had to find out the reason he was there. She carefully set her cup down and folded her hands in her lap. "You didn't come here to compliment me on my shortbread cookies, Mr. Garrett. Suppose you tell me the real reason you're here."

He set his cup down as well, then carefully brushed the crumbs from his fingers. "I brought along a generous slice of humble pie to serve with your tea."

SIX

"Humble pie?" Claire repeated. "I'm not sure I understand what you mean."

Cole stared down at the pine floorboards and shifted his weight on the uncomfortable settee. This was the moment he had dreaded. But, damn, he had no other options. Admitting he had made a mistake was never easy for him. Not today, not ever. He prided himself on carefully considering problems from every angle, weighing benefits against drawbacks, and reaching the correct conclusion. Following this philosophy, he managed to keep mistakes to a minimum. While this practice worked well in his professional dealings, it didn't seen to apply to personal areas. His marriage to Priscilla was a prime example of how his theory had failed.

He swung his gaze back to the woman patiently waiting for an explanation. After he humbled himself, he thought glumly, Claire Sorenson had every right to tell him to go to hell. He cleared his throat, then plunged in. "I'm here to make you an offer. A very generous one," he added.

"That isn't necessary, Mr. Garrett. You don't owe me a thing." Claire picked up her teacup and stirred the contents with enough vigor to create a miniature whirlpool. "I simply told Chief Tanner the truth when I said you were home at the time your wife was killed."

He was taken aback by her assumption. And her anger. "That isn't the reason I'm here," he said quietly.

She ceased her furious stirring and stared at him with frank curiosity. "Forgive me if I'm confused. Exactly what did bring you here?"

"I came to ask a favor of you."

"What sort of favor?" she asked warily.

"I realize in light of my past behavior, I have a lot of nerve to even broach the subject, but . . ."

"But . . . ?"

Damn! he swore silently. She wasn't going to make this easy for him, but then why should she? He surged to his feet and prowled the small parlor. He was used to issuing orders, being in control. Now the tables were turned. Claire held the power. "If you recall, you once offered to act as a temporary baby nurse for Daisy."

"An offer which you rejected," she calmly reminded him.

"Yes, well, I've had a chance to reconsider."

"Does this mean you no longer think I lack the necessary qualifications? Has my family suddenly gained respectability without my knowledge?"

His jaw clenched, he glared at the embroidered samplers on the wall, desperately wishing he could find the solution to his problems in the colorful stitching. Patience, he noticed, was another virtue missing from Matthew's list. Diplomacy wasn't among them either. Cole frequently found the two in short supply. Since time was getting short as well, he decided to be as blunt as she had been. "Listen, Claire, if you're still willing to act as Daisy's nursemaid, I'd be pleased to hire you."

Instead of the joyful acceptance he hoped for, she calmly poured herself more tea. "From what you've just said, I gather neither of the women from the employment agency was agreeable."

"No," he growled. "Besides, only one of them showed up."

"What happened to the other one?"

"The letter said she decided to stay on with her present

family. The wife apparently had just discovered she was expecting a second child."

"I see." Claire sipped her tea. "Then what about the one they did send? Didn't she like small towns?"

Cole felt his shoulders tighten. *Damn! She asked more questions than Tanner.* "The woman left on the next train bound for Chicago." What he didn't confess was that the prospective nursemaid refused to stay in a home where the husband was suspected of murdering his wife.

Claire helped herself to a shortbread cookie. "Perhaps Alma Dobbs knows of some local women who might be interested in working for you."

He jammed his hands into the pockets of his jacket where she wouldn't notice they had curled into fists. "Tried a couple of them, too."

She smoothed the napkin in her lap. "And . . . ?"

"And they didn't work out."

"Why is that?" she inquired innocently.

He skewered her with a look. "They just didn't."

She didn't say anything, just kept watching, waiting, for him to continue.

He let out a disgruntled sigh, resumed pacing. Claire Sorenson had a perverse streak hidden under all that softness on the outside. She wasn't about to let up until she had heard all the humiliating details. Very well, he decided, if that's what it took.

"Alma recommended two young women," he said. "The first flatly refused. Claimed I gave her the creeps. In spite of my alibi, she's convinced I killed Priscilla. The second one had agreed, but the next day decided to pay her cousin in Indiana an extended visit instead. I suspect Leonard Brock might have influenced her decision." To make matters worse, Cole thought glumly, Alma had given him an ultimatum. Either find a nursemaid without further delay, or he would find himself in need of a housekeeper as well.

Claire began to gather the tea things. "I can see where you must be feeling desperate."

Taking the cup and saucer from her hand, he set it down so forcibly the china rattled on the tray. "Look, Claire, I need your help. I've got a business to run, but can't make any headway when I have to come home early to change diapers and spoonfeed applesauce. Just name your price."

"Then I'm your a last resort," she said, looking him square in the eye.

Last resort? He nearly laughed out loud. Hell, she was the only resort. "Tell me how I can make it up to you for the things I said. I'm prepared to get down on my knees and beg if necessary."

"I accept."

Startled, he could only stare. "You want me on my knees . . . ?"

"I admit that was the revenge I originally wished for," she said with a small smile. "Let me rephrase. What I meant to say was that I am willing to act as Daisy's nursemaid for as long you need me."

He let out a long, slow breath. "Can you start immediately?"

"You mean tonight?"

"That's why I brought the carriage."

"*You* brought the carriage?" Claire rose and finished collecting the tea things. "Here, all this time I thought poor Tim O'Brien was waiting outdoors in the cold."

Cole added his cup and saucer to the tray, hoping to spirit her away before she changed her mind. Or her family returned. He wasn't in the mood to tangle with either Nils or Lud. "Tim's at the house, keeping on eye on Daisy."

"Tim!" She stopped what she was doing and shot him a look of dismay.

Cole shrugged. "It's dinnertime, and Alma had to be home because . . ."

". . . Harold expects his supper on the table."

He grinned at her. "Guess you've been around long enough to quote Alma chapter and verse."

"You must have been pretty persuasive to convince Tim to act as baby nurse."

"You better believe it," he said, nodding. "The new pair of snakeskin boots he's been admiring at the dry goods store were an added bonus."

She picked up the tray, her face alight. "You won't be sorry you hired me."

He frowned. "You understand, don't you, Claire, the position is only temporary. Just until the agency finds a suitable candidate."

"I understand." She kept her expression carefully schooled, her tone neutral. "You want only the best for your daughter."

Cole silently cursed his clumsiness as she hurried off to pack her belongings. He hadn't meant to hurt her feelings yet again. He reminded himself he had only warned her for her own good. It would be cruel to let her think the position would be permanent. Unfair to give her false hope. Claire was too young, and far too attractive, to be employed in a widower's household. People would talk, make unkind assumptions. As soon as a more suitable baby nurse, preferably a woman gray-haired and dowdy, could be found he'd send Claire off with glowing references and a generous bonus. She'd be able to move away from Brockton, away from the leeches who called themselves family, and start life anew.

Still, he regretted causing the glow of pleasure to fade from her pretty face.

Claire did what she always did when troubled—she turned to baking. Adding more molasses to the mixture in the bowl, she stirred vigorously. Since coming to work in the Garrett household, she hadn't heard a word from either her father or Nils. Their silence was beginning to worry her. She hadn't expected either of them to be overjoyed when they learned from her note that she was employed by

Cole Garrett, but she hoped they would accept her decision. With time they might even see the advantage of at least one member of the family bringing in a steady income.

In the week that followed her addition to the Garrett household, a pattern of sorts had emerged. Cole left for the sawmill early each morning and returned late each evening. During the day, Alma saw to the smooth running of the household—dusting, shopping, and preparing the evening meal, which was kept in a warming oven until Cole's return. Claire's sole responsibility was caring for Daisy, a task she delighted in. No chore was too tedious or unappealing. Each squeal and gurgle from the baby evoked an answering smile from Claire. With every passing day, she felt herself grow increasingly fond of her little charge. She feared that when the time came, the parting would be painful.

Claire even loved living in a big house in town, loved her spacious room on the third floor. She would have been perfectly content except for a nagging concern for her family. Placing a spoonful of dough between her palms, she rolled it into a ball which she then dipped in sugar and set on a cookie sheet. She had explained that the post required her to live in. Her father would have been angry, but surely his temper would have cooled by now. Wouldn't it? If Pa or Nils didn't contact her soon, she decided to seek them out. Her family might not amount to much in the eyes of the rest of the world, but it was the only one she had, and she didn't like being estranged.

She had just removed one pan from the oven and replaced it with another when the back door swung open and Cole entered on a draft of cold air.

"Something smells good." Cole snatched a cookie still warm from the oven and devoured half of it in one bite. "Umm."

Claire smiled at the image. Instead of a powerful lumber baron, he seemed more like a hungry, overgrown schoolboy.

"Shame on you, eating cookies before dinner," she chided him as she would Nils. "Didn't anyone ever tell you that will ruin your appetite?"

"If they told me, I didn't pay any attention." Unrepentant, he shrugged out of his coat and hung it on a hook next to Claire's jacket.

"Mrs. Dobbs left your dinner warming." She motioned toward the stove as she wiped cookie dough and sugar from her fingers with a kitchen towel. "Sit down, and I'll have it ready for you in just a minute."

"Don't bother. I'm used to fending for myself."

"It's no trouble." Careful not to burn herself, Claire removed a small cast iron bake oven, set it on the table, and ladled out a generous serving of lamb stew. "I'm used to looking after Pa and Nils," she explained, setting the steaming plate in front of Cole. "They're apt to come home at all hours, and are always hungry. Both are completely helpless in a kitchen. Between the two of them, they couldn't pry open a can of beans." She twisted the kitchen towel around and around. "I guess that's why I worry about them."

"They're grown men, Claire. It's time they start taking care of themselves."

"I know." She gave him a self-deprecatory smile. "It's just that I've watched over them ever since Mother died. It's become a habit of sorts."

He looked as though he was about to argue the point, then changed his mind. "Care to join me?" he said instead.

"No," she replied, startled by the invitation. "Thank you, but I ate earlier."

"I'm starved," he said, digging into his food with gusto. "I can't remember if I've had anything to eat since breakfast."

"If you'd like, I could fix a lunch for you to take with you."

"You're here to care for Daisy. I wouldn't want to take unfair advantage of you." He flashed a grin in her direction as he speared a chunk of carrot. "Although to be honest, it's rather nice having someone fuss over me at the end of a long day. Especially one coming on the heels of an even longer week."

She didn't know how to respond to his remark. To hide her uncertainty, she turned away and checked the tray of cookies browning in the oven.

"Unlike your father and brother, I'm a veritable wizard when it comes to cooking. I make a mean apple pie, though I have to confess my bread tends to be a bit on the heavy side." He broke apart a roll and slathered it with butter.

She looked at him in surprise. "Surely, you're teasing."

"On the contrary, I'm perfectly serious." He helped himself to more of Alma's stew, then laughed at the patent disbelief on her face. "Has anyone ever told you that you're transparent as glass. Whatever you're thinking is written across your face for all the world to see."

The cookies had finished baking so she removed the pan from the oven and slid them onto a rack to cool. "And if that isn't bad enough, I blush too easily. It's a curse."

"Well, it may be a curse, but it's a charming one."

Claire felt heat rise in her cheeks at the compliment. He laughed, apparently pleased with himself for provoking the desired response. Though she was exasperated with herself for falling easy victim, she also admitted she enjoyed his company. In addition to him being so handsome that her heart did strange little flip-flops, he was also very . . .

She cast about for the suitable word or phrase, and came up with "nice." The word seemed woefully inadequate. "Nice" seemed a more likely choice when describing a maiden aunt or favorite schoolteacher. But the fact remained, Cole Garrett was very likable. Of course, he could also be arrogant and infuriating, but at times like this he was definitely nice.

And that, in her estimation, made him even more attractive.

His dinner finished, he shoved his plate aside and reached for another cookie. "These are quite good. Perhaps sometime we can swap recipes."

"Mr. Garrett, would . . ."

"Cole," he interrupted. "Call me Cole."

Claire dumped the baking dishes into the pan of soapy water. It was one thing to think of him privately as Cole, and another thing entirely to address him face-to-face by his given name. "That would be inappropriate," she said primly. "I'm afraid I couldn't."

He dismissed her objection with a shrug. "If it makes you feel more comfortable, call me Mr. Garrett when others are around. The remainder of the time we can drop the formalities."

Sensing it would be futile to argue, she nodded. "Very well, since you insist."

"I insist. Now what were you about to say before I interrupted?"

"I was about to ask if you'd like coffee or tea?"

"Neither." Getting up, he went to the icebox and poured himself a tall glass of buttermilk. He started to loosen his necktie, then hesitated. "Do you mind?"

The simple request pleased her inordinately. He was treating her as though she were a fine lady, not a lowly servant. "Of course not, provided," she added as an afterthought, "you tell me how you learned your way around a kitchen."

He grinned at her, unaware of the devastating affect it had on her. "Believe me, I wore my share of aprons when I first started in the lumber business."

"You? In an apron?" The idea of this almost overwhelmingly masculine figure in an apron seemed so incongruous she struggled to contain her laughter.

"Think it's funny, do you?" Snagging his third cookie, he leaned a hip against the counter, one ankle casually crossed over the other. "Toughest job I ever tackled was cook's helper, or 'cookee,' as they're called, in Brownie's kitchen. At Camp Twenty, we had two hundred men to feed. I'd start in on the pies right after breakfast, sixty every morning. Got so I could make a pie a minute."

"A pie a minute?" She wasn't sure whether he was teasing or not.

"The camp had three big Adam Hall stoves that could bake twenty-four at a time. Raisin was always the men's favorite." He took a swig of buttermilk, then continued, his voice reflective. "After the pies, we'd start on the cookies and cupcakes, dozen upon dozen until the barrel was full. By then, the bread would be ready to pan. We'd make big loaves, five to a sheet-iron pan, forty or fifty in all. And that doesn't begin to describe the quantity of food we prepared for breakfast and supper."

She watched him drain his glass. "Pa never talked much about camp life. I had no idea what it was like."

"Sorry. Hope I didn't bore you."

"You didn't," she said with a smile. Indeed, she relished the camaraderie.

His dark head to one side, he studied her in a way that made her heartbeat quicken. "Most people would be asleep at this hour. What are you doing up so late?"

"I kept thinking about Pa and Nils, wondering how they were getting along. Baking always helps take my mind off worries." As she reached out to take his empty glass, her fingers brushed his. She drew in a deep breath and took an involuntary step backward. Electricity seemed to arc from his hand to hers. Startled by the unexpected response, she stared up at him, wondering if he, too, had felt the sharp tingle of awareness that had passed between them. The telltale darkening of his eyes to the shade of pewter suggested he had sensed it as well.

"Claire . . ." he began, his voice husky.

She looked at him, afraid to say anything, do anything, that might snap this tenuous bond between them.

He cleared his throat, glanced away. "I don't think I've thanked you for coming here to take care of Daisy. I hope it doesn't create problems for you with your family."

Claire felt deflated at his words, and promptly called herself a fool. What had she been hoping for? That Cole would acknowledge he felt a similar attraction toward her? Silly woman, she berated herself, life wasn't a fairy tale. She wasn't Cinderella, and he wasn't Prince Charming.

What had he just said? Something about her family . . . ? She forced herself to concentrate, then remembered. "Pa and Nils will be happy with my working here once they see food in the cupboard and money left over for beer."

"You work hard for your money." His expression hardened. "Your father and brother aren't entitled to a cent. They're able-bodied men. Let them earn their own."

She turned to the sink and began washing the bowl she had used for mixing the cookie dough. How could she explain that some things weren't options? Life was different for a man; women had fewer choices.

Cole headed toward the door, then hesitated. "Another thing," he said, "I should warn you, there's bound to be talk about our living under the same roof."

She didn't look up from scrubbing a stubborn stain from a baking sheet. "How can anyone object to you hiring a nursemaid?"

"That in itself wouldn't be cause for gossip, but, well, you're young . . . attractive. And moreover, people haven't forgiven you for providing me with an alibi for the night of Priscilla's murder."

"I should think everyone would be pleased that an innocent man isn't going to prison for a crime he didn't commit," she said with a trace of asperity.

"Perhaps. But by freeing me, you destroyed their peace of mind." His face etched with weariness, he slid his hands into his pants pockets. "When Tanner released me, it was as good as advertising that the real killer still walks the streets. Until he's caught, no one will feel safe."

She whirled about, unmindful of the dishrag in her hand dripping soapy water on the floor. "Surely you don't think that whoever killed Priscilla is still in Brockton?"

"It's possible." Cole shrugged, meeting her look with reluctance. "Sorry, I don't mean to frighten you, but you need to be careful. Keep the doors locked at all times. Be wary of strangers."

The thought of a murderer lurking in quiet little Brockton raised gooseflesh along her arms. She caught her lower lip between her teeth. "Alma mentioned that people were nervous."

"Folks here would feel much more at ease with someone—anyone—locked behind bars."

"—even if that person was innocent."

"Exactly," he concurred. "Some may even resent you for robbing them of their sense of complacency."

"Those people should pray that whoever murdered Priscilla is found quickly and brought to justice."

"I couldn't agree more. Tomorrow I intend to pay Tanner a visit and see if he's made any progress on solving the case. But I don't hold out much hope for an easy solution."

"Cole . . . ?" She raised troubled eyes to his. "Who do you think killed Priscilla? And why?"

"Wish I had the answers. All I seem to do is ask myself those same questions over and over again. Once Chief Tanner comes up with a possible motive, he'll be like a dog gnawing on a bone. I almost pity the man he suspects. Tanner can be relentless."

An involuntary shiver coursed over her.

Cole started to leave the kitchen, then stopped, withdrew an envelope from the pocket of his jacket, and handed it to her. "I almost forgot."

She stared at it blankly. "What is it?"

"Your first week's salary. You'll discover that I added a small clothing stipend." Having said that, he tossed the envelope on the kitchen table and went upstairs.

SEVEN

Claire's footsteps felt so light they almost bounced along the boardwalk lining Main Street. The weight of the pay envelope tucked deep in her pocket served to anchor her to the ground. She was about to treat herself to the unheard-of luxury of shopping for new clothes. After some argument, Cole had convinced her of the necessity of an appropriate wardrobe for her role as nursemaid. He claimed that more suitable attire would be an investment in her future.

"God knows, Claire, it's nothing to be ashamed of," Cole had told her when she hesitated. "I know firsthand that one can't buy new clothes if the pantry's empty."

When a qualified nursemaid was found to take her place, he had promised her a glowing reference. Armed with that and stylishly but modestly outfitted, she could head for Chicago, where no one knew her family's reputation, and sign on with an employment agency.

The thought of leaving everything familiar for the uncertainty of a big city was daunting, but Claire knew she had no future here in Brockton. Cole was offering a rare opportunity to improve her lot. She ought to be grateful, yet part of her felt torn. In all likelihood she would never see Daisy again—or the child's father. And therein lay the danger. Cole Garrett occupied her thoughts far too much of the time. If she wasn't careful, he might also capture her heart.

Claire turned up Main Street. Brockton formed a link in a chain of sawdust cities where pine was considered green gold. Smaller than some, bigger than others, its neat brick buildings announced its prosperity to anyone passing through. Claire likened the brick facades and brightly painted trim in the business district to soldiers standing straight and proud in parade dress. Closer to the river, the area her father liked to frequent, was a seamier side of town. There, bars and dance halls and brewing companies stood shoulder to shoulder.

She paused along the boardwalk to study the display windows of dress shops. All the garments thus far looked far too expensive, or too elaborate, for her limited budget. Besides, if she was frugal, she hoped to have enough left to purchase a coat. At the corner of Cedar and Main, she came upon Mildred Mason's Clothing Emporium. A sign in the window boasted a large inventory of ready-made garments at prices anyone can afford. "Perfect," she said under her breath as she pushed open the door.

The tinkle of a bell heralded her arrival.

"May I help you?" A tall, heavyset woman with dark hair, whom Claire assumed was the proprietress, approached wearing a slight frown.

Claire fought down a rush of nervousness at the woman's forbidding manner. "I'm here to look at dresses, and perhaps a coat."

Mildred swept an assessing look over her potential customer, taking in the worn jacket, the mended skirt. "My time is too valuable to waste on someone with nothing better to do than try on garments she can ill afford."

Stung by the woman's rudeness, Claire's first reaction was to flee in embarrassment. Then she drew herself upright, dug in her heels. Along with confidence, the money in her pocket brought a giddy sense of power. "Perhaps I've come to the wrong place. My money is too precious to waste in a store that doesn't value its patrons."

"Wait!" Mildred rapidly reassessed Claire. Though

clearly skeptical of her ability to pay, her tone softened somewhat when she addressed her again. "Since I'm experiencing a temporary lull in customers, I suppose I could direct you to the appropriate size."

Claire concealed her triumph. "Thank you. I would appreciate any help you could give me."

"Yes, well, come this way." Mildred led her across the store to a rack against the far wall. "You're slender. You might find something here to your liking. I bought these from a store in Grand Rapids that went bankrupt. Although I got a good deal on them, I realized when I got home that they tend to run on the small side."

Excitement bubbled through Claire's veins at the sight of so many pretty things. Glancing discreetly at the price tags, she let out a slow sigh of relief at knowing most were within the range she had set—barely. "Is there a fitting room?" she asked the shopkeeper.

Mildred indicated a door to her left. "Call if you need assistance."

Claire spent the next half-hour trying on a variety of dresses and skirts before finally selecting two dresses, one a soft grayish-blue, the other a rose-brown with a row of tiny buttons down the bodice, along with a dark skirt and several plain white blouses. The final item added to her growing pile was a dolman cloak of sturdy gray worsted. The new clothes would take every cent of the stipend, along with most of her pay envelope, but she remembered Cole's advice to look at an improved wardrobe as an investment in the future. Totaling the prices in her head one last time, she wasn't aware at first of the sudden hush that had fallen as she made her way toward the cash register.

Belatedly, she noticed Mildred Mason was surrounded by several women customers. Wordlessly, Mildred took the items from Claire and tallied the amount. "I assume you'll be taking everything with you?"

Nodding, Claire counted out the money, conscious of

the women's scrutiny. "I'm going to wear the coat, but you can wrap the rest."

"Very well." Mildred efficiently folded all the items into a neat bundle, then wrapped it in brown paper and tied it with string. "If you're interested, my spring items will be in within the next several weeks."

"I'll keep that in mind." Claire gave the proprietress a polite smile, nodded to the women customers, and headed for the door.

Just as Claire reached for the door handle, one of the women remarked, "Cousin Charlotte heard she left a will."

"A will . . . ?" the other echoed. "You don't say."

Their voices dropped to whispers, preventing Claire from overhearing more of their conversation. *A will?* Who had the women been gossiping about, she wondered as she made her way back up Main Street.

Her eyes widened in surprise as she saw her brother round a corner and walk toward her, his limp more marked than usual. His head down, he didn't notice her, which gave Claire the chance to observe him. She was shocked by his unkempt appearance. His blond hair was stringy, unwashed, and sadly in need of trimming, his clothing soiled and wrinkled. He might have passed right by her if she hadn't snagged hold of his sleeve.

"Nils!" she cried. "You look horrible. Have you been ill?"

He jerked free. "What's it to you?"

She recoiled at the sour smell of alcohol on his breath. "You've been drinking. Why aren't you at work?"

"Because I quit."

"Perhaps I could talk to Mr. Garrett . . ."

"I wouldn't accept a job from Garrett if his sawmill was the last one in Michigan." His bloodshot eyes narrowed to slits when he noticed she was wearing a new coat. "Gotta hand it to the man. Looks like he didn't waste any time taking care of my baby sister."

Her cheeks flamed. "I'm employed as nursemaid. How

I chose to spend my earnings is none of your business. You're just disappointed because you can't use them for a bottle."

"You're always harping I drink too much."

"Only because you do. It's the middle of the day, Nils, far too early to start drinking."

"As far as I'm concerned, anytime's a good time."

Claire sighed, knowing further discussion would only end in an argument. "How's Pa?" she asked, changing the subject.

"How do you think he is?" Nils snarled. "He's good and pissed you're working for Garrett."

"You needn't be vulgar." She glanced around surreptitiously, hoping no one was close enough to hear. "Next time I get paid, I'll send Pa money—that ought to make him a little happier. If I can't get away, I'll ask Tim O'Brien to deliver it."

Nils shrugged as though he couldn't care less. Leaning down, he absently rubbed his injured leg. "Rumor has it your friend Garrett's having a tough time finding enough men for the river drive."

This was the first Claire had heard of any difficulties. She couldn't help but wonder if that was the reason Cole seemed so preoccupied of late. "Are they saying why men aren't signing on?"

Nils lips curled into a thin smile. "Ask Garrett." Tired of talking, he pushed past her and entered the nearest tavern.

The remainder of the way home, Claire pondered everything she had heard downtown. Gossip, so it seemed, ran rampant, with rumors of wills and business problems. Added to that, her chance encounter with Nils had nothing to ease her concern. Nils no longer seemed to care about anything except his next drink. Before the accident that had crushed his leg, she had always looked up to him, admired his quick intellect and his effortless charm. Now he had become a virtual stranger.

By the time Claire reached the house, her initial pleasure in her new wardrobe had vanished, replaced by a nagging presentiment of trouble. Pushing open the back door, she found Alma Dobbs seated at the kitchen table, a piece of paper in her hand. Daisy apparently still hadn't awakened from her nap.

"'Bout time you got back," Alma grumbled, glancing up from a document she had been reading. "Took you long enough."

"Sorry." Setting her parcel on the counter, Claire removed her new coat and carefully hung it by the door. "I ran into my brother downtown. I haven't talked to Nils since I started here."

"Hmph," the housekeeper sniffed.

"Nils mentioned that Cole . . . I mean, Mr. Garrett," she corrected hastily, "is having trouble finding men for the river drive. Is that true?"

"I heard talk to that effect." Alma folded the paper she had been studying and replaced it in an envelope. "Seems almost as soon as he hires 'em, they get a better offer somewhere else."

"Another thing," Claire said as she lowered herself into the chair opposite Alma. "I heard women in the dress shop mention someone leaving a will. When they realized I was listening, they started whispering so I didn't find out who they were talking about."

Alma tapped the envelope in front of her with her stubby fingertips, making the paper rattle. "This here is what they was talkin' about."

Claire stared at the white oblong as though it would rear up and bite. It looked official, important—and vaguely menacing. "What is it?"

"A summons of sorts." Alma's plain face wore a dazed expression. "It's from Mr. Lamont, the lawyer. I'm to be in his office tomorrow afternoon at four o'clock for the readin' of Priscilla Garrett's will. Mr. Garrett got one, too. I left his on the hall table."

Claire's mind spun with possibilities. Priscilla Garrett

had been, after all, a wealthy woman. It was only natural for someone in her position to leave a will. Only natural that she'd leave a small bequest to a loyal employee such as Alma. And leave the remainder to her husband and child. Why, then, did she feel so uneasy? "I'm sure this was Mrs. Garrett's way of showing how much she appreciated your help and friendship."

Alma summoned a wobbly smile, her eyes suspiciously bright. "S'pose you're right, but it don't seem fittin'. Times it's hard to believe she's gone. And dyin' the way she did . . ." A shudder shook the housekeeper's plump shoulders.

"Were you with her very long?" Claire asked, her voice low, sympathetic.

"Woulda been ten years come summer." Alma dabbed her eyes with the corner of her apron. "I worked for her father, but when Mrs. Garrett married, she insisted I come with her."

"Then you two must have been close."

Alma's expression changed, became shuttered. Before Claire could voice any more questions, they were interrupted by a knock on the back door. Alma pushed to her feet, her face resolute. "That'd be Tim. Let him in while I go fetch my list."

Claire answered the door while Alma disappeared to find a shopping list she had prepared earlier. Tim O'Brien stood on the porch, his tweed cap clutched in his work-roughened hands. He gave her a deferential nod, but avoided meeting her eyes. "Afternoon, Miss."

"Come in," she invited, standing aside to allow him entry. "Mrs. Dobbs will be here in just a minute."

"That's all right, miss. Out here is fine."

"Nonsense." She opened the door wider. "No reason to stand out in the cold when you can be in a nice warm kitchen."

With obvious reluctance, he stepped inside. Tim O'Brien, she realized, was not a man who engaged in idle chatter, or one to initiate a conversation. She knew nothing about him other than that he was a trusted employee in the Garrett household. He kept the carriage polished to a glossy sheen, the horses sleek and well-groomed. Other than these meager facts, she was ignorant of any personal likes and dislikes. Silence stretched between them, stiff and thick as taffy.

Claire cast about for the means to break the awkward silence. Happening to glance downward, she spotted his shiny snakeskin boots and recalled the bribe Cole had offered in return for watching Daisy the afternoon of his visit. "Nice boots, Tim."

Tim's gaze followed the direction of hers. "Thank you, Miss."

Claire couldn't be absolutely certain, but she thought she had nearly tricked him into a smile. "No reason to be so formal. Please, call me Claire."

He bobbed his head in acknowledgment.

Emboldened, Claire latched onto the opportunity to say what she had wanted to for over a week now. Quickly, before Alma returned, she blurted, "I haven't had the chance to thank you before, but I appreciate your coming forward and telling Chief Tanner you saw me leave the house the morning of Mrs. Garrett's murder."

"Just told the man what I saw, is all."

"Still, if you hadn't verified my story, I don't think anyone would have believed me."

"Mr. Garrett's as fine as they come. I'd do anything for him. I owe him."

She was still puzzling over the meaning behind his words when Alma bustled into the kitchen, waving the list in her hand. Any further discussion with Tim would have to be postponed.

Cole waited in James Lamont's office. His expression deliberately bland, he flicked a speck of lint from his trousers and wished he was somewhere—anywhere—else.

Last night upon returning home, he had found a heavy white envelope propped against a Chinese bowl on the hall table. He had retreated to the library, where he built a small fire in the grate and poured himself a generous glass of bourbon. Only then did he finally open the envelope and read the contents. In it, James Lamont had informed him he was to be present the following day for the reading of Priscilla's final will and testament.

It had come as somewhat of a jolt. Until that moment, he hadn't been aware that Priscilla even had a will. Certainly she had never mentioned it. And neither had James, for that matter. Knowing how much Priscilla had despised him, he wondered what she could have possibly wanted him to have. That question had kept him tossing and turning until just before dawn. He had found himself wishing halfheartedly that Daisy would fuss and wake Claire. Somehow, talking with her helped put things in their proper perspective. In addition to being an attentive listener, her advice was sound, her approach practical.

And it felt good just being around her. Too good, perhaps. Cole shifted in his seat, uncomfortable with his own thoughts. He blamed his unwanted preoccupation with Claire Sorenson on being too long without a woman, he decided. Frowning, he tried to remember just how long it had been. Not since before his marriage to Priscilla—and not afterwards, either. Priscilla had made it clear from the start that she wanted nothing more from him other than his name.

Cole sighed, impatient with himself. This wasn't the time or place for such musings, but at the moment he welcomed any distraction.

Alma Dobbs, her short, sturdy figure clothed in her Sunday best, was the next person to be shown into the lawyer's office. After greeting Cole, she took the seat alongside him and folded her hands primly in her lap.

Cole looked up as the door opened for the second time. Leonard Brock entered, bringing with him the smell of cigar smoke, hair pomade, and sandalwood. Sparing Cole only a cursory glance, his former father-in-law took the chair farthest from Cole, obviously wanting as much space as possible between them. The muffled sound of voices, a man's deeper tones interspersed with a woman's softer ones, preceded the last of the arrivals.

Sophie Lamont, dressed from head to toe in dove gray, entered on her husband's arm. Sophie, Cole knew, had been Priscilla's closest friend, perhaps her only friend among dozens of acquaintances. On the surface they had been the unlikeliest of friends, but together they must have discovered a variety of shared interests. He felt grateful Priscilla had been thoughtful enough to honor the one woman who truly mourned her passage with a small bequest. Giving those present a tentative smile, Sophie sat on the remaining chair between Leonard and Alma.

James took his place behind the desk, then slipped on a pair of wire-rimmed spectacles and cleared his throat. "All of you know why you've been asked here this afternoon," he began, looking at each one in turn. "Shortly before her death, Priscilla came to me with the request to draw up her will and final testament. I tried to dissuade her, convince her she was much too young. But, as all of you know, Priscilla could be quite headstrong."

Sophie sniffled loudly, oblivious to Leonard Brock's frown of disapproval.

"Sophie, dear," James reproved gently. "Please, try to control your emotions."

"I'm sorry, James, truly I am, but Priscilla was my dearest friend." She fished a dainty, lace-embroidered handkerchief out of her handbag and dabbed her eyes.

James returned to the matter at hand, his expression solemn. "Regardless of my arguments to the contrary, Priscilla was adamant. She insisted she wanted her affairs in order should anything untoward occur. She claimed that once the will was signed and notarized, she wouldn't give the matter another thought until she was near her dotage."

At this, Sophie erupted in a fresh outburst of grief. Reaching over, Alma patted her hand by way of comfort. James gave his wife a stern look over the rims of his glasses, and waited impatiently for her weeping to subside.

Cole studied the carpet. The swirls of burgundy and navy blue in the floral pattern seemed symbolic of the way his life was going, around and around with no definite destination in sight. Just a hopeless maze of confusion and happenstance. He didn't want a dime of Priscilla's—all he wanted was to reclaim control over his own life.

"Can we get on with this matter?" Leonard inquired brusquely.

"Yes, sir. Certainly, sir." James Lamont admonished his wife with a look and once again focused his attention on the documents before him. After reading the opening statements attesting to Priscilla's being of sound mind, he got down to specifics. "The first of Mrs. Garrett's bequests is to her loyal and faithful housekeeper, Mrs. Alma Dobbs."

Alma leaned forward in anticipation, her expression hopeful. Cole listened dispassionately as the lawyer read off a generous monetary sum. A pleased smile wreathed the woman's plump face.

Next, James informed his wife that she had been left several pieces of costly jewelry as a token of Priscilla's friendship. Sophie, too, seemed happy with the gift, dabbing away a freshet of tears while murmuring her gratitude.

"To my father, Leonard Brock," James continued, his voice ponderous, deferential, "I leave the bonds and stock certificates gifted to me since childhood. Through his shrewd guidance and business acumen, these I am certain will have increased substantially in value."

Leonard nodded gravely. Judging from his expression, Cole surmised the man had expected nothing less from his daughter. Still, Cole couldn't help but wonder why he had been asked to attend the reading of Priscilla's will. Considering the nature of their relationship, it surprised him that Priscilla would want him here. Or had the invitation been designed to embarrass and humiliate him? Perhaps Priscilla wished to advertise the fact that she had left him nothing. And what about Daisy? Didn't the little girl merit something from her mother? Not that Priscilla had proved much of a mother, but still . . .

James gave a polite cough. "And now for the final bit of business at hand—the trust fund."

Cole sat up straighter. Until this moment, he hadn't known that Priscilla even had a trust fund. He was vaguely aware that the others in the room were staring at the lawyer with renewed interest. Even Sophie had ceased her weeping and watched her husband with alacrity.

James gave Cole a long look, then dropped his gaze to the papers in his hands. "I leave the remainder of my earthly possessions, including the trust fund established by my maternal grandmother, Louisa Abernathy, to be divided equally among any surviving offspring. I hereby appoint my husband, Cole Townsend Garrett, as executor of that trust until such time said offspring marry or come of legal age."

The lawyer's words fell like pebbles into a still pond, sending out an ever-widening circle of ripples. Cole sat stunned, already feeling the heavy yoke of responsibility. The two women turned to each other, each seemingly eager to voice a plethora of questions.

Leonard Brock was the first to recover from the surprise. "Son of a bitch!" he cried as he leapt to his feet, his face a disturbing shade of purple. "That trust fund of my daughter's represents a small fortune."

"Leonard, please." James adopted a placating tone. "Calm yourself. It's not wise getting this upset."

Ignoring the warning, Brock jabbed a stubby finger in Cole's direction. "What the hell was Priscilla thinking to put you in charge of her trust fund? She ought to have named me, for chrissake—I'm her father. Why, that child of hers is still an infant. By the time she reaches marrying age, you'll have squandered away her entire inheritance."

Cole eyed his former father-in-law coolly. "I've never been in the habit of 'squandering' anything, Leonard. I doubt I'll start now. For whatever reason, Priscilla felt confident I'd look out for Daisy's best interests."

Leonard's hands bunched into fists as he took a menacing step forward. "Are you implying I wouldn't?"

"Gentlemen, gentlemen." Alarmed, James's gaze shifted from one to the other. "Such talk is an insult to my client's last wishes."

Leonard shot James a look of such loathing that the lawyer seemed to visibly shrivel in his chair. The lawyer effectively silenced, Brock unleashed his venom once again on Cole. "You bastard! All this time you've been eyeing my little girl's bank account. I don't know how you did it, but somehow you managed to sweet-talk her into making this damn will. If it's the last thing I do, I'll prove you killed Priscilla for her money. Damned if I'll let you get away with this!"

He stormed from the office.

Bug-eyed, Alma watched him go, clearly fascinated at finding herself witness to the drama played out in front of her. Pretending polite disinterest, Sophie pawed through the contents of her pocketbook.

Obviously discomfitted by the scene, James cleared his throat yet again, then neatly aligned the sheets of paper in front of him. "You'll have to forgive Leonard's outburst, Cole. He's beside himself with grief. I'm sure he didn't mean anything by it."

Cole wished he could be as certain.

. . . A small fortune. You killed Priscilla for the money. The man's accusation rang in his ears long after he left the lawyer's office.

EIGHT

Her nerves wound tighter than a corkscrew, Claire jumped at the sharp crack of a door slamming shut. At last, Cole had returned. The baby, sensitive to Claire's mood, blinked up at her from the high chair. Her small face puckered, ready to burst into tears at the slightest provocation.

"It's all right, Daisy girl," she murmured, giving the child a smile meant to reassure.

Claire wiped the baby's sticky fingers with a damp cloth, removed her bib, and picked her up. The child had been fussy the entire afternoon, napping fitfully and gnawing on everything she could get into her mouth. It had taken all Claire's resources to amuse her. Even so, she welcomed anything that took her mind off the meeting at James Lamont's law office. Alma, dressed in her Sunday finery, had been unusually cheerful and chatty before she had left at the appointed hour. She obviously hoped to be generously compensated for being Priscilla Garrett's loyal and trusted employee. Claire couldn't help but wonder how well Cole had fared in his wife's will. In spite of the fact that the couple had shared the same roof, they hadn't seemed to harbor any genuine affection for each other.

Settling Daisy on one hip, Claire left the kitchen and started down the front hallway toward the stairs. She paused just outside the library. The door stood ajar. She saw Cole, his back turned, one hand braced against the mantel, standing before a low-burning fire. Something about his posture, perhaps the uncharacteristic droop of his broad shoulders, elicited her sympathy and concern.

"Mr. Garrett . . . ? Cole?"

He didn't glance up at hearing her voice.

Inner alarms sounded a warning. Taking a cautious step forward, she asked, "Cole, what's wrong?"

"What's wrong?" He let out a humorless laugh. "What makes you think something's wrong?"

Undeterred by his tone, Claire went closer. The library was swathed in murky shadow, the only illumination coming from the flames in the hearth. Not sure of a tactful way to approach the issue, she decided to go directly to the heart of the matter. "Whatever upset you must have to do with Mrs. Garrett's will. I take it things didn't go well."

"Now, *that's* an understatement if ever I heard one." Turning, he strode across the room, picked up a cut-glass decanter from the desk, and poured himself a drink.

Daisy caught a strand of hair that had come loose from the chignon at the base of her neck. Ignoring the gentle tug at the baby's hands, Claire forged ahead. "Are you disappointed at what your wife left you?"

"Disappointed . . . ?" Cole propped his weight against the heavy mahogany desk. "I would have been ecstatic if she had omitted my name entirely. And, Claire," he said, pinning her with a look of steel, "in the future, please don't refer to Priscilla as my wife. She's a part of my life I'd like to forget. Unfortunately, however, that's impossible."

Claire absently pulled her hair out of Daisy's grasp, only to have the baby reach for it again. She stood unmoving, the child in her arms, torn between leaving Cole alone to wrestle with private demons and the urge to stay. Drawing from a well of conflicting emotions, Claire realized she wanted to offer Cole comfort, support. And caring? Caring for such a man would lead to trouble. Was she willing to risk her heart on a man she barely knew? she asked herself. Someone who made her pulse race and her nerves tingle. A man who, in all likelihood, would never return her feelings. One who, even now, refused to share his thoughts.

"I'm sorry if I intruded on your privacy. You just seemed in need of a friend." She turned to leave.

"Claire, wait! Don't go." Setting his glass aside, he shoved away from the desk and narrowed the gap between them. "I had no call to take my frustration out on you. It's just that I'm so damned angry."

"What happened at Mr. Lamont's office?"

In an impatient gesture, he shoved long, square-tipped fingers through his hair. "Brock won't be content until he sees me locked behind bars."

"How can he blame you for what happened to his daughter?"

"He, better than anyone, knows our marriage was a sham from the start. Part of him believes I killed Priscilla to escape an untenable situation. After this afternoon, he's more convinced than ever."

Claire jiggled Daisy, who was getting restless. "Why would he think that?"

"Because of the money involved." Cole's expression turned even more grim.

Claire stared at him uncomprehendingly while Daisy, still not relinquishing hold of her hair, tried to stick her entire fist into her tiny mouth. "Money Priscilla left you?"

"Precisely." He tugged at the knot in his necktie. "This damn thing feels like a noose. It's choking me."

Claire simply waited for him to continue. Daisy, her eyelids starting to droop, nestled her head in the hollow of Claire's shoulder.

"God knows, there are few secrets here in Brockton. Better you hear the truth from me rather than a distorted version from the butcher or baker. In her will, Priscilla named me executor of a trust fund she left Daisy." He briefly outlined the details of the will, concluding with the fact that he was free to use the money as he saw fit until Daisy either married or came of age.

"I gather it's a substantial amount, or Leonard Brock wouldn't be so irate."

"Our esteemed mayor didn't waste any time voicing his displeasure. He stormed out of Lamont's office after accusing me of murder and probably headed straight for City Hall to talk with Tanner."

"But surely Mr. Tanner can reason with him. As chief of police, he knows you couldn't possibly have killed Mrs. Garrett."

"One of the first lessons I learned in the lumber trade was never to underestimate the power of money. Brock is a very influential man. He won't give up without a fight."

"But I explained to Chief Tanner you were home the night Mrs. Garrett died. He even found witnesses who saw me leave the next morning."

Cole gave her a pitying look. "Who do you think appointed Tanner?"

"The mayor . . ." Claire's eyes widened at the implication.

"Congratulations." Cole gave a grim nod of approval. "Edward Tanner owes his position as chief of police to Leonard Brock. If Tanner doesn't perform his duties to Brock's satisfaction, he can easily be dismissed."

Claire began a small rocking motion to soothe the sleepy baby as well as to soothe her own burgeoning fear. "The police chief—regardless of who appoints him—is sworn to uphold justice. It's his duty to find the guilty person. There's no justice, no fairness whatsoever, in prosecuting an innocent man."

"Unfortunately, it's not a perfect world where things are always fair and just." A wry smile touched his mouth for the briefest of moments, then disappeared. "As it is, Priscilla might as well have pointed a finger at me from the grave. Brock believes I killed her to gain control of her trust fund. Greed is one of the strongest motives there is for crime—including murder."

Sound asleep against Claire's shoulder, Daisy let out a

sound that was half gurgle, half sigh. Claire gently rubbed the baby's back in small, circular motions. "Poor thing, she's been cranky and out of sorts all day. I expect she'll sleep straight through 'til morning."

Cole smiled down at the little girl resting trustingly in the circle of Claire's arms. "I'm afraid Daisy has literally attached herself," he said, referring to the fistful of Claire's hair still twined in one hand.

"She likes to grab something soft to hold before she goes to sleep. Usually it's the ribbon trim on her baby blanket, but apparently," she said with a self-deprecatory laugh, "anything will do when she's desperate."

"Here," Cole said, moving closer. "Let me help get you untangled."

Without waiting for a reply, he carefully began to unwind strands of hair woven through tiny fingers. Claire's breath caught. He was so close she could see individual threads of his jacket, smell the tangy scent of his cologne, feel her pulse hammer. Feel heat radiate from his body. If she moved a fraction of an inch, she would brush against him.

Temptation crooked its evil finger.

What would it be like to lean into him, or be held in his embrace? To savor his hard, masculine strength against her softer, feminine curves? What would it be like, she wondered, to be possessed, totally and completely, by a man such as Cole Garrett?

And what would it be like to be loved?

"Now I understand why Daisy was holding on so tightly."

There was a husky quality to Cole's voice she hadn't heard before. Glancing upward, her eyes locked with those the color of woodsmoke. Cole now held the rebellious tendril that Daisy had once claimed. Gently he rubbed the shiny, ash-blond strand between his strong, work-roughened fingers. Claire's brain ceased to function. She felt a lump lodge in her throat the size of a grapefruit.

"Your hair feels like silk."

Just then the doorbell rang. Cole released her hair, and they sprang apart.

"Damn," Cole swore softly. "I'm not in the mood for visitors. Humor me, Claire. See who it is, then send them away. Please," he urged when she hesitated. "In the meantime, I'll take Daisy upstairs and put her in bed."

"Very well." Careful not to waken her little charge, Claire transferred Daisy into her father's arms.

Cole started for the stairs when he half-turned toward her. "You were right about my needing a friend tonight. After you get rid of our unwanted guest, will you join me downstairs for dinner?"

The doorbell pealed again—two quick, impatient jabs. Afraid the noise would wake Daisy, Claire abandoned any reservations she might have. Suddenly the thought of sitting across a dinner table from Cole and sharing a simple meal held enormous appeal. "I'd love to," she said with a smile.

He grinned in return, then disappeared upstairs with his daughter.

Removing the starched white apron she wore to protect her dress, Claire hurried to answer the front door before its incessant chiming succeeded in rousing Daisy—and ruined her prospect of dining with the baby's father.

"Mr. Lamont!" she gasped in surprise at finding the lawyer on the doorstep. He was nattily attired in a thick tweed Chesterfield buttoned to his chin and carried a gold-tipped malacca cane.

"And you must be Claire." He removed his bowler. "So . . ." he drawled, "you're the one everyone's talking about." His gaze traveled from her once-neat chignon with its escaping tendrils downward to rest on her scuffed leather shoes.

Dislike for the man began to mushroom. In addition to finding him arrogant, his condescending manner was undermining her confidence. "Mr. Garrett is indisposed. I'm afraid he isn't receiving callers this evening."

"He'll see me," James Lamont said with unshakable certainty. "Kindly inform him I'm here. Tell him I'm not leaving unless he does."

"Perhaps it would be better if you came back another time." Claire held her ground with grim determination. Drawing herself up to her full height, she met his stare boldly. The tightening of his handsome features told her that her efforts only antagonized him.

"Stand aside, Miss Sorenson. I doubt your employer will be pleased when I relate how obstinate you've been."

"It's all right, Claire." Cole's voice came from behind her. "Please show Mr. Lamont inside."

Claire stood aside as James Lamont brushed past her into the front hallway. The lawyer made no attempt whatsoever to hide his triumphant smirk.

Ignoring Claire, James addressed his remarks to Cole. "We have some important details to review regarding the trust fund. I thought the matter would be better handled in the privacy of your home rather than at the office."

Cole sighed wearily. "Whatever you think best. Let's go into the library, shall we?"

With Cole leading the way, the two men started down the hall toward the library. Before disappearing through the doorway, Cole stopped and turned. "And, Claire, I still plan to meet with you later as we discussed earlier."

Claire felt warmth flood her cheeks. Though relieved Cole hadn't changed his mind, she was glad James Lamont didn't know they planned to dine together. Somehow, she suspected, he wouldn't approve.

James shut the door securely behind him. "I don't want to add more grist for the rumor mill. God knows, there's enough talk already."

"If you're referring to Claire, you needn't worry. I trust her to keep anything she might overhear confidential."

"Claire, is it?" James raised a sandy brow askance. "How long have you and the Sorenson woman been on a first-name basis?"

Cole tried not to take offense at the lawyer's tone, reminding himself that James's curiosity was one of the qualities that made him good at what he did. "Join me for a brandy?"

James unbuttoned his topcoat and draped it over the back of a small settee in front of the fireplace. "Just a small one. If we're to discuss business, I need a clear head."

"Have a seat, then." Cole motioned him toward a pair of armchairs upholstered in hunter green leather and positioned at right angles to the settee. After pouring each of them brandy, he handed one to James and lowered himself into the chair opposite the lawyer.

Taking a sip, James crossed one impeccably clad leg over the other. "Are you sure it's wise to have that woman living here?"

"'That woman,' as you refer to her, has a name," Cole reminded him, his voice cool.

"She's Lud Sorenson's daughter, isn't she?" The question was purely rhetorical. James didn't wait for an answer before continuing. "From what I gather, her father can usually be found in one of the taverns down by the river. People say he spends more time drunk than sober."

"It isn't fair to judge Claire's merit based on the rest of her family." Cole scowled into the amber liquid in his glass. As loath as he was to admit it, he was no better than the man seated across from him. He, too, had been smug and judgmental. Assumed her character would prove a reflection of her father's. He couldn't have been more wrong.

"Nevertheless," James went on, "her background needs to be taken into account rather than ignored. I understand the brother's a regular chip off the block."

"Nils changed after his accident."

"Whatever persuaded you to ask Claire Sorenson to come and care for the baby?"

"Why did I *ask* her?" Cole let out a bark of mirthless laughter. "I was prepared to do more than ask. If need be, I was prepared to go down on my knees and beg."

James's brows shot up in surprise.

"What the devil was I supposed to do?" Cole inquired irritably. "Do you have any idea of the work involved in caring for an infant? Have you ever changed a diaper on a squirming baby? Miss Bartlesby hightailed it out of here after a tiff with Priscilla. Alma Dobbs makes no secret of the fact she hates children. She absolutely refuses to stay a minute past six o'clock. No one in town seems to want to be in the same house with a man suspected of murdering his wife. The situation called for desperate measures."

James nodded in sympathy. "But surely there must be someone better qualified? The Sorenson woman isn't trained for anything other than scrubbing floors and doing laundry."

"Claire happens to be quite competent when it comes to caring for infants."

"I must admit, your Claire isn't hard on the eyes." James smoothed his sandy-brown mustache with an index finger. "She's far more attractive than I had been lead to believe."

"Really? I hadn't noticed." Cole half-expected to be struck dead by a bolt of lightning for the blatant lie.

A small smile played across James's face. "The woman has a quiet, understated beauty one tends to overlook at first glance, but when seen close up she's really quite lovely."

It annoyed Cole to learn that James found Claire attractive. In certain quarters, James enjoyed a reputation with the ladies. It was rumored he was always in the midst of an affair with one woman or another. The fact that he had a wife didn't prick his conscience in the slightest. There was a time when Cole had suspected that James and Priscilla had been involved. But he hadn't cared enough to find out one way or the other. "What brings you here, James?" He swirled the brandy in his glass. "I assume you didn't come here to discuss Miss Sorenson's physical attributes."

"Before we begin discussing management of Priscilla's trust fund, I feel as your friend, as well as your lawyer, that I'm compelled to give you some sound advice."

"Advice about what?"

"Hear me out, Cole. Part of the reason I came tonight has to do with your choice of the baby's nurse." His handsome features arranged in an expression of concern, James leaned forward in his seat. "Not only is Claire Sorenson young and pretty, but she provided your alibi the night of your wife's murder. Think how it looks to others that she's living under the same roof."

Cole's temper started to simmer. "Get to the point, James."

"Knowing the people of this town as I do, it won't be long before they start to speculate that there's something going on between the two of you."

Cole jumped to his feet. "That's preposterous! Just because she's in my employ doesn't make us lovers."

"Of course not," James soothed. "Calm yourself, my friend. You know I'm only telling you this because I have your best interests at heart. You've been under a great deal of strain recently, and it may have impaired your judgment. I fear once Brock gets wind of who's taking care of his grandchild, he'll use it against you. He'll plant doubt about her credibility. Folks will wonder if she made up the entire story because she harbors tender feelings for you."

Cole walked to the desk and added more brandy to a drink he had yet to taste. "Brock can twist things all he likes. Witnesses who saw Claire leave that morning can substantiate her story."

James smoothed a wrinkle from his trousers. "Any lawyer with the ink still fresh on his diploma would have a field day with her so-called 'witnesses' once the case got to court."

A cold lump of fear settled deep in Cole's gut. "How's that?" he asked, his face impassive.

"Tim O'Brien and Karl Detmeijer," James sneered. "O'Brien's on your payroll. You hired the man when no one else would. The prosecution would claim he owes you and would lie if need be."

"And Karl? Does he owe me, too?"

"Ever notice the thick lenses Detmeijer wears? He's blind as a bat. Any lawyer worth his salt could shake his testimony that fast." He snapped his fingers to demonstrate.

A thick fog of despair engulfed Cole, obscuring his hopes of vindication. Despite Claire's coming forward with the truth, he still wasn't free from suspicion and doubt. And once Brock leaked word about the trust fund, the dam would burst and destroy him in the process.

James finished his brandy and got to his feet. "I can see your mind's already heavily burdened. We can review the details of the trust another time. One last thing before I leave, though," he said, reaching for his topcoat. "Have you given any consideration to the untenable position you're placing Miss Sorenson in?"

Cole shook his head. "I don't know what you're talking about."

"If people view you as a murderer, they could just as easily see her as your accomplice. You'll both be better off when she's no longer in the picture. The sooner you replace her, the better."

"I suppose you're right," Cole agreed in a dull voice. "I'll renew my efforts with an employment agency."

After buttoning his coat, James picked up his hat and cane. "We'll talk soon. You're in a hell of a predicament, my friend. Sorry I had to be blunt, but I'm only concerned about your well-being."

Cole walked with him to the front door. "I appreciate your efforts on my behalf."

James smiled suddenly. "I just had an idea. Why not let Sophie screen the candidates for nursemaid? She's not only experienced in hiring servants, but should there be any qualms on their part, she can assure them about your character as well."

"Fine," Cole agreed. "As you said, the sooner the better."

It wasn't until he closed the door after the lawyer's departure that he noticed Claire standing on the landing above. He couldn't tell from her expression how much of the conversation she had overheard. Why should that bother him? he asked himself irritably. He had been honest with her from the beginning. The position in his household wasn't a permanent one.

She came down the stairs slowly. "Mrs. Dobbs started a pot roast before she left for the day. I'll have dinner on the table in minutes."

After his lawyer's visit, the idea of a quiet evening in her company was more appealing than ever. James's assessment of Claire had been accurate. While Priscilla's brunette good looks had been striking, Claire's beauty was more subtle. Compared with the bolder, riotous shades of a summer garden, she was a delicate spring bouquet. Unfortunately, James had also been correct in that any association with him could prove disastrous. So he denied himself what he desired most.

"I'm afraid we'll have to postpone dinner until another time. I have some work that needs my attention."

"Of course," she replied with a bright smile. "Would you like me to fix you a tray?"

"Thank you, but no. It seems I've lost my appetite."

"Well then, good night."

"Good night, Claire."

As he watched her turn and climb the stairs, he wondered if her smile had been forced, or if he had only imagined it.

NINE

"Her ladyship's here to see you," Alma grumbled. "Not only does Madame Lamont arrive without any warning, but now she wants tea served. Doesn't she think I have anything else to do but wait on her?"

"Here, let me help." Claire put the teakettle on to boil, then started to set out the necessary items. She hadn't been surprised by Alma's announcement that Sophie Lamont had come to call. In fact, she had been expecting her visit.

"Ordering me about like she's the mistress of the house—who does she think she is? Sophie's always been one to put on airs." Picking up the rolling pin, Alma vented her irritation on the piecrust. She gave Claire a dubious look over her shoulder. "Are you sure you know what you're doing?"

"I'm positive. Besides," she added to further reassure the housekeeper, "my mother was English."

"Ah," Alma said, nodding. "That explains it then. Them English sure do like their tea and trumpets."

Claire's lips twitched with amusement. "Crumpets, Alma. They're called crumpets."

The housekeeper's face reddened as she applied the wooden rolling pin to the dough in front of her with renewed vigor. "That's what I said."

"Some afternoon, if you like, I'll make crumpets just the way my mother used to, piping hot and with lots of butter."

Alma seemed mollified by the offer. "All right. You know me, I'm always willin' to try new things."

Actually, Claire knew nothing of the sort, but wasn't eager to ruffle any more feathers. Instead, she chose a different topic while she waited for the water to boil. "Mrs. Lamont and Mrs. Garrett were close friends, weren't they?"

"Been friends since they were young girls."

Claire pried the lid from a tin of tea. "Then they must have been alike in many ways."

"Gracious, no." Alma paused to brush a strand of gray hair from her brow, and left a smudge of flour behind. "Sophie always was a quiet young miss, a bit on the timid side. Not at all like my Priscilla. Now, there was a girl for you. Always goin' here, goin' there. Not afraid to take her chances. Sophie was a watcher, but not my Priscilla. She was a doer."

"If they were so different, how did they ever become friends?"

"Their fathers were business partners at one time." Alma expertly eased the crust into a pie tin. "The girls, bein' the same age and all, did all the same things—dance lessons, piano lessons, voice lessons. Got invited to the same parties."

"Mrs. Lamont was the first to marry, wasn't she?"

Alma nodded. "She's been married comin' onto three years now. Priscilla wasn't as eager to settle down. Liked her freedom, she did."

Claire placed small plum cakes on a plate of fine bone china and added it to the tea tray. "Was it love at first sight for Mr. and Mrs. Lamont?"

"Hmph!" Alma sniffed. "If you ask me, more like love at first sight of her bank account. When Mr. Lamont first came to town he divided his attention between both girls. Not long afterwards, Sophie's father died and left her a fortune. Needless to say, his attention settled on Sophie."

"How did Mrs. Garrett react?"

"Let me tell you, she was none too happy. Her and Mrs. Lamont didn't speak to each other for a long time. Wasn't until Priscilla married Mr. Garrett that they mended their friendship."

Claire started to pick up the tray when a sudden thought struck her. "Does Mrs. Lamont have any children?"

"No, more's the pity." Picking up a large earthenware bowl, Alma spooned an apple mixture liberally spiced with cinnamon into the piecrust. "Fancy airs or not, Sophie'd make a fine mother. I've heard she's been wantin' a baby for years, but no luck. Priscilla, on the other hand, got pregnant quicker than you can blink an eye. If you ask me, I think Mrs. Lamont was always a little jealous."

Claire was still mulling over Alma's comments when she entered the parlor. Sophie Lamont stood before the fireplace, examining a collection of photographs in ornate filigree frames showing Priscilla at various ages. She turned as Claire entered. Claire couldn't help but think how well the current fashion of heavily boned, form-fitting basque bodices suited the woman's tall, angular figure. She looked modish in a royal blue pinstriped bodice and pleated skirt. A matching bonnet trimmed in black velvet ribbon completed her ensemble. A wavy fringe of brown hair fell over her forehead.

"How do you do?" she said, after subjecting Claire to careful scrutiny. "I don't believe we've met."

"No, I don't believe we have," Claire replied politely, knowing full well that any meeting between them would have been highly unlikely. "I'm Claire Sorenson. It's a pleasure to meet you, Mrs. Lamont."

Sophie lowered herself to the settee and gracefully arranged her skirt. "I see you brought the tea tray I requested. Just set it there," she said, motioning to a low table.

Claire placed it where Sophie indicated, then sat down in a high-backed chair. "How do you like your tea, Mrs. Lamont?" she asked, taking the initiative.

While Sophie Lamont watched with ill-concealed amazement, Claire flawlessly performed the ritual she had learned as a child.

"Well, I must admit," Sophie said as she accepted the teacup Claire offered, "you did that quite nicely."

Claire acknowledged the compliment with a slight nod. "I understand you wanted to speak with me."

"Yes, I'm sure you're wondering why I'm here." She took a dainty sip of tea. "I feel as though I owe it to my dear departed friend to oversee the welfare of her darling infant."

"How thoughtful of you to be so concerned. Let me assure you, Mrs. Lamont, her father always has Daisy's best interests at heart."

Sophie gave Claire a conspiratorial smile. "Men can't be expected to be attuned to the needs of the female members of their families, can they? Of course not," she answered before Claire had a chance to respond. "They're much too busy with their lumber businesses or their law practices. That's precisely why James asked my assistance in finding a replacement for Miss Bartlesby."

Claire stirred her tea. "You're very generous to offer your time."

"I love little Daisy almost as though she were my own. I feel it's my responsibility to see that she's well cared for." She was about to help herself to an iced cake when she realized how what she had just said must have sounded. "Oh, dear, how tactless of me. I didn't mean to imply Daisy wasn't well cared for with you in charge. I hope you aren't offended."

Claire studied the other woman for a long moment, but could find no trace of malice in the long, rather plain, face. "No offense taken, Mrs. Lamont. I understood what you meant."

Sophie tipped her head to one side. "You're not exactly what I expected to find, Miss Sorenson."

"Really?" Claire kept her expression impassive. "Just what did you expect?"

Sophie shrugged delicately. "Someone coarser, not as well-spoken—or as well-mannered." She clamped a hand over her bosom. "Oh, dear. There, I've insulted you again. I am so sorry."

Claire waved aside the apology. "Most people hold the same opinion as you. I frequently find myself judged by my father's—shortcomings. As much as I'd like to, it's impossible for me to change his ways—or that of my brother."

Sophie's demeanor changed. "You poor thing," she crooned sympathetically. "How unfair. If there's anything I can ever do . . ."

"Thank you, that's very kind." Claire found herself responding to the unexpected warmth. "Mr. Garrett has been honest from the start. He's made it quite clear this position is only until a replacement can be found."

"Whatever will you do when another baby nurse is hired?" Sophie helped herself to one of the plum cakes.

"I intend to leave Brockton for good." Basking in the understanding and sympathy in Sophie's dark eyes, Claire voiced her plans aloud for the first time. "When the time comes, Mr. Garrett promised me a letter of reference. I'll purchase a train ticket to a big city—Grand Rapids, Chicago, or maybe Detroit. Someplace where no one knows my family. Once there, I hope to find a position as nursemaid."

"That's very commendable, Miss Sorenson. I admire your courage. I, on the other hand," she confessed in a low voice, "was never brave enough to venture far from Brockton. After Father died, I was terrified at the thought of managing on my own. Fortunately, James was there for me."

"Even without Mr. Lamont's help, I'm sure you would have found the strength to cope," Claire said gently.

Sophie smiled, then grew thoughtful. "I'm so happy we

had this chance to become better acquainted. After talking with you, I've arrived at an entirely different conclusion than the one I expected."

"And that is?" Claire's heart leaped with hope.

"I think you're exactly what little Daisy needs right now. The last thing the poor child needs is to look up and find yet another stranger peering down at her over the top of her crib."

Claire experienced a sudden fear that she was only hearing what she wanted to hear. "You mean you think I should stay on?"

Finishing the last morsel of her teacake, Sophie daintily wiped her fingers on an embroidered napkin. "I know I gave James my solemn promise, but," she laughed, "he'll never know the difference. I agreed to interview the applicants. Can I help it if I accidentally say something I shouldn't and frighten them off?"

Claire was deeply touched by the offer. "You'd do that for me, Mrs. Lamont?"

"I'm doing it for sweet little Daisy. She is my goddaughter, by the way. It's only natural to want to do the right thing. Priscilla would have wanted me to look after her."

"I—I don't know how to thank you."

"Nonsense, no thanks are necessary." She reached over and patted Claire's hand. "And Claire, please call me Sophie. I have the feeling the two of us are going to become friends."

Before Claire could frame an adequate rejoinder, Cole burst into the parlor, then came to an abrupt halt. His cheeks were ruddy from the cold. His dark hair was tousled and windblown, leading her to believe that in spite of the damp chill he had been hatless.

"Sophie!" he exclaimed. "Alma said you were here."

Smiling, Sophie extended her hand. "Cole, what a pleasant surprise. I didn't expect to see you this afternoon. I thought you'd be at the mill, buried up to your neck in paperwork."

"That's exactly where I would be except for some estimates I forgot to bring with me." He shot Claire an uneasy glance. "I assume you explained to Miss Sorenson that you'll be interviewing women for the job of nursemaid."

"You know Priscilla and I were like sisters. Of course I'll do whatever's best for her baby girl."

Claire noted Sophie had neatly sidestepped Cole's assumption.

"I appreciate your help." His enigmatic gray gaze rested on Claire. "Perhaps Mrs. Lamont would like to see how Daisy is thriving these days."

The rebuke in his tone put Claire on the defensive. "She's been fussy all day. I just put her down for a nap minutes before Mrs. Lamont's arrival. I didn't want to disturb her."

Cole instantly turned into a worried parent. "She's not sick, is she?"

"I don't think it's anything to worry about."

"Do you think I should call the doctor?"

Claire set her cup aside, the tea having grown cold. "I suspect Daisy may be cutting her first tooth. It's a bit early, but some babies get them sooner than others."

Sophie rose to her feet and collected her gloves and handbag. "I'm clearly out of my element when it comes to babies. I'd be sending for the doctor at all hours of the day and night."

Alma poked her head into the parlor, a scowl on her face. "I hate to interrupt your tea party, ladies, but the child upstairs is wide awake and getting cranky."

Claire hastily stood. "If there's nothing more to discuss . . ."

"See to the baby," Cole ordered. "And, Claire, if there's any doubt, don't hesitate to ask Tim to fetch Doc Wetherbury."

After murmuring a polite good-bye to Sophie Lamont,

Claire hurried upstairs toward the source of the ever-increasing volume of a child's cries.

Claire dropped into bed, too tired to even braid her hair. No sooner had she closed her eyes when Daisy's wails carried to her from the floor below. Grabbing her wrapper, she shoved her arms into the sleeves as she navigated the dark, narrow flight of stairs leading from the servants' quarters.

Afraid the cries of her young charge would awaken Cole, she ran to the nursery. "What's the matter, Daisy girl?" she crooned to the unhappy, red-faced infant.

Daisy let out a hiccuping sob when she saw Claire's face smiling down at her. Claire continued talking, uttering nonsensensical words intended to soothe and distract. With her usual efficiency, she changed the baby's diaper, then picked her up and began walking with her. She brushed a kiss across Daisy's brow and was vaguely alarmed to find the baby's skin warmer than usual. Had she made a mistake, she wondered, in not sending for the doctor? Or was her intuition about teething correct? Ever since she had started working here, Daisy had been drooling copiously. And gnawing on everything she picked up in her tiny fist.

Thinking a darkened room more conducive to sleep, Claire didn't even dare light a lamp. The full moon outside the nursery window provided the only illumination. She paced. Rocked. Hummed. Recited nursery rhymes. Twice she thought she had succeeded in lulling Daisy to sleep, only to have her wake the instant she started to lower her into the crib. The reproach in the infant's big, blue eyes was enough to soften even the hardest of hearts. And where Daisy was concerned, Claire's heart was anything but hard.

From downstairs, the grandfather clock chimed the hour of two. Daisy alternately dozed and whimpered pathetically. Claire yawned as she crisscrossed the floor. Her arms felt as heavy as lead. Pausing a moment, she picked up the silver rattle from the dresser and offered it to the restless infant. Daisy latched onto it immediately and brought it to her mouth. Her face screwed into a grimace of pain when she bit down and encountered hard metal. Letting out a howl of rage and frustration, she tossed the rattle to the floor, where it landed with a loud clatter.

"Hush, Daisy," she pleaded. "You'll wake your daddy."

"Too late," Cole growled.

Claire whirled about to find him leaning against the doorjamb. Dark curls peeked from the deep vee formed by the shawl collar of a patterned damask dressing gown tied about his narrow waist with a silken cord. Embarrassed by her blatant interest, her gaze slid downward over muscular calves and bare feet. She knew with certainty he wore nothing under the heavy silk dressing gown. A tiny bud of desire, sweet and warm, unfurled low in her belly.

"Daisy giving you a rough time?"

She struggled to shrug off the sensual shroud that engulfed her. Struggled to concentrate on what he was saying. "I, ah, tried to keep her quiet. I'm sorry she woke you."

He advanced into the room with the grace of a stalking panther. Sleek, powerful, dangerous. A predator. It was all Claire could do not to back away. Mesmerized, her throat dry, she watched him approach. His mouth curved into a lazy half-smile that made her heart race.

"Seems I'm not the only one Daisy is keeping awake."

Claire retreated a step. She was suddenly conscious of her own state of dishabille. The cotton wrapper had been worn paper thin by repeated washings, the nightdress, equally worn, equally thin. Although swathed in voluminous folds and buttoned to the chin, she couldn't escape the feeling that what she wore was transparent.

"What seems to be the problem with our little princess here?" Cole reached out to stroke Daisy's flushed cheek.

Claire tightened her hold on Daisy, using the child as a shield of sorts. Daisy had temporarily ceased crying and regarded her father like a possible savior from her misery. Claire cleared her throat. "I don't think it's serious. Many babies are irritable for days, even weeks, before cutting a tooth."

"You mean this could go on for weeks?"

He looked so aghast at the possibility that Claire chuckled. "Every baby's different," she counseled. "Why not go back to bed, and I'll try rocking her again."

"Again?" His brows rose. "I take it you tried that method before—with limited success."

Claire nodded. Fatigue, she told herself, was responsible for her difficulty with speech. Cole's near-nakedness had nothing, nothing at all, to do with her brain's slowness to function.

Under no such constraint, Daisy let out a prolonged babble of baby sounds. "Da-da-da-da."

"Did you hear that?" Cole beamed. "She called my name."

He looked so proud, Claire didn't have the heart to tell him differently. Still grinning, Cole offered his hand, and Daisy immediately clutched his finger, pulled it into her mouth, and gnawed vigorously. The action drew Cole even closer until Claire felt surrounded in an invisible embrace. Her senses sharpened. She basked in the heat radiating from his body. Inhaled his unique male scent, which she found even more heady than the cologne he favored.

She desperately needed distance. "Perhaps something cold to suck on might help Daisy feel better," she suggested, relieved her voice sounded almost normal.

"Good idea," he agreed, taking the baby from her. "Meanwhile, it's time Daisy hears the tale of Paul Bunyan and Babe, his blue ox."

Claire laughed softly. "So much for more traditional stories such as Cinderella or Snow White."

"I prefer fairy tales where the hero stands twelve feet, eleven inches high," Cole replied with a straight face.

"And who happens to weigh eight hundred and eighty-eight pounds." She, too, had grown up hearing yarns about the legendary woodsman.

"Without his socks," he added, proving himself an authority on the subject of Paul Bunyan.

Still smiling, Claire left the nursery. When he allowed himself to relax, Cole Garrett had tremendous appeal. She hadn't expected to find a sense of humor under his businessman's armor. And the love he showed for his little daughter increased his appeal a hundredfold. If she didn't tread carefully upon the fragile barrier of her emotions, she could easily imagine herself in love with him.

TEN

After lecturing herself on the dangers of loving Cole Garrett, Claire returned to the nursery, carrying a small chunk of ice wrapped in a cloth and knotted securely.

At her approach Cole glanced up hopefully and relinquished the squirming infant into Claire's care. "How can someone with the face of an angel be such a little hellion?" he asked, but there was no bite to his words, only affection.

"Here, sweetie," Claire cooed, offering Daisy the iced cloth.

But after a tentative bite, Daisy didn't want any part of it. She knocked the ice to the floor with the same disdain she had had with the silver rattle earlier. Tears welled in her gentian-blue eyes; her lower lip quivered.

Cole raked his fingers through his hair. "Isn't there anything we can do? Some medicine to make her feel better?"

His question prompted Claire to remember a conversation she had overheard once between two young matrons about their infants. "Do you happen to have any flavored brandy?"

"I realize you must be exhausted, Claire, but do you really think brandy is the solution? Usually it has the opposite effect. Perhaps coffee or tea would be a better choice."

Startled by the advice, Claire stared at him, but from his expression, realized he was in earnest. Before she could prevent it, a bubble of laughter escaped. "The brandy isn't for me," she said, battling to control her mirth. "It's for the baby."

Cole went slack-jawed at her pronouncement. "Are you insane? You want to give brandy to a five-month-old child?"

She shook her head in exasperation. "I doubt if what I have in mind will turn Daisy into a hopeless drunk." When Cole continued to regard her with skepticism, she elaborated. "I simply want to rub a drop or two on her gums to ease the pain."

"It's worth a try, I suppose. I think there might be some elderberry brandy downstairs."

While he went off to search, Claire continued to pace back and forth, gently rubbing Daisy's back and murmuring words of comfort.

Cole returned five minutes later. He stood in the thick indigo shadows just beyond the nursery door, the shotglass in his hand forgotten. He took advantage of the opportunity to study Claire unobserved. God, she was pretty. Her glossy ash-blond hair fell to her waist in a silken waterfall. As she moved, the diaphanous folds of her nightdress swirled about her slender figure, eliciting tantalizing, erotic images of what lay beneath. Unbidden, images frolicked across his mind of her sprawled across his bed, her naked body draped with silvery moonbeams. Instantly, he felt himself respond.

Some faint sound must have drawn her attention because she stopped pacing and looked in his direction. "Cole . . . did you find any brandy?"

"Yes." He emerged from the shadows and into the nursery, steeling himself against the urge to touch her cheek. Was her skin as soft and smooth as it looked? Would it feel as cool as marble, or warm as a summer-ripe peach? Temptation goaded him to learn the answers. His fingers tightened around the shotglass, and he shoved the other hand into the pocket of his dressing gown.

As though sensing a change in his demeanor, Claire gave him an uncertain smile, then dipped the tip of her index finger into the brandy and rubbed it over the baby's lower gum. Daisy's small body shuddered at her first taste of the unfamiliar, but Claire persisted in massaging the area. "Poor baby," she murmured. "I know it hurts."

When Claire finished, Daisy grabbed a handful of her wrapper, and holding it tightly, began to suck her thumb. Ten minutes later, as Claire and Cole looked on, her eyelids fluttered, grew heavy, then drooped shut. Perhaps from the effects of the brandy, but more likely worn out from lack of sleep, Daisy finally fell asleep. Claire's eyes met his over the baby's head, and they shared a smile of victory.

Careful not to awaken the baby, Claire gently tugged her wrapper from the infant's grasp. Keeping his fingers crossed for luck, Cole waited while she placed Daisy in her crib. He breathed a sigh of relief when the little girl didn't stir as Claire pulled the blanket over her shoulders.

Then, wordlessly, their movements synchronized, they turned and left the nursery.

Neither spoke until they reached the end of the hallway outside Cole's bedroom. "Thank you for your help tonight," Claire said, avoiding his gaze.

"You did all the work." Cole was wide awake now and oddly reluctant to end the evening. "I only followed your suggestions."

Nervously, she dragged the tip of her tongue across her lower lip in a gesture both innocent and provocative. "Daisy's fortunate to have you for a father."

"I think I'm the one who's lucky." Unable to resist, Cole crooked his finger beneath her chin and raised her face to his.

She stared up at him. Her lovely silver-blue eyes mirrored trust and longing. And an elusive something he couldn't quite define. Need? Desire? His gaze unwavering, he slowly lowered his head, giving her ample time to retreat . . . to flee. But she did neither. Instead her lips parted in an invitation as old as mankind. Cole lightly traced her elegantly sculpted cheekbones with the pads of his thumbs. Her skin was warm satin under his callused fingertips. Fascinated, he watched the color of her eyes darken to the hue of a midnight sky. They beckoned, dark and mysterious.

And he was lost.

Just one taste, he told himself. Just one. His mouth brushed hers. The touch light as thistledown, the contact as explosive as gunpowder. Once, twice, then again, he went back for more. He slanted his lips across hers and deepened the kiss. Primal satisfaction surged through his veins as he felt her tremble beneath the onslaught.

Claire responded with an ardent yearning of her own. Her lips softened, yielded, clung. Her arms crept upward from his waist to clutch the lapels of his brocade dressing gown. A small whimper escaped from her that sounded suspiciously like a purr.

"Claire, sweet Claire . . ." he whispered. Diving both hands into the rich abundance of her hair, he cradled the back of her head. And his mouth devoured hers.

Only one taste. A delicate sip. That had been his intent. But a taste, a single sip, had transformed into an unquenchable thirst. His tongue slipped into her mouth, seeking a deeper draught of the nectar that was uniquely hers. His mouth played over hers with all the skill at his command. Stroking, savoring. Cajoling. When her tongue shyly met his, Cole feared he'd shatter from the force of his desire.

Then the last shred of reason asserted itself.

Danger, danger, danger! Cole's mind flashed a warning. His breathing ragged, his control a hair-thin wire ready to snap, he stepped back. Claire blinked up at him, her lips rosy and swollen as a result of his kisses. She was his for the taking. A rose waiting to be picked.

Stifling a groan, he raked his fingers through his hair. God, what had he done? Claire was sweet, generous, innocent. And far too trusting. Didn't she know, couldn't she sense, he had nothing to offer in return? His life was in chaos. His future in jeopardy. Any association with him would only lead to disaster. She deserved far better than a single night of unbridled passion. If nothing else, he could protect her from a mistake that could ultimately destroy her.

He had been a selfish bastard his entire life, taking what he wanted with single-minded determination. And although he wasn't proud of it, when the situation warranted, he had on occasion resorted to brute force. Over the years, he had accrued wealth and power and all the trappings that went with them. He had achieved his goal—lumber baron. He was proud of the title. With Claire, however, he felt a strong desire to place her needs above those of his own.

"Cole . . . What's wrong?"

"I neglected to warn you against confusing physical longing with more tender feelings of the heart."

She sucked in a sharp breath. "I—I don't understand."

Girding himself against her pain, he doggedly continued, "It was just a kiss, Claire. A simple kiss, that's all. Don't make it into something more."

She backed away from him, one hand clutching the folds of her wrapper tighter about her neck. "No, no, of course not," she murmured. "It was just a kiss, nothing more."

Whirling around, she fled toward the stairs leading to the servants' quarters.

Cole watched as her figure moved wraithlike through patches of moonlight and shadow. He should feel relieved she hadn't gotten wildly emotional and made a scene. But he felt hollow, deflated.

A simple kiss? Dammit! Who was he kidding? There had been nothing remotely simple about it. He was the consummate fool for thinking one taste could ever be enough. The first touch had stirred dormant desires, reawakened needs best left slumbering.

The following evening, the doorbell rang just as Claire was about to set her foot on the first stair. "Who could be calling at this hour, Daisy girl?" she asked the drowsy infant.

In reply, Daisy yawned and snuggled against Claire's

shoulder. Claire shifted the warm bottle of milk to her other hand and hurried to answer the door.

"Mr. Tanner," she gasped in surprise at finding the chief of police on the front porch.

"Miss Sorenson." He removed his hat. "May I come in?"

She sensed Tanner's visit wasn't a social call. Her first instinct was to slam the door and turn the key in the latch. But she lacked the authority to refuse him admittance, and standing with the door wide open ran the risk of Daisy catching a chill. "Yes, of course, do come in," she said, standing aside.

"Sorry to be calling at this time." Edward Tanner didn't sound the least repentant as his gaze roamed the front hallway, then returned to rest on Claire. "Looks like you were about to put the little one to bed for the night."

Daisy, already an accomplished flirt, favored the police chief with a beatific smile.

Not even a hardened policeman could resist the little girl's appeal. Claire could have sworn under his thick mustache Tanner's mouth curved in a smile. "Cute little tyke. Funny, she doesn't favor either of her parents, her being so blond and all."

Claire, too, had wondered about the dissimilarities between Daisy and her parents. And, whenever she did, felt disloyal. "What can I do for you, Chief?"

"I came to talk with Mr. Garrett. I assume he's home."

"I'm home." Cole's voice came behind them. "What do you want, Tanner?"

"There are some . . . points I want to review with you."

"Are they so important they couldn't wait until morning?"

"Just a few questions I want to ask about your wife."

"Haven't we been over this ground before? I told you everything I know."

"I'll be the best judge of that."

Claire clutched Daisy tighter as Tanner sauntered toward Cole. Cole, his coat and tie discarded, shirtsleeves rolled to the elbows, bounced lightly on the balls of his feet ready to do battle. She tensed. Were the two men about to come to blows?

Daisy, it seemed, had no such worries. "Da-da-da," she squealed.

Cole visibly relaxed. "Isn't it past her bedtime?" he said, acknowledging Claire for the first time.

Nodding, she edged closer to him, farther from Tanner. "I had just finished fixing Daisy's bottle and was on my way upstairs when the doorbell rang."

Cole reached out to stroke the baby's cheek. Smiling broadly, Daisy caught his finger and promptly put it in her mouth, then bit down—hard.

"Ouch!" Cole grimaced.

"Daisy cut her first tooth," Claire explained needlessly.

Their eyes met for a brief look. Both recalled last evening and the long hours spent pacing the floor. Both remembered what happened afterwards.

"Ahem," Tanner cleared his throat. "Is there somewhere we can talk—in private?"

"Let's go into the library, shall we?"

Cole gestured toward the open door behind him, and Tanner brushed past him and into the room.

"Don't worry," he whispered to Claire before he turned and followed Tanner.

Good advice, Claire reflected wryly, but advice easier to give than to follow. She wondered what ingredients she would find in the pantry once Daisy was snug in her crib. Tanner's visit—and the tension it created—called for an hour or two in the kitchen whipping up a batch of cookies.

Not waiting to be asked, Tanner removed his overcoat, draped it over the back of a chair, and settled himself in an armchair near the fireplace. He sat upright, his posture rigid, denying his body the simple pleasure of a comfortable chair.

"Care for a drink, Tanner?" Cole inquired.

"I'm here on business."

"Suit yourself." Cole poured himself a bourbon he didn't really want in order to give himself time to gather his wits. Drink in hand, he strolled across the room and sank down in the chair across from Tanner.

Tanner's deep-set eyes surveyed the room, taking in the half-eaten sandwich on Cole's desk, the cup of coffee now growing cold, and the papers strewn across the polished surface. Silence stretched between the two men, punctuated by the ticking of a distant clock. Cole, feeling somewhat at a disadvantage in shirtsleeves and vest, fought the urge to fidget. Tanner, on the other hand, had no problem with the protracted silence.

Finally Tanner asked, "Work here often?"

Cole shrugged. "No, not often."

"Work at home much when Mrs. Garrett was alive?"

"No," Cole snapped.

"Why not?"

"Why not what?"

"Don't play games, Garrett. Why didn't you work at home before your wife was killed?"

"I just didn't." What the devil was Tanner getting at? Cole wondered with growing unease. Dammit, it was none of his business where he chose to conduct his affairs. "I fail to see . . ."

Tanner crossed one leg over the other. "Just answer my question."

"Mrs. Garrett objected to my cluttering up the library with paperwork. She reminded me I had a perfectly adequate office at the sawmill."

"I see." Tanner nodded thoughtfully. "I assume Miss Sorenson doesn't share the same objections."

"I'm afraid I wouldn't know. You'll have to ask her," Cole said through clenched teeth. "You're forgetting this is my house, and I can do whatever I please."

"Not having a wife telling you what you can and can't do in your own home must be kind of nice."

Cole sat up straighter. "What are you insinuating?"

Tanner fixed him with a cold-eyed stare. "Heard you and Mrs. Garrett didn't get along."

"We had our differences. But what married couple doesn't?" Cole shrugged and swirled the amber liquid in his glass.

"Without your wife around, you're free to come and go as you please. There's no one to answer to. You found yourself a pretty young woman to share the same roof." His gaze never wavered from Cole's. "Doesn't appear to me that you're a grief-stricken husband."

"I won't pretend to feel something I don't." Too restless to remain seated, Cole sprang to his feet, set his glass aside, and, striding to the fireplace, placed another log on the fire. "Ours wasn't a love match if that's what you're getting at. It was an arrangement intended to be mutually beneficial."

"How so?"

Cole rested one arm against the mantelpiece and stared, unseeing, at the dancing flames. "I wanted a wife—she was ready to marry, raise a family."

Tanner frowned, mulling over Cole's blunt response. "Have you and the Sorenson woman known each other long?" he asked at length, changing tactics.

"No," Cole answered shortly. He didn't like this line of questioning any more than the other. James had warned him Claire's involvement might become suspect. Which, Cole decided, justified efforts to maintain a safe distance between them. A distance he had already trespassed on. Luckily, he was able to stop himself in time. A few more seconds and it would have been too late. There would have been no turning back.

"When did you and Miss Sorenson first meet?"

The question pulled Cole back to the present. Tanner was tenacious as a rottweiler. "When did we first meet . . . ?" He half-turned, leaned one shoulder against the mantel, and tried to assume a casual stance. "Let me think... Ah, yes, it was the night of the Howards' party. If you recall, that was also the night of Priscilla's murder. How coincidental."

"I've never been a great believer in coincidence." Tanner smoothed his pant leg with long, thin fingers. "You've already told me the story of returning from the office to find Miss Sorenson watching the baby, and your wife not home."

"Would you like to hear it again, Tanner?" Cole asked, his gray eyes as hard as flint. "Because it happens to be the truth. I'll gladly tell it over and over if that's what you want to hear."

Tanner ignored the sarcasm. "Claire Sorenson is an attractive young woman, don't you agree?"

Cole's patience was at an end. "This conversation has gone far enough. If you want to talk to me any more we can do it at your office—with my lawyer present."

"No need to be so touchy." Tanner stood and retrieved his overcoat. "I'm just doing my job."

"That's a lie," Cole snapped.

Tanner froze in the act of slipping into his coat, taken aback by Cole's outburst. "Pardon me?"

Cole closed the space separating them in long strides. Bunching his hands into fists, he shoved them into his pockets so he wouldn't be tempted to use them on Tanner. "If you were really doing your job, instead of acting as Brock's puppet, you'd be out looking for the real killer instead of harassing me. You make me sick, Tanner. You're more interested in saving your job than in finding Priscilla's murderer."

Tanner's face grew red. "I'll see myself out."

Cole stared after him, his thoughts in turmoil. He had been right about Leonard Brock. His former father-in-law was convinced he had murdered Priscilla. Brock wouldn't rest until a jury convicted him. In the meantime, a killer walked free.

He often suspected from Priscilla's furtive behavior that

she had been seeing someone. Had her lover also been her killer? Perhaps driven to murder in a fit of jealousy? Then again, it might have been someone she barely knew who had lured her to her death for reasons beknownst only to him. Poor Priscilla. Always searching, forever restless. Never happy with what she had. A pity she had died without finding what she sought. Every time he thought of her premature demise, he felt a profound sadness. It didn't matter that he didn't love her. For a short period of time, and because of a tiny baby girl, their lives had been intertwined.

Who had killed Priscilla? And why? Most frightening of all, if the police weren't interested in finding the answers, who was?

Returning to his desk, Cole slumped in his chair, propped his elbows on the polished surface, and put his head in his hands. Problems darted from so many directions, he wondered if a target was painted on his back. Added to the fact Brock wanted his hide, there were other, more immediate, issues to contend with. Once the ice melted from the rivers and streams, the river drive would begin. Even under ideal circumstances these drives were fraught with hazards, but this year it would be particularly risky. Several times he had been satisfied with a full roster of experienced men, only to discover they had been lured away. He suspected Brock was behind this defection, but so far hadn't been able to prove it. He would have to rely on a handful of loyal lumberjacks he had worked with in the past. And pray for the best. With a weary sigh, he picked up his pen and opened a ledger.

An hour later he slammed the ledger shut in frustration. He had added the same column of figures three times—and each time came up with a different sum.

Claire studied Cole from the library doorway. His dark hair, tousled from running his fingers through it countless times, looked in need of a trim. His face seemed leaner, his cheeks more hollowed. Worry was taking its toll. "Work not going well?"

Cole gave the ledger a shove. "You could say that."

She entered the room, carrying a tray. "I made some coffee."

"Mmm, fresh baked cookies," he said, eyeing the plate in her hand.

She set the tray down on the only corner of the desk that wasn't littered with papers.

"Maybe I should try your approach," Cole said as he helped himself to a cookie, "and bake my cares away."

Claire gave him a sidelong look as she handed him a steaming mug of coffee. "What did Chief Tanner want?"

Her question brought a scowl to his face. "Tanner has nothing better to do than waste his time and mine by asking questions to which he already knows the answers."

"I see . . ." She debated whether to pursue the subject or leave it alone.

"Don't let Tanner worry you. He's just following Brock's orders to make my life miserable." Snagging one of the still-warm oatmeal cookies, he devoured half of it in a single bite. "You'll be away from here soon."

Her conscience gave a painful twinge, but she kept silent. She hesitated to tell him Sophie Lamont was conspiring to keep her in the Garrett household. She wondered how Cole would react if he knew. Would he be angry? Or would a tiny part of him be pleased?

He stood and stretched, rolling his head around to relieve the tension. "My muscles feel tied in knots."

Once again, Cole reminded her of a big, sleek cat. Potentially dangerous, but capable of being tamed. "Sit down," she ordered, motioning to one of the armchairs.

He raised a dark brow and regarded her with a quizzical expression.

"Sit down," she repeated, taken aback by her own boldness. "I know how to untie those knots in your neck and shoulders."

Though clearly skeptical, he did as she requested. "If

you're half as good at that as you are at baking cookies, I'll be in your debt."

Resting her hands at the base of his neck, she slowly, rhythmically, kneaded his tense muscles. She concentrated on the task at hand, trying not to think of his almost feverishly warm skin beneath her touch. "Starting to feel better?"

"Mmm, wonderful," he murmured, letting his chin drop to his chest to give her better access.

Her fingers traveled the tops of his shoulders. Using her thumbs, she burrowed into stubborn knots of tension, alternately squeezing and relaxing. "I used to do this for Pa when I was young . . . before Mother died." Before he chose a bottle to drown his sorrow in, she added silently. Before he preferred a smoky barroom instead of his home.

"You'll make some lucky man a perfect wife," Cole said with a smile in his voice. "Not only do you make the best cookies this side of heaven, but your fingers work magic"

She forced a light tone. "Maybe I should track down Paul Bunyan and make him an offer."

When she finished, Cole appeared to be in a much more cheerful frame of mind. She wished she could say the same for her own. Touching him had been a bad idea. A very bad idea. The memory of his warm, firm, flesh would linger long after lights were out. Linger and make her yearn for something beyond her reach.

Cole, on the other hand, appeared totally unaffected. After bidding him good night, Claire glanced back at him from the library doorway. Lamplight glinted off his bent head, bringing out the mahogany and chestnut highlights in his dark hair. He busily entered figures into a ledger while holding a coffee mug in one hand, a half-finished plate of cookies nearby. He had already forgotten her presence.

As she went upstairs, Pa's warning, spoken years ago, played through her head. *You play with fire, girl, you're gonna get burned.*

ELEVEN

"Alma, would you mind if I left Daisy in your care for a short time?" Undaunted by the housekeeper's frown, Claire forged ahead. "She's taking her afternoon nap and shouldn't be any bother."

"A few minutes to you seems more like an hour to me." Parings flew like snowflakes from the potato in Alma's hand.

"I won't be long, I promise."

"Where you takin' off to now? Shoppin' again?"

Claire reached for her jacket. "I'm not going any farther than the carriage house. I need to ask Tim a favor, and thought I'd bring him some cookies as well."

"My guess is you're tryin' to bribe the man."

Claire piled cookies onto a plate, then covered them with a checkered napkin. "I thought he might have a sweet tooth."

"You and your bakin'." Alma shoved a lock of gray hair from her brow with the back of her hand. "At this rate, I'm goin' to have to restock the pantry."

"I'm sorry, I . . ."

Alma interrupted her apology. "Go, visit Tim. He ain't the only one with a sweet tooth. My Harold's the same way. Thought I'd bring him some cookies to go with his tea tonight."

Claire left the house before Alma could change her mind about Daisy. She stood on the back porch for a moment and drew in a deep breath. Her gloomy mood was reflected in the weather. The air was chill and damp, the sky overcast. Another dreary day in a seemingly endless chain of dreary days. With the exception of the morning of Priscilla Garrett's funeral, the sun had all but disappeared. In spite of the calendar, spring seemed eons away.

Heaving a sigh, she made her way down the steps and crossed the drive lined with mounds of mud-splattered snow. It felt good to be outdoors, even for a short time. She missed the long walks to and from town. Aside from the exercise, they had provided an excellent opportunity to think, to sort through problems, and to daydream. As soon as the weather improved, Claire vowed, she'd take Daisy for long strolls in her pretty wicker baby carriage.

Upon reaching the carriage house at the rear of the property, she pushed open the heavy door and stepped inside. Slush-colored light filtered through a series of high-set windows. "Mr. O'Brien," she called tentatively, "are you in here?"

She stood for a moment while her eyes adjusted to the dim interior. A conglomeration of smells assailed her nostrils: the characteristic scent of livestock, the pleasant aroma of saddle soap, the sweet smell of hay. "Mr. O'Brien," she called again.

Still no answer.

Claire slowly wandered down the center aisle. The roomy stalls of the carriage house could easily accommodate half a dozen horses. The Garrett carriage, buffed to a high gloss, stood at one end. A pair of matched bays contentedly munched their feed. Cole's horse was absent. She knew he preferred to ride back and forth from the sawmill rather than use the carriage.

She started to pass an empty stall when a soft *meow* drew her attention. She paused, her head to one side, and peered into the shadows. There, at the back corner, lay a mother cat curled next to a litter of six newborn kittens.

"Ohh," Claire breathed in delight. Her problems momentarily forgotten, she set the plate of cookies on a nearby bench and approached the mother cat. The striped tabby viewed Claire with lazy interest as she dropped to her knees beside her. "How precious."

Unable to resist the temptation, she scooped one of the tiny balls of fur into the palm of her hand. It was black except for a white face and a tail that looked as though the tip had been dipped in a bucket of whitewash. Enchanted with the kitten, Claire held it at eye level and ran her index finger lightly down its spine. She couldn't contain a smile when she felt its purr vibrate like a miniature motor.

"Like cats, do you?"

Startled, she glanced up and found Tim O'Brien observing her from the shadows. Feeling at a disadvantage, she scrambled to her feet, still holding the kitten. "Yes," she replied hastily. "I like them very much."

Tim propped his pitchfork against a nearby stall and moved closer. "Gertie, there," he said, indicating the mother cat with a nod, "is my best mouser."

"I never had a pet," Claire blurted, not sure what had prompted the confession.

"Why's that?"

She shrugged. "Pa doesn't care much for animals. Claims they're not worth all the bother."

Reaching out, Tim gently scratched behind the kitten's ear. "I plan to keep one of the females to help Gertie, but in another month or so the rest of these little fellas will be needing good homes."

"I wish I could help, but . . ."

He gave her a sly smile. "You might try asking Mr. Garrett if he'd be interested in one for that big house of his. Nothing like a good cat to keep the mice away."

"Maybe I could convince him Daisy should have a kitten." The notion instantly appealed to her. "Pets are good for children. Besides companionship, they teach responsibility."

His smile widened with approval. "I'm guessing you'd like a kitten for your sake as much as the little one's."

Her eyes clouded. Unless Sophie Lamont was able to perform a miracle, her position in the household was likely to end soon. "It's doubtful I'll be here long. Mr. Garrett made it clear that he'd prefer someone more qualified as a baby nurse."

O'Brien grunted. "Seems to me Garrett's got hisself a good one already."

Claire stroked the kitten's soft fur to hide her embarrassment. "That's very kind of you, Mr. O'Brien—"

"Tim," he interrupted. "Folks call me Tim, or just plain O'Brien. One or the other, whichever you prefer."

"Well, Tim, you can't fault Mr. Garrett for wanting only the best when it comes to caring for his daughter." Claire set the kitten next to its mother. Before straightening, she gently tweaked the ear of a kitten the color of marmalade. "I'm sure you know the reputation my father and brother have earned for themselves."

"Well, yeah." Tim tugged his earlobe. "I've heard they're both fond of their drink. Folks gossip. It's hard to keep something like that quiet in a small town."

"Actually, my father and brother are what brought me out here." Claire slipped her hand into her apron pocket. "I was wondering if you would do me a favor."

"What sort of favor?" he asked, suspicion replacing his previous affability.

"I hate to impose on you." She nervously fingered the envelope in her pocket. "If you'd rather not, don't hesitate to say so. I'll understand."

"Trust me—if it's something I don't want to do, I'll let you know."

Claire withdrew the envelope. "Would you give this to either my father or brother?"

Instead of accepting the envelope, Tim regarded it warily. "What's in it?"

"Just a little extra I've managed to set aside," she explained.

"You're handing over your hard-earned money?"

"Neither Pa nor Nils works regularly. In the past, my earnings went for food. I'm worried they might not have enough to get by on."

Tim's dark brows drew together. "You mean two grown men depend on you for the food in their bellies?"

"They pay whatever they can." Claire instantly leapt to their defense. "If you'd rather not deliver it, I'll ask someone else."

"No, I'll do it." Tim grudgingly accepted the envelope and stuffed it into his back pocket.

"Thank you," she said, relieved he hadn't called her bluff. She had no idea whom she would have asked if he had refused. "I'd do it myself except I can't leave Daisy unattended."

"No problem."

She offered him a tentative smile and was pleased when he returned it. "I hope you like oatmeal raisin cookies. I brought you some just in case and set them on that bench over there."

His brown eyes lit with appreciation. "Bake 'em yourself?"

She scuffed the hay with the toe of her shoe. "I'm afraid it's a habit of mine. Whenever I'm mulling over a problem, first thing I do is heat up the oven. Alma's complaining she'll have to restock the pantry."

"Well, I'll be happy to eat any that don't fit into the cookie jar."

She started to go, then turned back. "Would you mind if I brought Daisy out to see the kittens some afternoon?"

He seemed pleased by the request. "Anytime at all."

Before she could leave, another question, one she had wanted to ask for weeks, spilled out. "The night of Priscilla Garrett's murder, why did you take Mrs. Garrett to the Howards' but not bring her home?"

His mouth thinned. "'Cause she told me not to wait. Said her friends would see her home."

"Was it customary for Mrs. Garrett to return home with friends?"

Picking up the pitchfork he had propped against a stall, he slowly walked toward her. "Why the curiosity all of a sudden?"

Suddenly, Tim made her nervous. She berated herself for letting her imagination run rampant. Tim was a trusted employee. Certainly she had nothing to fear. "No special reason," she said, shrugging off the vague unease. "I just thought it odd that Mrs. Garrett ended up at the sawmill so late at night—and all alone."

Tim drove the tines of the pitchfork into a bale of hay, then folded his hands on top of the handle and studied her through narrowed eyes. "Mrs. Garrett liked to come and go as she pleased with no questions asked. She made it known she didn't answer to no one—not even Mr. Garrett."

"You don't sound as though you liked her very much."

"I didn't," he stated with finality. "Damned if I'll pretend otherwise."

"But I saw you at her funeral."

"My being there had nothing to do with her. Only went out of respect for Mr. Garrett."

Taking the pitchfork into both hands, he jabbed it into a mound of hay and heaved it into the nearest stall. Claire knew she would get no more information from him. From the shuttered expression on his face, she sensed he had already said more than he intended.

"Oh, dear," Sophie said, "I hope this isn't a bad time for me to call."

"No, of course not." Claire stood aside as the woman entered the front hallway. Sophie was dressed for an evening out in a plum-colored silk gown and matching cloak. An egret feather bobbed from a cluster of artfully arranged curls atop her head. Though undoubtedly expensive, the unflattering shade of purple gave her complexion a sallow cast. "Why don't we go into the parlor."

"I can only stay a minute," Sophie exclaimed as she followed Claire into the parlor, then took a seat on the settee. "The Bradfords are hosting a musicale in honor of Catherine's sister-in-law, who is visiting from Philadelphia. James, poor dear, had to work late, so I agreed to meet him there."

"Can I offer you tea?"

"That's very thoughtful, dear, but I'm afraid I don't have time." Sophie's brown eyes darted toward the doorway. "Is Cole home, by any chance?"

"No," Claire replied, taking the seat opposite her guest. "Like your husband, he often works late."

"I just wanted him to know I received a reply from the employment agency in Chicago. They're sending an applicant for an interview next week. Mrs. Abercrombie assured me the woman was eminently qualified to care for little Daisy."

The news, so casually relayed by Sophie, crushed Claire's fragile wish. She bit her lip and prayed she wouldn't disgrace herself by bursting into tears. "I see," she murmured. "I'm sure Mr. Garrett will be pleased to hear that."

Seeing Claire's crestfallen expression, Sophie reached over and patted her hand. "There, there, dear, don't worry. As I told you before, I'll do whatever I can to help. I have no intention of going back on my word."

Claire twisted her fingers together. "That's very kind of you, but what if this woman is as qualified as the agency claims . . . and wants the position?"

Sophie gave her a smug smile. "I doubt she'll be any more eager than her predecessors once she learns the rumors that surround her prospective employer."

"But Mrs. Lamont . . . Sophie," she corrected, "it isn't right to cast aspersions on Mr. Garrett's reputation."

"Of course not," Sophie replied, clucking her tongue.

"Why, I'd never do such a thing to Cole. It's in the best interests of all parties involved that the applicant be well informed. Even if the woman should accept the position, she will surely hear the gossip soon enough. Her bags would be packed in a wink, and she'd be on the next train out of town. Then poor Cole would find himself in the same predicament all over again."

Sophie succeeded in making her argument sound reasonable. Or maybe that was because it was what Claire wanted to believe. At any rate, she didn't raise any objections to Sophie's plan. "I appreciate your help. I've grown quite fond of Daisy, and it would break my heart to leave her in the care of another."

Smiling, Sophie rose to her feet. "As much as I'd like to visit longer, I really must be on my way. Catherine has an absolute fit whenever anyone is late for one of her gatherings. Please tell Cole that I dropped by."

After seeing Sophie out, Claire leaned against the door, her eyes closed. Would Sophie's ploy be effective? Even if she succeeded this time, would she the next time, or the time after? Claire painfully acknowledged that if she were going to be replaced, sooner would be better than later. Each day she stayed, the more difficult it was to contemplate leaving. She had been truthful when admitting to Sophie it would break her heart never to see Daisy again. What she had omitted to mention, however, was that leaving Cole would also create a void.

Cole returned late from his office at the sawmill to find Claire surrounded by a sea of baking paraphernalia. These days the house exuded a warmth and welcome that had been lacking when Priscilla was alive. Amazingly, he looked forward to coming home to find Claire waiting. "The cookie jar is still full from last time," he said with a smile.

Guilty color suffused her cheeks. "I was thinking of either cake or pie."

Cole tugged off his gloves, slipped out of his overcoat. In the short span of time that Claire had lived in his house, he had become aware of her personality quirks, including her proclivity to bake. Unfortunately, he had become aware of other assets as well. His thoughts strayed in her direction with increasing regularity. He found the notion disconcerting.

"I'm afraid Alma is starting to complain."

"And the whole time Alma's complaining, she's taking your baked goods home to her husband." Draping his coat over the back of a chair, he rubbed his hands to restore some warmth. "I'm surprised you're not as wide as she," he said, watching her as she tied an apron around her trim waist.

"Fortunately, I enjoy making pastries more than I do eating them."

Cole eyed her figure with bold, masculine appraisal. Even without the contrivances of stays and corsets, she possessed a slender, shapely form. He found himself wondering how she'd look without any clothes at all. With her hair loose and swirling around her shoulders. His body jolted with need, a fierce longing that astounded him. What sort of lover would she be? Affectionate and generous, or shy and passive? Did an adventurous streak lurk beneath a demure exterior? He yearned to discover the answers.

Unaware of his thoughts, Claire studied a list of ingredients written on a slip of paper. "If I had nutmeg, I'd bake an apple torte that used to be one of my mother's favorites."

With a supreme effort, Cole vanquished his unruly thoughts and concentrated on the present. "What upset you?"

"Nothing."

He knew her well enough to know her denial came a

shade too quickly. Well enough to know by her closed expression that she was unwilling to confide in him. He felt frustration and impatience simmer inside of him. He decided it best for the time being to change the subject. Heading to one side, he sniffed appreciatively. "Umm, something smells good."

She looked up from the recipe. "Have you eaten dinner? Alma made a pot of soup."

"Actually, I am hungry. Starving, as a matter of fact."

"I'll have your dinner on the table in no time."

"Only on one condition." Ignoring her look of surprise, he continued smoothly, "I insist that you join me."

"Me . . . ?"

"I'm in the mood for company tonight and don't want to eat alone."

Flustered, she gnawed her lower lip. "All right . . . if you insist."

"I insist." He flashed an approving grin. "And, Claire, for a change, I'd like to have dinner in the dining room."

A short time later they sat separated from each other by an expanse of mahogany gleaming beneath a heavy layer of lemon oil and beeswax. The burgundy velvet drapes had been pulled shut to block out the night. Flames danced atop candles in ornate silver holders. In addition to a steaming tureen of soup, Claire had arranged slices of cold roast beef and cheese on a flowered platter. A loaf of bread purchased from the bakery earlier that day completed the meal. While Claire prepared the simple meal, he had opened a bottle of wine and poured it into stemmed glasses. The atmosphere managed to be formal, yet, at the same time, curiously intimate.

Cole broke off a piece of bread as his gaze inventoried the room. The intricately carved breakfront with imported china and crystal encased behind beveled glass, the ponderous table large enough to seat twelve, silk brocade draperies, lush Oriental carpet. All the trappings of wealth.

"The entire time the house was being built, I envisioned

dinner here every evening. Sterling silver, starched linens, fancy dishes. A wife. Family. But, truth of the matter, unless Priscilla was entertaining, this room was never used. On the rare occasions she dined at home, Priscilla preferred to take her evening meal on a tray in her room."

Curious as to what Claire's reaction would be to his impromptu confession, he cast a surreptitious glance in her direction. However, while she appeared to be listening and sympathetic, she offered no comment.

Cole debated whether or not to continue the conversation. But once the cover had been removed from his box of memories, all the bitterness spilled out. "I had been proud, so damn proud, of owning a fine new home, hiring servants. Proud that a kid who had started as a cook's helper had achieved the status of 'lumber baron.' Marrying the daughter of Brockton's leading citizen seemed like frosting on a cake." Toying with the stem of his wineglass, he stared unseeing at the blood-red Bordeaux. "Maybe God paid me back for my conceit. Mortar and brick don't make a home. I discovered the house I was once so proud of was just another building. And my marriage . . ." his mouth twisted in a humorless smile ". . . only existed on a piece of paper."

Cole dragged his gaze from the wineglass to the silent woman seated across the table from him. She had yet to speak since the meal began. It was impossible to know her thoughts. Perhaps she found his table manners as revolting as Priscilla had. Priscilla had been quick to point out his shortcomings. He ate too fast. Ate too much. Possessed the table etiquette of a lumberjack. He began to feel like a fool for insisting he and Claire share a meal. And even more foolish for suggesting the dining room.

What had possessed him to bare his soul? And what response had he expected from her in return? Sympathy, understanding? Yes, dammit. He shoved his untouched soup aside. That's exactly what he had wanted—her sympathy as balm for his injured ego.

JUST BEFORE DAYBREAK

The silence between them stretched and stretched. A rubber band ready to snap.

Frustrated and short-tempered, he lashed out, "If you were opposed to the idea of our dining together, you could have refused. I'm not an ogre."

Putting down her spoon, she stared at him, distress etched across her delicate features. But still she maintained a stoic, and infuriating, silence.

"Come on, Claire, talk to me. Don't act as though we're strangers. For chrissake, don't act like Priscilla."

"I'm sorry," she said in a hushed voice.

"Sorry about what?"

"I didn't know what you expected from me." She lifted a shoulder and let it fall. "I was raised never to talk at the dinner table. Pa insisted upon our absolute silence during mealtime."

"Silence such as cooks impose in lumber camps." Now it all made sense. Cole let out a sigh as tension eased. "I've had enough silent meals to last a lifetime. Talk to me, Claire, let me hear the sound of your voice."

"All right," she smiled, "but only if you finish eating. You've barely touched your soup."

"Already giving orders, are you?" he said without reproach. He obliged by pulling the bowl closer.

Claire watched with approval as he dug into the hearty mix of vegetables and beef with renewed enthusiasm. "If either Nils or I forgot—and if Pa was in a good mood—we'd be sent from the table hungry. Other times, we'd get the strap. Only rarely did Pa make an exception to his rule."

"Your Pa sounds like a hard man." His soup finished, Cole made a sandwich with meat and cheese. "I can't imagine ever sending Daisy from the table hungry—much less taking a strap to her."

Claire chose not to comment on her father's character. "I've always admired this house from afar. I used to make up excuses to come by while it was being built. Right now there are a lot of unhappy memories attached, but once they fade, you'll feel differently."

"I hope you're right." He raised his wineglass and drained its contents. "If business doesn't improve, I stand to lose everything I've worked for. I could even be forced to declare bankruptcy."

Claire studied him thoughtfully. The flickering candlelight washed his features with light and shadow, illuminating planes, darkening hollows. He was brooding, troubled, and . . . vulnerable? "Tell me about your business," she said, leaning forward.

After refilling his wineglass, he resettled himself more comfortably in his chair. "Most of the logs are cut and stacked by the riverbanks, but unless I can float them downstream to the mill, I can't fulfill my contracts."

"River drives are an annual event. What makes this year so difficult?"

"No sooner do I have a full roster of experienced men signed on as river drivers than they start deserting me to hire on elsewhere."

"Do you have any idea why?" Claire took a tiny sample of wine while waiting for Cole to formulate his thoughts. Wrinkling her nose at the unfamiliar taste, she quickly set her glass down.

At her reaction, a smile tugged at the corner of his mouth before he turned serious again. "I suspect my former father-in-law is behind the men's sudden defection, but there's no way I can prove it. Even if I did, I'm not sure it would change things. No one challenges Leonard Brock. It would be my word against his."

"What will you do?"

"Wish I knew." He fiddled with the stem of his wineglass.

Half-formed ideas tumbled through her mind like autumn leaves in a gale. "Have you tried advertising in other parts of the state for a crew? Places like Saginaw or Bay City?"

"No," he admitted slowly. His gaze sharpened as he stared across the table at her. "So far I've limited my search to the western half of the state. What makes you think I'd be successful elsewhere?"

"Leonard Brock is a stranger to them. Maybe the men won't be so easily intimidated if they have an even stronger reason to stay."

"What kind of reason?" He sat up straighter. She had all his attention now.

"You're the businessman." A ghost of a smile hovered on her lips. "Surely you could think up some sort of incentive such as a reward or bonus. Perhaps a percentage of the profits."

"Percentage of the profits?" he echoed in patent disbelief. "That siphons money directly from my bank account."

"Unless you get your logs downriver and to the mill, there won't be any profits," she pointed out.

His gray eyes alight with hope, he pushed away from the table and stood. "Please excuse me if I seem rude, but there are some calculations that need my immediate attention."

Smiling, Claire rose to her feet also and began to collect the dinner dishes. "I'll bring you a pot of fresh coffee."

"And some cookies?" Cole asked, already halfway across the room. At the doorway, he stopped and reversed direction. Cupping her face in both hands, he gave her a quick, impulsive kiss. "Thank you."

She gazed after him with a bemused smile.

TWELVE

"Tim's downstairs."

Claire looked up from the quilt on the nursery floor where she had been playing peek-a-boo with Daisy. "Did he say what he wanted?"

Alma stood just outside the room, her arms folded across her plump bosom, her round face creased in a scowl. "I asked, but he ain't tellin'."

Claire felt a tickle of apprehension. What could Tim possibly want? She feared whatever brought him here this afternoon had to do with her family. She scrambled to her feet, scooped Daisy into her arms, and hurried out of the nursery and down the stairs.

Alma trailed after her with a steady litany of complaints. "If you ask my opinion, O'Brien's too close-mouthed. I told Priscilla time and again the man's secretive, sneaky. He's hidin' something, I said. But she only laughed and refused to listen to reason."

Claire paid scant heed to the housekeeper's diatribe. Her mind was too busy conjuring up various scenarios involving her father or brother—all of them unpleasant. No matter what they had done, she knew she'd do whatever she could to help.

Tim stood just inside the back door as though afraid to budge from the rag rug at his feet for fear of tracking mud on Alma's clean floor. He glanced up at her approach, his seamed face unsmiling. It occurred to Claire that he was a man unaccustomed to smiles, a stranger to laughter. One who, in all likelihood, had learned life's harsh lessons at an early age.

"Alma said you wanted to see me."

Daisy chortled noisily, a happy grin on her cherubic face, eager to charm the dour stranger.

Tim's fingers moved restlessly on the brim of the cap he held loosely in his hands. He shot a meaningful glance at Alma, who eavesdropped shamelessly. "What I have to tell you is best said in private."

"Well, excuse *me*," Alma sniffed. "Case you don't remember, this here is my kitchen. I have every right to be here."

"Alma, please, I'm sure Tim meant no offense." Claire gave the housekeeper a smile meant to soothe ruffled feathers. "If you would just give us a couple minutes, I'm sure this won't take long."

"Hmph!" Muttering under her breath, Alma stalked off in a huff.

Daisy made another bid to win the stranger's attention. Apparently unhappy with the stifling quiet that had befallen, she let out a long string of syllables. "Da-da-da-da."

The outburst drew Tim's attention to the child for the first time. He regarded the baby with a puzzled frown. A frown that turned into lengthy consideration. Vaguely uneasy with the scrutiny, Claire shifted the child from one arm to the other. "What was it you wanted to tell me?" she asked, her tone sharper than she intended.

He jerked his attention from the baby and back to Claire. "Sorry," he mumbled. "Just thinking how the kid doesn't take after either of her parents."

Claire refrained from comment. The same thought had occurred to her. "Does the reason you're here have anything to do with my father or Nils?"

Tim looked as though he wished he was somewhere else. "Overheard some gossip when I was in at the feed store this afternoon."

"What kind of gossip?" Claire wished she could keep the quiver from her voice.

"Gaa-gaaa!" Daisy squealed as her tiny fingers latched onto a loose tendril of Claire's hair.

The baby's action diverted Tim once again. "Don't know much about kids, but ain't she kind of young to be talking?"

"You didn't come here to discuss Daisy's vocal ability." Patiently, she unwound her hair from the baby's firm grasp.

Tim shuffled his feet. "It's your brother."

"Nils?" Her hold on Daisy involuntarily tightened, causing the child to squirm. "Is he all right? He isn't hurt, is he?"

"Tanner's got him locked up."

"He's in jail?" Dear Lord! Claire's eyes widened in dismay. When would Nils learn to stay out of trouble?

"Seems a fight broke out last night at Mulligan's Bar. Folks claim your brother started it. Stuff got broken, and the police were called. Your brother was arrested and hauled off to jail."

Her mind racing, Claire plunked Daisy down in her highchair. "I've got a little savings tucked away—not much, but some." Although she didn't say so out loud, it was all the money she had in the world. Savings she had set aside to finance her departure from Brockton should Sophie's plan fail.

"Doesn't your brother have anyone else to help him? What about your father?"

"Pa always told Nils that if he ever landed in jail not to call him. And he meant what he said." She removed a tin from the cupboard, took out a cracker, then broke it into small pieces and placed them on the tray of the high chair. "If I don't help Nils, no one will."

Tim tugged an earlobe. "Jail might not be all bad. It might teach your brother a lesson or two he needs to learn."

"You don't understand." She untied her apron, smoothed her hair. "When Mother died, Nils and I promised we'd look out for each other. I can't turn my back on him when he needs me. I'd never be able to look at myself in the mirror again."

"Well, if your mind's made up." Tim gave her a look, part pity, part admiration. "The police might be willing to release him if you pay his fine and arrange with Mulligan to pay for damages."

Impulsively, she reached out and placed her hand on his sleeve. "Tim, I don't know how to thank you. I appreciate your telling me about my brother. Poor Nils—he must be desperate by now."

His mouth grim, his eyes met hers and held. "Your brother needs you, all right, but does he deserve you?"

Then he was gone.

Claire didn't have time to ponder his remarks. She needed to retrieve her money from its hiding place on the third floor. Needed to find Alma and ask—no, not ask, insist that she watch Daisy until her return.

When she raced down the stairs, her savings tucked in the pocket of her cloak, Claire found the housekeeper in the parlor waving a feather duster over furniture already dusted earlier that day. "I'm terribly sorry, Alma, but a family emergency has come up. You'll have to look after Daisy until I get home."

"Me?" A horrified expression crossed Alma's face.

Claire struggled with the buttons of her cloak. "It can't be helped. My brother needs me."

Alma's cheeks grew red, and her ample chest heaved with righteous indignation. "How many times do I gotta tell you? I don't like babies."

"Daisy's an angel. She won't be a problem, I promise. Just feed her if she's hungry, change her when she's wet."

"How long you gonna be gone?" Alma wailed as Claire headed toward the door.

"Not long." But she crossed her fingers for luck.

* * *

Claire glanced skyward as she hurried toward town. Dark clouds the color of tarnished pewter blotted out the feeble rays of sunlight. Snow clouds, she mused. While the days were noticeably longer as the season inched toward spring, winter still maintained a stranglehold. A raw wind swept out of the north and across Lake Michigan bringing with it the threat of a late winter storm. She pulled the hood of her cloak closer around her face, grateful for its warmth.

In this section of town, the saloons and boarding houses sprouted like weeds along a roadside. Head bent, she quickened her pace. She didn't have enough money put aside, she knew, to cover the cost of both fines and damages. She only hoped the owner of Mulligan's Bar proved reasonable.

Mulligan's Bar was a frame building located midway down the block, between the fire hall and the Tucker Transfer Company. It was easily recognized by the emerald green shamrock hanging above the door. Before she could lose her courage, Claire shoved open the door. Even with gloves on, the door's handle felt sticky to the touch.

The instant she stepped inside, the odor of spilled beer and stale smoke assaulted her nostrils. The rumble of male voices droned to a halt. A hush fell. Knowing she was the object of curious stares, Claire's cheeks burned. She wanted desperately to flee, but sheer determination kept her rooted in place.

"Hey, girlie, can a fellow buy you a beer?"

The request and the ensuing laughter shattered the awkward silence. Claire squared her shoulders and slowly approached the bar. The sawdust sprinkled over the floor boards was spongy beneath her feet. For the first time since entering, she noticed bits of mirrored glass clinging to the rough-sawn wood behind the bar. A sinking sensation in her stomach told her that Nils was responsible for the breakage.

Ignoring the saloon's half-dozen or so gawking patrons,

she addressed the burly man tending bar. "I'd like to speak with Mr. Mulligan, if you please."

The bartender stopped polishing the glass in his hand to study her. Bright blue eyes set in a square face with a pugnacious jaw held a teasing glint. "And if I don't please?"

Could the man actually be flirting with her? she wondered in amazement. As impossible as it seemed, she couldn't discount the bold, masculine appraisal as his gaze raked over her. Or, afterwards, the twinkle of approval in his smile.

"What's the matter, sweetheart?" He grinned around the cigar stub clamped between large, yellowed teeth. "Cat got yer tongue?"

Aware of the men watching with open amusement, she decided to walk a narrow line, polite and businesslike, neither rude nor friendly. "If Mr. Mulligan isn't here, perhaps you could tell me where I might find him."

Snickers from the onlookers ceased at a reproving look from the bartender. "Could be I know his whereabouts," he nodded agreeably, "but first you'd have to tell me why you want to see him."

"It's a personal matter."

"Personal, eh?" His grin broadened. "Well then, lass, this is your lucky day. Meet Padraig Mulligan hisself."

"You're Mr. Mulligan?"

"In the flesh." He resumed polishing the glass, his eyes on her the entire time. "Now tell me what brings a pretty colleen such as yourself to my fine establishment."

She battled a sudden attack of nerves. "There's a matter I'd like to discuss with you. In private," she added with a meaningful look at the customers' unabashed eavesdropping.

"Now you've got my attention." He gestured toward a table at the rear of the bar. "Step into my office, lass, and we'll have ourselves a cozy chat, private as can be."

Coming out from behind the bar, he ushered Claire across the room. He wasn't a tall man, she noted, but what he lacked in stature he made up for in breadth. He looked as sturdy and solid as a brick wall. She sat on the edge of the chair, keeping her hands primly folded in her lap to avoid touching the table scarred with burn marks and water rings. Padraig Mulligan straddled the chair next to hers, his beefy arms folded across the back.

"Care to tell me who you are, and what business brings you to my place? If it's a job yer lookin' for, I might be able to help."

"My name is Claire. Claire Sorenson." Upon hearing her name, she watched a frost wither his flattery.

"Any chance you're the wife of that good-fer-nothin', no-count drunk?"

The disdain in his voice stiffened her spine. "Nils is my brother. And for your information, Mr. Mulligan, he's neither lazy nor a drunk."

"That's a matter of opinion." He shifted the cigar to the other side of his mouth. "Say what you came for, then be on your way. I got work to do."

Her carefully rehearsed appeal flew out of her head. "I just found out what happened here last night."

"Yeah, so?"

"I wondered if I could persuade you to drop the charges against my brother." The words tumbled out in a breathless rush.

He grunted. "When pigs fly."

Clutching her hands tighter, she leaned forward "Nils isn't a bad person, Mr. Mulligan. It's just that he's had a hard time since his accident last year. Things haven't been easy for him."

"Lumbering's a dangerous trade." He puffed his cigar and studied her through a haze of smoke. "Men are hurt every day, some killed. That don't give 'em license to come in here and bust up what I've worked hard for all my life."

"No, no, of course not," Claire interjected quickly. "I didn't mean to imply it did."

Mulligan removed his cigar, flicked ash on the floor. "Look, Miss, I've got a business to run. Where would I be if every drunk in town considered it his God-given right to trash the joint? Yer brother is to blame for breakin' my mirror, a dozen bottles of my best Irish whiskey, along with a table or two and some chairs. I special-ordered that mirror all the way from Chicago."

"I only hoped, perhaps . . ."

"Perhaps what? That I'd give him a slap on the knuckles, then offer to buy 'im a beer? Well, it don't work that way at Mulligan's." He started to rise, a signal the conversation was over.

Claire feared her appeal on Nils' behalf was falling on deaf ears. Padraig Mulligan was a hardheaded businessman, not easily swayed by pretty speeches. Since she failed to enlist his sympathy thus far, she changed tactics. "What if I give you my word you'll be reimbursed for any damages?"

He dropped back in his seat. "Now you're talkin' my talk."

"I don't have much," she cautioned, knowing a portion of her money would be needed to pay fines. "But there's no way Nils can begin to repay you if he's behind bars."

"True, but like I said before, your brother's nothing but a shiftless no-count. Why would I think he'd repay his debt once he's out of jail?"

For the first time since this discussion began, Claire sensed a softening. "If Nils doesn't, I promise I'll pay you myself."

Mulligan stared at Claire through narrowed eyes until she wanted to squirm. It took considerable effort on her part to keep her expression calm and unruffled. She clenched her fingers together to keep from fidgeting. At last, Mulligan broke the tense stalemate. "I don't trust your brother any farther than I could throw him. Convince me you're cut from a different cloth."

Claire drew a deep breath, let it out. "Just ask Mr. Cavanaugh at Cavanaugh's Food Emporium. He'll tell you I regularly pay on my account. I have a good job, Mr. Mulligan, one that earns a respectable wage."

The tip of his cigar glowed red as he puffed thoughtfully. "What kind of job?"

"I'm employed by Mr. Cole Garrett as a baby nurse."

"Garrett, eh? Worked for him long?"

Unable to sit still, she shifted uneasily in the chair. "Not long."

"I heard he sent to Chicago for someone with fancy credentials to look after his kid. Is that true?"

"Yes," she admitted. "But so far he hasn't found anyone suitable."

"But when he does . . . ?"

The question hung between them.

"Well . . ." he prodded.

She shrugged diffidently. "Then I'll find another position."

Taking the cigar from his mouth, he rolled it between his fingertips. "How do you propose to pay off your brother's debt in the meantime?"

"I'm not afraid of hard work," she bristled.

"And you're not hard on the eyes, either," he surprised her by saying. "Tell you what, Claire, I admire your spunk and your honesty. Here's the deal—you lose your job with Garrett before the debt's paid off, you come and work for me."

Claire blinked in surprise. "Pardon me?"

"What's so hard to understand? You lose your job with Garrett, you work here as barmaid until the bill is paid in full."

"B-but," she protested, appalled at the notion of working in such a place. "I've never worked in a bar. I wouldn't know what to do."

"You look like a smart lass. Figure it out." Standing, he dropped his cigar and crushed it under his heel. "Take it or leave it. What's it going to be?"

She stood, too, her face pale but resolute. "Very well. I agree to your terms."

JUST BEFORE DAYBREAK

* * *

"I'm here to see Chief Tanner."

Homer Bailey looked up from cleaning his grimy fingernails with his pocket knife. "Your brother got himself into a heap of trouble over at Mulligan's."

"I'm aware of that."

"Paddy's none too happy with all the damage. Specially that big mirror of his behind the bar."

"Would you please tell Chief Tanner I'd like to talk to him."

"Can't." Homer scraped debris from under his thumbnail.

"Why not?"

"He's in a meetin'. Said he didn't want to be disturbed."

"Do you have any idea how long this meeting will last?" Homer shrugged. "It'll be over when it's over."

Claire blew out an impatient breath. Alma must be having a conniption fit by now. It was almost time for her to go home to her Harold. But what choice did she have? Nils was in trouble. She couldn't turn her back on him when he needed her. "I'll wait," she told Homer.

"Suit yerself."

Claire plunked herself down on one of the straight-backed chairs along one wall, prepared to wait. Shadows collected in the hallway beyond, mute evidence the hour was growing late. City Hall was quiet, its workers having gone home to their warm houses and hot suppers. The only sound was the occasional irate male voice coming through the closed door.

Unable to sit still, she rose to her feet and paced the corridor. How well did Nils tolerate being incarcerated? she wondered. He must be frightened, abandoned by friends and family. When would he realize what he was doing to himself? His life was sliding out of control. When would he stop this destructive behavior? She rubbed her throbbing temples. It was becoming harder and harder to remember the person he had once been.

At the thought of her depleted finances, the drumming in her head pounded even more fiercely. The prospect of locating another position as baby nurse seemed remote. After tonight she wouldn't have enough money to buy a dozen eggs, much less purchase a train ticket. Even so, she was grateful Padraig Mulligan had been willing to accept her word that Nils's debt would be repaid. A promise she intended to honor—even if it meant working at Mulligan's Bar herself.

She stopped pacing at the sound of Tanner's office door opening, then closing, and turned in time to see Leonard Brock emerge. He paused in the act of putting on his tall beaver hat when he spotted her. His brow furrowed as he stared at her for a long moment. Homer Bailey ceased cleaning his fingernails to watch with avid interest. His eyes darted from Claire to Brock, then back again.

"Should I know you?"

"She's that Sorenson woman," Homer supplied before Claire could speak. "Her pa or brother probably worked for you one time or 'nother."

"Ah, yes." Brock's frown smoothed. "A pair of drunks, both of them."

Blood surged hotly to color Claire's cheeks. Taken aback by Leonard Brock's rudeness, she watched warily as he stepped closer. He wielded his considerable girth as a well-honed weapon to intimidate the cowardly. Claire held her ground and resisted the urge to retreat. "You also enjoy a certain reputation, Mr. Brock," she said, finding her voice at last.

He stopped. Surprise, then irritation, flickered in his pale-green eyes. "What the hell you talking about, girl?"

"No sass now," Homer warned. "As mayor of this here town, Mr. Brock deserves respect."

Ignoring the deputy, Claire addressed Brock. "I was referring to your reputation for being blunt. I don't believe we've been properly introduced. I'm Claire Sorenson."

"So you're the one." He regarded her as though she were a cockroach that had just crawled into the light. "If it weren't for you, my daughter's killer wouldn't be running around town a free man."

He stood close enough for Claire to smell the cigar smoke that clung to the tweed fibers of his coat. "With all due respect, Mr. Brock, without me, an innocent man would stand accused of a crime he didn't commit."

"What's he paying you to keep him out of jail?"

"He didn't pay me a cent."

"Nonsense!" His gaze raked over her with calculated shrewdness. "Everyone's services are for hire—for the right price."

From his tone and the glimmer in his pale-green eyes, the implication was clear to Claire's mind. He was offering a bribe if she would recant. "I beg to disagree, Mr. Brock. Not everyone has a price."

His ruddy complexion turned ruddier. His ginger-colored whiskers trembled from the force of his anger. "You change your mind, girl, you know where to find me."

Claire stared after his retreating back. In spite of all his power, all his wealth, she pitied him. Consumed by grief, driven by rage, Leonard Brock failed to value his greatest treasure of all—his own granddaughter. Not once had he inquired about the child's well-being. Not once had he attempted to see her.

Behind her, Homer Bailey noisily cleared his throat. "I'll see if the chief can see you now."

Claire drew a steadying breath. The encounter with Priscilla's father had been unnerving at the least. It was clear he hated Cole and would stop at nothing to see him behind bars. She found such single-mindedness frightening.

Homer disappeared into Tanner's office, then reappeared a moment later. "The boss said to send you in."

Shoving worry about Cole's safety into the far recesses of her mind, she concentrated on her problem at hand—Nils.

Chief Edward Tanner didn't look up from the sheaf of papers in his hands. He didn't extend the courtesy of offering her a chair, but made her stand before him like a supplicant begging for alms. "S'pose you're here because of your brother. Well, say whatever it is you come to say and be done with it. I've got work to do."

"I won't waste your valuable time, Chief Tanner. I'm here to ask you to release my brother."

Tanner's head jerked up, disbelief apparent on his hatchet-sharp features. "Just like that." He snapped his fingers. "You're naïve, girl, if you think you can just waltz in here and that brother of yours gets off scot-free."

"I'm not as naïve as you seem to think." She pulled a pocketful of crumpled bills and assorted coins from her pocket and triumphantly placed them on the desk in front of the police chief. "That should be enough to cover the fine for drunkenness."

He drummed his fingertips against the document on his desk, making the papers rustle. "Even if it were, there's still the matter of the considerable damage your brother inflicted upon Padraig Mulligan's property. Last I know, Padraig was none too happy."

"I just came from talking with Mr. Mulligan. He has kindly agreed to drop charges against Nils. He's more interested in being compensated for the costs and knows my brother can't do that if he's behind bars."

Behind his thick mustache, Tanner's lips thinned into a straight line. "I'm going to speak to Mulligan personally and find out if what you say is true. Wait here."

THIRTEEN

Her feet felt like blocks of ice. Claire stomped to restore the circulation. Nearly an hour had elapsed since Homer Bailey had instructed her to wait for Nils behind City Hall, where the jail was located. Not even a smattering of stars relieved the inky darkness. A blustery wind swirled the light dusting of snow into small eddies along the frozen ground. Since leaving the Garrett house, the temperature had plummeted. The bitter cold seeped through her woolen cloak and into her bones.

She knew Alma would be furious with her when she returned. She had been gone much longer than she had anticipated. Her hands were stiff and numb inside her thin gloves. She blew on them for warmth while rehearsing ways to placate the irate housekeeper.

At last the door behind her opened, and her brother emerged.

"Nils." She hurried toward him, anxiously inventorying him for damages. Other than a black eye and puffy lip, he looked no worse for his ordeal. "I've been so worried about you."

"I can look after myself." He tugged the collar of his jacket higher around his neck.

"I came as soon as I heard." She fell into step next to him as he limped down the street. "Are you all right?"

"Garrett couldn't wait, could he, to let you know your

brother landed in jail. Probably thought good riddance to bad rubbish."

"This has nothing to do with Cole," she retorted, stung by his tone.

"Cole," he sneered. "Since when did he become *Cole?"*

"Tim O'Brien told me about the fight at Mulligan's."

"Same difference." He kept his head bent against the wind. "From what I hear, O'Brien worships the ground Garrett walks on."

"What's wrong with you?" She grabbed his sleeve and spun him around to face her. "Why are you acting like this?"

Wind whipped his pale hair around his thin face. "I didn't ask for your help. I don't want your help. You should have let me rot in jail."

Claire struggled to understand her brother. She had expected gratitude and relief that she had intervened on his behalf, but instead he seemed resentful. "I love you, Nils. I couldn't stand by without trying to help. Instead of being grateful, you're angry."

He jerked his arm free from her grasp. "As you well know, little sister, I hate the man's guts. Knowing the money used to bail me out of jail was once in his bank account makes me want to puke."

Nils walked away as quickly as his damaged leg would allow. Hurt and confused, Claire stared after him until he turned the corner and was lost from view. Her sacrifice had been in vain. She had gladly surrendered her entire savings to free her brother, only to have him throw her generosity in her face. She had been a fool to expect more. She was left with an incredible emptiness deep inside.

And feeling unutterably alone.

With a heavy heart, she headed in the opposite direction her brother had taken.

Claire blew into the cozy kitchen on a cold blast of arctic air. Upon seeing her, Daisy let out a delighted crow from her perch in the high chair. Judging from Cole's scowl, she guessed he didn't share his daughter's enthusiasm. Alma's presence, she noted, was conspicuously absent.

"It's snowing." The inane comment was all she could think to say as she self-consciously brushed the wet flakes from her cloak.

"Really?" Cole's voice dripped with sarcasm.

Claire eyed him warily as she tugged off her gloves. His shirtsleeves, rolled to the elbow, revealed a pair of brawny arms. The food splatters decorating his shirt front, however, were anything but masculine. They suspiciously matched the colors smeared across Daisy's little face. Pea green and carrot orange.

"Do you have any idea of the time?" Pulling a gold pocket watch from his vest, he pointedly checked the hour.

Claire felt chilled in spite of the warm kitchen. She held her hands toward the iron cookstove where a coffeepot simmered on a back burner. "I'm sorry. I know it's late, but it couldn't be helped."

Daisy squealed loudly, then proceeded to rub a fistful of strained vegetables into her blond curls.

Cole hissed with frustration at the mess the baby had created. "Alma makes no secret of the fact she dislikes children," he said through gritted teeth. "Yet you take off on some mysterious errand and don't return for hours."

"It couldn't be helped." Slipping out of her cloak, she folded it carefully and placed it over the back of a chair before donning an apron. "Here," she held out her hand for the silver baby spoon he held, "I'll finish feeding Daisy."

He relinquished the spoon with ill-concealed relief. "The poor child could have starved to death, no thanks to you."

Oblivious to the undercurrents between the two adults, Daisy opened her mouth in eager anticipation of more food.

"What do you mean?" Claire asked, scooping strained peas from the baby's dish.

Cole leaned against the sink, arms folded across his chest, a frown in place. "I got home later than I planned to find Daisy screaming at the top of her lungs. I'm surprised Tim didn't hear her from the carriage house."

"Where was Alma?" The heavy weight of dread settled on her chest.

"Sitting here at the kitchen table with her coat on. 'I don't take care of babies,' she tells me before I even open my mouth. Well, she sure as hell proved it tonight."

"And where was Daisy all this time?"

"Upstairs in her crib, crying. Her diaper was soaked through and she hadn't had her supper. She was so happy to see a friendly face that the smile she gave me could have melted stone." His mouth twisted into a grim smile at the memory.

Claire swallowed a lump of guilt that threatened to choke her. "I'm so sorry. Even though Alma doesn't like babies, I never thought for a second that she'd neglect Daisy."

"Well, she did."

She bit down on her lower lip to keep it from quivering. The thought of Daisy wet and hungry made her want to weep. But what else could she have done under the circumstances? From the shelter of hindsight, she knew she should have waited until Cole returned home, but at the time she had been too upset to think clearly. Instead, her actions had been governed by a sense of urgency. Nils was in trouble; he needed her. "I'm terribly, terribly sorry. You have my word, I'll never leave her again."

"You disappointed me, Claire." He turned his back on her, poured himself coffee from the pot on the stove. "I believed you were more responsible. You were hired to take care of my child, not ignore her."

In spite of her efforts to remain calm, her hands shook as she wiped Daisy's sticky hands and face. "Are you telling me I'm fired?"

He looked over his shoulder and speared her with his

steel-gray eyes. "Seeing as I've already lost one employee tonight, I'm not in the mood to make it two."

"Alma quit?" She froze in the act of lifting Daisy from her high chair. The headache brewing behind her eyes suddenly intensified.

"She quit only seconds before I would have fired her." Cup in hand, he stared at a fixed spot on the kitchen floor. "No one, *no one,* treats my child the way she did."

Claire bounced Daisy on one hip. "I didn't think I would be gone so long," she murmured.

"Didn't think at all, is more like it."

"I accept full responsibility." She wanted to hang her head in shame. Cole had been good to her, kind and generous, and she had let him down. Worst of all, Daisy had suffered as a result of her rash decision. "The fault is all mine. If I had been here, none of this would have happened."

"Then why the hell weren't you?"

She hesitated, remembering the enmity between Cole and her brother. Absently, she ran her hand over Daisy's hair, but the blond tufts defied her efforts and remained a halo of orange and green spikes instead.

Cole waited impatiently. Raising the coffee cup, he took a sip. "Damn!" he swore, spitting it out. "This stuff tastes like sludge."

Claire studied his harsh expression with troubled eyes. Knowing how he and Nils disliked each other, she doubted if Cole would be sympathetic to her plight.

"Never mind," he growled. "Keep your reasons to yourself. I don't think I want to know."

Tossing the rest of the coffee into a pan in the sink, he stalked off.

Her knees wobbly, Claire sank into a nearby chair and cuddled Daisy in her lap. Considering the circumstances, Cole had every right to be angry. Even though she had been the target of his fury, she couldn't help but admire the way he sprang to his child's defense. But no amount of understanding or admiration could salve her guilt.

She brushed a kiss across the baby's food-encrusted locks. "Poor baby, I'm sorry I deserted you and left you with mean old Alma. Somehow, though, I didn't think your father would appreciate me taking you to visit a jail."

Reaching up, Daisy patted her cheek with chubby fingers. Whether to offer solace or merely wanting Claire's undivided attention it was impossible to guess, but Claire smiled for the first time in hours.

By the time Cole climbed the stairs an hour later, his temper had cooled considerably. While still irritated, he was no longer furious. From the stricken look on Claire's face, he knew she regretted her decision to leave the child in Alma's care. He had gone a little crazy at discovering Daisy wet and hungry, tears rolling down her flushed cheeks. Funny, he mused, the strength of a parent's protective urges. He'd slay dragons for that little girl. He started down the hall, already unfastening the buttons of his shirt, which still bore traces of Daisy's dinner.

He paused just outside the nursery door, his head to one side, listening. Noiselessly, he moved closer and peered inside. Claire sat in a rocking chair holding Daisy, who drowsily sucked from a bottle. In a sweet, lilting soprano, Claire sang to the sleepy infant.

Hush, bye-bye, don't you cry,
Go to sleep, little baby,
When you wake, you'll have sweet cake,
And all the pretty little horses.

A band tightened around his chest at the sight. A beautiful woman, an adorable child, an elegant home. This was what he had slaved for, dreamed about all his life. Only the woman in front of him wasn't his wife. The child wasn't his. And as for the home, well, he admitted with brutal honesty, it was only bricks and mortar. He had taken such pride in building a fine, new house. Such pride in marrying a woman of indisputable social standing. *Pride goeth before a fall.* Would pride lead to his ultimate downfall? he wondered grimly.

Giving himself a mental shake, he realized Claire's lullaby had ended. He watched her rise to her feet and place the sleeping baby in her crib. Quietly, he entered the room and stood next to her while she pulled the blanket over the tiny form. Unable to resist, he reached down and gently stroked Daisy's cheek with the back of his finger. Her skin felt soft as a rose petal. Her wispy curls gleamed spun gold. She smelled fresh and vaguely of flowers, he thought, realizing Claire had bathed her before rocking her to sleep.

"You love her very much, don't you?" Claire asked in a whisper.

"Yes." He cleared his throat. "Yes, I do." The love he felt for this small creature had caught him by surprise. Nothing in his experience had prepared him for that unexpected rush of emotion. The overwhelming tenderness. It had kicked him in the stomach. Hit him square between the eyes. And it had happened in an instant.

He remembered that exact moment with blinding clarity. Daisy had been squalling her lungs out in that quavering, high-pitched wail of a newborn. Priscilla had turned a deaf ear and a blind eye to her daughter's distress while the baby nurse sulked in her room over a petty misunderstanding. Feeling clumsy and awkward, Cole had picked the baby up and held her. So trusting, so vulnerable. So very tiny. In that split second, Daisy had become the child of his heart—if not from his loins.

"She's a sweet child," Claire murmured. "I'll miss her when I leave."

Noiselessly, they left the nursery together.

He was beginning to feel a bit ashamed for his earlier outburst. The full brunt of his anger at Alma Dobbs had been leveled at Claire instead. He hadn't even offered her ample opportunity to explain her absence. Though loath to admit it, he had felt a sharp prick of worry when he had come home and found her gone. He feared she might be gone for good. Daisy would miss her—and so would he.

Where had that thought sprung from? What the hell was wrong with him, anyway? For chrissake, she was a servant—and a temporary one at that. Disgusted with his train of thought, he rolled up his shirtsleeves with quick, angry motions. He caught Claire watching him, trepidation on her pretty face. His conscience nagged at him. He considered himself a fair and reasonable employer. The least he could do was give her a chance to justify her actions.

"We need to talk. Come to the library after you're finished with your duties."

She swiped her palms on the sides of her apron. "If you wish," she replied. Her voice was steady, almost resigned.

Claire found Cole waiting, his back turned to the room, staring out the window at nothingness. Hungry orange flames licked logs piled in the grate. Their hiss and crackle mingled with the ping of ice pellets striking glass panes. It might have been only her imagination, a trick of the lighting, but with his shoulders bowed, his head bent, he appeared a strong man laboring beneath a too heavy burden.

"You wanted to see me?"

He jerked the heavy drapery closed, then turned to face her. "It occurred to me that you still haven't explained why you left Daisy in Alma's care this afternoon. I think—as your employer—I'm entitled to an explanation."

She stepped farther into the room. His expression was difficult to interpret in the dim light, a mix of shadow, mystery, and rugged male. Attractive. Potentially dangerous. She ran the tip of her tongue over her bottom lip. Over the years, she had learned men could be unpredictable— and often cruel—when provoked.

Her hesitation apparently annoyed him, because he snapped, "For heaven's sake, Claire, quit looking at me as though I bite."

Cautiously advancing toward him, she stopped to rest her hands along the back of a chair. "My brother needed my help."

"Nils?" he grunted. "What this time?"

Her grip tightened on the chair back. "He was in jail."

"Can't say that surprises me." He walked over to the sideboard along one wall and splashed liquid into a glass. "Precisely what did he do to land himself in jail?"

Her chin raised a fraction at his tone. "Nils got into a scuffle at Mulligan's Bar, which resulted in considerable damage. He was arrested for drunk and disorderly conduct."

"And begged his sister to come to the rescue."

"No, you're wrong. Nils didn't ask for my help." *Quite the contrary,* she added silently.

He studied her over the rim of his glass, then shrugged. "Your brother has been heading in that direction for quite some time. It shouldn't have come as a surprise."

"Just as it doesn't come as a surprise to hear you say those things. I'm well aware that there's bad blood between the two of you."

"Bad blood or not, you can't run at the drop of a hat every time he's in trouble. Comes a time a man has to stand on his own two feet."

"That's all very easy for you to say." It had been a trying day, and suddenly she had had enough. "You're a lumber baron. You don't have to worry about how to pay for a broken mirror. Or not having money for a lawyer. You're a strong, able-bodied man with two perfectly good legs. You don't have physical limitations like Nils." Her chest heaved from the force of her anger. "It's very easy for you to criticize someone less fortunate."

Her display of temper served to rekindle his. "Stop treating your brother like a child. Nils is a grown man.

It's time he acted like one. Time he grew up. I've seen other men injured a hell of a lot worse who don't feel entitled to spend the rest of their lives feeling sorry for themselves."

It irritated her that Cole's words struck close to the truth. Yet loyalty ran thick through her veins. "What Nils does, or doesn't do, is none of your business."

"Damn right it is." Setting his glass down, he narrowed the distance between them until all that separated them was a chair. "It becomes my business when you neglect your duties and run off to clean up his mess. Tell me, Claire, what did you do, bail him out?"

"The money I earn is mine to do with as I please."

"And what about the damages Nils did at the bar? From what I hear, Padraig Mulligan's a hard-headed man when it comes to doing business."

Her chin came up another notch. "I found him both fair and reasonable."

"Funny," he let out a harsh laugh, "but those aren't the words I've heard used to describe him. One of my men said Mulligan has a cash register in place of a heart." His eyes narrowed as a sudden thought struck him. "Did you offer to pay him for Nils's share of the damages?"

Uncomfortable under his cross-examination, she shifted her weight but remained silent.

"Was that the reason Mulligan agreed to drop the charges? Because you agreed to pay your brother's debt?"

"Once Nils finds steady work, he'll gladly repay what he owes." She dropped her gaze and traced an invisible pattern along the ridge of the chair. Truth was, she had no idea whatsoever if Nils would give a dime toward costs. He certainly hadn't been in any mood to discuss finances when last seen. She hoped after his temper cooled he'd be in a more rational frame of mind.

"When are you going to take off the blinders, Claire? Your family uses you, and will go on using you, but give nothing in return. Mention the name Sorenson, decent people look in the other direction. They don't want anything to do with you or your family."

"I've listened to you long enough. I'm tired of hearing you criticize my family." She turned to leave, but he moved like lightning, blocking her retreat. His hands curled around her upper arms; she felt the strength, the heat, burn through the sleeve of her dress.

"Your father ruined any chance you might ever have of leading a normal life. Most men, even if they are interested in courting you, think twice about having to confront him. Same goes for Nils. Unless something changes soon, you're going to end up a spinster, cleaning up after them for the rest of your life."

"What I choose to do with my life is no concern of yours." She tried to pull away from his hot hands, his hateful words. Words that were an arrow to the heart. His grip, while painless, was nevertheless inexorable. "I've already apologized for leaving Daisy with Alma. I don't know what else I can say other than if I had to do it over again, I'd do things differently."

"If you could do things over again, I'd advise you to find yourself a different brother. Maybe an entirely different family. Your father isn't exactly a prize, either."

"Is that all?" she said between gritted teeth. Anger lent her strength. This time, when she pulled back she succeeded in breaking free from his hold.

"Go to bed, Claire," he said, his voice low, controlled. Only his eyes still blazed with banked temper, reminding her of molten steel. "I've already said far more than I intended."

FOURTEEN

Claire rubbed frost from the windowpane and stared into the raging storm. Outside, the wind howled, rattling the rafters and shaking the shutters. Inwardly she felt equally as rattled and shaken. Her exchange with Cole had left her wide awake and unable to sleep. Restless.

Drawing the woolen shawl more snugly over her shoulders to ward off the draft, she paced the length of her quarters. The folds of her nightgown swirled around her bare feet with each step. Cole's words had left her furious, made her want to strike back.

Not because they were untrue, but because they were.

As long as she remained in Brockton, she would never have any sort of life. She'd always feel obligated to cook, clean, and defend her family. And Nils, she feared, would never make any attempt to repay Padraig Mulligan what he owed the bar owner. He would be content to leave it up to her to pay his debt, even if it meant her working as a barmaid.

She squeezed her eyes shut as another home truth slammed into her. It was unlikely that any decent, law-abiding suitor would ever seek to make her his wife. Her father's uncertain temper discouraged even the most intrepid lumberjacks. There were too many other women to court who were unencumbered by a drunken father and trouble-seeking brother.

Enough! she berated herself. Wallowing in self-pity

would get her nowhere. Somehow, some way, she'd find a solution. In the meantime, a nice cup of hot milk might help her fall into sleep and escape her problems, at least for a few hours.

She paused on the second floor to check on Daisy. Impervious to the early spring blizzard, the baby lay sound asleep on her stomach, her little round bottom hunched in the air. Claire couldn't help but smile, remembering Cole standing next to his daughter's crib. He was clearly devoted to the child. She found it touching that such a big, strapping man could at the same time be so gentle—so vulnerable.

"Know what, Daisy?" she whispered. "You're a very lucky girl to have a daddy like yours."

Leaving the nursery, she made her way down the servants' staircase to the kitchen. A short time later, balancing a plate of cookies on top of a steaming mug of hot milk, she wandered into the library. A book might be just the thing to help her fall asleep. She stood for a moment on the threshold, eyes and ears straining to detect any sign of Cole's presence. But all was quiet.

Reassured she was alone, she stepped farther into the room. The library smelled pleasantly of woodsmoke and leather and an elusive scent that belonged to Cole exclusively. The fire burned low in the hearth, but emitted enough light to read the gold-embossed titles of books on the shelves that flanked the door. One in particular drew her attention. *Daisy Miller* by the novelist Henry James. As she reached for the leather-bound volume, she wondered if the work had influenced the name of her charge.

"What are you doing in here?"

Startled by the low rumble of Cole's voice directly behind her, Claire spun around. The mug of hot milk and cookies flew from her hands. The mug landed on its edge with enough force to send its steaming contents shooting upward.

"Ohh . . . !" she cried out as scalding hot liquid came in contact with her bare feet and her right ankle.

Cole assessed her predicament with a glance. Swinging her up into his arms, he crossed the room with long strides. "I should have known better than to come up behind you." Concern roughened his voice.

"I thought you had gone upstairs to bed," she managed to gasp.

"I dozed off in front of the fire." He deposited her on the sofa in front of the fireplace, then, kneeling next to her, examined the burns on her feet with exquisite gentleness. "These must hurt like the devil."

"A little," she admitted. The initial shock of the injury was wearing off. She battled tears as pain dug in with wicked talons.

"Claire, I'm so sorry. This is all my fault." With the pad of his thumb, he brushed away a stray tear that rolled down her cheek in spite of her effort to control them.

"I couldn't sleep," she admitted raggedly.

"Shh." He forestalled further talk by placing his index finger lightly against her lips. "I know just the thing. Don't move, I'll be right back."

The pain clawed at her, burning, stinging, driving everything else from her mind. Cole returned minutes later, bare to the waist. He held his bunched-up shirt, now filled with snow, in one fist.

Kneeling alongside the sofa, he folded the snow-filled garment like an overlarge bandage and placed it over her scalded feet and ankle. "This is a remedy I learned when I was a kid working in the cookhouse."

Her breath hissed out at the first touch of the icy cold compress.

"Trust me, Claire." He smoothed back a strand of hair from her face. "This will help, but give it time."

"H-how long?" she asked dubiously through teeth that had begun to chatter in the aftermath of shock and pain and cold.

"Not long, I promise."

She shuddered violently as a delayed reaction set in.

"Damn," he swore softly. "I'm such a clumsy oaf. Next, you'll catch pneumonia thanks to my carelessness." Retrieving her shawl, which had dropped to the floor, he spread it over her shoulders. "There, that better?"

"I'm fine, r-really," she insisted, but she couldn't seem to stop her teeth from clicking together. "Y-you don't have to fuss over me."

"Nonsense. Everyone needs someone to fuss over them once in a while."

He gave her the type of smile usually reserved for Daisy. A smile radiating tenderness, affection. A smile that started a warm glow inside.

Absently, he took one of her hands and chafed it lightly with his much larger one. "You're always busy taking care of others. This once, let someone take care of you."

Amazing! He wanted to take care of her. His words brought an ache to her chest. Sweeter than flowers. More precious than jewels. It had been a lifetime ago since anyone had offered to take care of her. "All right," she agreed, relaxing back against the cushions. "Just for a little while if you don't mind."

"My pleasure," he murmured, his gaze fastened on hers.

Mesmerized, Claire stared into gray eyes that had deepened to the color of shadow. An intense, brooding shade that hid more than it revealed. His ruggedly handsome face was a charcoal sketch composed of oblique planes and uncompromising angles. And his body . . . She refused to let herself dwell on the powerfully sculpted torso that was mere inches away.

He stood abruptly. "The fire's burned low," he said, his voice oddly hoarse. "Guess it's time to add another log."

Claire observed the play of muscle and tendon beneath bronzed flesh as Cole bent, then placed a chunk of firewood in the grate. He jabbed the wood with a poker, sending a shower of orange sparks flying. Flames greedily devoured the log, causing the oak to snap and pop. She eased herself up on an elbow, vaguely aware that her gaze was as greedy as the dancing flames.

"I know another remedy that might ease the pain." Cole crossed the room to a sideboard. Crystal clinked as he removed the stopper from a decanter, then poured a generous splash of amber liquid into a snifter. He came toward her, slowly rotating the glass between his palms, then offered it to her. "Nothing like good brandy on a cold night."

"No!" she declined with an adamant shake of her head. "I never touch spirits."

"A teetotaler, eh?" His mouth quirked at one corner. "It won't hurt if, just once, you make an exception to your rule."

She stared at the drink in his hand with a look akin to terror. Knowing her father and brother's weakness for liquor, she harbored the fear that she, too, might have inherited the same character flaw.

Cole's smile vanished as he guessed the true reason for her hesitation. His expression serious, he lowered himself to the edge of the sofa. "You're nothing like the rest of your family, Claire. Believe me, you're as different as night from day."

"I know it's silly," she confessed. "But I worry all the same."

"Think of it as medicine, if you like. Please, Claire," he coaxed. "It'll make me feel less like a villain."

This time when he offered, she accepted.

"Good girl," he applauded when she took a cautious sip. "Humor me. Take one more swallow before I check the burns on your feet."

Liquid heat trickled down her throat and pooled in the pit of her stomach. While she doubted brandy would replace her fondness for tea, the taste wasn't unpleasant. "This isn't so bad after all," she admitted.

"What isn't bad?" He raised a brow. "Two toasted feet?"

The pain had subsided into a dull, steady throb. In its place, she felt almost languorous, filled with an intoxicating sense of well-being. "No," she retorted, stifling the absurd impulse to giggle. "I meant the brandy—as well as being warm and snug in front of a fire, while it's cold and stormy outside."

Gingerly he removed the snowy compress that he had fashioned from his shirt. He placed his hand beneath her instep and, ignoring her sharply indrawn breath, raised her foot for his inspection. Satisfied, he repeated the process with the other.

Scooting into a sitting position, Claire leaned forward to look for herself. "Thanks to your quick thinking, I don't think they'll blister."

"I'd hate for such pretty feet to bear scars." Glancing upward, his gaze locked with hers.

His gray eyes were dark; his stare veiled and intense. Emotion, hot and wild, lurked beneath a thin layer of civility. At a loss for words, Claire dragged the tip of her tongue across her lower lip. The action pulled his attention to her mouth.

Absently, Cole reached out and brushed aside the heavy sweep of dark blond hair that fell forward to partially cover her face. He lingered to stroke the smooth curve of her cheek. "Your skin is soft and smooth as silk."

His touch jolted her clear to the center of her being. "I— I should go up to my room," she said, her voice strained. But she wanted to stay, wanted to be touched. Wanted to hear extravagant compliments.

He traced the pad of his thumb over her full bottom lip. "Right or wrong, I want you, Claire. I need you. You can't possibly know how much."

Want? Need? The words were foreign to her. So was the undisguised longing he made no effort to conceal. Primal and raw. A yearning of her own welled up, sharp and swift and violent. In that instant, she wanted to be needed. Needed to be wanted. So basic, so complex.

So irresistible.

"Yes," she whispered, moving toward him. "Yes," she sighed as his lips crushed hers.

Cole didn't pause to question his good fortune. His mouth moved over hers with barely controlled hunger. Blood drummed in his ears. Her lips parted eagerly beneath his. She tasted of summer berries and aged brandy. While her flavor was intoxicating, her responsiveness was pure nectar.

His mouth left hers to trail a fiery path along her jaw. He felt her quiver like a plucked bowstring when he discovered the sensitive spot behind her right ear. Knowing his affect on her, a heady sense of power surged through him.

He elicited a series of tiny sighs from her as his lips traveled down the slender column of her throat. Claire pressed closer. Encouraged, Cole locked his arms around her waist and tugged, pulling her off balance. Together they tumbled to the floor in front of the hearth, his weight cushioning hers.

Claire lay sprawled on top of him. Her waist-length tresses formed an amber curtain about them lending an aura of intimacy. He framed her face between his hands. "I can't remember ever needing a woman the way I . . ."

"Shh." She silenced him with a kiss. "No promises."

He frowned. "But, you . . ."

"No promises," she repeated softly. "And no regrets."

"No regrets," Cole echoed. *And no strings attached.* Disappointment flickered in a secret place deep inside. A simple release. A physical joining between man and woman as ancient as time itself. *That was what he wanted, wasn't it?* He should be relieved Claire understood, and accepted, the situation for what it was. Yet, he felt oddly . . . dissatisfied? He shrugged off his brooding thoughts. Later there would be ample time to sort out his conflicting emotions. Right now, the prospect of more enjoyable matters claimed his attention. Shifting his weight, he turned so that Claire rolled off, and they now lay facing each other.

He smiled into a pair of silver-blue eyes glazed with surprise and with what he hoped was passion. "You have the most tempting mouth," he said, then proved it by claiming hers for a mind-emptying kiss. Plundering, commanding, cajoling. Claire responded with an innocent ardor that inflamed senses already burning out of control.

Through the thin layer of fabric that separated their straining bodies, he could feel the imprint of her slender form. He was already hard, so hard his arousal was painful. Cupping her breast in one hand, he squeezed gently, experimentally.

Claire drew in a sharp breath, then froze. He waited, forced himself to be patient, even though the act required almost Herculean effort. Gradually he sensed her relax, accept his touch. Her breast, surprisingly round and firm in spite of her slender build, filled his palm as though designed for him alone. Curious, he flicked his thumb back and forth. Instantly the nipple furled into a tight bud.

The desire to claim her, brand her body with possession, flared hotter, brighter. With nimble fingers, he unfastened the row of tiny buttons at the yoke of her nightgown. He slid the garment down one shoulder, then the other. Then, with ill-concealed impatience, he dragged it over her hips, flung it aside.

He stared unabashedly at the bounty exposed to his hungry perusal. Perfectly formed breasts, a narrow waist his hands could span, gently curved hips, and long, shapely limbs. He exhaled a ragged breath. "God, Claire. You're beautiful."

Embarrassed, she lowered her lashes and instinctively raised a hand to shield her nakedness.

"Don't. Please don't, sweetheart," he pleaded.

"No one has ever seen me undressed," she confessed shyly.

Now it was his turn to freeze. She was an innocent. A virgin. This shouldn't come as a surprise. If he had stopped to consider, he would have guessed as much. Yet her admission humbled him, rocked him. "Are you sure, Claire? It still isn't too late for second thoughts."

Damn! he swore silently. He couldn't believe the words coming out of his mouth. A warm and willing woman offered herself to him, and here he was, giving her an opportunity to change her mind. What the devil was wrong with him?

Her eyes glowed as though lit within. Smiling, she wound her arms around his neck. "I'm certain."

Cole's body shuddered as he drew her into his embrace. Sweet, lovely Claire had chosen to give herself freely with no false promises or lies between them. He didn't know what he had done to deserve such a marvelous gift, but he wasn't strong enough to refuse. Slanting his mouth over hers, he kissed her deeply, passionately.

And her ardor matched his.

His large hand returned to fondle her breast. This time when it closed over the soft mound, she pressed closer to the source of rough heat. Before she had a chance to divine his intent, he drew back slightly, bent his head, drew her nipple into his mouth, and sucked.

"Cole," she gasped. She tangled her fingers through his hair, then flexed them as though undecided whether to repel his advances or entreat them to continue.

Cole turned his attention to her other breast, laving the nipple until it, too, turned pebble-hard. Her breathing hitched. Closing her eyes, she arched her back like a pagan offering. He took quick advantage. While continuing the exquisite torture with lips and tongue, and teeth, he slid one hand along the smooth skin of her abdomen. The tiny nerve endings just under her skin's surface seemed infinitely responsive to his touch. As her body began to undulate to a timeless rhythm, he pressed his fingers into the hot, wet center of her femininity.

She bucked, instinctively trying to dislodge this unfamiliar invasion from her body.

"Steady, sweetheart," he soothed. Instead of withdrawing, he slowly, skillfully, moved his finger back and forth until she was liquid and pliant and wanting.

She opened her eyes, her lids heavy, the irises smoky, unfocused. "I want to please you, but I don't know how."

"You make me feel like a randy schoolboy." He rested his forehead against hers, fought to regain a minute semblance of control. It would be easier to hold back a runaway team on an icy slope, he thought, than to contain this fierce need that had taken possession of his body.

She kneaded the thick ridge of muscle along his back. "Tell me what to do," she whispered brokenly.

He found the tiny nub nestled in the damp nest of tawny curls. Circled, teased. "Don't do a thing, sweetheart. Let yourself fly."

Superbly sensitive to each touch, each caress, she moved against his hand, tentatively at first, then with increasing confidence as sensation mounted, one wave of emotion on top of another. She rolled her head side to side. Her hands dug into his back, the nails scoring his flesh. Cole neither noticed nor cared.

Using his mouth and hands, he played her like a finely honed instrument until she writhed with pleasure and sobbed his name. At some point, the impulse to take had been mysteriously transformed into the urge to give. The moment, he knew, would be sweeter, the reward greater, if pleasure was shared.

Her back arched, her eyes shut, she convulsed in a paroxysm of pure pleasure. Cole's lips pulled back from his teeth in primal satisfaction as he watched her shatter.

With her body still quaking in the aftershock of passion, he quickly stripped off his pants, then parted her legs and knelt between her thighs. His engorged shaft nudged her portal. "Open for me, sweetheart."

And miraculously she obeyed. Her eyes trustingly fastened on his, she spread her legs to allow him entrance. Holding impatience on a tight leash, he proceeded slowly while every instinct urged him to rush. Perspiration beaded his brow. Instead of plunging into her heat, he eased in with controlled, gradual increments until he encountered the fragile membrane guarding paradise.

His elbows braced on either side of her face, he kissed her deeply, partly to distract her from the pain to come, partly to beg her forgiveness. Then, with one swift thrust, he pierced the delicate tissue. He swallowed her muffled cry of pain. He paused, waiting for her discomfort to subside, prayed it would happen quickly. Claire stirred beneath him and tilted her pelvis fractionally. It was his undoing. His hips began to pump, faster and faster. Her inner muscles clenched around him like a tight fist. Like hot, wet velvet. Like nothing he had ever experienced.

"Take me, Cole," she murmured against his lips. "Make me fly."

And together they soared.

Drowsily, Claire opened her eyes and smiled, replete. Cole returned the smile with a lazy one of his own. His hand rested possessively at the curve of her waist. They lay facing each other in front of a fire that had burned to embers. Like the flames in the hearth, the passion between them no longer flared intense and bright, but still radiated a glowing heat.

Reaching out, she stroked his jaw, savoring the raspy feel of his unshaven beard. It was such an obstinate jaw, she mused, square and strong. Somehow it suited him. He was too big, too rugged, to be judged handsome by conventional standards, yet his strength was what appealed to her. Strength coupled with a hint of vulnerability.

He caught her hand and pressed a kiss into her palm. At the unexpectedly tender act, sensation shivered through her anew.

"How thoughtless of me," he said, misinterpreting her reaction. He climbed to his feet and extended his hand to assist her up. "It's late, and the floor is cold."

Was this how such things were supposed to end? she wondered dismally as he swung her to her feet. With awkwardness and haste? She had no clue what rules of etiquette applied after losing one's virginity. "Yes, it is quite late," she said, attempting to keep her tone neutral.

She clutched her shawl to her breast in a vain attempt to cover herself while her eyes frantically searched for her carelessly discarded nightdress. Cole, she couldn't help but notice, appeared entirely at ease with his state of undress.

"Is this by chance what you're looking for?" He retrieved the garment from where it lay half-hidden on the floor.

"Yes, thank you," she replied, her cheeks blazing. She tried to snatch it from him but he held it just beyond her grasp.

He grinned down at her, obviously enjoying the little game. "From the sound of it, the storm seems to be getting worse. My guess is, it'll probably last well into tomorrow." The teasing glint in his eyes turned serious. "What do you say, Claire? Shall we make the most of our time together?"

She stared at him in mute surprise. Joy swept over her with the realization he didn't want to end this interlude any more than she did. He hadn't tired of her, it seemed. He still wanted her.

He must have seen her answer reflected in her eyes because he swept her off her feet, into his arms, and headed for the stairs. Claire looped her arms around his neck, enjoying the crisp texture of his hair along the nape. Sighing with contentment, she nestled her head in the hollow of his shoulder.

They had reached the door of his bedroom when her bubble of optimism burst. "Cole . . . ?"

A slight frown drew his dark brows together. "What is it, sweetheart? Don't tell me you've changed your mind? You know I'd never force you to do anything you don't want to do."

"No, no. It's not that," she hastened to assure him. "It's just . . ."

He waited as she struggled to explain her sudden reluctance.

"For some reason, it seems wrong to make love in the same bed you shared with your wife." Her words tumbled over one another in their haste to be said.

His frown smoothed. "Priscilla and I occupied separate rooms. We never shared the same bed."

Before she could assimilate this startling bit of information, he nudged the door aside with his shoulder. Carrying her into the room, he deposited her on the bed, then lowered himself to the mattress and wrapped her in his arms. Doubts and questions scattered like the blowing snow that pelted the windowpanes.

FIFTEEN

Claire floated on a current of contentment. Suspended between sleep and wakefulness, her mind reenacted a scene played out in the hours between midnight and dawn.

Somewhere in the middle of the night, Cole's warm breath had fanned across her temple. "Awake?"

"Mmm," she murmured as her blood began to stir.

From the darkness, she heard nature's symphony: the soughing of the wind through bare branches, the sting of sleet against the windowpane. But inside, she felt the incredible heat of Cole's strong body curled around her, spoon-fashion.

He had nuzzled the nape of her neck, discovered the wildly beating pulse at the base of her throat, fondled, teased, tormented until passion rekindled, then blazed anew. Soft sighs and whispered endearments sang counterpoint to the blizzard's fury. This time when he had entered her, there had been no pain, no discomfort, only an explosion of intense pleasure.

Even now, hours later, her body tingled from the memory of his possession.

Rolling onto her back, Claire stretched lazily. Opening her eyes, she glanced around the room with a vague sense of disorientation. The bed's towering headboard was elaborately carved. In addition to the huge bed, the room contained a bureau, wardrobe, and washstand, all fashioned from glossy black walnut. A marble-topped nightstand stood next to the bed. The furnishings were dark, massive, solid. Much like the room's occupant, she mused.

Knowledge she had been the only woman to share this bed brought with it a primal surge of satisfaction. She frowned slightly, trying to recall Cole's words from the previous night. *Priscilla and I never shared the same bed.* The notion delighted her—then she sobered. Not sharing the same bed didn't meant they hadn't slept together. After all, their union had produced a child. She had worked in enough upper-class homes to know it was common for married couples to occupy separate bedrooms. She was no longer naïve enough to think children were necessarily conceived in a bed.

Or within the bounds of matrimony.

Claire's eyes rested on an enameled clock on the nightstand. Eight-thirty! She came fully alert. She should have been up hours ago. Daisy rarely slept past seven. Springing out of bed, she searched frantically for something to put on. Her nightgown was nowhere to be found. Desperation prompted her to snatch one of Cole's shirts from a bureau drawer. The sleeves came well past her fingertips, the hem to her knees, but concern for the baby outweighed modesty.

Barefoot, she raced down the hall toward the nursery. The crib was empty. Worry spiked into panic. Her heart hammered against her ribcage. She whirled around and flew down the stairs, all the while berating herself. Once again she had neglected Daisy. She didn't deserve the title of nursemaid.

She stumbled to a halt when she reached the kitchen. Cole stood at the cast-iron cookstove frying bacon, a long fork in one hand, a coffee cup in the other. Daisy sat in her highchair, smiling and content.

Cole turned with a smile. "Good morning."

Her stomach did an odd little flip at the sight of him. Freshly shaven, he wore a starched white shirt, the sleeves rolled to the elbows, the neck unbuttoned to reveal a vee of dark curls. In spite of his lack of sleep, he looked remarkably well rested. And strikingly handsome.

"I—ah . . ." She made a futile attempt to tame the unruly tangle of tawny hair that streamed around her shoulders

Cole's smile faded as he studied her dishabille. He let out a low whistle of appreciation while his gaze raked over her flushed cheeks, disheveled hair, and lingered on the exposed expanse of bare leg. "You look good enough to eat."

"Sorry. I couldn't find my nightgown, so I borrowed this." She nervously tugged at the hem of his shirt. She tried to convince herself the breathlessness in her voice was due to her breakneck race through the house and not the hungry way he stared at her. "It's rare that I oversleep. I'm usually an early riser." She was babbling, but couldn't seem to stop herself. "I can't imagine what you must think."

A small smile played around his mouth. "Sweetheart," he drawled, "I could probably be arrested for what I'm thinking right now."

Her flush deepened from both embarrassment and pleasure—mostly the latter. "I—I'll go get dressed."

"Don't hurry away. I like the way you look in my shirt."

Daisy, tired of being ignored, pounded on the tray of her highchair.

"See?" he said with a grin. "Even Daisy approves of your attire." He jerked his head toward the back door, his tone wheedling. "It's just the three of us today, Claire. No one else. We have the world to ourselves."

Her gaze shifted toward the window. Not even the coach house across the yard was visible through the heavy curtain of snow that fell fast and furious. They were swathed in a thick cocoon of white; everything was leached of color. Cole was right. No one was going to be out on such a day. They had the world to themselves. The idea held enormous appeal. "We must have gotten at least a foot of snow already," she marveled.

"And it shows no signs of letting up." Cole sounded inordinately pleased at the prospect.

Daisy smiled happily, displaying her single tooth.

"Sit down," he said, turning back to the stove. "Breakfast will be ready in just a few minutes. I assume you like bacon and eggs."

She sank into the nearest chair. "You actually fixed breakfast?"

"And made coffee." He plunked a steaming mug on the table in front of her. "Here, have a cup. By the way, how do your feet feel this morning?"

"They barely hurt at all, thanks to you." She took a small sip, discovered it strong but not overly so, then took another. "I must admit this is a novelty. You're a man of many talents, Mr. Garrett."

"Didn't believe me, did you, when I told you I apprenticed as a cookee at a lumber camp?" He poked at the bacon sizzling in the skillet.

"Seeing a demonstration has banished the last of my doubts." Reaching up, Claire stroked Daisy's halo of golden curls. The infant seemed content and free from any disagreeable odors. Still, duty tugged at her conscience. "I should tend to Daisy. She usually likes her breakfast early."

"At the risk of bragging, she's already been fed and her diaper changed." Cole gave Claire a smug look from over his shoulder. "I admit I'm rather proud of my accomplishments, though I confess I've learned a trick or two from watching you. Daisy's mealtimes still tend to be a great deal messier when I'm the one feeding her."

"Yes, I've noticed." Claire laughed, remembering his multicolored, vegetable-stained shirt.

He studied her from over his shoulder, his expression arrested. "You ought to do that more often."

"Do what?" She smiled over the rim of her cup.

"It just occurred to me how seldom I've heard you laugh."

She glanced away. Lately, she reflected, with life fraught with more problems than solutions, humor seemed difficult to find. Purposely, she shoved disturbing thoughts aside. The day held too much promise to let anything spoil it. She smiled instead and changed the subject. "What can I do to help with breakfast?"

"Just keep Daisy amused while I cook the eggs."

Conversation flowed freely between them while they shared the simple meal. Once he was convinced her interest was genuine, Cole expounded on Claire's questions regarding the lumber industry. Although she had grown up hearing her father and brother talk about life in the lumber camps, listening to Cole gained her a whole new perspective.

"I've taken your advice," he said casually as he helped himself to the last slice of bacon.

"*My* advice?" The notion pleased her.

"I advertised as far away as Bay City and Saginaw for river drivers. I'm willing to pay twenty-five cents an hour above the current rate."

"I would think you'd be flooded with offers."

Breaking off bits of toast, Claire rolled them into tiny balls and put them on the tray of Daisy's high chair. Daisy, her lower lip jutting out in concentration, diligently tried to pick them up between her thumb and forefinger. For the time being, the simple task kept her occupied.

"Never underestimate the power of Leonard Brock." Cole's mouth set in a grim line at the thought of his former father-in-law. "He has connections all over the state. Even Governor Croswell listens when he has something to say."

"What happens if you can't find enough men?"

"It's been a productive winter. I've got lumber piled higher than you can see, all up and down the riverbank. But if I can't get it downriver to my sawmill in a timely fashion, I don't stand to make a profit—or repay loans from the bank. I could be forced to recruit a partner. And, if worse comes to worst, declare bankruptcy."

Claire nibbled a piece of toast. "How hard would it be to find a partner?"

"Like trying to pull a rabbit out of the hat." Cole refilled his coffee cup. "Finding a backer willing to pump unlimited funds into a failing venture is next to impossible.

There's no way, however, that I'm going to lose everything I've worked for without a fight. Even if it means becoming a damn good magician."

"You'll succeed. I know you will."

"Funny, I used to have all the confidence in the world. Never doubted that if I worked hard, kept my eye on the target, I'd succeed. For a while I actually believed I accomplished everything I set out to. From cook's helper to lumber baron. Now," he spread his hands, "I could lose everything. It's made me doubt myself. Made me look at things differently. Made things that were once important seem . . . inconsequential."

She leaned forward and placed her hand over his. "You'll come out of this a stronger person, Cole. I have faith in you."

Their eyes met and held. Cole opened his mouth to speak, but whatever he was about to say was cut off by Daisy's unhappy shriek. Tired of playing with bits of rolled bread, she knocked them off her high chair with a sweep of her tiny hand.

"What's the matter, Daisy?" Claire rose to her feet and lifted the baby out of the high chair. "Aren't you getting your share of attention?"

Daisy's bottom lip quivered, and tears pooled in her big, blue eyes. The baby managed to look reproachful, yet adorable at the same time.

Hugging her close, Claire pressed a kiss to the top of her head. "Didn't you have your bottle this morning?"

"Bottle?" Cole smacked his forehead with the heel of his hand. "I had a feeling I missed something. I managed the diaper and a small dish of pabulum, but forgot the bottle."

"Well, that's easy to remedy." The baby riding on one hip, Claire removed a bottle she had prepared the evening before from the squat oak icebox. "Fortunately, Alma was planning to make pudding yesterday and asked Karl Detmeijer to leave extra milk."

Cole got up from the table and took the baby from her. "Here, I'll hold Daisy while you heat her bottle."

Claire watched Cole surreptitiously while she went about warming the bottle. He seemed perfectly at ease carrying Daisy and patting her back as he strolled around the kitchen. The pair formed such a contrast: Cole, a big, powerful man who exuded masculinity with every breath, and, Daisy, his tiny, fair-haired daughter. He was a good man, a good father. Tender and caring. A fierce champion who would rise to battle if need be. Qualities Claire found enormously endearing.

A band tightened around her heart. She sucked in a breath as a realization staggered her. With blinding clarity, she knew what she had only suspected before. She loved Cole Garrett. The truth was as pristine as the snow blanketing the ground, as bright as tomorrow's sunshine.

She loved him.

"Claire . . . ?"

Aware that Cole was looking at her strangely, she shook her head to bring herself back to the present. "I—I'm fine," she stammered. But she wasn't fine at all. Acknowledging the depth of her feelings had left her curiously off balance. Her head spun. Her heart reeled. Dazed by the discovery, she automatically removed the baby's bottle from the pan on the stove and tested the temperature of the milk on the inner aspect of her wrist.

Yawning widely, Daisy rubbed her eyes.

"Looks like the little princess might be ready for a nap." Cole relinquished the baby into Claire's arms.

Daisy promptly nuzzled her head against Claire's shoulder and sucked her fist. Above the baby's head, Cole's eyes met hers and held them captive.

Claire felt a fluttery sensation in the pit of her stomach. "Is anything wrong?"

"No," he said in a low voice. Reaching out, he tucked a long strand of her hair behind one ear, the action familiar, casual. "For the first time in a long while, everything seems right."

Claire swallowed, afraid to move, reluctant to blink, for fear of snapping the fragile thread of intimacy that bound them together.

"This storm is a blessing in disguise," he continued in that same low, compelling tone. "What I'm asking for, Claire, is one more day, another night, before the world intrudes on us."

She tried to marshal a defense against his request. Attempted to summon an argument against its appeal. But her heart overruled logic. Why deny what she, too, wanted most?

"Well, Claire, what do you say?" Cole's gray eyes shimmered like liquid mercury. Full of questions, uncertainty. Hope.

"Yes," she whispered, her voice barely audible. She cleared her throat. "Yes," she repeated with growing confidence. "One more day. Another night."

Bending his head, he kissed her. His lips brushed hers lightly, then returned to linger until Daisy, who was trapped between them, squirmed and let out a howl of indignation.

Cole drew back, smiling. "Let's hope Daisy settles down for a long nap after her bottle."

If she lived to be a hundred, Claire knew she would always look back with fondness on this snowy April day. A day whiled away talking, getting to know one another—and making love.

While Cole answered correspondence and jotted notes in a ledger, Claire played with Daisy on a blanket spread on the library floor. His work finished, he, too, got down on the blanket. He tickled Daisy until she gurgled with glee, her arms and legs miniature windmills flailing the air. By unspoken agreement, neither of them mentioned problems lurking outside the frosty windows.

After Daisy was bathed and asleep for the night, they shared a late supper. Claire lingered over her dessert, reluctant for the perfect day to end. When Cole went to fetch more firewood, she wandered to the dining room window and pulled back the heavy drapery. She scraped away a patch of frost and pressed her nose against the glass. It was impossible to tell whether or not the snow had stopped. Letting the drape fall back into place, she closed her eyes and wished it would snow until next Christmas.

Absorbed in her fantasy, she failed to hear Cole sneak up behind her and slide his arms around her waist. Sighing, she leaned back against him. *I don't want this ever to end.*

"I wish things could stay like this," Cole murmured, his thoughts unconsciously mirroring hers. His lips grazed her temple. "No worrying about Brock's vendetta. Or Tanner's determination to arrest me, guilty or not, for Priscilla's murder."

She turned in the haven of his embrace, and placed her fingertips against his mouth. "Shh," she said. "Let's not spoil our last night together worrying about tomorrow."

He teasingly bit the pad of her finger with his teeth. Shocked, she drew in a sharp breath. Amused by her reaction, he smiled, his good humor restored. "The lady, it seems, is wise as well as beautiful."

Claire tilted her head to one side and studied him. "Such pretty words will make the lady's head swell." Catching his hand in hers, she drew him away from the window. "It's late. Don't you think it's time to retire for the evening?"

"Excellent idea, sweetheart. The lady is indeed wise, beautiful—and brilliant," he amended, his eyes alight with anticipation.

Slowly they made their way up the stairs, pausing every two or three steps to kiss each other breathless. Midway to the top, Cole succeeded in pulling the ribbon from her hair and tunneling his fingers into the heavy mass. "Your hair is like silk, thick and shiny."

By the time they reached the upper landing, he had the

buttons of her blouse unfastened. He eased it from her shoulders to reveal a chemise worn soft and paper-thin from repeated laundering. His hand closed over her breast, and instantly she felt its nipple harden.

"Lace," he said, his voice thick. "You should have only the finest lace against your skin. Or, perhaps, pearls. Pearls and nothing else."

Laughingly, she knocked his hands aside and, tugging his shirt from the waistband of his pants, pulled it over his tautly muscled abdomen and up over his ribcage.

He assisted her efforts by drawing the shirt over his head and flinging it aside. "Like what you see?"

"Oh, yes," she whispered. His chest was an ocean of bronzed skin and hard muscle covered by a springy mat of dark curls. Just looking at him made her mouth water. Unable to resist, she ran the palms of her hands over his chest. Her inquisitive fingers encountered flat, brown nipples nearly hidden in the dark nest.

His lids lowered over eyes gone smoky. He ran his hands up and down her arms. "Ah, sweetheart, see the effect you have on me?"

She angled forward, forcing him to take a half-step backward so that his body was pressed against the wall of the upstairs hallway. "What have we here?" she murmured playfully. Not hesitating to consider her actions, she flicked her tongue across his nipple.

His entire body went rigid as he sucked in a breath.. "God, Claire, do you have any idea what you're doing to me?"

"Show me." *One more night,* an inner voice whispered. *Be bold. Make it memorable.* She burned with a desire fueled by desperation.

Discarded articles of clothing formed a path to his bedroom. Naked, they fell backward onto the bed in a tangle of arms and legs.

Cole trailed kisses down her throat. "I can't seem to get my fill of you."

Claire arched her neck, welcoming, inviting. Her hands

roamed up and down his back, reveling in the sleek, smooth warmth of his skin. "Your body is beautiful. I love touching you, looking at you."

"Beautiful?" He nipped the wildly beating pulse at the juncture of her neck and shoulder, then soothed it with his tongue. "Surely you must have me confused with someone else."

A delicate shiver rippled through her. "I could never confuse you with anyone else."

Further conversation ceased as Cole's hands and mouth took possession of her senses. Claire was caught up in a maelstrom of delight. Hard, callused fingers lightly danced across the smooth skin of her stomach until the nerve endings quivered. The faint rasp of whiskers along the highly sensitized underside of her breast was exquisite torture.

His mouth claimed hers. His clever tongue teasing, stroking, driving her mad with longing. While his kiss stole the breath from her body, his need captured her heart.

A soft moan escaped as she surrendered to the intoxicating onslaught of pleasure. Her breasts felt heavy and turgid, awaiting his caress. Desire twisted into a hot coil at the apex of her thighs. Slick, hot, throbbing. Her entire being felt gloriously alive. Reality dropped away. She moved, restless and craving more.

"Let me touch you, sweetheart," Cole whispered. "Touch you the way your body begs to be touched."

"Please, Cole, I . . ." Her voice broke when his mouth closed over her nipple. Plunging her fingers into his thick, mahogany locks, she clasped him closer, wordlessly communicating her need.

Raising his head, he feathered kisses from the valley between her breasts and down across her abdomen. He played her body as though it were a rare violin, drawing out chords, eliciting notes, until she resonated. She began to writhe in helpless abandon, her senses ravaged from this assault.

Suddenly she wanted to touch, to explore, wanted to

know his body as intimately as he knew hers. "May I?" she asked. She scarcely recognized the throaty sound of her own voice.

"Anything," he murmured. "Everything."

She shyly took his manhood in her hand. Instantly, his body turned rigid as stone. "Oh, my God, Claire . . ."

She released him at once, alarm piercing the sensual fog that surrounded her. "Am I hurting you?"

"Touch me again, please. No pain has ever been this sweet."

At his whispered encouragement, her fingers curled around his shaft. Hard as steel. Soft as velvet. The contrast fascinated her. Knowing the physical effect she had on him amazed her even more.

"Much more of this, and my control will snap." Shifting, he rolled so that she lay flat on her back with his body sprawled across her, his knee wedged between hers. "Now, it's my turn."

With devilish glee, Cole let his fingers delicately skate across her stomach and lower abdomen in an unerring path to a nest of dark gold and the treasure buried within. A wicked smile curved his mouth as she bit her lower lip to stifle a groan. Her mind emptied. He teased the small nub of passion, circling, circling, until whimpering, she tilted her hips in unconscious entreaty.

She practically sobbed with need, yet he continued to tease and torment, driving her higher and higher, until she teetered at the ultimate summit. Then, he plunged into her. Wrapping her legs around him, she held him fast as their cries of release intermingled.

Afterwards, they held each other for a long time as shadows frolicked across the ceiling above the bed. Neither spoke. Both knew their time together was near an end.

SIXTEEN

Claire woke to the sound of snow shovels scraping. Without opening her eyes, without turning her head, she knew she was alone. The idyllic time with Cole had come to an end. Just as she had always known it would.

No promises. No regrets.

Resolutely, she opened her eyes and swung her legs over the edge of the bed. Buttery yellow sunlight speared through a crack in the curtains. Its brightness mocked her gloomy mood. Padding across the room, she eased the curtains farther apart and peeked out. In the yard below, Cole, assisted by Tim, lifted heavy shovels of snow from the drive and walkway. The town was starting to dig its way out from beneath a mountain of snow. Soon roadways would be cleared, and citizens would resume their normal lives.

Her gaze lingered on Cole. Hatless as usual, he wore a red plaid mackinaw, undoubtedly a remnant from his days in the lumber camps. Pale April sunlight glinted off his windblown hair. She watched the flex and release of muscle as he bent, then straightened, visible even with his jacket on. His movements were smooth, economical, effortless. Graceful.

Sighing, she dropped the curtain back in place. Daisy would soon be wide awake and demanding to be fed and changed. If she hurried, she still had time to return to her attic room, wash, and dress before the baby woke. She stumbled to a halt just outside the bedroom door when something caught her eye. Stooping down, she retrieved the small object from the edge of the runner. She recognized it immediately as a button from the blouse she had been wearing last night. A button that had gone flying in their haste to undress, to touch. A lump wedged in her throat. Swallowing it back, she curled her fingers around the button and fled upstairs to her attic quarters.

A short time later, Claire was down in the kitchen. Daisy, fed and diapered, banged against the tray of her high chair with a wooden spoon. Claire had a pot of coffee brewing on the stove. The best way to avoid dwelling on what could never be, she decided, was to keep busy. Too busy to think, too busy to feel. Now that Alma Dobbs no longer worked there, she would also have housekeeping chores to tend to. After Daisy was asleep each night, she planned to work until she was ready to drop with fatigue. It was best that way.

The sound of the snow shovel seemed to slow. A quick glance out the window told her the men were nearly finished with the task. The drive had been cleared to the street; a path led to the coach house. The men now attacked the snow remaining on the porch and steps.

"Time for some fresh air, Daisy girl." The baby welcomed the idea with a drooly smile.

Claire wrapped Daisy snug in a warm blanket, then pulled a cap of pink angora wool over her feathery blond curls. After shrugging into Nils's old jacket, she hefted Daisy up in the crook of one arm, snagged two enameled mugs, and picked up the coffeepot with the other. Thus armed, she stepped outside onto the porch and into the blinding glare of the sun.

"I thought you gentlemen deserved a reward for your hard work."

"If that's coffee, I sure could use a cup." Tim drove his shovel into a snowbank at the foot of the steps and approached the porch with an eager tread. "This is mighty thoughtful of you."

Cole ignored her offer. Instead, he rapped the shovel against the ground to knock off the snow and ice particles clinging to it.

Tim blew on his coffee, took an experimental sip. "Tastes almost as good as your cookies."

The bright sunlight revealed a network of fine lines and wrinkles that fanned out from the corners of his eyes when he grinned. Claire wondered about Tim's age. In spite of the threads of silver in his hair and the wrinkles around his eyes, she suspected he was younger than he appeared. Suspected life hadn't always treated him kindly.

Tim rested one booted foot on the lower step. "By any chance, have you mentioned anything to Mr. Garrett about taking one of the kittens?"

"Not yet." Claire darted a glance at Cole, but he didn't look her way.

Tim's large, work-worn hands cradled the coffee mug. "Won't be long those little critters'll be ready for good homes."

"I'd like to bring Daisy out to see them one day soon."

"Fine by me. Come by anytime."

Claire noticed his cup was nearly empty. "Care for more?"

"Don't mind if I do." He held out his cup for a refill. "You'll make some lucky man a good wife."

The last comment was said just as Cole finished shoveling and started toward the steps. Claire felt herself blush, then was annoyed for allowing him to have this effect on her.

He stomped the snow from his feet, the clatter causing Daisy to babble with glee. But not even Daisy could erase the frown he wore.

"Isn't it too cold out here for a baby?"

The undertone of criticism cut her to the quick. Instinctively, she tried to hide her hurt behind a smile. "As you can see, she's all bundled up. A little fresh air will be good for her."

He looked as though he might argue the point, but grunted instead.

The sun had already begun to melt the icicles that hung from the porch roof like Monday's laundry. Water dripped from their tips and landed on the snow below. Each gentle *plop* seemed overly loud in the tense silence.

Claire shifted Daisy's weight to her other arm. "I thought you and Tim might enjoy a hot cup of coffee after you finished."

"Thanks, but I'll have mine when I get to the office. I've got a lot of work to catch up on."

His brusque tone was as effective as a slap. Color surged to her face anew. Knowing Tim eavesdropped shamelessly only added to her embarrassment. "All right," she said, proud her voice sounded calm in spite of her inner turmoil. "Since Alma won't be coming, I'll have your dinner waiting tonight."

"Don't bother." He tugged off his work gloves.

"It's no bother. I'm used to cooking for Pa and Nils."

Cole let out an impatient breath. "I plan to work late. If I'm hungry, I'll have my secretary bring me something from town."

Claire kept her expression carefully schooled. Tim scuffed the toe of his boot against the step. "Well, in that case," Claire said, "I think I'll take Daisy inside."

"Bring the little one out to see me anytime." As Tim handed her his empty mug, Claire glimpsed what might have been sympathy in his dark eyes before he turned toward the coach house.

Cole grabbed the coffeepot from the porch rail where she had set it. He jerked open the kitchen door, then stood aside for her to enter. He waited until they were inside, the door closed, before speaking. "I realize how I must have sounded just now, maybe even rude, but I didn't know how else to act considering the circumstances."

Tired of being swaddled in a blanket, Daisy began to fuss. Claire was only too happy to have an excuse to avoid looking at Cole directly. Sitting the baby on the edge of the table, she removed the cumbersome wrapping. "You don't owe me an explanation."

"The last thing either of us needs is any suspicion concerning the two of us."

"I agree with you completely." She derived a perverse sense of satisfaction from the surprised look on his face.

"Good, good." He nodded absently. "I trust Tim explicitly, but one word to the wrong person could lead to trouble."

She pulled off Daisy's pink wooly cap and fluffed her curls. "It isn't necessary to make excuses, Cole. I understand." Unfortunately, she understood only too well. He had his reputation to protect. The last thing he needed was additional scandal to tarnish it even more than it already was.

"Good," he repeated. Keeping his back turned to her, he tugged off his muffler, shrugged out of his mackinaw, and hung it from a peg near the door. "Then you do understand, too, that what happened between us can't continue?"

"One more day, another night. I believe that's how you phrased it. And no regrets, remember? Regardless of what you might think, I'm not so naïve as to expect more. Now, if you'll excuse me . . ." She picked Daisy up and left before he could see how much the effort cost her.

No regrets? That was a blatant lie. Claire bitterly regretted that he didn't love her in return. She longed for more than one more day, another night. Selfishly, she wanted all the tomorrows. But, she reminded herself as she rushed up the stairs, life wasn't a fairy tale with a happily-ever-after ending.

And Cole Garrett wasn't a handsome prince ready to pledge his undying devotion.

The coffee tasted bitter. Cole set the cup down with disgust. It was probably the dregs from the bottom of a pot made hours ago. Dinner was no better. The meal his secretary, Arthur Bowman, had brought him before leaving for the day consisted of a blanket of congealed gravy spread over stringy roast beef and day-old bread. But he had no one to blame but himself for the poor fare.

He tossed his pen down in disgust. He'd give his right arm about now for a cup of Claire's delicious brew. She had even offered to have a hot meal waiting, and he had refused that as well. Stupid on his part. She was a fine cook. She also had a way with babies, and was damn good company besides. Tim's remark that morning about her making some man a good wife had struck a chord. He didn't like the idea of Claire with another man. Guess that made him a selfish bastard as well as a stupid one.

Picking up his pen again, he dipped it into the inkwell. He hadn't accomplished half the work he had set out to. All day long, his thoughts kept circling back to Claire. Guilt gave him a swift kick in the backside when he remembered the stricken look he had glimpsed on her face before she tried to hide it. He had handled the situation poorly. He had been blunt almost to the point of cruelty. Under similar circumstances, many women would have created a scene, resorted to hysterics, but not Claire. She had handled an awkward situation with aplomb.

Startled by a knock on his office door, he cursed when a large blob of ink fell on his neat column of figures.

"Come in," he snarled.

Cole's mood turned even more sour when Edward Tanner strolled into his office.

"Working kind of late, aren't you?" Tanner took a seat without waiting to be asked.

"What do you want, Tanner? As you can see, I'm busy."

Tanner crossed one leg over the other. "Stopped by your house. Miss Sorenson told me I might find you here."

"Well, now that you've found me, say what you came to say."

Tanner ignored the rudeness. "After our last conversation, I got the impression you preferred to work at home."

Cole leaned back in his chair and studied the man seated across from him. Tanner's deep-set eyes were dark and shrewd. And suspicious. "I'm sure you're not here to discuss my work habits. Get to the point."

"Does my being here make you nervous? An innocent man has nothing to hide."

"I'm not nervous." Cole bit out each word. "I'm irritated. There's a vast difference."

"I wondered if you might have remembered something, some small detail perhaps, that might shed light on your wife's murder."

"We've covered this ground before. I've already told you everything I know."

"In my line of work, it's not unheard-of for people to recall a pertinent fact or two at a later date."

"If I should remember something of value, I know how to find City Hall," Cole told him. Edward Tanner's condescending manner never failed to put him on the defensive. Deciding to give his temper time to cool, he picked up his coffee and took a swig. He spit it back into his cup, grimacing.

Tanner's luxurious mustache twitched to hide a smile. "Coffee that bad can rot the gut."

"Yeah, well, I'll keep that in mind."

"By the way, Garrett, with Alma Dobbs out of the picture, I gather you and Miss Sorenson have that great big house all to yourselves."

Cole's instinct for danger flared. "I fail to see where that's any of your business."

"Started me wondering, is all. She's an attractive young woman. Any man worth his salt could see that."

"I resent your implication, Tanner." Cole sprang to his feet. "You've got a filthy mind."

"In case you've forgotten, I've got a murder to solve—your wife's. It's my job to look at it from every possible angle. Could be the Sorenson woman's sweet on you, maybe fancies herself the next Mrs. Cole Garrett. It would be quite a coup, considering her background." Squinting into the near distance, he made a sweeping motion with his hand. "I can picture the headlines now, DAUGHTER OF TOWN DRUNK WEDS LUMBER BARON."

"That's preposterous!" Cole clasped his hands behind his back to keep from hauling Tanner up by the scruff of his neck.

"Is it?" The police chief's thin face remained impassive. "That would explain why she's willing to do, or say, anything to save your hide."

"You're grasping at straws, and you damn well know it." Anger simmered, seasoned with a pinch of fear. The bastard was trying to discredit Claire's ability to provide an alibi. Questioning her motives. What next? he wondered. Would he hint they had conspired to kill Priscilla? The thought made his blood run cold. "When—and if—I decide to remarry, it won't be to Claire Sorenson."

"What's wrong with her? She's pretty, in a quiet sort of way. Seems polite, speaks well. You could do worse."

True, he agreed silently, Claire was all that and more. But damned if he was going to openly admit that Edward Tanner was right. "Nothing against her personally, of course," he said, attempting to deflect the man's thoughts away from Claire. "She's just not the sort I envision as a wife. A man in my position looks for certain qualifications in a woman, things such as culture, education, and family background."

"In other words, another such as your late, unlamented wife?"

"Exactly," Cole concurred. *And as it had been with Priscilla, any such marriage would undoubtedly be another colossal blunder.*

"The Sorenson woman is good enough to bed, but not good enough to wed?" Tanner got to his feet. "Guess I had you pegged from the start, Garrett. You're a user, that's what you are."

Tanner's accusation brought a dull flush to Cole's

cheeks. He felt his shoulders tense. But angry as he was, it was far better that Tanner believe the worst of him than for Claire's motives to become suspect. "Don't get me wrong, Chief. Claire's a fine young woman. All I meant was that we're from different worlds."

"Yeah," Tanner grunted. "You're rich, she's poor."

"I've had enough insults for one evening." Cole came out from behind his desk. "Either arrest me, Tanner, or get the hell out of my office."

Tanner stopped at the door, his hand on the knob, and turned. "By the way, how did you manage to get rid of Alma Dobbs?"

"If you're so interested, you'll have to ask Alma."

"Maybe I will."

A sly smile on his face, Tanner disappeared. Needing to vent his frustration, Cole kicked the door shut after him. The man was like a bird dog on a scent. He'd sniff around until he found a way to pin Priscilla's death on him. Then, like a well-trained bird dog, he'd go straight to his master, in this case Leonard Brock, wagging his tail for a pat on the head.

Cole slumped down at his desk, his head in his hands. With a concerted effort, he willed his knotted muscles to relax. It was then that he realized his mistake. Tanner, clever bastard that he was, had led him into a neatly baited trap. Thinking back to their conversation, Cole had failed to dispute the police chief's assumption that he had slept with Claire. He groaned aloud at his own stupidity. In his zeal to protect her, he had only succeeded in placing her in greater jeopardy.

"I could smell something baking from outside."

"I'm nearly finished." Claire forced a smile and tried to hide her dismay. She had hoped to have the last of the pans and dishes washed and put away before he returned.

It was difficult to act as though nothing had happened when the day before he had stolen her heart.

He spotted loaves cooling on a rack. "Banana bread?"

She turned back to the sink. "It was either use the bananas or throw them out. I hate to see things wasted."

Cole tugged off his gloves, unwrapped the woolen muffler from around his neck, then slipped off his overcoat and draped it over a chair. "It smells delicious. Mind if I have a piece?"

"Of course not. It's hardly as if you need my permission."

If he had detected the edge in her voice, he gave no indication as he removed a plate from the cupboard and cut himself a generous slice. Steam rose from the still warm bread, and the air was fragrant with fruit and walnuts. "I found my secretary's version of dinner less than satisfactory."

"Would you like me to fix you coffee, or perhaps tea?"

"Thanks for offering, but don't bother." He sat down at the table, but instead of eating, pushed the plate aside. "Quit scrubbing that bowl for a minute. We need to talk."

"I can talk as well as scrub."

"Sit down, Claire."

Claire couldn't mistake his tone. It wasn't a request, but an order. Perched on the edge of a chair, she twisted the striped dishcloth in her hands. "We've already discussed our . . . situation. If you're worried . . ."

"Don't!" He softened his next words after seeing her recoil at his sharp tone. "I don't doubt for a minute that you'll honor the terms our . . . agreement. That isn't what I wanted to talk about."

She smoothed a strand of hair behind her ear with an unsteady hand. Embarrassment stained her cheeks fiery pink. "I'm sorry if I jumped to conclusions. What is it you wish to discuss?"

"There are several matters, actually." He ran his hand through his wind-tousled hair, an action that had become familiar to her whenever he felt uneasy. "First of all, I leave for the lumber camps day after tomorrow. How well my visit goes determines whether I participate in the river drive. Chances are, however, that I won't return until it's over."

"But the river drive—"

"Don't worry, I can handle myself," he said, cutting off her objections. "I've been a river pig before, even worked a couple years as head push."

Claire caught her lower lip between her teeth. She had no right to object, yet she couldn't help but worry. Everyone knew a river drive was the most treacherous part of the lumbering business. Many things could go wrong.

And often did.

Some men lost limbs. Others wound up in shallow graves along the riverbank, their only monument caulked boots nailed to a nearby tree. The drive was best left to veterans, not men grown soft sipping expensive brandy while debating the cost of board feet.

Setting her fears aside, at least temporarily, she said, "You mentioned there were several matters you wanted to discuss."

He drummed his fingertips on the table, cleared his throat, and avoided meeting her eyes. "I paid Alma Dobbs a visit on my way home."

"I see," she murmured, though she didn't see at all. She had thought he wanted nothing more to do with the woman.

"She's returning tomorrow to resume her duties as housekeeper."

"What?" she gasped.

Cole held up a hand to forestall her protest. "Alma's sole function will be to attend to housekeeping duties. Under no circumstances is she to have anything to do with Daisy's care. That will be entirely in your hands. If you must go somewhere, you'll have to either take the baby with you, or make arrangements with someone other than Alma. Understood?"

"No! I don't understand." She stopped twisting the striped towel and flung it aside. "Why would you ask her back after she woefully neglected Daisy?"

His jaw set in an obstinate line. "Because . . ."

"Because?" she snapped. "That's no answer. Granted Daisy's your child, and you don't owe me an explanation, but I can't help but wonder why you changed you mind."

He came to his feet and paced the length of the kitchen. "I have none other than Brockton's chief of police, Edward Tanner, to thank for my change of heart."

"Tanner . . ." she whispered. A sharp dart of anxiety struck a nerve, making it quiver with dread. "What does he have to do with any of this?"

"Dammit, Claire!" Cole pivoted and changed direction. "Can't you see, this is the only sensible thing to do. People are starting to gossip about the two of us living here alone. I don't want them to get the wrong idea. Alma will provide a buffer, a semblance of respectability. A chaperone of sorts."

She sat up straighter, watched him pace. "We're both adults. Certainly we can weather a little gossip."

"Let it go, Claire. I don't want to discuss this anymore."

"Very well." It was clear to her that his mind was made up and nothing she could say would change it. Getting to her feet, she placed the loaves of bread into gaily painted tins.

Cole watched from across the room. "There's one more thing you should know. After I left Alma, I stopped at the Lamonts'."

Claire waited while her future hung in the balance.

"I instructed Sophie to wait until after the river drive before interviewing the applicant for nursemaid. I also told her that I want the opportunity to talk with the woman personally."

Cole left the kitchen, muttering under his breath. Claire couldn't be certain, but she thought she heard him mumble something about gray hair and fallen arches.

Long after the baking dishes had been washed and

stored away, Claire sat in the darkened kitchen. She couldn't rid herself of the nagging suspicion that Cole hadn't been entirely forthcoming about his reasons for rehiring Alma Dobbs. He didn't seem the sort to worry over idle gossip. Hard as she tried, she couldn't dispel the notion that he was keeping something from her. And that something had to do with Edward Tanner's visit.

SEVENTEEN

Aimlessly, Claire crossed the nursery, pulled aside the lacy curtain, and stared out the window. Spring had made a tardy appearance. Days bright with golden yellow sunlight alternated with dull, rainy ones. Spears of green poked through a bristly brown carpet of dried grass. Jonquils, daffodils, and tulips bravely defied the uncertain elements and began appearing in flowerbeds and along garden paths.

The house, which she once thought so spacious, seemed to shrink around her. She felt restless, on edge. Bored. Lonely. She missed Cole's company. Though she tried to fill her days with activity, at night her thoughts circled back to him. One week had stretched into two, two had turned into three. She suspected his prolonged absence was his way of avoiding her. She wished she could forget him as easily.

Just as she was about to drop the curtain into place, she spied Gertie, Tim's prize mouser. The feline leisurely groomed herself in the doorway of the carriage house. Suddenly, Claire remembered her promise to Tim. Now would be the perfect time to take Daisy to view the kittens. She was surprised the idea hadn't occurred to her sooner.

She turned a smile on the baby sprawled on a quilt and contentedly gnawing the ear of a gingham rabbit. "Daisy girl, what do you say we pay a long-overdue visit to the carriage house?"

Daisy ceased assaulting the stuffed toy and blew a spit bubble.

Within minutes, Claire had the baby bundled in a warm woolen sweater the same shade as her eyes and pulled a matching cap over her wispy blond curls. She made a mental note to remind Cole that his daughter was rapidly outgrowing her wardrobe. Certain items needed to be replenished. Scooping Daisy up, she hurried downstairs. She found Alma in the dining room, polishing silver.

"I'm taking Daisy out to the carriage house to see the kittens."

The housekeeper didn't look up from her polishing. "No matter to me what you do."

"Would you like to come with us?"

"Horses, hay, and such make me sneeze."

"We won't be long."

"Suit yourself."

Claire sighed as she turned away. Alma had been surly ever since her return. She cleaned, prepared meals, but kept to herself. The woman was obviously nursing a grudge and blamed Claire for nearly costing her her job. On the way through the kitchen, Claire paused to cut a generous wedge of apple pie to take with her. After a moment's debate, she added a slice of cheese. She draped a shawl around her shoulders, then, with Daisy in one arm and holding the pie with the other, she slipped outdoors.

Buds swollen and ready to burst covered the branches of the maple tree in the backyard. A robin landed on the ground nearby and tugged on a fat worm. Dainty yellow blossoms sprouted from a forsythia bush next to the porch. Claire silently wondered who might have planted it. Priscilla Garrett had never struck her as a woman who soiled her hands gardening.

Gertie, the striped tabby, regarded their approach through slanted green eyes, then rose with feline dignity and ushered them inside. Tim came out of the tack room, a bridle in one hand. He grinned when he saw his visitors.

"I wondered when you'd bring the little one. Thought you might've forgot. Or changed your mind."

"I was giving the kittens a chance to grow a bit before introducing them to Daisy."

Tim's dark eyes gleamed with anticipation when they settled on the plate in her hand. "See you were in another of your baking moods, eh?"

"Apple pie," she said, handing him the plate. "I added a piece of cheddar cheese from Mr. Cavanaugh's market."

"Nothin' better. Used to dream of apple pie with a thick slice of cheddar. Not that your cookies aren't always a treat," he hastened to add.

He set the pie on a bench and led them past the stalls of two meticulously groomed horses to a far corner of the coach house. "It's nearly time to find good homes for Gertie's offspring. You mention anything yet to Mr. Garrett about having one up at the house?"

"No, not yet. But I will as soon as he gets back."

Gertie sat like a queen on a throne while the kittens cavorted around her. Claire knelt in the straw, the baby in her lap. Daisy's eyes rounded with wonder when she saw them.

Daisy grinned, waving her arms.

"Well, ain't that somethin'," Tim chuckled. "She's taken to 'em already."

Claire smiled, too. The kittens, though still tiny, had grown considerably since she had last seen them. The black kitten pranced closer, its white-tipped tail whipping back and forth. Unable to contain her excitement, Daisy bounced up and down in Claire's lap. Another kitten, this one a palette of black, white, and orange, daintily swiped its front paw with a raspberry pink tongue while maintaining a safe distance. Several others frolicked, batting pieces of straw.

"They're all adorable. The hardest part will be deciding which one to choose."

Tim tugged his earlobe. "Well, I'd be more'n happy to let you take the whole litter if I thought Mr. Garrett would agree. But even if he did, knowin' Alma, she'd have a thing or two to say."

Claire picked up a kitten the color of woodsmoke. She felt an unexpected pang when she realized the gray matched the shade of Cole's eyes. God, how she missed him. Struggling to control her wayward thoughts, she took Daisy's hand and guided it lightly over the kitten's back. "Gentle," she coached when the baby tried to grab a fistful of fur.

Tim beamed down at them.

"Just be sure to tell Mr. Garrett what you said before. That pets are good for kids, teaches 'em responsibility. Remind him pets make for good company. It's not likely this little tyke is going to have a flock of brothers and sisters to keep her company—at least for a while yet."

Claire cleared her throat, but didn't attempt an answer. The thought that Cole would someday remarry and have more children was one she didn't wish to dwell upon.

Tim squatted on his haunches and rubbed Gertie's ears. "Bothers me that Tanner and Brock are out to cause a good man trouble."

Claire raised her eyes to his seamed face. "It bothers me, too," she confessed, "but, short of finding the real killer, I don't know what to do."

"Blind as bats, both of 'em, if they can't see Garrett's a decent man. Couldn't find better anywhere."

"Have you known him long?"

"Not long. Just since . . ." He broke off abruptly.

"Since . . . ?"

Tim picked up a tabby identical to the mother cat in his large, work-worn hands. "If I was choosing one of these little fellas for a pet, I'd take either the black or the calico."

Claire noted the sudden change of subject. Absently, she showed Daisy how to pet the kitten without harming it. Content, Daisy patted the soft fur and blew drool bubbles.

"You've made no secret of how you feel about Mr. Garrett, Tim, but what about Mrs. Garrett? Did you hold her in high esteem as well?"

Claire watched in fascination as Tim's expression turned to stone and his mouth compressed into a mere slash. "Far as I'm concerned, Priscilla Garrett was a first-class bitch. I hated her guts."

Stunned by his vehemence, Claire sat straighter and regarded him as she might a stranger. Even Daisy's round baby face registered uncertainty and fright at his harsh tone. "Why?" Claire asked. The question seemed to burst out of its own volition.

"Priscilla Garrett treated me like dirt. Thought all she had to do was crook a finger, and I'd be at her beck and call. In spite of her fancy pedigree, all she brought was grief. Mr. Garrett could have done better."

In that instant, Claire realized how very little she knew about this man. She had just seen another aspect of Tim's character. This one intimidating—and just a little menacing. *You're being fanciful,* she scolded herself. Just because the man didn't particularly like the wife of his employer didn't mean he was dangerous. Careful to keep her voice casual and her gaze trained on the calico kitten, she asked, "Did you work in the lumber camps before being hired by Mr. Garrett?"

"Nope." Tim set the tabby on the floor. "Never worked in the camps."

"How did you happen to meet Mr. Garrett?"

"Was lookin' for a job. Woulda taken anything, but no one wanted to hire me." He climbed to his feet, a faraway look in his dark eyes. "When Garrett heard I was raised on a farm and knew livestock, he offered me work. I owe 'im. I'd do anything for 'im—anything at all."

Having said that, he turned and walked off, leaving Claire to puzzle over his words. *I'd do anything—anything at all.* Did that include lying to Tanner about seeing her leave the morning after Priscilla's murder? And if he had, how long before Tanner discovered the truth?

* * *

"River's at driving pitch."

It was a phrase Claire heard repeated over and over as she pushed the baby buggy up the incline. The last of the ice had melted; the rivers and streams were swollen. Their waters ran fast and high. The distinct grumble of waterborne logs heralded the approach of the river drive. At the sound, men, women, and children, young and old, rich and poor alike, dropped whatever they were doing and congregated along the banks of the Brockton River to view the entertainment. In logging communities such as Brockton, the annual drive was the equivalent of the circus come to town. Its audience would be treated to drama, adventure, death-defying feats of bravery—and occasionally death itself.

"Garrett's the head push," declared a bewhiskered man in a plaid shirt and overalls.

At the mention of Cole's name, Claire paused to eavesdrop shamelessly. Bending over the carriage, she fussed with the baby's blanket.

"Don't say." His companion aimed a stream of tobacco juice at an oak tree. "Garrett always was the best whitewater man I ever did see. He could ride logs through the rapids like nobody's business."

Rocking back on his heels, his grizzled companion wagged his head. "With all his sawbucks, you'd think he'd sit tight and let others risk their necks."

Claire moved away. Overhearing their conversation only added to her apprehension. What had possessed Cole to volunteer to be the foreman, or "head push" as people more commonly referred to the job?

A vanguard of pine floated past, carried along by the swift current. Soon an army of logs would follow, most sixteen feet in length, some four or five feet across. Shading her eyes, Claire noticed several members of the jam crew armed with peavey hooks, skillfully herding the logs through the waterway. She had hoped for a glimpse of Cole, but was disappointed.

As Claire maneuvered the wicker baby carriage over the

uneven ground, one of the front wheels became snagged on a protruding root. Padraig Mulligan, having observed her struggle, separated himself from a group of his cronies and came to her aid. Tipping his hat, he gave her a broad smile. "I must say you're looking fit, Miss Sorenson."

"Mr. Mulligan," she replied with a polite nod. Gripping the handle of the carriage more firmly, she tried to jockey it over the impeding root while being careful not to upset it.

"Call me Padraig. Here," he said, "let me help." Not waiting for her reply, he lifted the entire carriage and set it down on smoother terrain.

Gratitude warred with mild annoyance, but finally won. "Thank you."

He peeked into the carriage. "Cute kid."

She tried to continue on her way, but he blocked her path. Seeing him reminded her of the debt she owed him. Or rather, the debt Nils owed. The speculative gleam in Padraig Mulligan's bright blue eyes was making her uncomfortable. He was looking at her the way a man looks at a woman he finds attractive. Or, she wondered, had he guessed the nature of her relationship with Cole Garrett?

"Tim O'Brien, Garrett's man, came by my place and dropped off your first payment." He removed a thick cigar from the inner pocket of his jacket, struck a match with a thumbnail, and puffed it to life. "Your brother, on the other hand, has yet to pay me a dime."

Claire cringed inwardly at the thought of working off Nils's debt as a barmaid. "I'm sure Nils will find work soon and when he does . . ."

Padraig cut her off with a wave of his hand. "Personally, I hope he doesn't."

His words brought a frown to her face. "But why would you say that?"

"Simple, lass." He grinned at her through a pungent haze of cigar smoke. "I rather fancy the notion of you working in my saloon. You'll give the place a touch of class."

Giving her a broad wink, he sauntered off to join his

friends, leaving Claire staring after him in dismay. Not paying attention to where she was going, she narrowly avoided colliding with a pair of well-dressed matrons.

"Hilda, dear, look at the baby."

Claire recognized one of the women as Hilda Schmidt. On several occasions, she had been hired to help at the Schmidt residence while they entertained. The other woman, Martha Sims, was involved in various charitable events. The two women peered into the carriage. Daisy obliged them with one of her cherubic smiles.

"What an angel!" Hilda cooed.

"Isn't she just precious?" Martha reached into the carriage and pinched Daisy's cheek.

Neither of the women acknowledged Claire's presence.

"If I'm not mistaken, she is Priscilla Brock's daughter. I heard Priscilla named her . . . let me think . . ." She tapped her cheek with a gloved finger. "Yes, now I recall. Daisy, she named the baby Daisy."

"Tsk, tsk," Martha clucked her tongue. "Such a common name, don't you think, Martha? Daisies are hardly more than weeds along the roadside."

"How true." Hilda nodded emphatically. "I would have thought Priscilla would have chosen something more suitable for her daughter."

"Strange, isn't it? The child doesn't favor either of her parents."

Though Claire knew Daisy couldn't possibly comprehend what the women were saying, she wanted to get her away from their malicious comments. As she steered tight-lipped around them, she heard Hilda Schmidt remark, "If my arithmetic doesn't fail me, wasn't the child premature?"

Martha nodded sagely. "Only as far as the marriage was concerned."

"Well, dear, we both know babies take nine months. Except for the first," Hilda tittered.

Furious, Claire pushed the baby carriage along the path

toward the top of the dam. No one would have dared such insults in Cole's presence, or, for that matter, the child's grandfather's. She only hoped Daisy wouldn't be subjected to such cruel barbs as she grew older. But people could be insensitive. Small towns, she knew, tended to have long memories.

Upon reaching the crest of the hill, she searched for a vantage point from which to observe the proceedings. Logs filled the river in increasing numbers, twisting and jostling for space in the rushing water. To her surprise, she spied Nils nearby in the shade of a tall elm. He glanced up at the crunch of carriage wheels. Though he didn't smile when he saw her, neither did he retreat.

Another surprise followed quickly on the heels of the first when she realized he was sober. Her brother's eyes were clear, his clothes neat, and his fair hair, if too long, at least was clean and combed. "You're looking well, Nils."

"Can't complain." He shrugged his narrow shoulders. "Garrett treating you all right?"

She imitated his shrug. "Like you, I have no complaints."

Claire took advantage of the uneasy truce to check on her small charge. She needn't have worried. Daisy had fallen fast asleep, a silver rattle clutched in one dimpled hand.

"Rumor has it Garrett's head push. Ask my opinion," Nils went on, "the man likes the attention. He'll do anything to show off in front of a crowd."

"How's Pa?" Claire asked, refusing to be drawn into a discussion destined to end in an argument.

"Same as always. The old man's never going to change."

"Maybe not, Nils, but it's not too late for you."

"Don't give me another one of your lectures."

"You're young yet," she admonished "You can still turn your life around. Make it into something that matters."

"A cripple isn't left with many options."

"That's a poor excuse for becoming a hopeless drunk. You have a perfectly good mind."

He stared sullenly at the floating mass of timber. "Pa's not happy that you haven't been home in a while. Never any food in the cupboard, place is a pigsty. Money's scarce."

"You mean there's no money for liquor." Her hands curled tight around the handle of the baby carriage. She drew in a deep breath, then let it out. The time had come for Nils to face reality. She was tired of cleaning up after him, making excuses. "Fact of the matter, dear brother, there is no extra money."

"Why's that? Garrett quit paying you?"

Her patience snapped. Nils had become a parasite, a leech, just like her father. Both men expected to be coddled, cared for, always taking, never giving anything in return. Not even affection or gratitude.

"Have you ever wondered why Padraig Mulligan didn't press charges for the damages you inflicted?" Her voice shook with barely suppressed anger.

"Mulligan made too much out of a simple fight."

"Nothing 'simple' about the cost of replacing an eight-foot-long mirror that had to be ordered all the way from Chicago. Nothing 'simple' about paying for the bottles of liquor that used to fill the shelves on either side of it. Not to mention the table and chairs that were smashed. The total sum was considerable." It took every ounce of effort to keep her voice low so that others wouldn't overhear. "Are you so dimwitted that you believe Mr. Mulligan is going to forgive a debt that size out of the goodness of his heart?"

His handsome face took on a mulish expression. "Mulligan's got more money than he knows what to do with. Probably has the first dollar he ever earned."

"Padraig Mulligan is a businessman who doesn't countenance fools. If I hadn't assured him the bill would be paid in full, you'd still be sitting in some filthy jail cell."

At her sharp reminder, dull color crept up his neck.

"You promised to pay him back, not me. As far as I'm concerned, that's your problem."

Her anger evaporated, leaving her nauseous instead. The debt was hers, and hers alone. Nils had no intention of repaying Mulligan. Not now, not ever. Yet she had given the man her word, and refused to go back on it. As a matter of pride, she intended to prove she was cut from different cloth than the rest of her family.

"Fights break out in bars all the time. It's a risk that goes with the business. Seven years bad luck!" Nils gave a humorless laugh. "I should be the one complaining, not the Irishman. Take my advice, Sis. Ignore the bastard, same as me. What's the worst that can happen?"

Daisy's whimper just then proved a welcome distraction. Claire went around to the front of the carriage and adjusted the angle of the flounced pink parasol that protected the baby from the sun. "Is that better, sweetie?" Claire asked the infant, who was now awake.

"So that's Garrett's brat, eh?"

"Her name's Daisy," she said stiffly.

From a bower of tufted pink brocade, Daisy returned Nils's stare with a solemn one of her own.

Nils cleared his throat. "The kid looks more like a rose than a daisy."

On this particular issue, Claire agreed with her brother. Daisy did indeed look soft and sweet as a rosebud. Golden curls peeked out from a frilly bonnet that framed the baby's angelic face. Round cheeks were flushed from sleep; her pretty blue eyes were bright and inquisitive.

"How old is she?" He tentatively reached into the buggy, and smiled when the baby grasped his finger.

"She just turned six months old."

He blinked. "Six months, you say?"

Had the wind sifted through the canopy of branches overhead, momentarily blocking the sun? Or had the color drained from her brother's face? "Nils . . ." Concerned, she placed her hand on his shoulder. "Are you all right?"

"Odd," he muttered. "I always thought the kid would have dark hair like her mother . . . or Garrett."

"Children don't always favor either of their parents." She tucked the satin-trimmed blanket more snugly around the baby. "Sometimes they take after a distant relative—an aunt or maybe a grandmother."

Nils was too engrossed with the baby to respond.

Claire laughed when Daisy drew Nils's finger into her mouth and chomped down, making him wince. "I should have warned you. Daisy prefers fingers to teething biscuits."

His gaze still fastened on the baby, he smiled wanly at her attempted humor. "Don't know much about babies, but Daisy's a pretty little thing, isn't she?"

"Yes, pretty as a picture with a disposition to match."

Nils slowly extracted his finger from the baby's grasp and stepped back. "I've gotta go."

She looked at him, puzzled. "Aren't you staying to watch the river drive?"

"I'm going into town for a beer. Suddenly I've developed a thirst."

Claire watched as he turned, then threaded his way through the crowd and was lost from view. "What do you suppose got into him, Daisy girl? Seems I hardly know my own brother anymore."

EIGHTEEN

Claire was still puzzling over her brother's odd behavior when Sophie and James strolled up.

"A perfect vantage point," Sophie exclaimed. "Let's watch from here." One gloved hand rested possessively on her husband's arm, the other twirled a ruffled silk parasol.

James patted her hand. "Whatever you say, my dear."

As much as she liked Sophie, Claire had to admit in all honesty that James was the more striking of the pair. Tall, slender, elegant, he wore a camel-brown sack coat and vest with tweed trousers in a darker tone. Sophie's taste tended toward frills, flounces, and the bright, harsh colors which were currently all the rage. Her magenta cashmere dress featured a fitted basque with shirred panels down the front and a pleated skirt draped just below the hips. A small bonnet trimmed with ostrich plumes perched atop an elaborate arrangement of brown curls. Compared with Sophie, Claire felt plain in her simple white blouse, gray skirt, and plaid shawl. A sparrow next to a peacock.

"Miss Sorenson," James said, tipping his curved-brim bowler.

"Mr. Lamont," Claire returned the greeting.

"Oh, James, just look at little Daisy." Sophie hugged her husband's arm in a display of affection. "See, I told you she was adorable."

"Mmm." James gave the baby a cursory glance, obviously more to please his wife than from genuine interest. "I'm afraid I must confess—all babies look alike to me."

"Perhaps the poor little thing will have an opportunity to see her father this afternoon. Cole's been away for some time, hasn't he?" Her tone carried a note of censure with it.

"I'm sure Mr. Garrett wouldn't leave his daughter for an extended period of time if it weren't necessary," Claire said, compelled to defend Cole's prolonged absence.

"No, of course not," James interjected smoothly. "No man in his senses would leave a comfortable home for the wilds of a lumber camp."

"It's such a lovely day. I thought this would be a good time to take Daisy for a stroll in her new carriage. Fresh air and sunshine are good for babies."

"I admire your knowledge of infants, Claire. You're exactly the type I'd hire to take care of a child of our own. Don't you agree, James?"

"Absolutely, my dear. Miss Sorenson would make a perfect choice."

"That's very kind of you," Claire murmured. James Lamont's gaze had lingered on her a fraction too long, his voice seemed a shade too warm. From the look Sophie shot her husband, Claire knew she had noticed as well.

"Is it true, Claire, that Cole is actually one of the crew?"

"Like you, I've heard rumors."

"Can't say I applaud his decision." James's mouth firmed in disapproval. "Cole has a certain reputation to uphold in the community. He doesn't need to soil his hands in lumber camps. He's risen above laborers who earn a dollar and a half a day."

Sophie concurred with a vigorous nod that set the ostrich plumes on her hat dancing. "If she were still alive, Priscilla would have been mortified to know Cole lowered himself to the ranks of unskilled labor."

"'Unskilled' is hardly the appropriate term, Sophie dear." James gave his wife a condescending smile. "Though I'm loath to correct you, it requires a great deal of skill to be a river hog—or river rat, if you prefer—and survive."

Sophie shuddered delicately. "Rat, hog, pig, whatever you call it, Priscilla would turn in her grave to hear her husband referred to that way."

James chuckled. "Be that as it may, my sweet, the foreman of a river drive is a man worthy of respect . . . regardless of the sobriquet."

"Priscilla always said a man couldn't buy class. Not even marrying her could make a silk purse out of a sow's ear."

"Sophie, really," James chided. "Miss Sorenson will think you the worst kind of snob."

Listening to the conversation between the Lamonts had been enlightening. Claire sensed that she was seeing under the sophisticated veneer to the true character beneath. In her opinion, they were both snobs and well-deserving of each other. "I think it's admirable that Mr. Garrett is willing to work alongside his crew. To let his men know every job, no matter how trivial it may seem to others, is important."

Sophie stared at her as though she had grown two heads. James recovered his aplomb more quickly than his wife. "Don't misunderstand, Claire," he said, using the same persuasive tone he might use to sway a jury. "Like others who have risen from the ranks by dint of hard work, Cole is to be commended. As a valued client, I hold him in the highest regard."

Sophie took her cue from her husband. "I admire Cole, truly I do. Perhaps I was unwise to repeat the comments of a dear friend. Priscilla only wished Cole was more . . . genteel. Like my James," she added, beaming up at him.

"Here she comes!"

The shout reverberated along the riverbank. Conversation ceased as everyone turned to watch the annual pageant being played out on the water. Logs bobbed on the surface in great numbers. Men swarmed over them, wielding peavey hooks and pike poles as skillfully as knights of old with lances and swords. All wore similar attire, colored shirts or bright plaid mackinaws, stagged pants or overalls cut off just above the boot tops, and caulked boots, the pride of river drivers. These shin-high boots, studded with sharp, quarter-inch steel spikes, anchored them to the floating logs like the claws of a cat. Soon the entire surface, shore to shore, was a churning, writhing mass of pine.

"Runner on the loose!"

Claire felt a ripple of excitement at the familiar cry. She eagerly scanned the scene in front of her, searching for the fearless river driver who, surefooted as a squirrel, could lightly run along a log barely able to support his weight.

"Oh, look!" Sophie exclaimed, pointing at a figure precariously balanced on a small log.

Claire gasped. "Cole!"

"No, it can't be." Squinting, James leaned forward for a better look.

But regardless of the thick beard and crude clothing, Claire recognized him in an instant. He had a certain fluidity of movement, an arrogant tilt to his chin, that was more distinctive to her than his signature.

"Well, I'll be," James said with a trace of awe. "It is him."

"Doesn't he know the dam is just ahead?" Sophie wondered aloud.

"The dam . . ." Just a little farther downstream there was a three-foot drop to the water below. "Surely, he must realize it's close by."

Just as the log Cole was riding on seemed about to sink, he leapt to another. The crowd cheered, delighted at the daring antics. James and Sophie applauded as well. Letting out a shaky breath, Claire relaxed her death grip on the carriage.

"Claire, dear, are you all right?" Sophie's plain face wore a concerned look. "You look as though you've seen a ghost."

"I'm fine, really," Claire replied. With each passing minute, Cole drew nearer to the edge of the dam. Though the drop wasn't excessive, one misstep, one wrong move in the log-strewn river could be catastrophic.

"Watch this, ladies." James stepped forward for an unhindered view. "You're about to see some derring-do."

Claire's fingernails dug into the polished wood handle of the baby carriage until her knuckles gleamed white. She watched, her heart in her throat. "Dear Lord . . ."

Knees flexed, a jam pike across his chest for balance, Cole skated through the narrow channel of open water. His caulked boots bit into the bark beneath his feet. Using his superbly muscled legs, he steered the log as easily as though it were a child's toy. Then, crouching slightly, he sailed over the rim of the dam. For a seemingly impossible time, he hung suspended, his figure silhouetted against a backdrop of woods and sky, then plunged into the seething water below.

And disappeared from view.

Agonizing seconds later, he reappeared in their line of sight, triumphantly guiding his log through the maze of others that had preceded it. Those on shore erupted into an enthusiastic burst of hand-clapping. Claire released her pent-up breath and wondered just how much excitement her wildly beating heart could withstand.

Sophie laughed with pleasure. "That's what draws everyone year after year. As I always tell James, a river drive is far more thrilling than watching a stuffy old play at the theater. Where else would one see a real life-and-death drama?"

The river stopped moving.

Cole felt it deep in his bones the instant it happened. Next came the cold knot of fear. A log jam. The most dreaded occurrence on a river drive. And the most deadly.

While he watched, a massive log swung sideways, then snagged on another log already blocking the river. At Cole's shouted command, men scrambled to pry it loose with the pointed iron tips of their peavey hooks. Before they could free it, however, other logs coming at a fast clip in the rushing water piled behind it.

"Damn it!" Cole swore softly. He had sent an advance crew to inspect every foot along the river bank for possible obstructions. They had reported that the way was clear. Now this . . .

Even though his river rats worked at a feverish pace, sixteen-foot lengths of timber began to form a haphazard mound. Spectators along both sides of the river yelled out advice. One of the river hogs, a man who went by the name of Frenchie, was momentarily distracted by the commotion. The particular log he was standing on began to roll, then spin. His feet frantically fought for purchase, but not even the metal spikes on his boots could save him. Arms windmilling, he plunged backwards into the chill waters. His head struck a log behind him with a sickening crunch. A sea of white pine closed over him, sealing off his escape.

"You, Iverson," Cole shouted. "Fish him out."

Cole was already picking his way across the jumble of wood. The men nearby rushed to help.

"Got 'im, boss." Iverson tugged on his cant hook. By sheer luck, he had succeeded in snagging the neck of his friend's shirt with the curved tip. Frenchie emerged like an oversized fish, unconscious, blood dripping from his head.

"Good job." Cole gave Iverson a nod of approval before turning to the others who had come to the rescue. "We got to get him out—fast."

Legs braced, he dug the end of his peavey into the log in front of him and used his weight as a lever to create a space large enough to drag the unconscious crew member through. A half-dozen others imitated his actions. Shoving. Pushing. Muscles straining. Finally, an opening of sufficient size emerged.

"Pull!" Cole yelled.

Two men, one on either side, grabbed onto Frenchie's shoulders. Behind them, Cole heard logs crashing together. He knew they would have only one chance before the open area would slam shut like the jaws of a trap, and the man's body would be crushed, pulverized, by tons of wood. Muscles burned as they fought against time. Cole shook the sting of sweat from his eyes. The spectre of death breathed down his neck. He waged a fierce battle against losing one of his crew.

"Almost there, Boss," Eugene Leduc huffed.

Just as they pulled Frenchie free, the mass shifted. A huge log shot past, propelled by an enormous buildup of pressure from behind, striking the man's arm as it went. The sickening crack of breaking bone was loud enough to be heard by those on shore.

"Leduc, haul him out of here. Iverson, fetch Doc Wetherbury."

Leduc and Iverson hurried to carry out Cole's orders. The rest waited for instructions. As head push, Cole knew it was up to him to untangle this mess. And untangle it quickly. The longer the jam continued, the more difficult it would be to break up. He recalled last year when the Jump River had clogged for thirteen miles. Tales still circulated of the Red Cedar back in '76 which was stacked with logs thirty feet high. Jams could take days to break up, even weeks.

Some were widow-makers.

He sent the river rats to work the center of the river with peaveys and poles. Using the pointed steel tips, they picked away at logs the size of giant jackstraws, hoping to find the key log. Once the key log was pried free, the jam would clear in minutes. If prying failed, it could be hacked to pieces. Dynamite would be used only as a last resort. All they needed was to find that one vital hunk of pine that locked the others in place. Contrary to the popular myth, Cole knew that sometimes there was more than one.

"Take that spruce!" Cole hollered, pointing his arm.

Tools rattled and clanked as men struggled to remove the spruce from the tangle. The jam shifted, groaned.

JUST BEFORE DAYBREAK 227

Every eye turned to Cole for direction. Nerves strung taut, he waited, watched, listened.

The mass settled, locked once again in a wooden embrace.

"Now that pine," he shouted, indicating a giant log at least five feet across.

The men changed direction and attacked the one he indicated. Prodding, lifting, cutting, pulling. The chore continued. Yet the jam steadily worsened.

Cole wiped the sweat from his brow with his plaid shirtsleeve. From the edge of the jam, he surveyed the situation and reviewed his options. Sometimes a jam gave way of its own accord. But lately, luck hadn't been on his side. He had no reason to think things were about to change. Glancing over his shoulder toward the riverbank, his gaze locked with that of his former father-in-law.

Leonard Brock, puffing on his ever-present cigar, stood surrounded by cronies. The group included Edward Tanner. With a self-satisfied smile wreathing his florid face, Brock calmly reached into his vest and pulled out a gold pocket watch. "Tick, tock," he mouthed.

Even from a distance, Cole could read his lips. Brock made no attempt to conceal the fact that he relished seeing him in this predicament. The drive was at a virtual standstill with time the enemy. Getting a good price for the timber depended on delivering it to the mills before the market was glutted and prices dropped. He stood to lose everything. He'd be branded as inept, held up for ridicule, and right back in the lumber camps where he had started. Brock would gloat if that happened.

"Bastard," he muttered. He was about to return to the task at hand when a woman standing under a tall cottonwood caught his attention. Claire. She stood out—even in a crowd. A single, glowing diamond amidst a clutter of colored glass.

Seeing him, she smiled. But unlike Brock's smile, hers radiated encouragement, confidence. Caring. Renewed his belief in himself when he had started to doubt. He smiled in return, then squared his shoulders.

"Smith," he yelled. "Fetch the horses and oxen. Leduc, bring the jam dog. We're wasting time."

"Cole must be getting desperate by now." Sophie Lamont idly twirled the handle of her parasol.

They had watched while the "jam dog," an apparatus which consisted of a thick rope with two sturdy iron hooks in the center, was stretched across the water. Under Cole's supervision, the hooks were drilled into the key log and hitched to oxen on one side of the river and horses on the other. For an hour, man and beast had battled to dislodge the jam. The animals worked on either side of the river, alternately pulling, tugging, then changing direction to start the process anew. The jam stubbornly refused to yield.

James nodded sagely. "If this fails, Cole will be forced to blast it loose. Mill owners won't be happy if that happens. They don't want their winter's profits turned into a heap of kindling."

Not wanting to contemplate that dire possibility, Claire turned her attention to Daisy, who had started to fuss. Thankfully, the fresh air agreed with the little girl, and she had slept much of the afternoon. Even so, Claire was glad she had had the foresight to bring an extra bottle of milk. The river drive showed no sign of ending soon. "Hush now, sweetie," she whispered. "Your daddy is going to find a way to fix this."

As she bent and picked up the baby, Claire felt eyes boring into her. She tried to ignore the sensation, yet the feeling persisted. The fine hairs pricked at the back of her neck. Scanning the throng of onlookers, she found Leonard Brock watching her with an unblinking stare. Instinctively, she held Daisy closer. If the man wanted to see his granddaughter, she could hardly refuse. Thus far he had exhibited no interest in his daughter's offspring. Relief mingled with confusion when he made no effort to approach. His look was cold, hostile almost, and reserved exclusively for her.

"Well, I'll be," James cried out. "I think Cole's nearly got it licked."

Claire pulled her gaze from Leonard Brock back to the action on the river. The crowd had grown quiet, alert. A single log held the others in place.

"Any volunteers?" Cole's voice rang out.

The men kept their eyes averted. None stepped forward.

"He's the river boss," Sophie said plaintively. "Why doesn't he just order one of them do it?"

"Because he knows whoever cuts that log in two could be killed," Claire answered softly. "He doesn't want their deaths on his conscience."

James expelled a snort of disgust. "A river drive's no place for cowards. You sign up, you take your chances."

Before she could reply, a heavy rope was looped beneath Cole's armpits. A crew of men held onto the end, ready to pull him to safety if the situation warranted. Cole made his way into the midst of the jam. He moved from log to log with the agility and grace of a circus performer. Daisy wriggled in Claire's tight grasp. "Sorry, sweet," she whispered, the words thick in her throat.

"Just think, ladies," James spoke in a lowered voice. "One piece of pine holding back tons of floating projectiles. Never know what will happen once it lets loose."

No one spoke as Cole raised his axe. The only sound to be heard was that of steel biting into pine.

Claire forgot to breathe. The notch deepened beneath sure, steady strokes. Halfway through, a loud cracking ricocheted through the stillness. Cole paused, ready to jump at a second's notice, but the log held. Again, he raised his axe high and brought it down. With a boom like thunder, the wall of logs let loose. Pushed by the tremendous water pressure, lengths of pine hurtled forward like sticks.

In the aftermath, Cole was nowhere to be seen.

"Where'd he go?"

"Gotta been killed."

"No way a man could live through the likes of that."

Claire heard the comments as though in a trance. Had Cole sacrificed his life for a river of logs? She was unaware of tears streaming down her pale cheeks.

A man pointed. "That 'im over yonder?"

Her gaze flew in the direction the man had indicated. She glimpsed a red plaid sleeve seconds before it bobbed beneath the sea of logs. "Please, God," she whispered.

"Yank on the rope, men!" Leduc exhorted his fellow river rats. "Pull! Put your back into it!"

The men pulled. Then, as a single unit, staggered backwards. Empty. The rope that had been tied around Cole's chest came away empty. The crowd stared at it in disbelief. Claire pressed a hand to her mouth to hold back the sobs.

"He's a goner."

The old man's pronouncement echoed the consensus of those watching. Cole was trapped beneath tons of timber. His fate was the same as a man caught beneath a solid mass of ice. With no way out, no air, he was doomed.

Claire was vaguely aware of a flurry of activity on the opposite bank. Then she noticed people swarming from all directions, a kaleidoscope of color before her dazed eyes.

"By George!" A wizened old logger slapped his knee. "If that ain't 'im."

All attention focused on a dripping-wet figure dragging himself up the muddy riverbank. Claire gulped air. Blinking moisture from her eyes, she saw that it was Cole. Battered, bruised, bleeding, but otherwise unharmed.

Safe.

Her knees felt ready to collapse. She offered up a silent prayer of thanksgiving as she pressed a kiss to the crown of the baby's head. "See, Daisy girl?" she whispered. "I told you your daddy would fix everything."

A cheer from the crowd was nearly drowned out by the noise of rushing water and jostling logs. A friend of

JUST BEFORE DAYBREAK 231

James's came up and greeted him. The two men slapped each other on the back as though they personally had freed the jam. Together they wandered off, leaving the women behind while they engaged in an animated discussion about the hazards of a river drive.

"Claire . . ." Sophie lightly touched her arm. "You look overwrought. Perhaps you should find a place to sit."

Claire dashed away tears she didn't remember shedding. "I thought Cole had been killed."

"Cole?" Sophie raised an eyebrow.

It took Claire a moment to realized her blunder. "Did I say Cole? I meant Mr. Garrett, of course. You're right—I *am* overwrought. I'm sorry if I sounded overly familiar. I was just so worried." She was babbling and knew it.

"No need to apologize, dear." Sophie patted her arm. "There, there, I didn't mean to be sharp with you." She paused a beat, then asked, "You don't fancy yourself in love with the man, do you?"

"No! Of course not!" Even to her own ears, the denial came a shade too quickly, too vehemently. "That would be utter foolishness on my part. I merely take care of Mr. Garrett's daughter. True, I worried that he might have lost his life just now, but only because of Daisy."

"Daisy?"

Turning away, Claire resettled the baby inside her carriage. "Naturally, I was concerned about what would become of her if anything should happen to Mr. Garrett. The child's own grandfather shows no interest in her."

"That's true, certainly, though for the life of me, I can't explain why. James and I are Daisy's godparents. If anything, God forbid, happens to Cole, we're ready to welcome Daisy into our home and raise her as our own."

"That's very generous of you."

"I'm sure Priscilla would want it that way. After all, we were like sisters."

Claire adjusted the baby's blanket. "It's ridiculous to think there could ever be anything between Mr. Garrett and myself. When the time comes for him to seek another wife, he'll choose another like his first."

"Maybe, maybe not." Sophie pursed her lips and considered the matter. "While there's considerable merit to what you've just said, it's been my observation that men often make stupid choices where women are concerned."

"We're worlds apart," Claire said, repeating the phrase she told herself time and again. "You surely must know the reputation of my father and brother."

Sophie had the grace to look embarrassed.

Still shaken by the afternoon's events, Claire left soon afterwards with Daisy. Later, she couldn't recall whether or not she had bid Sophie good-bye. She did know, however, that she had revealed more of her personal feelings than she had intended. She had seen suspicion, then confirmation, reflected in the woman's shrewd brown eyes.

NINETEEN

Three days had passed since the river drive, but her terror hadn't. Every time Claire thought about it, her heart would race, her chest tighten. She felt like screaming. Cole had taken foolish chances. Risked his life. He could have been killed. While she admired his willingness to perform any job required, in this instance she agreed with Sophie. As the foreman, he should have ordered someone else to take the chances. At the thought that he might have died, part of her died, too.

"Bla!" Daisy raised her tiny arm and splashed.

Claire ducked as droplets of bathwater flew everywhere. Too late. Beads of water streamed down her cheeks. Wet tendrils of hair framed either side of her face. Even the apron she wore over her serviceable blouse and skirt was damp from the baby's antics. "Daisy," she scolded, smiling, "you turn into a menace at bath time."

"Bla!" Again Daisy slapped the water with her chubby palm, sending it spewing.

"Here," Claire said, finding the toy wood duck that had found refuge behind the infant. She propelled the favorite bath toy around the tub. "This little duck goes quack, quack, quack!"

Daisy chortled, then let out an ear-piercing squeal of glee when Claire pretended the duck pecked at her bare tummy. Claire joined in the laughter.

"Looks like you're having fun," a familiar voice commented from the bathroom doorway. "Can anyone play?"

Claire let out a startled gasp. Cole lounged against the door frame. If possible, he looked even scruffier than the last time she had seen him. Except for the caulked boots, he still wore the same clothes he had worn during the river drive. The fact that he was in stocking feet explained why she hadn't heard him come up the stairs. His shirt was torn, his stagged pants ragged, his beard and mustache dark and thick. A rogue. A pirate. A reprobate. Dangerous, reckless, extraordinarily masculine. He quite simply stole her breath away.

His effect on Daisy was quite the opposite. At the sight of her father, her lower lip trembled and her eyes filled with tears. Her fists pumped frantically as she held out her arms to Claire.

Grabbing a towel, Claire wrapped it around the terrified infant and scooped her from the tub. "There, there, sweetie, it's all right."

Clutching her savior with all her might, Daisy burrowed against Claire's shoulder.

Worried by his daughter's reaction, Cole stepped farther into the room. "What's wrong? Is she in pain?"

Claire's eyes met his over the top of the baby's head. At close range, he appeared exhausted, with dark circles under his eyes. His face was thinner, too, transformed into an intriguing blend of angles and planes. But his wonderful smoke-gray eyes could still make her heartbeat erratic. "Be patient with her, Cole. You look different."

Daisy timidly peeked at the man who sounded like her father, but looked like a stranger.

"What's the matter, Peanut? Miss your father?" Cole reached out to touch the baby's cheek.

At the first contact, Daisy threw back her head and howled.

"What did I do?" Baffled, Cole shook his head. "I've seen her give friendlier greetings to perfect strangers."

"Babies go through different stages." Claire shushed the baby until her cries subsided somewhat. "She's still not quite sure who you are."

He scrubbed a chapped, calloused hand over his bearded jaw. "Guess I do look a bit different."

"Considerably."

He chuckled at her acerbic tone, then sobered. "What about you, Claire? Did you recognize me?"

Her gaze never faltered. "I'd recognize you anywhere."

He looked as though he were waging a silent debate within himself. A ghost of a smile flitted across his face as he tucked a damp tendril of her hair behind her ear. "It's good to be home."

She wanted to hurl herself into his arms, be crushed against his chest, hear the reassuring thud of his heart against her ear. Wanted to confess she had missed him, feared for his safety. Loved him. But she did none of these. If she knew what was good for her, she'd keep her distance. Those magical, wonderful hours they had shared were over. Like a flame that had burned hot and bright, then was extinguished.

"Daisy's worked herself into quite a state. She'll be better once you've had a chance to bathe and change."

Raking his fingers through hair too long and shaggy, he gave her a rueful grin. "I think you're both implying I need a shave. You, however, are much more tactful than my daughter. I'll see you both after I make myself presentable."

Claire watched him saunter off. Daisy's sobs had changed into hiccups. Using the corner of the towel, Claire mopped up the little girl's tears. "You little imp," she chided gently. "You gave your father a fine welcome home. One he's not likely to forget for some time."

At the reproof, Daisy's lower lip jutted as though she would start wailing again at the slightest provocation.

"Still out of sorts?" Claire lovingly brushed the baby's

damp curls. "Let's get you dried off, little one, and into your nightclothes. And then a nice bottle of warm milk."

When Cole entered the nursery a short time later, he experienced such a profound sense of peace and homecoming that it staggered him. Claire sat in a rocking chair holding Daisy, all flushed and sleepy, as she sucked contentedly on a bottle. A perfect picture. A perfect family. And it had nothing to do with wealth, social position, or ambition. He had once believed that by marrying Priscilla Brock, settling in his fine new home, and raising a family, he'd achieved the pinnacle of success. He had it all. A perfect family, a perfect life. Somewhere, somehow, his priorities had shifted, changed. He was wiser now, but had wisdom come too late? And at what price?

Claire glanced up at him, her expression as calm and serene as a madonna's. She was so lovely his heart ached with longing. He had left home, stayed away as long as possible, struggled to put her out of his mind. He had tried to forget her, but the harder he tried, the more he remembered. The softness, the sweetness, the generosity had become an addiction. It required all his control not to tell her how he felt. But that would be playing with fire. Until he was no longer suspected of Priscilla's death, he had no right to involve her, or anyone, in his life.

Daisy turned her head. Her face lit up in a smile when she saw him.

Cole grinned back, unabashedly the doting father. This tiny creature had effortlessly become the center of his world. He'd do anything, everything, to keep her safe. He wanted to watch her grow into a healthy, happy, caring young woman. One as beautiful inside as she was outside.

One like . . . Claire.

He cleared his throat at the onslaught of emotion, then advanced into the room. Wordlessly, he reached down and picked up his baby daughter.

"Da-da-da-da." Daisy patted his cheek.

Cole knew babies of Daisy's tender age couldn't speak. Knew the stream of babble was sound with no particular meaning. Yet he couldn't stifle the happiness he felt at hearing them. "That's a much better way to greet your father, Peanut."

Claire rose from the rocking chair and brushed at her wrinkled apron. "I'll give you two time to get reacquainted. Then I'll be back to put Daisy down for the night."

"That won't be necessary." Taking the seat she had just vacated, Cole picked up Daisy's half-finished bottle. "I'll tuck her in."

"Very well," she said, turning toward the door. "If there's nothing else you need . . ."

"Well, there is one thing you might do for me."

She stopped, looked at him expectantly.

"I haven't had dinner. If it isn't too much trouble, I wondered if you could fix me a sandwich or something." He knew he shouldn't. That he had no right to ask anything of her. Not even a simple favor. Truth was, he wasn't even hungry, but wanted an excuse, albeit a lame one, to spend time in her company. Selfish bastard that he was, he simply wanted her near.

"It's no trouble," she replied.

"And Claire," he said as she started to move away, "would you wait for me downstairs? I'd like to talk with you."

"If you wish."

"I was hoping you'd tell me everything that's happened while I was away," he improvised.

"I'll see you downstairs."

After Claire left, Cole sat with Daisy cradled in the crook of his arm while she finished her bottle. The baby's eyelids fluttered, then drooped. He continued to rock her even after she was asleep. He hadn't been prepared for such an emotional homecoming. He blamed it on having been away too long. He had missed them, both of them, more than he cared to admit. Daisy, the child of his heart, he could understand. But he had no right to feel anything for Claire. What he felt went far beyond the physical need of a man for an attractive woman.

And it scared the daylights out of him.

With Daisy sleeping soundly, Cole left the nursery. He found Claire in the kitchen where he had known he would. He stood for a moment, content just to watch her. She performed even the simplest acts with an innate grace, an economy of movement, whether it was bathing an infant or baking cookies. He found himself wondering what it would be like to hold her while they waltzed around a ballroom blazing with light.

"There was leftover chicken in the icebox along with potato salad Alma made yesterday," she said without turning.

"Sounds perfect." All of a sudden he was famished. Plunking himself down on a chair, he reached for a thick slice of bread and slathered it with butter.

"Would you like tea or coffee? Or there's buttermilk, if you'd prefer something cold."

"Buttermilk," he answered, biting into a drumstick. It was then he noticed the plate of oatmeal cookies studded with fat raisins, just the way he liked them.

She put the glass of buttermilk on the table, then stood back.

"Sit, sit." He motioned with the chicken leg to the chair next to his. "Keep me company while I eat."

"You said there were matters you wanted to discuss." With obvious reluctance, she did as he asked.

It pained him to see her so aloof when they had once been intimate. He understood though that he was the reason for the barriers she had erected. "Just talk to me. Tell me what's happened while I've been gone."

"There's not much to tell." She stared down at her fingers laced together in her lap. "What is it you wish to know?"

"Anything. Everything." She could recite nursery rhymes—he didn't care.

"Alma and Tim are both fine. Alma arrives each morning at eight and leaves promptly at six. She doesn't say much. I don't think she's forgiven me for leaving her with Daisy when Nils was in jail."

"She'll get over it. Don't let her bother you." He polished off the last of the potato salad and washed it down with buttermilk. "What's Tim been up to these past weeks?"

"He . . . keeps busy."

Cole noted her slight hesitancy before answering. "Claire," he asked quietly, "is there something you want to tell me?"

"Tim wondered if perhaps you might consider taking one of Gertie's litter for a house cat." She moistened her lower lip with the tip of her tongue, then, ignoring the surprise that must have registered on his face, plunged ahead. "I took Daisy to see the kittens while you were gone. You should have seen her expression when she saw them. She's absolutely fascinated. Pets are wonderful companions for children."

"A kitten . . . ?"

She nodded enthusiastically. "There are six to choose from, all adorable."

He leaned back, mulling over the possibility. "I never had a pet."

"Neither did I," she confessed.

"I must admit I don't know the first thing about cats."

"Tim assures me there's very little to do. He says cats are self-sufficient."

"Very well, then, I'll let you choose the one you think best."

"Just like that?"

"Just like that." He smiled in amusement, enjoying her reaction. She had been armed for battle, but not prepared for easy victory.

"Oh . . . good. Tim will be pleased." She sprang to her feet and returned the buttermilk to the icebox. Keeping her back to him, she stood at the sink, folding and refolding a kitchen towel.

"I know you well enough to know something's bothering you." Getting up from his chair, he came up behind her, placed both hands on her shoulders, and forced her to face him. "What is it, Claire?"

"I'm *so* angry with you!" So angry, in fact, her voice shook.

"Why?" Cole blinked, caught off guard by her vehement response. Of all things, he hadn't expected this. "Because of what happened between us before I left?"

"The fact that we made love has nothing to do with how I feel. Nothing," she repeated fiercely. She tried to shrug loose from his tight grip.

Cole doubted he'd ever understand the workings of the female mind. He dredged up patience from his short supply. "Then suppose you explain exactly what I did to make you angry."

"Did you stop to think—even for an instant—that you might have been killed? Whatever possessed you to accept the job of head push on the river drive?" Her eyes blazed like twin blue flames. "I watched you break up that log jam, watched you disappear from sight. I thought you were dead."

He fought the urge to take her in his arms, hold her, comfort her. But he knew where that would lead. He couldn't hold her without wanting to kiss her, couldn't kiss her without wanting to make love to her. Couldn't take without anything to offer in return.

And he had nothing to give any woman, much less one as special as Claire.

His hands gentled on her shoulders. "Sometimes we do what we have to in order to survive. Even though the stakes are high, the rewards outweigh the risks. I knew what I was doing, Claire. It's not the first time I broke up a jam."

"You're considered a lumber baron. None of the others take those chances."

"I'm not like one of the others." He sighed wearily. "When I wasn't able to round up my share of men for the drive, I made a deal with the other sawmill owners. If I acted as head push, they were willing to overlook the fact that I had less than my quota of manpower. I had a vested interest in the success of the drive. A financial interest I couldn't ignore."

"Oh . . . I didn't know."

He felt her tension dissolve. As he watched, embarrassment replaced the anguish he had glimpsed in the depths of her slate-blue eyes. And he was humbled. No one else had cared whether he lived or died since he was a child. The knowledge warmed him clear through to his bones. "Worried about me, Claire?" he asked softly.

"Of course I was worried." She wrenched free from his grasp and stepped away. "Did you stop to consider Daisy's fate should something happen to you? You're the only parent she has. She needs you."

He watched her turn and march off, head high, spine ramrod straight. Had he been an arrogant fool in assuming her concern was for him when it was really Daisy she was concerned over? He rubbed his freshly shaved jaw. Possibly, he admitted. Still, he clung to the hope that she hadn't been completely truthful. He wanted her to care.

Admitting that came as the biggest shock of all.

No sooner had Claire fallen asleep when she was awakened by a banging noise coming from the rear of the house. She lay there for a moment, trying to gather her wits about her. It was dark outside, the middle of the night. Who could possibly be pounding on the back door at this hour?

When the banging started anew, she hastily got out of bed, crossed the room, opened the window, and peeked out. "Pa," she whispered. She was filled with dismay at finding his familiar figure on the porch below.

"Hush, Pa," she called down, her voice an exaggerated whisper. "You'll wake the entire household."

"Get down here, girl," he bellowed.

Grabbing her shawl, she flew down the stairs. She raced through the kitchen and flung open the door. Lud Sorenson pushed his way inside. The strong odor of whiskey sent her senses reeling. Automatically, she steeled herself for trouble. Her father had an unpredictable temper in the best of times. Alcohol made it worse.

"Pa, what's wrong? Is Nils in trouble again?"

"No, it ain't your goddamn brother," he roared.

She placed a finger to her mouth. "Shh, Pa, please. Mr. Garrett's asleep."

"Hmph!" he sneered. "From the looks of you, my guess'd be you were, too."

She didn't need to light a lamp to know the degree of her father's drunkenness. She could hear it in the slurred words, smell its rank odor. "It's late, Pa," she said, attempting to make her tone conciliatory. "Most people have been in bed for hours. You should be, too."

"I ain't most people." He staggered backwards, fell up against the kitchen table. "Bars just closed, so it ain't late."

Claire winced at the loud clatter and cast a worried glance toward the hallway. The last thing she wanted was for Cole to be awakened from an exhausted sleep by her father's rantings. Added to that, Daisy was cutting another tooth. She didn't relish the thought of spending the rest of the night pacing the nursery floor. Pulling the shawl more firmly about her shoulders, she hugged her arms around herself. "If it's money you want . . ."

Lud snorted. "His money, you mean."

"If it isn't Nils, and it isn't money, what is it?"

He shook a thick finger under her nose. "Don't you sass me, girl."

Claire sighed and closed her eyes briefly. When she was

younger, he used to terrify her when he was in one of these moods, but no longer. Tonight she felt calm, almost detached. "Sorry, Pa," she said, opening her eyes. "I didn't mean to be disrespectful."

Mollified, he nodded so vigorously that a shock of white hair fell across his brow. "I'm your pa. Don't you go forgettin' it. Just because you live in a rich man's house—share a rich man's bed—don't make you better'n your old man."

It took a moment for the full impact of his words to sink in. She had only been half listening, letting him rant and rave, hoping he would soon tire and leave. She stared at him in disbelief. "You think . . . ?"

"Don't think, *know*," he said, cutting off her flow of words. "How stupid do you think I am, girl?"

He lurched closer, but she held her ground. "You're wrong, Pa."

"That right?" Eyes narrowed, he studied her as carefully as a cat ready to pounce.

Claire silently damned the telltale blush that spread across her cheekbones. Even to her own ears, her denial lacked conviction. Those two glorious nights during the blizzard would forever be emblazoned in her memory.

"You've made me a laughingstock. Cain't even get a beer without everyone talkin' about your goin's-on."

"I work for Mr. Garrett, Pa. I take care of his little girl. Hired help is all I am." And that, God help her, was the unvarnished truth. "Who are you going to believe, Pa? A bunch of drunken lumberjacks in a smelly barroom, or your own flesh and blood?"

"You're lyin'. I can always tell." He stuck his face in front of hers. "Is Garrett payin' you, girl, or are you givin' it away for free?"

"Go home, Pa. Sleep it off." She clamped her jaws together, afraid of what she might say if she wasn't careful.

"Don't go givin' me orders."

Lud's face mottled with rage. For the first time since

opening the door, she felt a cold tickle of fear along her spine. "It's late, Pa. We'll talk next time I get a day off."

Lud didn't budge. "My own daughter, the town whore. People are laughin' at me behind my back."

Suddenly, Claire had had enough of her father's insults. A hot flood of anger washed away all caution. "Like they laugh behind mine because you're a drunk?"

Enraged, Lud hauled off and backhanded her across the face. The force of the blow sent her crashing up against the sink. Pain exploded along her ribcage. Stars danced in front of her eyes. The entire side of her face felt numb. The blessed numbness was replaced by a fiery burning and throbbing that brought tears to her eyes.

Cole charged into the kitchen. He had been awakened from a deep sleep by a man's irate voice. The first thing he saw was Claire huddled against the sink. Lud loomed over her, his hand poised to strike again. Without stopping to think, Cole grabbed Lud by the scruff of his shirt collar, picked him up bodily, and heaved him out the back door and down the steps.

Lud landed in the dirt, then scrambled awkwardly to his feet. Cole bounded down the stairs after him.

"Cole, don't!" Claire called from the top step.

Her plea didn't penetrate the red haze of rage fogging his brain. Lud took a swing, but Cole dodged and the punch went wide, glancing harmlessly off his shoulder. Cole's aim, however, was true to its mark. The blow connected squarely with Lud's jaw, sending him once more sprawling to the ground.

Tim came flying out of the coach house, stuffing his nightshirt into his trousers as he ran. "I heard the ruckus and figured there'd be a problem," he panted.

Cole jerked his arm back, cocked his fist. "I ought to kill the bastard for what he just did."

Tim grabbed Cole's arm. "It ain't worth it, Boss. Trust me, it ain't worth it."

"He's right, Cole." Claire, blood oozing from a cut lip, rushed to his side. "Let him be—he's drunk."

Cole drew back. The blood still drummed in his ears. If Lud Sorenson did so much as utter one swear word, he was ready to pummel him into oblivion.

"Believe me, Boss," Tim said earnestly. "You're doing the right thing."

"Get him out of my sight."

"Yessir!" Tim's head bobbed emphatically. "Soon's I hitch the team I'll haul his sorry ass outta here."

Lud already forgotten, Cole turned his attention to Claire. Gently, he touched her bruised cheek, her swollen lip. Like a willow to the wind, she swayed toward him. "You all right, sweetheart?"

Her tentative smile tugged at his heart.

Tim watched the exchange with interest, but no outward show of surprise. "See to your woman," he advised Cole with a cheeky grin. "She needs you."

Cole acknowledged Tim's advice with a jerk of his head. Then he draped one arm protectively around her shoulders and lead her toward the darkened house. He debated whether to pick her up and carry her, but was afraid it might add to her discomfort.

Once back inside, he lightly traced the contours of her face with his fingertips, needing to reassure himself she wasn't seriously injured. He had been a hair's breadth from losing total control when he found Lud ready to strike Claire a second time. If Tim hadn't intervened . . . He shuddered to think what the result might have been. Only a monster would want to injure someone so fragile, so fine. "I'm sorry I wasn't able to stop your father before he did this."

"It's my fault. I should have known better than to goad him."

"Don't *ever* let me hear you make excuses for him. Your father is responsible for his actions, not you."

"It's a habit of mine." She tried to smile, but winced. "... A bad habit, but one I'm determined to break."

"That's my girl." He smoothed back a lock of her silky blond hair. "Now let me get some ice to keep the swelling down."

Letting out a shaky sigh, Claire gingerly lowered herself to a chair.

Cole paused in the act of chipping ice and placing it in a kitchen towel when he heard her breath hitch. He stopped what he was doing, knelt on the floor in front of her, and took both her hands in his. "Claire, maybe we should send for Doc Wetherbury."

"No, no, I'm fine," she protested. "I hit the edge of the sink when I fell. I'm bruised, but nothing's broken. I'll be a little sore, that's all."

Cole studied her intently, then nodded. It distressed him to see a bruise mar the perfection of her face. Helpless to stop himself, he leaned in and brushed a feather-light kiss against her mouth, then drew back before he succumbed to temptation.

He sat back on his heels, his hands still holding hers. "You never said what brought your father here at this hour."

She averted her gaze. "He was drunk."

"I'm sure he's been drunk on many occasions since you've been here. Why tonight, Claire?"

"Pa heard some gossip," she said after a lengthy pause.

He frowned. "What sort of gossip?"

Again a pause. "About you and me . . ."

She didn't have to elaborate. Cole could well imagine the ugly rumors circulating.

"He called me . . . names. Horrible, disgusting names." Her voice was low, choked with unshed tears. "And I couldn't deny them."

She pulled her hands free from his and stood.

Guilt crashed down on him as heavy as any avalanche of logs. He had never meant to hurt her. Would never harm a single hair on her head. Yet his actions had been the source of pain just as surely as Lud Sorenson's hand. Claire had been a virgin. He should have shown more restraint than to take advantage of her innocence, her generosity. Should have anticipated the damage.

He watched her walk away, holding herself carefully erect. He had to stop her, apologize, tell her . . .

He grabbed the ice-filled towel and raced after her. "Claire . . . wait!"

She stopped at the base of the stairway, one hand on the newel post, and gazed at him through shadowed eyes.

Cole swallowed. He didn't know how to unlock the words that clamored to be said. So many unruly emotions scrambled to break free—too many; he didn't know where to begin. He needed time to sort through them, control them. So he did nothing.

"You forgot this." Berating himself for being a coward, he shoved the dripping towel at her.

He stared after her as she made her slow, painful ascent. One emotion crystallized deep inside of him. He loved her. A simple truth. Shining and clear. A simple truth that staggered him. Terrified him.

He loved her.

TWENTY

"I came this afternoon because I was concerned about you." Sophie gave Claire a sympathetic smile over the rim of her teacup.

"How thoughtful of you. But as you can see, I'm fine."

"Did you know you gave me quite a fright at the river drive? I thought for a moment you were about to swoon."

"That's ridiculous," Claire said with a small laugh. "I've never fainted in my life."

"Nevertheless, you turned ghastly pale." Sophie nudged the plate of chocolate eclairs she had brought as a special treat from Murdoch's Bakery closer to Claire.

Not wanting to appear ungracious, Claire helped herself to one of her guest's pastries. "Umm, delicious," she said after sampling the eclair.

"If you had fainted, I certainly would have understood. Everyone was certain Cole was dead after watching him disappear in front of their very eyes." She shuddered delicately at the recollection.

Claire's appetite faded. Sophie's reminder brought back the scene in vivid detail. "I feared that as well," she confessed.

"You were absolutely distraught."

"I'm certain I wasn't the only one who felt that way." Sophie's watchful gaze made her self-conscious. Claire couldn't rid herself of the notion that Sophie was waiting for her to say or do the wrong thing. "No one wants to see another person meet their death," she said.

"Of course not," Sophie concurred. "But as James said that day, men know the risks when they sign up. It's not as though they haven't seen graves all along the river. Even I know death isn't permitted to slow down the drive."

Claire was appalled by Sophie's comments. They revealed a callous side of the woman's nature she hadn't suspected. Or, she thought more charitably, Sophie might simply be parroting the sentiments of her husband, a man she obviously adored.

"They bury men right where they take them out of the river," Sophie continued. "Then tack their boots to the nearest tree. James told me about a fellow they called Flour-barrel Fred. Fred, so the story goes, had no relatives, so they made a casket out of two flour barrels. They shoved one barrel over his head, the other over his feet. Thank goodness," she giggled, "Fred wasn't very tall."

"Let's change the subject, shall we?" Weary of tales of death and mayhem, Claire started to set her plate aside.

"Claire!" Sophie admonished. "If you don't finish your treat, you'll make me think you didn't like them."

Claire obediently took another bite of the rich, custard-filled dessert covered with an even richer chocolate icing. "You and your husband make an attractive couple," she said, striving to find a more agreeable topic.

Sophie preened under the compliment. "James is quite handsome, isn't he? I never swoon, either, but I thought I might the first time I saw him."

"You've never told me how you and James met."

Sophie took another sip of tea, her expression dreamy. "James had escorted Priscilla to a musicale I was hosting. We exchanged pleasantries while going through the buffet line. He complimented me on the diamond necklace I was wearing that had once belonged to Mother."

"Did you fall in love with him immediately?" Claire asked. *As she had with Cole.*

"It was love at first sight." Sophie gave a girlish laugh. "Later James admitted it was for him, too. At the time, however, he was new in town and just establishing his law practice. He said he didn't want to appear overeager. That he wanted to prove himself worthy of me. For a while, I despaired he might never come courting. But all that changed when Father died unexpectedly."

"That must have been a difficult period for you," Claire murmured. She set her half-finished pastry on the table and poured them both more tea.

"I don't know how I would have managed without him. James was everything a woman could ask for—polite, attentive, charming—absolutely perfect. He proposed to me as soon as it was proper. Our life is wonderful, except..." A cloud passed over her features.

"Except...?" Claire prodded gently.

Sophie dismissed Claire's question with a wave of her hand. "Our life *is* wonderful in every way. In every way," she repeated emphatically.

"I'm sure it is." Claire thoughtfully stirred her tea and kept her tone neutral.

Sophie daintily blotted her mouth with a linen napkin. "Naturally, James stopped seeing Priscilla and began courting me after Father died."

Intrigued by the story, Claire asked, "Was Mrs. Garrett upset when that happened?"

"For a while, but she got over it." Sophie gave a nonchalant shrug. "Priscilla never lacked for suitors. She liked men," she confided, dropping her voice, "and not always ones that were in the same class as my James."

Claire filed the information away with the intention of examining it later. "I admit I'm overly curious about Priscilla Garrett. I know very little about the woman whose daughter I care for."

"Priscilla and I mended our friendship and promised each other never to let anything stand in the way of it again." Rising, Sophie arranged the folds of her mauve silk skirt. "I'd love to stay and chat, but I really must get ready for Alice Howard's dinner party. Alice is eager to show off her new cook. She ordered oysters shipped all the way from Boston. Have you ever tried oysters, Claire?"

"No, I haven't."

"The first time I tried them I didn't really care for them." Sophie collected her bag and parasol. "They're . . . I'm not certain how to describe them . . . slimy. Slimy, salty, and a bit chewy. They tend to slide right down one's throat."

Slimy? Chewy? Claire's stomach revolted at the description.

Sophie must have noticed her expression. "You're looking a trifle peaked, Claire. Perhaps you should rest a while before darling Daisy wakes from her nap."

"I might do just that," Claire murmured as she accompanied her guest to the door. Never in her life had she taken a nap in the middle of the day, but right now the idea held enormous appeal. A short rest might help calm her suddenly queasy stomach.

One foot out the door, Sophie turned. "Shame on you, Claire," she scolded. "You kept me so busy talking about James that I almost forgot the real reason for my visit."

Claire felt a dull ache build behind her eyes. She wished Sophie would hurry and leave so she could lie down. "And that was . . . ?"

"I know I promised to do all I could, but . . ."

Apprehension increased the pounding inside her skull. "Go ahead, Sophie, say what you must."

"I hate to upset you when you're looking so wan," Sophie demurred.

"I insist." Claire wanted to shake the woman. Instead, she gritted her teeth and waited patiently.

"Since you insist, dear. There is a candidate for your job who looks quite promising. Mabel Holland has excellent credentials and glowing recommendations. She's expected to arrive sometime within the next ten days. Cole is adamant about interviewing her personally. I tried my best, but I'm afraid I can't find fault with her application."

"I see." Claire clutched the door handle. She had secretly known this moment would come. It was inevitable, really. Yet with every passing day, she had dared dream. Parting with Daisy would be painful. And leaving Cole would be like cutting out part of her heart.

"Maybe once Mrs. Holland arrives, she'll decide she isn't suited for life in a small town. One can always hope."

Claire nodded weakly. Even the slightest motion aggravated her nausea. She needed more than hope; she needed a miracle.

"You know I'm on your side, don't you?"

"Of course I do. You've been a friend to me."

"It'll all work out for the best, you'll see." Sophie patted her on the cheek. "Now go take that nap while you still can."

By the time Claire reached her third-floor room, her insides were twisting into knots, and the knots were being drawn tighter. She barely made it to the chamber pot before heaving the contents of her stomach. She knelt on the floor, wracked by spasm after spasm of vomiting.

Finally, weak and exhausted, she fell onto her bed and promptly fell asleep.

No sooner, it seemed, had her eyes closed when she was awakened by a loud pounding. At first she thought it was her head, then she realized the noise came from the closed bedroom door.

Claire groaned. Swinging her legs over the edge of the bed, she stumbled across the room. Opening the door, she found an irate Alma Dobbs glowering at her.

"The kid's awake and bawling her head off."

"I'll be right down," Claire mumbled, smoothing her disheveled hair with shaky hands.

The housekeeper's expression, however, underwent a subtle transformation once she got a good look at Claire's face. "You look like crap," she announced without preamble.

Claire managed a sickly smile. "Funny, that's exactly the way I feel."

"Whatsa matter? Somethin' you ate?"

Rich golden custard, heavy chocolate icing. The mere thought of the eclair she had just consumed sent Claire racing for the chamber pot. When she raised her head, Alma handed her a damp towel. "Thanks," she whispered.

"Get back to bed."

"But Daisy . . ."

"She's fine. Wide awake and playin' with that stuffed rabbit she likes."

Claire sank down on the mattress, her head in her hands as she struggled to think through the nausea and bone-splitting ache in her temples. "But I thought you said . . ."

"So I lied to you. Whatya gonna do, shoot me?" Alma squinted down at her and studied her with a practiced eye. "What happened to your face?"

Claire lightly touched her bruised cheek. She had nearly forgotten last night's altercation with her father. Strange, Sophie hadn't said a word. But maybe she was too well-bred to mention it. "I . . . ah. I ran into a wall."

"Hmph," Alma sniffed. "Looks to me like you ran into somebody's fist."

"It's of little consequence."

"Never known Mr. Garrett to raise his hand to a lady."

"Mr. Garrett had nothing to do with this."

"Then who hit you? Your no-count father, or was it your brother?"

"Please, Alma, I don't want to talk about it."

"Thought as much." Alma stuffed her hands into her apron pockets. "Didn't think, even for a minute, it was Mr. Garrett who done that to you. Cole Garrett might not have grown up with all the advantages, but he's a gentleman through and through all the same. Never known him to lose control around a woman. He treated Priscilla well, probably better than she deserved."

Claire wrapped her arms over her midsection and

rocked back and forth, only vaguely aware of what the housekeeper was saying. Cramps sharp as a double-bitted axe slammed into her. She knew any minute she was going to be sick again.

"Lie down," Alma said, her voice heavy with resignation. "I'll take care of the kid 'til Mr. Garrett comes home."

Cole was astonished to find Alma Dobbs waiting his return, and even more surprised to see Daisy in her arms. "It's after six," he said, frowning. "Did Claire get called away?"

Alma bobbed her head. "In a matter of speaking, you could say that."

"I'm in no mood for riddles, Alma. Just tell me in plain English—what the hell is going on?"

She jiggled the baby, the action a bit awkward and unpracticed. "Claire took sick."

"Sick . . . ?" His irritation vanished in a heartbeat. "If her father or brother had anything to do with this, so help me . . ."

"She's been heaving her guts out ever since Mrs. Lamont's visit," Alma interrupted impatiently. "Made her chamomile tea with a drop or two of peppermint. She couldn't even keep that down."

"Where is she? Do you think I should send for the doctor?"

"That ain't up to me." Alma thrust Daisy into Cole's arms with obvious relief. "She's up in her room. You might want to check on her."

Cheerful and free from unpleasant odors, Daisy appeared no worse for having been in Alma's care. A vast improvement over the last time, Cole noted absently. "It was good of you to take care of Daisy."

"Hmph!" Alma snorted. She untied her apron and, slipping out of it, hung it from a peg near the door. "Just don't go makin' a habit of it. Still don't like babies."

Before the door slammed behind her, Cole, with Daisy in the crook of his arm, bounded up the stairs two at a time. He barged in, not bothering to knock. He stumbled to a halt when he found Claire curled on her side, her face leached of color.

"Claire..."

A fresh paroxysm of pain contorted her face as she tried to rise up on one elbow. The attempt left her panting for breath. Cole had seen enough. "I'm sending Tim to fetch Doc Wetherbury."

Too weak, too ill, to protest, Claire rushed for the chamber pot.

Cole waited downstairs while Doc Wetherbury examined his patient. In the interim, he had fed Daisy her supper and was contemplating giving her a bottle and putting her to bed early.

Daisy yanked on his tie with a tiny hand, then launched into a volley of syllables only she could understand.

"I need you to be a good girl tonight, Peanut, so I can take care of Claire." He pried his tie free, but gave up when she attacked it again seconds later.

Hearing Doc's footsteps, he stopped pacing and met him at the foot of the stairs. "Well, Doc, what's wrong? Is she going to be all right?"

"Little one's growing like a weed." Doc gently chucked Daisy's chin. "As for Miss Sorenson, let her rest. When she feels up to it, have her take small sips of the chamomile tea Mrs. Dobbs prepared. Time will do the rest."

"But she will be all right, won't she?"

"In most cases, this runs its course."

Cole expelled a deep breath, then another thought hit him as Daisy gave his tie a playful tug. "The baby...? What Claire has isn't contagious is it?"

"Doubt it." Doc retrieved his derby from the ornately carved hat rack.

"Why's that?"

"When I asked what she had to eat today, Miss Sorenson said the last thing she ate was a cream-filled eclair Mrs. Lamont brought over." He tilted his derby over one brow. "I expect soon I'll be paying a call at the Lamont residence."

When Claire opened her eyes, it was dark outside. Sensing she was not alone, she turned her head and watched a familiar figure separate itself from the shadows.

"Feeling better?" Cole asked quietly.

"A little," she returned in a raspy voice she scarcely recognized as her own. To her profound relief, she discovered she did feel better. The wicked pounding in her head had subsided to a gentle throb. Her stomach, while still unsettled, was less rebellious than it had been earlier.

"Good, then try a little of Alma's tea. Here, let me help you."

Before she could protest, he eased her into a sitting position, held the cup to her mouth, and urged her to drink. She drained the contents thirstily, then sank back down. "From now on, I swear the only baked goods I eat are those I make myself."

The corner of his mouth lifted in a small smile. "Yours probably taste better anyway."

As he sponged her brow with a moistened cloth, Claire wondered if she had gone to heaven. Being pampered was a luxury, a novelty. The thoughtfulness of the act brought tears to her eyes. "I could easily grow accustomed to this kind of treatment."

"You deserve to be taken care of for a change."

Claire's eyes flew wide. "Daisy . . . ?"

"Sleeping like a baby." He grinned at his own humor, then grew serious. "Sleep late tomorrow morning—and that's an order. I'll stay home until Mrs. Dobbs arrives. I think perhaps I can prevail upon her to help with Daisy.

JUST BEFORE DAYBREAK 257

She doesn't seem to mind as long as you're close by. In the meantime, I'll sit here until you fall asleep."

Again she was touched to the verge of tears by his thoughtfulness. She blamed the uncharacteristic weakness on her present condition. "You don't have to sit with me," she said, clearing her throat. "I'm not an infant, or an invalid."

"Humor me." He pulled up the blanket and tucked it around her shoulders with the same tenderness he accorded Daisy. "Unless you object, I'll stay until you're asleep. I don't like the idea of you being ill and all alone."

He brushed a kiss across her brow. "Sleep well, love."

Sleep well, love. Hard as Claire tried, she couldn't recall if Cole had actually whispered those words as she dropped off to sleep the night before, or if they'd been part of a dream.

Though still fatigued after the violent bout of illness, she felt remarkably better. Tea and toast, then later a bowl of Alma's chicken soup, had miraculously stayed in her stomach. Her gaze wandered over the pretty pink-and-white nursery where she sat rocking Daisy, a book of fairy tales opened in front of her. If Sophie was correct, and there was no reason to doubt her, she would soon be leaving. When that day came, it wouldn't take long to gather her belongings. Since she had no savings and still hadn't paid off Nils's debt, she imagined her next job would be barmaid in Padraig Mulligan's saloon. A prospect she didn't relish.

"You got a visitor."

Closing the book, Claire found Alma hovering in the doorway. "Who is it?"

"Homer Bailey. Says Chief Tanner sent 'im with a message."

Claire's throat went dry at the mention of the chief of

police. She had dreaded a visit from her father. This was worse, much worse. "What sort of message, did he say?"

"Won't tell me a blamed thing. Closemouthed as a clam, that one."

Claire clutched Daisy tightly as she hurried through the upstairs hallway and down the stairs. Alma bustled close at her heels. Homer Bailey, his narrow chest puffed with importance, stood in the entryway. He stopped eyeing the furnishings in the parlor when the women drew near.

Claire forced her voice to remain cool and unruffled. "Mrs. Dobbs said you had a message for me from Chief Tanner."

He handed her a sealed white envelope with her name in bold, black script. "Chief asked me to deliver this personally. Said to give it to you—and," he shot a telling look at the housekeeper, "no one but you."

Alma scowled at him. "What do you take me for, you sawed-off runt, someone who'd read another person's mail?"

"Just followin' orders, ma'am."

"You're tracking dirt on my clean floor. Consider your job done and get your bony arse out of here."

Confronted with Alma's irascible disposition, Homer's self-confidence slipped a notch. With a mumbled good-bye, he departed with undue haste.

With trembling fingers, Claire tore open the envelope and quickly scanned the paper inside. She felt sick after reading the brief message. Not a physical illness this time, but one that pervaded the spirit.

"Well, what's so all-fired important that Bailey refused to hand it over?" Alma asked querulously.

"Chief Tanner wants to see me in his office at four o'clock."

Alma held up her hands in protest and backed away. "Don't ask me to watch that kid again. I told Mr. Garrett last night I wasn't going to make it into a habit."

"I wouldn't dream of imposing on your generous nature," Claire replied, amused in spite of the seriousness of the situation. Alma looked . . . terrified? . . . at the prospect of caring for one tiny baby girl. "I'll take Daisy with me. The fresh air will do us both good."

Tanner kept Claire waiting in the hall, even though she had arrived promptly for their appointment. Unable to sit still, she walked up and down the corridor with the baby in her arms.

"Well, Daisy girl, if Chief Tanner thinks this will make me even more nervous, he's absolutely right."

Daisy, tired of being held, was starting to squirm when the outer door to his office finally opened.

"The chief will see you now," a moon-faced clerk announced, looking a shade embarrassed for the long wait.

Thanking the man, Claire squared her shoulders and followed him. She was ushered into a roomy office where Tanner stood, his back turned, hands clasped behind him, staring out a bank of windows to the street below.

Tanner didn't invite her to take a chair, so she stood, shifting Daisy's weight from one arm to the other while she waited for him to speak.

"Explain again why Cole Garrett couldn't have murdered his wife," he said at last.

"I've already told you all this."

"Then you shouldn't mind repeating it."

"Very well . . ." Puzzled at the request, she related the sequence of events from the time Priscilla Garrett had left the house until Claire had left early the following morning.

He waited for her to finish, then turned around and fixed her with a cold-eyed stare. "You're absolutely certain of the times."

"I'm positive. Mr. Garrett arrived home shortly before midnight. I didn't leave the house until the next morning."

"It isn't too late, Miss Sorenson, to change your story. Witnesses often relate erroneous details after an event. If that's the case, I'm willing to excuse your faulty memory."

"There is nothing faulty about my memory, Chief. Are you still certain Mrs. Garrett was killed after midnight?"

"Without a doubt."

"How can you be so sure?" Claire was curious. She didn't recall ever actually hearing how Tanner knew the time Priscilla died.

He studied her for a long moment, but finally answered. "Mrs. Garrett was wearing a small gold watch pinned to the bodice of her dress. It was broken during the attack. The hands read exactly twelve-fifteen."

Claire's gaze locked with his. "Cole Garrett was home well before the hall clock chimed the hour of midnight."

"I have only your word for that."

Daisy spotted an inkwell on the police chief's desk and reached for it. Claire struggled to hold the straining infant, who seemed to grow heavier by the minute. Tanner had a devious mind, she suspected. Why did he choose now to question Cole's alibi? She needed to remain calm, rational. "I remember distinctly you telling me there were witnesses who saw me leave the Garrett home on the morning in question."

The smile he gave her could have put frost on a pumpkin. "Therein lies the crux of the problem, Miss Sorenson."

Apprehension tightened around her chest like a tourniquet, making breathing difficult. "Please come to the point, Chief Tanner. The baby isn't going to be patient much longer. She tends to be very, very insistent when it's her dinner time."

Tanner's mouth tightened as he shot a quick glance at the restive infant. Apparently deciding Claire's wasn't an idle threat, he ceased playing coy. "After further questioning, Karl Detmeijer, the milkman, states his eyesight is weak. He said he may have been mistaken about seeing you leave the Garrett home."

Her knees suddenly jelly, Claire sank uninvited into a hard chair. "And Mr. O'Brien? Has he been subjected to further questioning as well? Is he also claiming weak eyesight?"

"There's no call for sarcasm, Miss." Tanner sat down at his desk, steepled his fingertips, and stared at her across an expanse of polished oak. "With Mr. O'Brien's recollection, I fear there's a problem of a different sort." He waited a beat before adding, "Are you aware Tim O'Brien has a prison record?"

Claire gaped.

"I see this comes as a shock." He leaned back in his swivel chair, his gaze never leaving hers. "Mr. O'Brien served time in the state penitentiary. Only recently was he eligible for parole. Cole Garrett, it seems, was the sole person willing to hire him. Without a job, O'Brien would still be locked away."

"What does this have to do with whether or not he saw me leave?" Even as she asked the question, Claire anticipated the answer.

"O'Brien feels a great deal of loyalty to his employer. He'd do—or say—anything to protect him, including claim he watched you leave on any given morning. Considering his background, he would have no credibility in a court of law."

"I see," Claire said, her voice faint. Stunned, she tried to absorb everything Tanner had just told her. "Just one more question, Chief Tanner. Of what crime was Mr. O'Brien guilty?"

"Murder."

Claire imagined she saw a glint of malice in Tanner's deep-set eyes.

TWENTY-ONE

Claire sprang from the chair the instant she heard the sound of horse's hooves on the drive. From the kitchen window, she watched impatiently while Cole dismounted his bay and handed the reins over to Tim. She fired her first question at him as he came through the door.

"You've known from the beginning, haven't you?"

He quietly closed the door behind him. His eyes scanned the countertops, taking in the jar of fresh-baked cookies and a cherry pie still steaming from the oven. "I must say," he said in a mild tone, "this is a vast improvement over last night when you turned green at the mere mention of food."

She refused to be diverted from the subject foremost in her mind. "Chief Tanner summoned me to his office this afternoon."

His expression underwent a change at the mention of the chief of police. "Did he, now?" he drawled. "And what matter occupied the chief's calculating mind?"

"Tim O'Brien."

"The sawmill is in full operation." Hooking a forefinger, he tugged the knot of his tie loose. "I could use a drink. Shall we go into the library? We can talk there."

Claire hesitated a moment, then followed his broad back down the hallway and into the library. He went directly to the sideboard and removed a stopper from a crystal decanter. "Care to join me?"

"No, thank you," she retorted.

"Nothing worse than a teetotaler—unless it's a reformed teetotaler." He splashed a generous portion of brandy into a glass, took a sip, then turned to her. "Care to elaborate on what Chief Edward Tanner had to say about Tim?"

She knew then and there she had guessed right. Cole had known all along about Tim's prison record. He showed no surprise and little interest about a man who was an integral part of his household. "He said Tim was a murderer."

"Sit down, Claire. You're poised like a deer ready to flee a hunter's rifle."

She sank down into a leather chair that flanked the settee. Not only did Cole show no surprise at the news, but even more damning, he made no attempt to deny the allegation. *Prison? Murder?* Until now, she had nursed a kernel of hope that Tanner had lied. But that tiny kernel had turned out to be an empty hull.

Cole took the chair opposite her and leaned forward, his elbows resting on his knees, his eyes riveted on hers. "What Tanner told you, Claire, is true. But surely you must realize things aren't always black or white, but many shades of gray."

She linked her fingers together in her lap. "Will you please explain why you'd hire a man guilty of murder?"

"Because Tim's a decent man. No one else would give him a chance."

"But he killed someone."

He rose to wander about the room, drink in hand. "Precisely what did Tanner tell you?"

She frowned, trying to recall their exact conversation. At the time, she had been too stunned to ask for details. Her mind had grappled with the concept of a man she not only knew, but liked, being capable of such a heinous crime. "Actually, Chief Tanner told me very little. He seemed to be enjoying a version of cat and mouse—with him as the cat and me the mouse."

He swore under his breath. "Tanner's a sneaky bastard. He deliberately led you to think the worst."

"You mean Tim didn't kill anyone? He's innocent?"

"It's not that simple."

Hope rekindled, shriveled. "I'm confused. Suppose you explain the varying shades of gray."

Cole ceased his restless prowling and rested his weight against the desk, his ankles crossed, in a deceptively relaxed pose. "Tim killed a man, all right. But in a fair fight. Both parties had been drinking heavily at the time. When the other man insulted Tim's sister, a drunken barroom brawl ensued. Versions differ as to who took the first swing. It doesn't really matter. What does matter is that the man was knocked to the ground, struck his head on a rock, and died. Tim was held accountable."

Claire silently digested all Cole had just told her. Fistfights, she knew, were a common occurrence not only in Brockton but in every sawdust city along Lake Michigan's shoreline. Lumbermen tended to resolve their differences with their fists rather than a gun. The same scenario could just as easily apply to Nils.

"Tim paid his debt, served his sentence," Cole continued grimly. "One of the conditions for his parole was that he have a job, some source of responsible employment."

"And that's where you came in."

"No one else wanted to hire him. No one was willing to give him a second chance."

"So you volunteered."

"Yes, and I've never regretted my decision."

Claire digested this for a moment, then cleared her throat and asked, "Did Mrs. Garrett object to having a convict as her coachman?"

His broad shoulders lifted in a negligent shrug while his smoke-gray gaze remained fixed on her face. "She never objected because I didn't tell her."

"I see," she murmured. But she wasn't sure she did, not really. Part of her argued that Cole should have been honest with his wife about the background of a man hired specifically to drive her about. Another part admired Cole's determination to give another man a second chance. Even if that chance involved subterfuge.

Cole rubbed the back of his neck. "I suppose that was wrong of me, but . . ."

She shook her head to stem his apology. "As you said, there are many shades of gray. What you did may have been wrong, but your motives were sound."

"All Tim wants is to do his job and put the past behind him."

"Tanner implied Tim would be willing to lie for you."

Nonplused, Cole sipped his brandy. "I suppose he would. Tim's extremely loyal."

"You don't suppose, do you," Claire nervously pleated the folds of her skirt, "that he might have been the one who . . . killed . . . Mrs. Garrett?"

"No!" Cole shoved away from the desk. "I'd stake my life on it."

Claire drew a shaky breath. She wished she could let the subject drop, but couldn't. Not yet. "Don't you find it rather odd that Tanner, knowing Tim's prison record, isn't considering him as a possible suspect?"

Cole's mouth twisted in a humorless smile. "I don't find it strange at all. Think about it, Claire. Tim killed a man in a barroom brawl. That's an altogether different matter than driving a peavey hook into the back of a woman he barely knew."

Claire had to admit his reasoning made sense. "I see your point, but there is still one more thing that bothers me."

Cole took another swallow of brandy and studied her thoughtfully over the rim of his glass. "Out with it, Claire. Don't disappoint me now by suddenly being afraid to speak your mind."

She wasn't certain, but thought she detected a trace of

admiration layered beneath the sarcasm. "Tim disliked Priscilla. He told me so himself."

"Disliking a person and killing them aren't necessarily related. While I don't like Edward Tanner, I certainly don't plan to shoot him dead." He resumed prowling the room, picking up objects at random, then setting them back down. "Brock has convinced Tanner I'm guilty. He's positive that killing Priscilla was my way out of a loveless marriage and a means to take control of her fortune in the process. As far as Brock and Tanner are concerned, I'm the only logical candidate."

"Someone hated Priscilla enough to want her dead. Maybe . . ."

"Let it go, Claire," he growled. "I won't have anyone cast aspersions on Tim's character—not even you."

She caught her lower lip between her teeth to hold back a volley of questions and doubts. From the stubborn thrust of Cole's jaw, she recognized that further argument would be useless. The day's revelations tumbled like rocks through her mind and refused to settle. The Tim O'Brien she knew was indeed a gentle man. Thus far, nothing in his conduct suggested otherwise. He acted genuinely pleased when she plied him with cookies or pie. She recalled the utmost care with which he handled a newborn kitten. Perhaps Tanner had been right in saying Tim would lie to protect Cole's alibi. But wasn't intense loyalty more virtue than fault?

Yet Priscilla Garrett's murder remained unsolved. Someone, probably someone she knew well, had taken her life. But who? Could Tim O'Brien's dislike have turned into hatred?

The house was dark by the time Cole returned from the sawmill. He wished now that he had returned home earlier to spend time with his daughter, hold her, rock her, kiss her good night. Time was precious. And he had the horrible feeling it was quickly running out.

Not bothering to light a lamp, he wandered into the darkened library and poured a drink he didn't really want. He slumped down on the settee where he stared unseeingly into the cold, empty hearth. What would become of Daisy if Brock had his way, and he was sent to prison? Would Brock step up and do the right thing for his only grandchild? The thought of Daisy growing into girlhood in those austere surroundings was daunting. Would his contented, happy baby become a sad and lonely child? Perhaps Sophie and James Lamont could be prevailed upon to oversee Daisy's growing up.

His thoughts bleak, he rested his head against the back of the settee. He had selfishly hoped that Claire would be there to greet him upon his return home. Somehow, she always managed to cheer him. She filled a hole, an emptiness, deep inside. He had never needed a woman before, never needed anyone, until she came along. She shed light where there was darkness, warmth where there was cold. Lovely, sweet, giving. Everything a man could want in a woman. And want her he did with every cell in his body. He ached for her. Yearned for her.

Loved her.

How the devil had that happened? It was all wrong. Hopeless. Impossible. He had nothing to offer her but grief, heartache, and possible scandal. The greatest gift he could bestow would be to send her away before her future was as tainted as his. People were already talking about them. What if they linked her with Priscilla's death? The mere thought made his mouth go dry. No, he decided, he had to send her away. Soon.

"I heard you come in."

He turned at the sound of her voice and found her standing in the doorway. He had no idea how long he had sat alone in the dark. "I tried to be quiet."

"I thought you might have worked through dinner. I

brought you something to eat." She set the tray on a small table. "Bread and toasted cheese, just like my mother used to fix whenever I was unhappy."

He patted the settee next to him. "I'll eat if you promise to keep me company."

"All right."

Setting his untouched brandy aside, he picked up one of the thin slices of bread. He nibbled only to be polite, then realized he was starving. He couldn't recall if he had eaten anything since a hurried breakfast many hours ago. "Umm," he sighed. "These taste great."

Claire looked on as he polished off the entire plate of sandwiches, then wiped his hands on a napkin. "It's nice to see my efforts weren't wasted."

"You always know how to make me feel better." Reaching for her hand, he brought it to his lips, brushed a kiss across her knuckles, and pressed another in her palm. He felt her shudder in response. "I wish I could give you something special in return," he whispered.

Turning to face him, she placed her hand gently on his cheek. "I don't want anything you can't give freely." Then, leaning into him, she lightly grazed his mouth with hers.

Cole felt as though he were about to explode. The contact had been slight, the result incendiary. Spark to dynamite. His arms went around her, locking her in his embrace, and he deepened the kiss. His mouth ravaged hers, needing—no demanding—a response. He traced the slick inner lining, savored the raspy texture of her tongue. Absorbed the small hum of pleasure, a contented purr, at the back of her throat. Claire held nothing back, showing him without words that her hunger was as insatiable as his.

They were both breathless when he finally dragged his mouth from hers. "We shouldn't," he whispered raggedly. "I shouldn't."

"Hush." She silenced him by placing her finger against his mouth. Then, smiling, she began to remove the pins from her hair one by one.

He swallowed hard as her hair, that glorious silky riot of dark gold, tumbled around her shoulders. The soft gleam in her eyes was no longer that of an innocent, naïve girl, but that of a woman. A woman experienced in ways of the flesh. One who knows how to give as well as receive.

"Claire, are you sure . . . ?"

With tantalizing slowness, she started to unbutton her blouse. "Look at me, Cole," she demanded softly. "Look at me and tell me you don't want this as much as I do."

Cole's blood heated at her boldness. Any denial strangled in his throat. For a man who took pride in his self-control, all his vaulted discipline vanished in a heartbeat. He wanted her, all right, wanted her with a desperation that bordered on painful. "You're like a drug, an addiction," he confessed. "Whenever I'm near you, I feel green as a schoolboy in the throes of his first crush. I can't get you out of my head during the day. At night my body aches for the feel of yours."

"Just as mine does for yours." Rising to her feet, she took his hand.

Cole slowly got to his feet, but resisted her effort to draw him with her. It was hard to think rationally when she stood before him with her hair wildly streaming down her back and her blouse open to reveal round, firm breasts that pushed against the thin fabric of her chemise. Desire bore down on him like a river of logs blasted from a jam. "We need to be sensible," he protested feebly. "People are already starting to gossip."

Claire scrutinized the shadow-filled library with exaggerated care. "Funny, but I don't see anyone here but the two of us."

"I'm just trying to be sensible." Did she have any idea how difficult it was to refuse her? His head urged caution; the lower half of his body urged something else entirely. "Your reputation will be ruined beyond repair."

"Isn't it a little late to worry about my reputation?"

"I thought it only fair to remind you of the risks involved."

"I don't want to be sensible. You said in certain situations that the risks are worth the danger." Stretching up on tiptoe, she kissed him again, let her mouth linger, then drew back. "Is it so wrong to want to steal one more night?"

Her softly spoken plea was his undoing. All his resolve unraveled at hearing a yearning in her voice that echoed his own. "No," he replied. "How can something that feels so right be wrong?"

Picking her up, he swept her off her feet and carried her upstairs. Once in the privacy of Cole's bedroom, they quickly divested each other of clothing. Their mouths hot and hungry, their bodies pressed together, they tumbled onto the bed. Cole's lips left hers to travel along the sweep of her jaw, then journeyed down her throat, stopping to revisit the highly sensitive spot at its base where the pulse beat a frantic rhythm.

Claire's eyelids fluttered shut, and a low-pitched hum escaped. He marveled at her responsiveness to every touch, each caress. Her body was an instrument specifically designed for his pleasure.

Lowering his head, he laved her nipple, then suckled gently. She fisted her hands in his hair, her back arched in silent offering. When he turned his attention to the other breast, her hands moved restively up and down along his sides. Her need to touch, to feel, communicated an urgency that matched his.

Together they explored each other's bodies, charting smooth planes, exploring hollows, discovering the new and delighting in the familiar. Sighs and endearments. Moans of delight, whispered encouragement. The sounds, the music, of love.

Her hair smelled faintly of lily-of-the-valley. Like a blind man, he ran his hands over her flesh, memorizing each sweet nuance. He loved the smooth perfection of her skin, the baby-softness at the undersides of her breasts.

JUST BEFORE DAYBREAK

But above all else, he loved her passion. She was just as eager to taste and touch in return. They were partners in an erotic, choreographed dance where the participants moved to a primal rhythm only they could hear. Each caress, each gentle flick of the tongue, brought them a step closer to a breathless, heart-stopping finale.

He kissed her again, deeply, searchingly. The world dropped away, leaving only the two of them dizzily whirling in an ageless dance of love.

Then, bracing his hands on either side of her, he slid down her slender body. Dipping his head, he sipped the beads of desire. Her fingers tangled in his hair. Another delicate taste, and she cried out as her body convulsed with pleasure.

Covering her writhing body with his, he plunged into her. The muscles of her pelvis contracted around his shaft, held him gloriously captive. He fought to prolong the exquisite pleasure, then surrendered to a force beyond his control. His breathing harsh, ragged, he pumped his hips back and forth while his blood drummed to a quickened tempo. Faster, faster, faster.

Claire held him in a fierce embrace, her arms twined around his shoulders, her legs locked around his waist. Together they sprinted, senses spinning, spiraling, toward the ultimate fulfillment. Together they shattered into a million shiny fragments of pleasure so intense it left them reeling . . .

. . . and marveling at the magic.

An interminable time passed before Claire, her head nestled in the hollow of Cole's shoulder, murmured, "Is it always like this when two people make love?"

"It's never been this way for me before."

A simple sentence, the words priceless, an invaluable gift. She placed her hand over his heart, felt the strong, steady, beat pulsate beneath her palm. "I love to touch you, feel you," she confessed. "Your body is perfect. Like a marble statue in some faraway museum."

"Now, that's a novel thought." He gave a harsh laugh at her description. "Priscilla turned away in disgust at the sight of my bare chest. She claimed I was too brawny—nothing more than a rough, uncouth lumberjack. She preferred less muscular men with lean, aesthetic builds."

Drowsily replete, she caressed his splendidly sculpted torso, savoring the textures, the crispy mat of dark curls, the taut, bronzed skin beneath. "In my opinion, your body is a testament to strength. It speaks of your ability and determination to overcome all obstacles in your path. I can't think of anything more appealing."

He picked up a lock of her hair and played with it. "You never fail to amaze me."

She drew a deep breath, let it out in a sigh, and decided to be brave. The moment seemed a rare time for confidences. "Cole . . ." she began haltingly.

"Umm, yes, sweetheart?"

"You said once that you and Priscilla never shared the same bed. Yet the two of you created a child together. Surely you must have cared for each other at some point in your lives."

He grew still. Even his breathing seemed to slow. Claire feared he wasn't going to respond when he surprised her. "Daisy isn't my child."

Claire's hand ceased its idle exploration. *Daisy wasn't his?* How could that be? Had she possibly misunderstood? Countless times she had watched them together, seen the outpouring of love. Of course Daisy was his. There was no other logical explanation for the affection she had witnessed. "I—I don't understand," she said at last.

"Daisy is my child in every way that matters, Claire, but I didn't father her." The admission came hard. "Priscilla was pregnant with another man's child when we married."

"Ohh." Claire didn't know what to say.

"Priscilla's pregnancy prompted our marriage. Her father was livid when he learned she was pregnant. She absolutely refused to name the baby's father, so Brock assumed the man was already married. Instead of sending her away, he decided marriage to a respectable businessman of his choosing might tame her wild streak."

"And you were the 'respectable businessman' chosen for the task."

"I was hand-picked. I was unmarried, had achieved the status of lumber baron, and would benefit from a wife of Priscilla's social standing. Business, pure and simple. A disaster from the start."

Claire wished she could see Cole's expression, but knew from the bitterness in his voice that he regretted the decision. Everything was starting to make sense to her now. It explained the antipathy Priscilla felt toward Cole, the man her father had coerced her into marrying. Cole had become the target of all her pent-up anger and resentment.

"To sweeten the pot, Brock made me an offer he knew I couldn't resist. He signed over several valuable timber tracts. He even financed a loan on equipment I needed for the sawmill. All I had to do was marry his daughter and give her child my name. I'm not proud of my actions. I have only my ambition and greed to blame."

"Stop punishing yourself, Cole. Many marriages begin for reasons other than love. Knowing you as I do, I'm sure you tried your best to be a good husband just as you're a good father to her child."

"After Priscilla and I eloped to Chicago, her father spread word around town that ours was a wild, impulsive love affair. When we returned from our so-called honeymoon, he hosted the largest reception Brockton has ever seen. That marked the beginning of the most miserable period of my life. I'm sure Priscilla shared my sentiments. In fact," he gave a harsh laugh, "that was probably the only thing we shared. We had absolutely nothing in common. She couldn't even bear to be in the same room."

For the first time, Claire felt sympathy toward Priscilla Brock Garrett. Both Priscilla and Cole were hopelessly trapped in a loveless marriage. He by ambition and

Leonard Brock's machinations. She because of her willful nature . . .

. . . and a child conceived out of wedlock.

Cole toyed with a strand of her hair, watching it sift through his fingers. "After," he cleared his throat, "after they found her dead, I was sorry, of course, but a small part of me secretly rejoiced she was out of my life. To this day, I despise myself for feeling that way."

The torment reverberated in his voice. Claire knew with certainty that he still harbored guilt, not that he had wanted her dead, but because he couldn't truly mourn her passing. "Priscilla caused you pain. You only wanted the pain to ease."

He released a long, shuddering sigh. "Brock blames me for everything that happened. I feel there's a dark cloud over my head ready to burst . . . and I'm going to lose everything that matters to me."

Drawing away, Claire levered herself on one elbow so she could see his face. The bleak resignation etched across his features tore at her heart. Tenderly, as she might with a small child, she smoothed the hair from his brow. "Somehow, Cole, you must have faith. Everything will work out for the best, you'll see. Remember, it's always darkest just before daybreak."

TWENTY-TWO

"Well, boy, if you think you're getting off scot-free for killing my daughter, think again."

Cole glanced up from the sheaf of papers in his hand as Leonard Brock entered his office and closed the door behind him. The ear-piercing whine of circular saws and the perpetual cloud of sawdust that hovered in the air had given him a pounding headache. And, as if that wasn't enough, now he had his former father-in-law's visit to contend with. "I've told you before, Leonard, and I'll say it again. I didn't kill Priscilla."

Not waiting for an invitation, Brock lowered his substantial girth into a chair across from Cole's desk. He sat like a giant Buddha, hands folded over his abdomen, a pocket watch on a heavy gold chain swagged across his paunch. "No . . . ? That's not the way I see things."

"Well, you're mistaken."

"Am I?" Brock raised a bushy, ginger-colored brow.

"I've a business to run." Cole gestured toward his cluttered desktop. "I'm too busy to play games. Say what you came for, then let me get back to work."

Brock fixed his pale green gaze on Cole's face. "Heard there's something going on between you and that Sorenson woman."

"She's Daisy's nurse," Cole retorted, his voice clipped.

"She's your whore."

Bounding to his feet, Cole tossed the papers down on

his desk, sending other pages fluttering to the floor unheeded. "Get out, Brock! I refuse to tolerate your insults."

"So it is true," Brock chuckled. "I figured that might get a rise out of you. You didn't disappoint me."

"Don't you have anything better than slander to occupy your time?"

Brock laboriously climbed to his feet. "I thought you needed a personal reminder that justice will be served. It's only a matter of time, you know."

Cole studied his visitor more carefully. He hadn't seen Brock since the reading of the will. In the interim, Brock's normally ruddy complexion had taken on an unhealthy rubious undertone. Extra flesh seemed to have accumulated on his already large frame, giving him a bloated look. For the first time, Cole questioned the man's mental stability. Had Priscilla's death warped Brock's mind? His actions and accusations were those of a man obsessed. "Didn't I honor my part of our agreement? Why are you so convinced I'm guilty of killing Priscilla?"

"No one else has a better motive, boy. It's not the first time a cuckolded husband killed an unfaithful wife. Won't be the last." He lumbered toward the door. "Had my suspicions from the start, but hearing Lamont read my girl's will erased any doubt."

"You think I killed her for the money." Cole's voice was flat, void of emotion. The pounding in his head intensified.

"As I recall, she left you in charge of a sizable trust fund. You got rid of a wife you never really wanted and got a heap of money in the bargain. But you'll pay, boy, I'll see to it that you pay."

"Get out," Cole snapped, but Brock had already left.

"I realize this must be unpleasant, dear. But surely you can't be surprised. You must have realized this day would come."

Speechless, Claire stared at Sophie Lamont. Words deserted her. Where was the woman who had befriended her? Who had volunteered to help her remain on as Daisy's nursemaid? "But . . . I thought," she faltered.

"Considering the circumstances, we're fortunate to find an applicant with Mrs. Holland's impeccable background."

Claire's gaze shifted to the redoubtable Mrs. Holland. Mabel Holland, a tall, spare woman, appeared to be a matron in her fifties. A small, straw bonnet sat flat on top of her head of salt-and-pepper hair that had been pulled back into a neat bun. Her gray traveling costume was simple and unadorned except for a small enameled brooch pinned over her heart. Though she had a no-nonsense air about her, she had the grace to look discomfited at being privy to her predecessor's dismissal.

"As you well know, Claire, this is for the best." Sophie gave Claire a knowing look that spoke volumes. "Mr. Garrett mentioned something about putting Mrs. Holland up at the Pinewood Hotel overnight. But after talking matters over, Mabel and I decided there was no reason to delay her employment. Isn't that right, Mrs. Holland?"

Mabel nodded. "Throwing away good money for a hotel would be frivolous."

"So she's agreed to start at once." Sophie beamed her approval.

"I see." Claire barely managed to squeeze out the words.

The shock of meeting her replacement had left her emotions encased in ice, a fact for which she was grateful. There would be time later for tears. Seeing that the matter was settled, there didn't seem to be much else for her to do other than go upstairs and pack her belongings. And bid good-bye to Daisy.

"I know from experience how difficult this is, Miss Sorenson. Trust me," Mabel Holland advised, "the sooner the child becomes accustomed to another nursemaid, the better."

Claire nodded. "If you ladies will excuse me, I'll gather my things."

She forced herself to maintain a dignified pace as she exited the parlor. She silently swept past Alma, who loitered in the front hallway, feather duster in hand. No doubt the housekeeper had eavesdropped shamelessly on their conversation. Claire, not trusting herself to speak, continued up the stairs.

Even with the new additions she had purchased, her belongings were few. It took less than twenty minutes to remove every trace of her presence. She stood on the threshold of the attic room she had occupied and looked around. A lump lodged in her throat. She would miss the large, airy room with its big windows overlooking the backyard. The lilacs were just beginning to bloom, and robins were building a nest in the big maple tree. Servants' quarters or not, she had been the happiest here she had ever been. Each day had been precious, filled with small treasures such as a baby's smile—or a lover's caress.

Sadly, she picked up her battered valise, then, stiffening her back in resolution, went to say farewell to her tiny charge.

Claire left the valise just outside the door and tiptoed into the nursery. Daisy lay sound asleep in the midst of her afternoon nap. The lump in Claire's throat seemed to grow into the size of a watermelon as she watched the child sleep. She bit down on her lower lip to keep it from trembling. To Claire's mind, Daisy resembled a tiny princess, all pink and white with her cheeks flushed with sleep, her mouth soft and sweet as a rosebud.

Reaching out, she touched the baby's downy curls. It hadn't been wise to fall in love with a child that wasn't hers—would never be hers—but she had been unable to resist the infant's appeal.

Just as she hadn't been able to resist the child's father.

"Love you, Daisy girl," she said in a strained whisper.

Knowing that the longer she stayed, the closer she was to losing control, she left the nursery as quietly as she had entered. She needed to keep her emotions under tight rein.

Under no conditions did she intend to create a scene in front of Sophie Lamont or Mabel Holland. She heard the murmur of their voices coming from the parlor, but kept walking. She wanted to slip quietly out the kitchen door with little or no fanfare.

Alma Dobbs waited for her in the kitchen, her arms folded over her ample bosom. "The kid's gonna miss you somethin' fierce."

Claire shifted her valise from one hand to the other. "I'll miss her, too."

"Too bad you couldn't have stayed on. I was just gettin' used to you."

This was high praise indeed coming from the housekeeper. Claire cleared her throat. "Mrs. Holland seems highly competent."

"Yeah, but does she bake?"

In spite of her heavy heart, Claire had to smile. "Goodbye, Alma."

Alma saw her to the door. "Tim would be happy to give you a ride. I can ask 'im."

"Thank you, but I'd rather walk."

And she did. Down the porch steps and out the drive without a backward glance. It wasn't until she left Brockton behind that she let the tears fall.

"Where's Claire?" Cole asked the instant he stepped foot inside the house after a long, frustrating day.

Alma shot him a fulminating look as she hung up her apron. "Supper's on the back burner. Should still be hot."

"Dammit, Alma." He shoved an impatient hand through his hair. "I need to talk with Claire. Is she in the nursery?"

"Nope." Alma picked up her handbag.

Cole's patience was at an end. "Then, where the hell is she?"

"She's gone."

"Gone . . . ?"

"And if you ask me, which you haven't, it was a pretty shoddy way to get rid of her. You oughta be ashamed of yerself."

"What are you talking about?"

"Claire Sorenson was good enough to take care of the kid when no one else would. You mighta at least had the decency to tell her yerself that her services were no longer needed. But, no, you sent Sophie Lamont to do yer dirty work. Thought you had more guts." Alma sailed out, slamming the door in her wake.

Gone? How could that be?

Determined to find out, Cole bounded up the stairs two at a time. His answer came in the form of Mabel Holland. He found the woman he had interviewed earlier that day humming to herself while she bent over the crib and changed Daisy's diaper.

"Mrs. Holland . . . ?" he said, stepping into the nursery. "I'd like a word with you."

"Certainly, Mr. Garrett." After expertly securing the flannel diaper, she turned to him with an expectant look on her face. "Is anything wrong?"

"Why aren't you at the Pinewood Hotel? I specifically remember telling you that your duties wouldn't start until tomorrow."

Daisy's legs furiously kicked air. "Gaa!"

Immediately, Cole went over and picked her up. Delighted at her father's attention, Daisy grabbed at his nose.

"I hope I'm not overstepping my bounds, Mr. Garrett, but you're spoiling the baby. It isn't wise to hold a child every time it makes the slightest sound. They're apt to become little tyrants."

"I'll take my chances," he retorted, his voice cold.

Mabel Holland's lips firmed in disapproval, but she wisely held her tongue. "As to what I'm doing here, sir, Mrs. Lamont questioned the sensibility of spending a night in a hotel when I could begin immediately. I agreed. It would be a waste of money."

He groaned inwardly. Claire had been kicked to the curb like yesterday's garbage. That had never been his intention. He had planned to tell her personally about Mrs. Holland. To break the news gently, tell her how grateful he was for her help, then offer her a generous severance bonus. He couldn't imagine how she must feel. Knowing her as he did, she must have been devastated to part from Daisy.

"Sir, if there's nothing else you wish to say, it's time for the baby's dinner. I like to establish a set routine as soon as I come into a household."

Cole relinquished a none-too-happy Daisy into the arms of her new nursemaid. "There is one more thing, Mrs. Holland. The 'baby' has a name. I suggest you use it."

"Yes, sir."

Cole stood for a long time, hands in his pockets, and wondered what he should do. He wanted to find Claire and explain what had happened. Why would Sophie deliberately countermand his instructions? Did she have Daisy's best interests at heart, or were her actions prompted by more devious reasons?

Head bent in thought, he left the nursery and started down the hall toward his bedroom. Midway there, he paused. Metal glittered in a shaft of light. Stooping down, he retrieved a hairpin lying at the edge of the carpeted runner and nearly concealed by the swirling floral pattern. A hairpin such as Claire used. Had it dropped unnoticed the last time they made love? He curled his fingers around it and pressed it into his palm. His indecision fled.

"What are you doing here?" Claire stared aghast at finding Cole on her doorstep.

"Are you all right?"

"Yes. Yes, of course I am." Her mind felt sluggish. She hoped her eyes still weren't red and puffy from tears she had shed earlier.

"May I come in?" he asked quietly. "I need to talk to you."

"This isn't wise." She darted a glance over her shoulder. Neither her father nor Nils was home. She had no idea where they were, but knew they wouldn't be happy to return and find Cole Garrett in the parlor.

"Please, Claire. I'm not leaving until I do."

She heard the determination in his voice, a personality trait of his that she found both endearing and exasperating. "Very well," she relented. "Let's go for a walk."

Seeing some of the tension leave his face told her he hadn't been nearly as confident as he had tried to seem. Her barriers slipped a notch, knowing he was vulnerable. Snatching her shawl as she closed the door behind her, she joined Cole outside. She set a brisk pace away from the house, following a narrow path along the garden's edge toward the fringe of woods beyond.

It was a beautiful night. A peaceful night. Stars glowed like millions of sparks against the black velvet canopy of sky. The air was permeated with the gentle, sweet fragrance unique to early spring. The smell of soft earth and delicate blooms. Twigs snapped and leaves rustled as night creatures scuttled back and forth. A moon, silver and bright, dangled over the treetops like a broken locket. But Claire was impervious to the evening's spell. An unsettling disquiet settled over her like an invisible cloak.

"Where are we going?"

She slowed her pace once they reached the cover of trees. "There's a small clearing just ahead with a stream running through it. No one will see us there."

"I'm not afraid of your father, or Nils. We've done nothing wrong."

"Why ask for more trouble?"

Cole didn't argue.

Upon reaching the clearing, she turned to confront him. She hoped to hide her tumultuous emotions behind a mask of calm, but wasn't sure she could succeed. Cole had a way of peeling away pretense. Stripping off the thin layer of civility to expose raw emotion. Anger, passion, love. Especially love.

Cole took a step closer, then stopped. Something in her expression must have warned him to keep his distance. He dug into his pocket, held out the hairpin. "I thought this might be yours."

She stared at the object in his palm in frank amazement. "You came all the way out here, risked the wrath of my family, to return a hairpin?"

He shifted uncomfortably. "It gave me an excuse, albeit a lame one, to see you again."

Her barriers slipped yet another notch or two. She was touched that he wanted to see her. Even though she knew it had ended, she yearned for him—and the intimacy they had once shared. "Now," she said, taking the hairpin and slipping it into her pocket, "tell me the real reason for your visit."

"I wanted to explain about Mrs. Holland. And I want to tell you how sorry I am."

"You don't owe me an apology." She hugged her shawl around her, let out a sigh. "You were honest from the start. I always knew my position was tenuous. That I could be replaced at any time."

"Dammit, Claire, I didn't intend for it to happen that way. I planned to break the news to you as gently as possible, give you time to grow accustomed to the notion."

"It wouldn't have hurt any less." The stream babbled over its rocky bed. Not even the soothing murmur could ease the ache in her heart.

"I gave Sophie specific instructions to take Mrs. Holland to the Pinewood Hotel until I had a chance to tell you myself. I don't know how she could have misunderstood."

"Today, tomorrow, the end result would have been the same." What choice did she have, she wondered, other than to accept the inevitable. "An amputation is best done quickly."

He winced at the analogy. "I understand how you must have felt. I'd feel the same if—when—I'm ever parted from Daisy."

Cole's admission shocked Claire out of her apathy. She had been so absorbed in her own misery, she had forgotten the peril he faced. His future rested in the capricious hands of fate. More specifically, in the hands of Police Chief Edward Tanner. "Forgive me," she said quietly. "I've been selfish. How is Daisy handling the changes?"

The corner of his mouth quirked at the mention of his daughter. "Cranky. I think she misses you."

Not trusting herself to speak, Claire let her gaze drift across the stream toward the darkened stand of trees. Then, drawing a ragged breath, she turned her head to meet Cole's compelling smoke-gray eyes. "Mrs. Holland seems competent. As a matter of fact, I liked her. Daisy will, too, once she's adjusted to someone new."

"I suppose," Cole agreed, but sounded doubtful.

"It was wrong of me to let her grow so attached. Love is such a powerful emotion. I didn't know how to stop it from happening until it was too late." The same could be applied to the child's father, she admitted silently. But if she had to make a choice, she'd gladly do the same all over again. *Some rewards outweigh the risks.* Cole's words resounded through the recesses of her mind.

"Brock paid me a visit today," Cole said, breaking the lengthy silence.

All her senses sharpened at hearing the name. The man was a viper waiting to strike. "What did he want?"

Cole broke off a branch from a nearby bush and absently tapped it against his thigh. "I have no way to prove it, but I suspect that Brock was somehow responsible for the log jam."

"But why? How?"

He shrugged. "Just a feeling I have. It never should have happened. I sent an advance crew to scour both sides of the river and remove any possible obstructions. They reported the way was clear. Yet the log jam occurred in spite of my precautions."

The night air seemed fractionally cooler. Claire drew her shawl more firmly about her. "Didn't Brock stand to lose financially if the drive wasn't a success?"

"Brock has deep pockets. He's not above finding a man's weak spot, then offering a bribe. Take me, for a prime example," he said, his voice bitter. "Bought and paid for. A husband for his daughter."

"Brock frightens me," she confessed, recalling the way he had watched her at the river drive. His intensity had seemed to bore a hole through her. "Be careful, Cole. I fear he's capable of almost anything."

"I'm afraid you're right."

"What did he want today?"

"Brock wanted to remind me that justice would be served. That Priscilla's death wouldn't go unpunished." He snapped the branch he held, the sound unnaturally loud in the strained aftermath of his words. "Maybe he's right, Claire. Maybe I am partially to blame for what happened to her."

"Why would you even think such a thing?" she asked, appalled.

He tossed the broken stick aside. "If I had tried harder, been more attentive, maybe Priscilla wouldn't have felt compelled to look elsewhere. I should have made a greater effort to be the type of man she admired."

Claire moved closer, started to put her hand on his sleeve, but stopped herself in the nick of time. "Marriage should be a partnership. You can't assume the entire blame for its failure."

He smiled. "How did you get to be such an authority on the state of matrimony?"

"I'm not," she admitted sheepishly. "It's just a theory of mine."

"I rather like your theory."

With his smile, the last of her barriers came tumbling

down. She wanted to smooth the tiny lines of worry bracketing his mouth. Brush back the shock of dark hair that fell rakishly over his brow. She didn't trust herself near him. "We should head back toward the house," she said at last. "No telling what Pa might think or do if he finds me gone again."

They walked through the woods side by side. For a while neither spoke.

"Why does Leonard Brock hate you so?" Claire said at last, breaking the silence. "Why is he so determined to hold you responsible for his daughter's death?"

"I think he blames himself for what happened to Priscilla. Sometimes I think he even blames Daisy for ever having been born. That if he hadn't insisted that Priscilla marry me, things might have turned out differently. In his mind, he's managed to twist it around somehow so that this is my fault—or Daisy's. I think beneath his gruff exterior, he truly loved his daughter, but didn't show it. Now it's too late. Maybe like the rest of us mortals, he wishes things could have been different."

"If wishes were horses . . ."

". . . beggars would ride," Cole completed the saying.

"It seems to me," Claire mused, "there's a wealth of guilt being manufactured between the two of you. I'm not denying that Priscilla's death was a tragedy, but did you stop to consider that perhaps she was responsible for the events leading to her own demise? It's possible that it had nothing to do with you, or her father, but stemmed from her own selfish desires. I don't mean to speak ill of the dead, but isn't it conceivable that she could have made someone angry enough to want her dead?"

He enfolded her hand in his, the action as natural as the sun coming up every morning. "I only wish to God they'd catch the bastard."

Her fingers twined with his. *A simple touch. What could be the harm?* "Do you have any idea who Daisy's father is?"

"None."

Claire peered through the darkness and tried to read his expression, but his face was swathed in shadow. "Do you think Priscilla had a lover?"

"I wondered if there might be someone, but didn't care enough to find out. Sad state of affairs, isn't it, when a man couldn't care less who his wife is having an affair with?"

They emerged from the woods and, with the moon as their guide, continued along the path leading toward the house. Claire frowned, her mind racing. "Priscilla must have been meeting someone. Or else why go to the sawmill at that hour? Brockton is a small town. Surely someone knows more than they're willing to tell."

Cole stopped walking abruptly, jerking her to a halt. "Claire, you're starting to worry me. We're talking about murder. Promise me you'll leave the matter in Tanner's hands. If a person killed once, they might not hesitate to do it again."

Shrugging off his concern, Claire adopted a conciliatory tone. "There's no call to worry. Whoever killed Priscilla is probably far away by now."

"Promise me you won't do anything foolish." His grip on her hand tightened.

"Very well. Since you insist, you have my word."

"Good." He relaxed visibly. "There's one more matter I wish to settle." Reaching into an inner pocket of his jacket, he withdrew an envelope and offered it to her.

She stared at it with blatant suspicion, but made no move to accept it. A coldness settled over her.

"Go ahead," he urged. "I want you to have this."

"You're offering me . . . money?"

"Consider it a bonus for a job well done. I don't know how I would have managed without you all these weeks."

She withdrew her hand from his. "I was well compensated for my time."

"Humor me, Claire. Take the damn money. I know you need it."

Temper danced along her nerve endings, sparked in her eyes. "Don't insult me—or what we shared—by offering me money. If I accept it, then I'm no better than the whore some seem to think I am."

"Whore . . . ?" A muscle ticked in his jaw. "Is that how you view yourself?"

They faced off, angry, hurt, ready to lash out and wound. Neither noticed the figure that bore down on them.

TWENTY-THREE

Nils charged out of the darkness like an enraged bull and flung his cane aside. Shoving Cole and Claire apart, he pushed himself between them. "Keep your hands off my sister, you bastard!"

"Nils!" Claire tugged on her brother's arm, but to no avail. It felt like tempered steel beneath her touch. He refused to budge.

The two men stood toe to toe. Nils seemed oblivious of the fact that he was four inches shorter and at least thirty pounds lighter than his adversary. Cole, while he didn't appear eager for a fight, didn't look like he would shy away from one, either.

"Stay away from her, Garrett! Haven't you caused enough trouble already?"

"Your sister, Sorenson, has a mind of her own. She doesn't take orders from a drunk."

"In case you haven't noticed, I'm stone-cold sober. But drunk or sober, the advice is the same."

"Nils, you're embarrassing me."

Nils ignored Claire's protest. "You're only sniffing after her skirts because no decent woman will have anything to do with you."

Cole drew back his arm and struck Nils solidly on the jaw. The lightning-quick blow landed the younger man on his backside in the dirt. Cole loomed over him, ready to strike again. "You ought to be ashamed of yourself. In case you haven't noticed, your sister's as fine as they come. I refuse to stand by and let anyone insult her—especially those who should know better."

Nils wiped the trickle of blood from his mouth with the back of his hand. "Can't you see, Sis?" he appealed directly to Claire as she helped him to his feet. "He's only using you. Deep down, Cole Garrett considers himself too good for the likes of us. He's a rich, powerful lumber baron. You're only good enough for scrubbing floors, changing dirty diapers, and when he needs a warm, willing female in his bed."

Claire saw Cole's hands bunch into fists. "No, Cole, don't."

Cole let out a pent-up breath and stepped back.

Did Nils's words carry a grain of truth? Claire felt ill at the possibility. Cole had never spoken of anything permanent between them. Never expressed how he felt. Their time together had always been measured in increments of hours and days. Never weeks, months, a lifetime. Had she deceived herself into believing he cared for her at least a little?

"What kind of game are you playing, Garrett? Are you trying to ruin her life just like you ruined mine?"

"If you weren't so bullheaded, you'd admit I didn't ruin your life. I'm sorry about your leg, but it was an accident, pure and simple."

Anger vibrated through Nils like the plucked string of a fiddle. "If you had been doing the job like you were supposed to instead of showing off, I'd still have full use of both legs. Damn you!" he cried.

Nils launched himself at Cole, his hands going for his throat. Both men went down, rolling over and over in the unplowed garden plot. Cole put the palm of one hand against Nils's face and shoved. With his other hand, he tried to pry Nils's fingers from his neck. Claire grabbed onto her brother's shirt and tugged. The fabric gave with a loud rip, and she was left clutching a strip of plaid cloth.

"Nils, Cole, stop this," she pleaded. "Stop before one of you gets hurt."

"I hate you. I hate you. I hate you." Nils punctuated each outburst with a jab to Cole's ribs.

The pair continued to fight in spite of Claire's pleas for them to cease.

"It's all your fault," Nils panted.

Claire watched, helpless at the sight of the two men she loved most beating each other to a pulp. She had never seen her brother like this. He was a terrier ferociously attacking a much larger, stronger breed with more valor than sense. Gradually, she realized Nils was landing the brunt of the blows. Cole, on the other hand, appeared to be on the defensive, protecting himself as much as possible from the pummeling.

After what seemed hours, Cole levered the weight of his body, flipping Nils onto his stomach and pinning his arm behind him. "Are you finished?" he asked, breathing heavily. "Got it out of your system?"

"Let me up," Nils half-sobbed in frustration.

"Are you finished?" Cole repeated.

"Yes," Nils hissed. "Now get off me."

They slowly climbed to their feet. Eyeing each other warily, they knocked clods of dirt from their clothing. Blood dripped from Nils's lip, and his eye was already beginning to discolor. Cole's face bore a series of minor cuts and scrapes. Lining peeked from a tear in the shoulder of his jacket.

"What happened to you, Nils, was an accident." Cole looked Nils in the eye. Each word was slow and distinct.

"You were the top loader that day," Nils spat. "It was your job to make sure the load was balanced. If you had done what you were supposed to, my so-called 'accident' never would have happened. Do you have any idea what it's like to have thirty logs come crashing on top of you?" Nils voice turned ragged. "To think every breath you take will be your last?"

"How much do you remember about that afternoon?"

"Enough." Nils's mouth hardened into a line. "I remember it well enough to know someone else had the job of top loader until you arrived. You just couldn't resist the chance to show off in front of the crew. Had to prove, didn't you, that you could do any job in the camp, and do it better."

Cole's gaze wavered as Nils's barb found its target. "Pride be damned, I can't deny what you say is true. I won't ask another to do a task that I haven't mastered."

"I was lead teamster. I was waiting for the sleigh to be loaded, then was supposed to drive the horses down Miller's Hill to the riverbank. You watched for a while, then sent the top loader on an errand and took over the job yourself."

Claire glanced from one to the other. She stood rooted to the ground, avidly listening, hearing the details of that fateful event for the first time.

"I thought by sending him away I was doing everyone a favor." Cole jerked off his necktie, which had come loose in the scuffle, and stuffed it in his pocket. "The man assigned to the task, Ben Hinkle, was a greenhorn. I didn't want to embarrass the foreman in front of the others by questioning his choice, so I asked Hinkle to go to the blacksmith to get a chain that had been sent for repair. And that was my mistake."

"I don't understand," Claire said, breaking her silence. "How could that have been wrong?"

Cole brushed hair from his brow, only to have it immediately fall back again. "Because Hinkle brought back the wrong one. Instead of the chain that had been repaired, he returned with one that had a weak link and used it to fasten the load."

Nils looked at Cole with dawning comprehension. "Are you saying . . . ?"

"That's exactly what I'm saying." Cole's voice sounded weary now. "The chain snapped when the horses started down the steep slope, and the load gave way. You know the rest."

Nils's Adam's apple bobbed as he swallowed convulsively. "I sat perched high on top of the load. The instant I felt the logs shift I tried to jump free. They flew every which way."

Cole nodded slowly. "You did some pretty fancy footwork. I thought for a moment you were going to make it."

"Almost did." Nils's face took on a faraway expression. "Almost did," he repeated softly.

"I didn't discover the mistake until later when the blacksmith brought it to my attention. I fired Hinkle, of course, but there was nothing to be gained from making an issue of it. It wouldn't have saved your leg."

Nils was silent, brooding. Claire moved to stand next to him. Her heart went out to her brother. He had fed on anger and self-pity for more than a year. They had been his crutch just as surely as the cane he frequently used. Now that support had been abruptly withdrawn, leaving him off balance and tentative. She took his arm. This time he made no attempt to shake it free as he had done so often in the past.

"It's time for you to leave." Nils words were quiet but firm.

Cole's eyes moved from Nils to Claire. "Is that what you want, too?"

She nodded, her expression veiled. "There's no more to be said."

He looked at her long and hard, his eyes dark and intense, then turned and left.

Claire and Nils stood alongside the uncultivated patch of earth, neither speaking as Cole mounted his bay and headed toward town. It was only when the sound of the horse's hooves faded that Nils stooped to retrieve his cane and they started toward the rented farmhouse they called home.

Claire was grateful that clouds partially obscured the

moon. She didn't want Nils to glimpse the turmoil she was sure must be visible. She felt bereft. There had been an undercurrent of finality to this meeting with Cole.

A sense that a bond had been severed.

"You're better off without him, Sis," Nils said quietly.

"How can you say such a thing? You don't even know him." She felt perilously close to tears.

"There's talk he murdered his wife. I'll be happier knowing you're a safe distance."

"Cole didn't kill his wife. He isn't capable of killing anyone. He's an honorable man."

"If he's so honorable, why doesn't he leave you alone? "

She had no answer. How could she explain the strong, irresistible attraction she felt for Cole Garrett? It annihilated common sense, shredded willpower, yet made her come totally alive, made her glow.

"Nothing you can say will make me change my mind about Garrett," he said as they reached the back porch. "When all this is settled, he'll pretend he never knew you. He'll look the other way when he sees you on the street. Time comes to choose a wife, it'll be another thoroughbred like Priscilla Brock, not a mongrel from the outskirts of town."

Claire whirled to face him, unshed tears swimming in her eyes. "Is that what I am—a mongrel?"

"Hell, no, Sis. That's not what I meant, and you know it."

"Then what *did* you mean?" She hated hearing the fear in her own voice.

Nils's expression was earnest. "All I'm telling you is that Cole Garrett can have his pick of women. Mark my words, the next woman he marries will be another like his first."

Another like his first. It wasn't what she wanted to hear, but she couldn't refute the likelihood. She and Cole had been thrown together by unusual circumstances. The chemistry between them had been them powerful. Explosive. And like an explosion, devastating but brief.

"It's late," she said at last. "Good night, Nils."

***

Claire slept poorly. Just before dawn, she gave up trying. She dressed in the dark, then went into the kitchen. She could hear her father's snores reverberate through the thin walls of the bedroom he shared with Nils. Pulling out a chair, she sat down, drew up her knees, and stared across the small yard to the woods beyond. Something nagged at her. A faint bubble of memory. Whenever she was just about to touch it, it would burst, leaving her grasping at air.

From just outside the kitchen window, Claire heard twigs snap. She canted her head, all her senses alert, and waited for Nils to appear. He hadn't come into the house after his fight with Cole last night. And still wasn't home. She assumed he had gone into town to drown his sorrows at one of the few bars that would still give him credit. But except for the muted rustling and crackle of twigs, there was no sign of him.

Getting up from the chair, Claire peered into the predawn darkness. Twin yellow-green orbs stared back her. Startled, she retreated a step. Then, recovering from her fright, she laughed at her own foolishness. A small herd of deer had wandered close to the house. A large buck with an impressive rack of antlers gazed calmly back at her. Careful not to make a sound, she watched a doe and her fawn munch the branches of a young cedar tree. Then, at some indecipherable signal, the herd turned as one and bounded into the woods and disappeared.

Deer . . . ? Claire sat back down, wrapped her arms around her waist, and rocked back and forth. The half-remembered memory that had haunted the edges of her sleep returned. Closer this time, less fragile. Something to do with . . . deer?

Closing her eyes, she willed herself to concentrate. The morning following Priscilla Garrett's death, she had arrived home to discover Nils burying something out back.

Later he claimed it was the entrails of a deer he and a friend had shot. That in itself wasn't cause for alarm. Deer were plentiful in Michigan. Venison often supplemented a family's winter food supply.

Yet . . .

In spite of the cold temperature, Nils had been in shirtsleeves. And those sleeves had been stained with blood. It wasn't Nils's actions, however, that gave her pause, but his reaction. He had been ill-tempered. Secretive. Distraught. Claire's eyes snapped open, and she sat straighter. What if Nils had lied? The cold finger of fear tickled her spine, chilling her clear to the marrow of her bones. What if he hadn't buried the guts of a deer, but something far more sinister?

Nils still hadn't returned by the time Lud trudged off to work. Claire had barely concealed her impatience while her father ate his breakfast. For once she had been grateful about enforced silence at mealtime. The minute her father disappeared from view, she hurried from the house to the storage shed where the tools were kept. Removing a shovel, she began digging at the spot just behind the shed where weeds had begun to sprout from a barren patch of earth.

Bend, straighten, lift, and throw.

Her mind blank, Claire focused on the task at hand. She didn't want to think about what she might find. Didn't want to face the terrible possibility Nils had lied. Yet she couldn't rest until she learned the truth.

Bend, straighten, lift, and throw.

The mound of dirt grew with each shovelful. Blisters formed along the pads of her hands. Sweat beaded her brow. She was almost ready to admit defeat when her shovel encountered resistance.

Kneeling alongside the hole she had created, she used her hands to brush dirt aside. Her breath caught in her throat at the sight of a familiar item. Reaching down, she pulled out Nils's favorite blue jacket. A jacket covered with dirt. A jacket stiff and caked with stains. Coffee-colored stains. Stains the color of dried blood. Human blood? What other conclusion could she draw, she wondered bleakly, when there was no sign of decomposing matter?

She sat back on her heels and stared in horror at the jacket in her lap. At first her mind refused to comprehend what her eyes were seeing. But the numbing mindlessness quickly fled, leaving her besieged with doubt and fear. Nils had been burying his bloody jacket the morning after Priscilla Garrett's murder. Were the bloodstains coincidence or somehow related to her death? Her mind balked at the thought. That just didn't make sense. Why would Nils kill a woman he didn't know?

"Oh my God, Nils, what have you done?" she whispered.

Less than an hour later, the kitchen door flew open and Nils appeared. He paused when he saw her sitting idly at the table, an empty coffee mug in front of her. "Something wrong, Sis?"

"You might say that." She regarded him sadly. Where was the man who could win friends with a smile? The man with a quick wit and devilish charm. Who was this haggard, furtive interloper he had become?

Nils crossed to the coffeepot sitting on the stove. His limp seemed more pronounced, as it often did when he was tired. "Still mad because I took a swing at Garrett?"

"I want to talk to you, Nils."

He emptied the contents of the pot into an enameled mug. "If you expect an apology for what I said afterwards, you won't get one. I meant it, Sis. Garrett's trouble. He's only going to hurt you."

Nils's eyes were bloodshot, his clothes rumpled, but at least he didn't reek of cheap beer. Good, she thought—she didn't want his mind fuzzy from drink for the conversation they were about to have. Reaching down, she retrieved the jacket from the floor near her feet. "Recognize this?"

The mug slipped from Nils's hand, spewing coffee on the floor, then rolled to a stop near a box of kindling. His mouth worked soundlessly.

Claire rose to her feet, the jacket clenched in one fist. "You claimed you shot and gutted a deer. That you were burying its entrails. Why bury your jacket instead?"

Nils's face had gone deathly pale. "B-b-because," he raised a hand toward the garment, then let it drop to his side, "because it has blood all over it. It's ruined. I can't wear it like that."

"Then why not just throw it away, or burn it? Why go to all the trouble of burying it?"

"Why not?" Nils avoided her gaze. He grabbed a towel from a rack and used it to mop up the spilled coffee.

"Stop lying to me, Nils." Fury, fear, and frustration warred for dominance as Claire snatched the cloth from his hands. "I found you burying your jacket the morning after Priscilla Garrett's murder. Tell me, convince me, you had nothing to do with her death," she pleaded, her voice breaking.

At the mention of Priscilla's name, myriad emotions chased across Nils's face like clouds before a storm. Then, while Claire looked on in amazement, he sank down on a chair, buried his face in his hands, and bawled like a baby.

Of all the reactions she had envisioned, this outpouring of grief hadn't been among them. But was it rooted in guilt or in fear of the consequences? She simply couldn't fathom which. Never before had she seen Nils lose control. Not even after the accident when Doc Wetherbury had told him he might lose his leg or, at best, never regain its full use. Dear Lord, what had he done to merit this outburst?

No matter what, she loved her brother and vowed to stand by him. His gut-wrenching sobs tore at her heart. Unable to bear the sound of them any longer, she put her arms around Nils's quaking shoulders and rested her cheek against his hair. "Shh, Nils, it'll be all right." She repeated the phrase over and over as she would to comfort a child.

At last he gulped air as his torrent of tears subsided. Wiping the wetness from his face with a shirtsleeve, he kept his head bent, his gaze fixed on the floor.

More convinced than ever that her brother was guilty of a heinous offense, Claire sank down in front of him and took both his hands in hers. "Nils, you've got to go to the authorities. I'm sure whatever happened to Priscilla was an accident. You must make them understand that you never meant to kill her."

He lifted his head slowly and stared at her with dawning horror. "Good God, Sis, you think I killed Priscilla?"

"Are you telling me you didn't?" Her grip on his hands tightened spasmodically, but he didn't seem to notice.

"I loved Priscilla. I'd never harm her in a million years."

"Loved her . . . ?" Claire repeated, her voice faint.

Nils nodded. "We planned to run away together—until I got hurt, that is. Then everything changed."

The admission left Claire floundering in a quagmire of confusion. "I—I didn't think you two knew each other."

"Oh, we knew each other, all right," he said with a hoarse bark of laughter. "Better than you can imagine."

Relaxing her grip on his hands, she sat back on her heels and studied him. She was no longer as naïve as she had once been. She had experienced firsthand the irresistible, irrefutable pull of desire between a man and a woman.

And how quickly desire could flare out of control.

"You don't believe me, do you?"

She looked into her brother's tear-ravaged face, but couldn't come to terms with the fact that he had once been involved with the woman Cole had eventually married. "I'd like to believe you, but it's hard to imagine you and Priscilla Garrett."

"Priscilla Brock." Nils's voice was sharp as the blade of an axe. "Her name was Priscilla Brock back then. She barely knew Garrett, except as one of her father's business associates."

"Talk to me, Nils. Tell me everything."

He rubbed his eyes with the heel of his hand, then sniffed back fresh tears. "It started with a little innocent flirting. Not to brag, Sis, but I had my pick of the ladies before I got hurt."

"I know," Claire murmured. She remembered watching his flirtatious charm any number of times.

"Priscilla and I took an instant liking to each other. At first I was surprised that she agreed to meet me. I think it was all a game to her. A way of rebelling against her father, or maybe getting even with him for not paying her enough attention. Whatever her reason, I was different from the type she usually socialized with, different from the sort her father chose for her. We'd get together wherever, whenever, we could. It was exciting, titillating, at the beginning. Later . . ."

"Later?"

"Later it changed—at least it did for me."

Claire's cheeks burned with embarrassment, but she needed to hear him answer her question. "W—were you . . . ?" she stammered.

"Yeah." He dragged a hand though his shaggy hair. "We were lovers."

Needing time to adjust to Nils's startling revelations, she climbed to her feet and began to grind beans for a fresh pot of coffee. "What happened after your accident?"

Nils stared into space. "By the time I quite literally got back on my feet, she had run off and eloped with Garrett. After that, she wouldn't give me the time of day. Next thing I heard, she's pregnant with his kid."

Claire's hand jerked. The coffee she had been about to pour into the pot scattered across the floor. "Daisy isn't Cole's child," she said, forcing a calmness into her voice that she didn't feel.

Nils went absolutely still. "Are you certain?"

"I'm positive." Claire abandoned her attempt at making

coffee. "Priscilla was pregnant with another man's child when they married. Leonard Brock forced Priscilla to marry a man of his choosing or face scandal."

"And Cole Garrett was hand-picked for the job." Nils looked up and met her eyes. "You know what this means, don't you?"

Claire nodded slowly. "You could be Daisy's father."

And she could be her aunt!

Nils rubbed his unshaven jaw. "I gotta admit it came as a shock seeing the baby at the river drive, her being so fair and all. She doesn't look anything like her mother—or Garrett, for that matter. After a few beers I convinced myself I was crazy to even consider the possibility she might be mine."

"You can't be sure she is. There's no way to prove you're the father."

Nils's chin dropped to his chest. "Yeah, you're right," he said at last. "Even if I could prove it, the kid's better off without me. Garrett treats her like a princess."

"Brock, and later Cole, assumed the baby's father was married, and that was the reason Priscilla refused to name him. They never suspected it might be . . ." She let her voice trail off.

". . . a common lumberjack like me."

Claire wrapped her arms around her waist and studied the floor. "You still haven't explained how the blood came to be on your jacket. Was it Priscilla's blood?"

"Yes." He swallowed convulsively. "But I swear to God I didn't kill her. If I tell you the whole story, will you promise not to tell another soul? Please, Sis," he said, seeing her hesitation. "Promise? My life depends on it."

At her nod of assent, he drew a ragged breath. "I'm the one who found her body."

TWENTY-FOUR

Hugging a small package, Claire lurked behind skids piled six feet high with fresh-sawn lumber. She was determined to wait as long as necessary for the screech of giant saws to cease. She needed to speak to Cole, needed to win his cooperation. Nils's revelations of that morning had created a whirlwind of uncertainty. But enough time had elapsed for the turmoil to settle and a plan of action to form. A plan sculpted by sheer desperation.

The lives of the two men she loved most were at stake.

How could she keep Nils's secret at the expense of Cole's freedom? The answer was painfully obvious. The only way to protect both her brother and Cole was to find the real murderer.

She had listened, fascinated and horrified, as Nils recounted how he had followed Priscilla to the sawmill that fateful night. From her furtive manner, he surmised she was meeting someone. Regardless, he had resolved to talk to her, to plead for another chance. He hid in the shadows outside the sawmill, but she never came out. Thinking she might have left through another entrance, he went inside to investigate.

And he found her. Impaled on a peavey hook. The discovery was grotesque. Obscene.

Claire shuddered. It was difficult to imagine finding a body—any body, much less that of a loved one—who had been killed in such a barbaric fashion. Nils had been devastated. Unable to bear seeing his beloved with a metal shaft protruding from her chest, he had removed the peavey hook. He lovingly placed Priscilla's body on a pallet in a storage shed, then covered her with a canvas tarpaulin. Then, still in a state of shock, he returned to the sawmill, cleaned off the peavey hook, and sprinkled a thick layer of sawdust over the pooled blood on the floor. It was almost, he had said trying to explain his irrational behavior, that if he could erase the signs of violence, he could also eradicate the outcome.

When she had asked him, Nils claimed he hadn't seen the person responsible. He assumed the killer might have already been at the sawmill, patiently waiting his victim's arrival, then left unnoticed by a rear entrance.

And Claire believed him. Nils wasn't a killer. And neither was Cole.

What had happened that night? she wondered. A spurned lover. A jealous rage. Ingredients for mayhem. Her brother was terrified no one would believe his story, and he'd be sent to prison. Who would take the word of a drunk? Sadly, Claire agreed. If the police doubted her veracity regarding Cole's alibi, why would they believe Nils's declaration of innocence?

Finally, workers weary after a twelve-hour day and eager for a hot meal began to file out of the sawmill. Claire bided her time, knowing Cole was usually the last to leave. When ten minutes had passed and no more workers trickled out, she slipped out from concealment and wended her way around the skids of lumber. She stepped inside the cavernous building and looked around to get her bearings. The smell of fresh-cut wood hung heavy in the air. Twilight filtered through a series of windows set high in the walls, washing the interior in shades of purple. Sawdust had been swept from the floors and placed in huge barrels destined to be sold for insulation. Heavy machinery occupied the entire first floor.

Not seeing any sign of an office, Claire climbed the stairs

to her left. She breathed a sigh of relief at spotting a crack of light shining beneath a door at the far end of the second floor. A thin layer of sawdust muffled the sound of her approach. She saw the words, C. T. Garrett, Owner, stenciled in bold, black letters above the office entrance.

Her tentative knock was met with gruff impatience. "What is it?"

Drawing a fortifying breath, she opened the door and bared the lion in its den.

Cole sat behind a desk, buried under stacks of ledgers and mounds of paper. "I thought you had already left for the day, Bowman," he said without looking up. "Forget something?"

She cleared her throat. "I'm not Bowman."

His head jerked up at hearing her voice. "Claire!" A smile of welcome softened his features.

"Am I disturbing you?"

"Nonsense," he said, flinging down his pen and coming out from behind his desk.

Instead of moving toward him as she longed to do, she remained standing on the threshold. Guilt surged through her at seeing his face crease into a warm smile. Part of her felt as though by promising to keep Nils's secret she had somehow betrayed him. If the police knew what she knew, suspicion of murder would shift from him to her brother. How could she sacrifice one to save the other? She was trapped in a dilemma with only one way out.

Cole paused and looked at her strangely. "Is anything wrong?"

She offered him the small package. "I brought you this."

He lifted the cover and peeked inside. "Chocolate cake!" he exclaimed in pleasure. "My favorite. Don't tell me you walked all the way into town just to bring me a piece of cake?"

She blushed. "It's a flimsy excuse, I know, but no worse than you returning my hairpin."

"Touché." He gave her a sheepish grin, one that she

found endearing, then sobered. "Knowing you as I do, you must have been pretty upset to bake something this fancy."

"Do you mind if I have a seat?"

"No, of course not." He motioned to a chair in front of his desk. "Are you still upset about the scuffle I had with your brother last night?"

"Trouble has been brewing between the two of you for some time. It had to erupt sooner or later. I'm glad the truth is out in the open." She laced her fingers together to keep from fidgeting. She watched him lean his hip against the edge of his desk. So strong, so solid, so dear. And so terribly vulnerable. If he was to come away from this ordeal unscathed, he needed her help. She was his only chance.

"I'd like to think you're here because you've reconsidered and decided to accept the bonus I offered you, but I know how proud and stubborn you are. Out with it, Claire. Suppose you tell me what's bothering you."

She had rehearsed her lines over and over, but now that she was actually here, her little speech stuck in her throat. She drew in a deep breath to steady her nerves. "It's about what we talked about last night."

A wry smile tugged at the corner of his mouth. "Ah, sweetheart, we talked about a lot of things last night. You and I are rarely at a loss for words."

"About Priscilla," she blurted.

In the space of a heartbeat, his expression went from warm to remote. He picked up the pen from his desk and ran it through his fingers. "I don't think there's any more to be said on the subject."

"Oh, but there is," she contradicted.

He raised a brow, but said nothing and waited for her to continue.

"I'm convinced Priscilla holds the answer, the key, that will lead to her killer." She held up her hand to forestall the protest she saw forming. "Just hear me out. I've given the matter a great deal of thought. The only way you'll ever be free is for us to find the real killer."

"Claire, you're talking foolishness. We're not trained detectives. This isn't some child's game you're suggesting. The matter is best handled by professionals."

"Such as Tanner!" she scoffed. She saw his gray eyes grow dark and turbulent. "Is this how you want to live? Never knowing when you'll be arrested and sent to jail for a crime you didn't commit?"

"Of course not." He flung the pen down.

The monologue she had practiced on her walk into town broke free and spilled out with fervor. "Do you want Daisy to grow up without you? People talk. She's bound to hear rumors and gossip. Do you want her to hear whispers that her father is in prison for murdering her mother? If you don't do this for your sake, do it for hers. We need to take action—and we need to take it now."

"We . . . ?"

"Yes," she said, nodding vigorously. "The two of us stand a better chance to learn the truth. I think that by working together we might uncover some small detail that's been overlooked thus far. Tanner isn't even pretending to search for other suspects. And Brock, well, he's so convinced of your guilt that he's blind to any other possibility."

"Why are you doing this, Claire? This is my problem, not yours."

Because I love you.

Because I can't bear the thought of you in prison.

She bit her lower lip to keep the confession bottled inside. She didn't want him to feel obligated to love her in return. Didn't want him to feel guilty that he didn't, couldn't. Didn't want what he wasn't able to give freely and honestly. She only wished he weren't watching her so intently. "Think of your daughter, Cole. When the time comes to leave Brockton, I want to know she's cared for by the one person in the world who truly loves her. Every child deserves that much."

Cole studied her for a long time before answering, then

nodded slowly, his expression inscrutable. "All right, then. For Daisy."

Claire exhaled a pent-up breath and allowed her tense muscles to relax. "My theory is that Priscilla was killed by someone she was well acquainted with."

Cole frowned. "To my knowledge, none of Priscilla's friends has suddenly left town. If you're correct, that would indicate the killer is still in Brockton."

She leaned forward slightly. "Why is Mr. Brock so certain you killed his daughter? Is it because Priscilla named you executor of Daisy's trust fund?"

"It wouldn't be the first time money was a motive for murder." Shoving away from the desk, he prowled the cluttered office. "Initially, Brock blamed me for not being the sort of husband to satisfy Priscilla. After the reading of the will, he turned even more vindictive. That was when he first accused me of killing her for the money."

"I don't understand—if Priscilla hated you as much as you say, why did she leave Daisy's trust fund in your hands?"

"I'm not sure I understand any better than you. I wish to God she hadn't." He dragged a hand through his hair. "It's as though she's pointing a finger at me from the grave."

A chill raced along Claire's spine at the image his words conjured.

Cole picked up a gnarled wood paperweight, absently tossing it from one hand to the other. "The money supplied Tanner with a motive. However, thanks to you, I have an alibi for the time Priscilla was killed. But deep in my gut I know—Tanner's looking for a way around it."

Inwardly, Claire agreed, but knew voicing her opinion would only add to Cole's worries. "Mr. Lamont drew up Priscilla's will. Has he ever explained why she named you to oversee her trust fund?"

Cole paused, deep in thought. "I don't think he's ever said. But then, I've had so much on my mind, I might not have asked. Perhaps it's time I pay James a visit and pin down an answer."

"Is there a person Priscilla might have confided in if she were having an affair? Sophie, perhaps?"

"Possibly," Cole replied after giving the matter a moment's thought.

"What about Alma?" Claire persisted. "She's worked for Priscilla for years."

Cole resumed pacing. "Alma's loyalty to Priscilla was unshakable. If she knows any secrets, she'll carry them with her to the end."

"Surely there must be someone who can help us." Claire raised troubled eyes to his. "What about Tim? He took Priscilla wherever she wanted to go. I know for a fact he disliked her."

"No, not Tim. I'm sure if he knew anything useful, he would have mentioned it by now."

Claire didn't argue the point. Still, she entertained certain reservations about Tim. No matter how hard she tried, she couldn't dispel the feeling he knew more than he was willing to tell. "At least we have a place to start. Why don't you talk to James? Find out why Priscilla chose you as guardian of Daisy's trust. In the meantime, I'll visit Alma. Maybe I can coax her into confiding in me. Or, at the very least, give me a hint who Priscilla might have been seeing." She rose to her feet. "I'd better be on my way."

"Claire . . ." Cole stopped her just as she reached the door. "Thank you for having faith in me. You can't imagine how much it means."

She swallowed the lump in her throat and tried to summon a smile, but wasn't successful. She watched as he set the wood paperweight on the desk and slowly walked toward her.

Reaching up, he touched her cheek. "Do you have any idea how special you are?"

A tight band around her chest seemed to cut off her breathing. Even her heart seemed to stutter to a standstill. Turning her head, she pressed her lips in his cupped palm. "Special? Funny, I always think of you that way."

Framing her face with his hands, he lowered his mouth to hers. His lips brushed hers, the contact light, gentle. Incendiary. Spark to tinder. Instantly the tenor of the kiss changed, deepened. Cole pulled her into his arms. Heat flared, fusing them together. Hot and demanding, his mouth devoured hers as though he could never get enough of the taste. As though this kiss might be his last. His need fueled hers. Claire responded, caught up in the blaze of passion.

At the sound of heavy footsteps on the stairs, they guiltily sprang apart.

The partially opened door to the office slammed back on its hinges. "Well, well, well," Tanner drawled. "What have we here? A pair of lovebirds?"

Claire's gaze swept over the three men who stepped into the room. Tanner was accompanied by Homer Bailey and a third man, a policeman whose face she recognized but whose name she didn't know. All appeared formidable and unsmiling.

Cole positioned his body so that he stood between Claire and the trio. "What do you want, Tanner?"

"We're here on official business, Garrett. You can either come peaceably or make it hard on yourself. Either way, you're under arrest."

A soft moan of protest escaped as Claire grabbed onto Cole's arm. Her heart pounded furiously against her ribcage.

Bailey caught Cole's other arm and tugged. "C'mon, Garrett. Quit wastin' time."

Cole jerked free, only to freeze when the third man drew his gun.

Homer smirked at Cole. "We're here to escort you to your new home—or should I say *jail cell?*"

Tanner stepped forward. "Cole Garrett, you're under arrest for the murder of Priscilla Brock Garrett."

Bailey snapped handcuffs on Cole's wrists while Claire looked on in stunned disbelief.

Cole met the police chief's cold-eyed appraisal with false bravado. "Seems to me we've done this before, Tanner. If memory serves, you were forced to release me since I was nowhere near the sawmill at the time Priscilla died."

Tanner didn't even blink. "After the display of affection me and my men just witnessed, Miss Sorenson's story has lost credibility. Any fool could see the woman's sweet on you. She'll be lucky she isn't charged for obstructing justice by providing you with a false alibi."

At a nod from Tanner, the two policemen, one on either side of Cole, began dragging him away. "Why now, Tanner? Why after all this time?"

Tanner's thin lips curled into a smile. "Because we found the murder weapon."

Cole's jaw dropped. His face turned the shade of day-old oatmeal. Twisting in the policemen's grasp, he addressed Claire over his shoulder, "Go find James. Tell him what happened."

Before she could respond, he was hustled down the stairs and out of sight.

Claire hurried down Maple Street. She didn't have much time. Padraig Mulligan was expecting her to start work promptly at eight o'clock. But first she had to let James Lamont know Cole had been arrested. And find out why Priscilla named Cole guardian of Daisy's trust. If she was late and Padraig unhappy, then so be it. She had promised him every cent of Nils's debt would be repaid. And she meant it. To her, it was a matter of honor.

The Lamont home was far bigger and much more grand than the Garretts'. It was an imposing structure a full three and a half stories tall, if one included the solid stone foundation. Studying it, Claire wondered if the owners couldn't decide which feature they liked best so they incorporated all of them. The house was an amazing collection of turrets and gables and balconies, bay windows and stained glass transoms, and a porch that wrapped around one side. Cornices were trimmed with elaborate fretwork. Fanciful and ornate. If the house was intended to intimidate, Claire agreed it had succeeded.

She debated briefly whether she should march up the front steps or go around to the servants' entrance at the rear. She reminded herself that she had come on business, not as hired help. Squaring her shoulders, she went up the front steps and pulled the doorbell.

The bell was answered on the second ring by a housemaid dressed in a black uniform with a crisp white organdy cap and apron. "Yes?" She swept a practiced eye over Claire, quickly assessing her simple blouse and dark skirt.

"I'm here to see Mr. James Lamont. Please inform him Claire Sorenson would like to speak with him on a matter of utmost importance."

The maid pursed her lips together. For a moment, Claire feared the woman was going to refuse her request or tell her the Lamonts weren't home. "Wait here," the maid said at last, then shut the door in Claire's face, leaving her standing on the porch.

After what seemed an inordinately long time, the maid returned and ushered Claire inside and down a long hallway to a small parlor. "The Lamonts are entertaining," the servant said with a trace of disapproval in her tone. "Mr. Lamont said he'll be with you shortly."

Claire was left alone to wait. And worry. It was impossible to imagine what Cole must be going through. Though he had tried to hide it, she had glimpsed the panic—and despair—in his eyes as he was dragged off.

Tanner had said the murder weapon had been found. But if what Nils had told her was true, that was impossible. She distinctly recalled him describing how he had wiped all traces of blood from the peavey hook and replaced it in a rack of similar tools. None of this made sense, unless . . .

"Claire, this is a surprise." James entered the small parlor. He closed the door behind him, shutting out the murmur of voices engaged in light conversation. He took one look at her face and knew instantly something was wrong. "Sit down, my dear, and tell me what's happened."

Claire sank down gratefully on a settee of crushed velvet. "It's Cole," she said, in a choked voice. "He's been arrested."

"No wonder you look so distressed. Can I offer you something to drink? Sherry? Tea, perhaps?"

"That's very kind of you, but I don't have much time."

He sat next to her, took her cold hands in his, and rubbed gently. "There, there. Suppose you tell me exactly what happened."

Everything spilled out in a rush. James listened attentively, interrupting every so often to ask a pertinent question.

"A murder weapon, eh?" he mused. "Don't worry, my dear. I'll go down to Tanner's office and see what I can find out. But," he squeezed her hands reassuringly, " I must warn you, it doesn't look good."

Sophie swung open the parlor door. "What's this all about?" she inquired in a brittle voice, her eyes darting from one to the other.

James immediately released Claire's hands and stood. "I'm afraid Miss Sorenson came with some rather shocking news."

"Really?" She arched a dark brow.

Claire got to her feet. "Cole's been arrested."

"Oh, dear, what a pity." Sophie smoothed a hand over her sleek French twist. "But surely this didn't come as a surprise. Leonard Brock usually gets what he wants."

Claire was appalled by her friend's seeming indifference to Cole's plight. But this was hardly the time to demand an explanation. Instead, she turned and offered her hand to James. "Thank you for seeing me, Mr. Lamont. You will do what you can to help Cole, won't you?"

"Of course." He smiled at her, the picture of concern. "I'll go immediately."

"But James, we have guests," Sophie protested.

He gave his wife a look of mild reproach. "I'm sure you

can entertain our guests in my absence. Cole has been a client for years. I simply can't turn my back on him in his hour of need."

"Of course you can't, dear." Sophie bestowed a loving smile on her handsome husband, then turned to Claire. "I'll have Anna show you to the door."

Claire's smile felt as though it were plastered on. "That's quite all right, Mrs. Lamont. See to your guests—I can see myself out."

It wasn't until after she left the Lamont home that Claire remembered she hadn't asked James about the trust fund. What if the answer turned out to be so simple, so obvious, that everyone had missed it? What if Priscilla had simply named the one person, the only person, who truly had Daisy's best interests at heart to guard her inheritance? Who better than Cole? He was the most logical one to oversee the child's welfare. Instead of insuring her daughter's future, Priscilla had inadvertently put it in greater jeopardy. How ironic.

Mulligan's Bar was already crowded and noisy by the time Claire arrived a half-hour late. Padraig, leaning on the bar, his ever-present cigar clamped between his teeth, spotted her immediately as she wound her way through the mass of patrons.

"Yer late," he said by way of greeting.

"It couldn't be helped." Claire tied on an apron and reached for a tray.

He nodded, his shrewd blue eyes never leaving her face. "Just don't go makin' it a habit. I might not always be so understandin'."

"I won't, I promise."

Shifting his cigar to the corner of his mouth, he stared at her long and hard as though trying to make up his mind about something. She returned the look without flinching.

"Fine, then," he growled. "Get to work and remember to smile like I told you earlier."

By the time closing came, Claire couldn't decide which hurt more, her feet or her head. But the merry jingle of coins in her apron pocket more than compensated for any discomfort.

"You done good, lass." Padraig gave her a broad wink. "Had my doubts when those two clowns were hamming it up to get your attention, but you handled them just fine."

Claire smiled, her first genuine smile of the evening. "They both had to be close to seventy."

Padraig grinned back. "But you made them feel like a pair of randy young bucks." He took out his cigar and studied the tip. "Heard about Garrett bein' arrested. Couldn't been easy, workin' tonight. You shoulda said somethin'."

She kept her expression schooled as she unloaded a tray of dirty glasses into a pan of sudsy water. "Working kept my mind occupied." Her mouth curved in a wry smile. "Usually when I'm worried, I bake. I already filled the cookie jar today. And made a chocolate cake besides."

Picking up a rag, Padraig polished the already shiny stretch of walnut. "Bet you're a pretty fair cook, too."

Claire took off her apron, folded it neatly, then stowed it under the bar. "You've been very kind, Mr. Mulligan."

"Padraig," he corrected her. "Friends call me Padraig. Or Paddy. Don't spread the word around you think me kind. I got a certain reputation to protect. Have to admit, though, I'm rather taken with the notion, seein' how the compliment comes from a pretty lass like yourself."

Why, Claire thought, astonished, he was flirting with her again. After the day's horrendous events, she teetered precariously on the brink of hysterical laughter.

"You look ready to drop. Go home, Claire, and get some rest. You'll find Mike Donahue waitin' for you outside. He lives not far from your place and agreed to see you home safe and sound."

Padraig Mulligan's thoughtfulness was nearly her undo-

JUST BEFORE DAYBREAK 315

ing. Claire impulsively rose on tiptoe and brushed a kiss across his cheek. Then she ran out before she embarrassed them both by bursting into tears.

TWENTY-FIVE

Claire chose late afternoon to visit Tim O'Brien. Try as she might, she couldn't rid her mind of the notion that Tim might somehow be involved in Priscilla's death. Or, at the very least, harbor secrets that might help prove Cole's innocence. At any rate, she had decided to ignore Cole's advice and confront him with her suspicions. She could ill afford to ignore any possibilities. Not when Cole's freedom—his life—was at stake.

She swept a glance over the Garrett house, but there was no sign of either Alma or Mabel Holland. Slipping around the back, she entered the carriage house. Gertie, Tim's tabby, peeked out at her from the stall nearest the door. Her marmalade-colored kitten batted at a shadow in a square of fading sunlight.

Though she didn't see Tim, she followed a tapping sound coming from a tack room at the rear of the building. She found him hunched over a bench repairing a leather harness. He looked up from his work when he caught sight of her, but there was no smile of welcome on his lean face. They studied each other for a long moment in silence, each taking the other's measure, gauging character, trust, loyalty, friendship.

"S'pose you heard about Mr. Garrett." Tim's opening gambit was more statement than question.

"That's why I'm here."

He didn't reply, but went back to his work.

"Cole didn't kill his wife."

"I know that," he muttered, not looking up.

She never took her eyes from him. "I have a feeling you know a great deal more than you're letting on."

His mouth set in a stubborn line. Avoiding her questioning stare, he picked up a cloth and began to rub saddle soap into the leather.

"You once told me you'd do anything for Cole. You said you owed him. Is this how you repay his kindness?" Stepping farther into the room, she fought the urge to grab the polishing rag from his hands and fling it aside. She wanted to force him to look at her. Make him tell her what she needed to know.

"Nothin' I can do."

"Isn't there?" She was relentless. "Cole gave you a second chance when no one else would give you the time of day. If not for him, you'd still be in prison. I know you're keeping something from me. I can feel it. How can you do nothing when Cole could spend the rest of his life in prison for a crime he didn't commit?"

"Go 'way. Leave me alone."

"What are you hiding, Tim?"

Tim tossed the harness down and brushed past her. Claire, more determined than ever, followed close on his heels. Picking up a pitchfork, he worked hay loose from one of the bales stacked nearby.

"Did you kill her, Tim?"

He stopped what he was doing to look at her in amazement. "Is that what you think? That I killed her?"

His shock seemed genuine. It took Claire a moment or two to gird herself against a rush of sympathy and press on. "Cole didn't kill Priscilla—but someone did."

Tim's expression turned mulish. "Don't mean I killed her."

"You didn't like Priscilla Garrett," Claire persisted. "You told me so yourself."

His grip tightened on the pitchfork's handle. A muscle in his jaw worked spasmodically. He pointed the sharp tines at her. "I *didn't* kill the bitch!" Each word was punctuated with a jabbing motion.

Claire belatedly felt an inkling of fear. She had ignored Cole's warning to leave Tim alone. She had conveniently set aside the fact that Tim O'Brien had killed a man in a fit of rage. She eyed him with renewed suspicion. His body was compact, wiry, tough. Strong enough to drive a peavey hook into a woman's unprotected back. It had been foolhardy to come here alone and goad the man into revealing his dark secrets.

She surreptitiously glanced around, searching for an escape route, but Tim stood between her and the nearest exit. She took a half-step backward. If she could manage to reach the relative safety of the house, she'd have the added protection of Alma Dobbs and Mrs. Holland. She moistened her lower lip with the tip of her tongue. "At least tell me why you disliked Priscilla so much." she said, keeping her voice calm with effort.

Just then, Gertie, oblivious to the tension in the air, sauntered up to Tim and wound in and out between his legs. Tim tossed the pitchfork aside. Bending down, he scooped up the cat and started petting it. Gertie purred with contentment.

"I'm not proud of what I done," he mumbled, his eyes on the cat's sleek coat. "Mr. Garrett deserved better from me."

Claire was struck by the odd contrast between Tim's innate gentleness with animals and the violence she knew him capable of. "If you know anything, anything at all, that might help Cole, please tell me."

After a silent debate with himself, Tim raised his eyes to hers. "The bitch was blackmailing me."

"Blackmail . . . ?" Now it was Claire's turn to be surprised.

He nodded. "No one but Tanner and Mr. Garrett were supposed to know about my prison record. Don't know how, but Mrs. Garrett found out. She threatened to spread it all over town. Said she'd see me driven out of Brockton if I didn't keep my mouth shut. Claimed folks wouldn't take kindly to having a murderer in their midst."

No longer frightened, but curious, Claire asked, "What did you have to do in return?

"My job was to drop her off at one place or another, then come back and pick her up. If I mentioned word of her doin's to Mr. Garrett, she'd see to it I was run out of town. Never felt right keepin' it from Mr. Garrett, but I knew she'd make good her threat without battin' an eyelash."

Claire felt deflated by the admission. Instead of a murder confession, she had learned Tim had been a victim of blackmail. "And this is what you've been hiding all this time?"

"Yep." He set Gertie down and watched her wander off. "I seen the Garretts together often enough. I finally figured Mr. Garrett didn't give a tinker's dam what his wife did. Told myself, what's the harm? All the time, it's been eatin' away at me. Never felt right about what I did, but without a job, it's back to jail for me. I'd do 'most anything short of murder to keep from goin' back."

And Claire believed him. However, that brought her no closer to learning the truth. Tim had proved another dead end in the hunt for Priscilla's killer. She was grasping at straws to find the one responsible. God forgive her—first, her own brother, and now Tim O'Brien. "From what you've just said, it's clear Priscilla was meeting a lover. Do you know who he was?"

"Don't have a clue." Tim picked up the pitchfork and heaved hay into a stall. "Sneaky bastards, they were. Never saw the man."

Claire's shoulders slumped in defeat. "Think, Tim—is there anything else you can tell me?"

He paused to consider the matter. "They usually met during the day, mostly in the afternoons. Rarely at night. Makes me think he mighta been married with a wife at home."

There were dozens of married men who might have succumbed to Priscilla Garrett's wiles. Dejected, she started to turn away. "If you didn't kill her, and I know Cole didn't, who do you think did?"

She didn't realize she had spoken the words aloud until she heard Tim reply. "Asked myself the same question a dozen times," he said, "but never came up with an answer."

She turned back to him, placed a hand on his arm. "Forgive me, Tim, for everything I said earlier. I've done you a grave injustice."

He smiled for the first time that afternoon. A small, bitter twist of his lips, but a smile just the same. "Make no nevermind. I'm used to people thinkin' the worst."

If anything, she felt even more guilty for the things she had said to him. "If it helps to know, Cole's faith in you never wavered. I should have listened to what he was trying to tell me. I just can't bear the thought of Cole spending the rest of his life in prison."

Tim folded his hands on top of the pitchfork and gave her a knowing look. "Love 'im that much, do you?"

A denial sprang to the tip of her tongue. For an instant she thought of hiding behind Daisy, claiming she was worried about the child's future without a father. But why lie? Tim had easily guessed her secret. Was it so obvious that others knew as well?

"Garrett's a lucky man, havin' a woman like you in his corner. Wish I could have been more help, but all I know is Mrs. Garrett went to a lot of trouble so no one would find out who she was seein'. Figure it musta been somebody important. Or maybe somebody who already had a wife."

Despair nipped at her spirit with razor-sharp teeth. The sky had grown overcast since her talk with Tim. The leaves were turning their backsides to the wind. A sure sign of rain, Claire knew. Since it was still too early to report to work at Mulligan's, she decided to pay a call on Alma Dobbs. Alma, like Tim, must know many of Priscilla's secrets. Maybe for Cole's sake she could be cajoled into sharing a few of them. It was worth a try.

Though she had never been there, Claire knew Alma and her husband Harold occupied a small home on Fourth Street. A neighbor directed her to a single-story house built in the Greek Revival style. A pot of purple petunias bloomed by the door. Claire spotted a flash of red as a cardinal flitted through the branches of an elm tree in the front yard.

Going up the steps, she knocked on the front door. She waited patiently, but no one answered. She had almost decided no one was home when she finally heard someone coming. The door was opened by a wizened gnome of a man leaning heavily on a gnarled walking stick. The man's hands were grotesquely deformed with rheumatism. But in spite of his affliction, he sported a friendly smile.

"I—I'm not sure if I'm at the correct address. I'm looking for Alma Dobbs."

"You're in the right place, dear. Come in, sit a spell." He stood aside for Claire to enter. "Alma should be here shortly. She mentioned stopping at the market on her way home."

"If you're sure you don't mind."

"Nothing I love better than company. It gets lonely here by myself while she's working. I'm Harold, Alma's husband of thirty-odd years. Now, who might you be?"

She followed him into a tiny parlor crammed with overstuffed chairs and a settee. Every conceivable surface was draped with crocheted doilies or fringed paisley. Pictures of stern-faced ancestors in heavy wood frames hung suspended from the moldings with silken cords. "I'm Claire, Mr. Dobbs. Claire Sorenson."

"Ah, I thought so. Alma said you were a comely young miss." He lowered himself slowly and painfully into a sturdy chair, then drew his legs up on an ottoman. He held up his hands with the misshapen knuckles for her to see. "I'd offer you tea, but I'm not much use in the kitchen these days."

"That's quite all right." She sat on the settee, her hands in her lap. Harold Dobbs was hardly the ogre she expected to find, based on Alma's comments. "I hope my dropping by uninvited won't interfere with your dinner," she said, recalling that Alma insisted Harold demanded his meals served promptly.

"Not at all." He waved aside her concern with a broad grin. "Alma always likes to sit for a spell after coming home from a day's work. She often brings dinner from the Garretts' so all she has to do is heat it up a bit. Neither of us is fussy about what time we take our supper. We enjoy our time together."

Claire smiled weakly. Interesting, she thought. Apparently all this time it was Alma, not her husband, who made the rule about leaving promptly at six o'clock.

"My Alma is sure fond of little Daisy," Harold said conversationally. "Said she's smart as a steel trap. Bet you miss her something fierce. Alma said you were like a mother to her. She hated to see you leave."

Claire felt a warm glow of pleasure at hearing Alma considered her a good nursemaid. Especially knowing that she had once protested Claire wasn't fit to watch the child. Even more amazing, however, was the housekeeper's proclaimed fondness for Daisy. "I must have been mistaken," she said, choosing her words with care. "All this time, I had the impression Alma didn't like babies."

"Alma? Not like babies?" Harold chuckled. "Gracious, no."

"Really?"

"You betcha. Why, if we could've had our way, we would have had a flock of our own. But," he added, the smile fading from his eyes, "things don't always work out the way you think. As it was, we only had one."

Harold Dobbs was delivering one surprise after another. Claire leaned back on the settee. "You and Mrs. Dobbs have a child?"

Harold nodded slowly. "Had a child . . . a girl. Little Sarah Jane. Not much older than the Garrett baby when we lost her."

"I'm so sorry," Claire murmured. "I had no idea."

His eyes took on a faraway look. "The wife doesn't talk about it much. Still blames herself for what happened."

"I'm sure whatever happened, it wasn't her fault. I would think Mrs. Dobbs made a very conscientious mother."

"Couldn't of asked for better," Harold stated with quiet conviction. "To this day, Alma can't stand being around infants for fear of accidentally doing something that might harm them."

Claire took a moment to digest this last tidbit of information Harold had fed her. *Alma was afraid she might harm the baby?* This explained why she kept her distance from Daisy. And, on one occasion, ignored her to the point of neglect. Claire shook her head in bewilderment. "I never would have guessed."

"Babies scare the daylights out of her."

"What happened to Sarah Jane?" Claire asked quietly.

"The wife put her down for the night. Next morning we found the baby dead in her crib. Alma can't get it out of her head she did something wrong. Nothing rips you up inside like losing a child."

Claire blinked back tears. She hadn't meant to dredge up sad memories. She wished she knew a magic formula to erase the pain etched across his wizened features. At times like this, words were a hollow echo of sympathy. Leaning closer, she placed her hand on his arm and squeezed gently. "I'm so sorry."

Before Harold could respond, the door opened and Alma sailed in with a cloth shopping bag looped over one arm. Her forehead creased into a frown at finding Claire in her parlor. "My, this is a surprise. What's the occasion?"

"Hello, sweetums," Harold greeted his wife with obvious affection. "Claire and I are just getting acquainted."

"I hope I'm not intruding." Claire jumped to her feet, uncertain of her reception. "I was hoping we could talk."

"Talk?" Alma's round face mirrored her suspicion. "About what?"

Claire took a deep breath and went straight to the heart of the matter. "Surely, Alma, you know as well as I do that Cole Garrett didn't kill his wife."

Alma settled her shopping bag on a small table. "The police don't seem to think he's innocent. Not after finding a peavey hook hidden in a shed behind the sawmill with blood all over it."

"He's a good man, Alma. You can't think him capable of such violence."

"I'm ready for a cup of tea." Having said that, Alma turned and marched toward what Claire assumed was the kitchen.

Harold caught Claire's eye and motioned for her to follow his wife. "Go," he whispered. "All she needs is a bit of coaxing."

Claire flashed him a quick smile of gratitude, then hurried after Alma. She found her in the tiny kitchen, busily filling a teakettle. "Alma, you know full well I was at the Garrett house at the time Priscilla was killed. There's no possibility Cole would have murdered her. Please, I'm begging you to help me find the truth."

Her lips pursed, Alma measured tea into a china pot. Then she sighed so deeply her ample bosom rose and fell. "Cole Garrett proved a better husband than Priscilla deserved. Fond as I was of her, she wasn't an easy one to live with. What do you want to know?"

"Tell me about Priscilla. Everything points to the fact that she was seeing someone. Do you have any idea who he was?"

Alma shrugged. "Men were a challenge, a game to Priscilla. The more dangerous, the better she liked it."

"Did she ever get careless, mention a name?"

"A couple times she confided in me, named names, but not this time. This time was different."

"Then you asked her?"

"'Course I did, but she clammed up on me. Told me to mind my own business."

Now it was Claire's turn to sigh. Another dead end, just like with Tim. "Tim seems to think the man she was having an affair with might be married," she ventured.

"Wouldn't surprise me none." Alma set out a sugar bowl, then poured cream into a matching pitcher. "Priscilla was partial to men her father wouldn't approve of. Only she got caught once."

"She became pregnant."

Alma nodded. "There was a time, just before that, when she seemed genuinely happy. But next thing I knew, she was havin' a baby, and her father was hellbent on her marryin' Mr. Garrett. To this day, Leonard Brock doesn't want anything to do with little Daisy. Never even came to 'er christenin'."

"I've often wondered at his attitude."

"Pigheaded, coldhearted man." Alma clucked her tongue. "Blames a poor little baby for everythin' bad that's happened to Priscilla."

Claire caught her lower lip between her teeth. Was Alma referring to Nils? If not for a freak accident, both their lives might have turned out quite differently.

"Wish I could help, but all I know for sure is Priscilla went to great lengths to keep the man's name a secret. Said if I knew, I wouldn't approve, and she wasn't in the mood for one of my lectures."

Claire declined to stay for tea. After thanking Alma, she said good-bye to Harold and left, no closer to solving the puzzle.

Clouds the hue of tarnished silver blotted out the sun. Twilight descended earlier than usual. Claire slowly walked toward downtown. All the shops were locked for the night. Main Street was virtually deserted. Seeing this only added to her sense of isolation. Cole was right. She wasn't equipped for detective work. Her sleuthing had confirmed what she already suspected—Priscilla had been having an affair. And probably with someone already married. She couldn't get rid of the feeling that if she found the lover, she would find the murderer.

Glancing up, she sighted City Hall standing in solitary splendor across the street. Since it was still too early to begin work at Padraig Mulligan's bar, she decided to prevail upon Cole's jailers to allow her a brief visit. At the back of City Hall, she descended a short flight of stairs, taking her below ground level. Bracing herself to beg if necessary, she pushed open the heavy door. She found the policeman who had arrested Cole with his legs propped on a scarred desk sipping coffee and reading the Brockton *Gazette*.

"Guess it won't do no harm," he said after hearing her request. "Follow me."

Claire followed him through a doorway and down a short corridor with two jail cells on either side. Except for Cole, the jail was empty. The walls shrunk around her. The air smelled of musk and mold and despair.

"Ten minutes is all. Don't wanna get in trouble over this." The policeman ambled off, accompanied by the jingle of keys at his waist.

Cole rose from his bunk where a tray of food sat untouched. His eyes lit upon seeing her. "Claire . . ." There was a wealth of emotion in that single word.

She swallowed hard against the lump in her throat. Her heart twisted at the sight of him. Even with his clothes rumpled and dark stubble covering his jaw, he still had the power to stir her blood.

He curled his hands around the bars of his cell and gave her a heart-stopping smile. "Ah, sweetheart, what are you doing here? You shouldn't be in a place like this."

She drank in every aspect of his appearance. He looked tired, haggard. He still wore the same clothes he had on yesterday when arrested. His once immaculately starched white shirt was wilted and none too fresh. His dark hair was hopelessly mussed, no doubt from raking his fingers through it countless times. But it was the desolate look in his eyes that gave her pause. They were the stark, bleak gray of a wintery landscape. Needing to touch, needing a connection, she curved her fingers around his. "I had to come."

He seemed just as thirsty to see her as she was him. "Have I ever told you how pretty you are? You light up a room whenever you enter." His lips twisted into a wry smile. "Even a place like this."

"Have I neglected to tell you that you're the most handsome man I've ever seen?" She gave him a wistful smile. "Aren't we a pair?"

For a long minute, they were content simply to gaze into each other's eyes and take solace with what they found there. Then, recalling they had only a short time together, Claire knew she had to make every minute count. She cleared her throat. "Tomorrow I'll ask Tim to bring you a change of clothes along with your razor." She nearly faltered before adding, "I stopped to talk with him this afternoon."

"How many times do I have to tell you he's not involved with Priscilla's death." The reproof sounded more weary than angry.

"He told me Priscilla was blackmailing him."

"What?"

Claire rushed on. "Somehow she found out about his prison record. She threatened to make it public, knowing he'd be driven out of town once people found out he killed a man."

Cole uttered a curse. His fingers tightened around the bars.

"In exchange for her silence, Tim agreed to take her wherever and whenever she went to meet her lover. He was terrified that without a job, he'd be returned to prison. I believe him when he said he didn't kill her."

"No, I can't believe he did, either."

"Afterwards I went to visit Alma." She spoke rapidly, knowing there wasn't much time. "Alma said Priscilla was exceptionally secretive about her lover's identity. Everything I've learned so far points to the fact that the man is most likely married. I don't know where else to turn. Cole, do you have any idea who it could be?"

He rested his forehead against the bars of his cell and closed his eyes. "For a time I thought there might be something between Priscilla and James Lamont, but I never had any proof."

"The husband of her best friend . . . ?"

He opened his eyes and shrugged. "Priscilla and Sophie weren't always on the best of terms. It wasn't until shortly before Daisy's birth that they mended their friendship."

"I remember Alma saying something to that effect. She said James had been courting Priscilla, then Sophie's father died suddenly."

"And she came into a rather large inheritance."

They looked at each other. "Are you thinking the same thing I am?" Claire asked in a hushed tone. "But if we're right and they were lovers, why would James kill her?"

"Who knows? Maybe he wanted to leave her. Maybe she was the one who had grown restless and wanted to end it. They might have argued and in the heat of passion, the unthinkable happened."

Claire felt a flood of optimism drown lingering doubts. "I'm going to have to call on Mr. James Lamont and see what I can find out."

With a sudden movement, he twisted his arm and captured her wrist. "You'll do nothing of the kind. Promise me you'll stay away from him."

"Cole, it's our only chance."

The grip on her wrist tightened. "He's dangerous, Claire. There's no telling what he might do if cornered."

"Time's up," the policeman called from the end of the corridor.

Claire used the timely interruption to jerk free from Cole's grasp. She hurriedly left the jail with the sound of Cole shouting her name.

TWENTY-SIX

"Are you sure you want to go through with this, Sis?"

"I'm positive." It had taken Claire until the next day to implement her plan. But now everything was in place. There would be no turning back.

Nils struggled to keep pace beside her as they wound their way through the back streets of town. "As much as I hate to admit it, for once I agree with Garrett. This idea of yours is dangerous."

"That's why I'm taking you along," she returned without breaking stride. "You're my insurance. My protection."

He gave a bitter laugh. "Some protection I am. What do you expect me to do if things get out of hand? Beat Lamont over the head with my cane?"

"If that's what it takes, yes, by all means."

"There's no reasoning with you when you're like this," Nils grumbled.

"On the contrary, I'm being quite reasonable."

"That's not how I see it."

"We've been over this before, Nils. I'm safe as long as you're with me. All you have to do is keep hidden from view and eavesdrop on my conversation with James Lamont. If he should reveal he was Priscilla's lover—or killer—then I need you to repeat what you heard to Chief Tanner. Everyone knows how much you hate Cole. You certainly would never lie to protect him."

"I still think you're crazy."

"Maybe I am," she said with a grim smile. "Blame it on the full moon."

They lapsed into silence.

The sawmill, a dark hulk of a building, came into view as they neared the end of River Street. Claire's steps slowed. All work there had ceased with Cole's arrest. The place was virtually deserted. The moonlight gave the scene an eerie, ghostly appearance. But even as those thoughts flitted through her mind, clouds floated across the moon's shiny surface, leaving shadows in their wake. Unless James had something to hide, why would he select such a secluded spot for their rendezvous? A spot not only secluded, but the site of Priscilla's murder. She shuddered at the thought.

"It isn't too late to change your mind." Nils seemed to be having second thoughts as well.

"Do you want to find out who killed Priscilla or not?" she retorted. "You said you loved her. If so, then you must want to see the guilty party punished."

The numerous stacks of lumber in the yard surrounding the mill provided a perfect hiding place. "This gives me the creeps," Nils whispered. He reached inside his jacket and pulled out a bottle.

Claire shot her brother a quelling look. "You don't need your wits addled with drink."

He scowled, but replaced the bottle without sampling it first. "Don't start preaching."

"Wait here. After you see James arrive, move close enough to hear what he says, but not so close that he knows you're present."

"Where will you be?" Both of them spoke in whispers.

"The note said to meet him inside, near the stairs leading to Cole's office."

"It's dark as pitch in there. Sure you can find your way?"

"If my instincts are right, the stairway isn't the only thing I'm going to find before this night is over." Claire left him concealed amidst skids of lumber before he had a chance to lodge any more protests.

She stood just inside the huge building and let her eyes adjust to the dim light. Moonlight filtered weakly through windows set high in the walls. She was able to discern the bulky shapes of machinery, saws and such, that snoozed on the floor like sleeping giants.

The waiting for James Lamont to arrive stretched her nerves until they felt ready to snap. She had sent a note earlier, requesting he meet with her to discuss a delicate matter that required the utmost privacy. She intended to begin their discussion by asking him to explain why Priscilla had delegated Cole to oversee Daisy's trust fund. Next, she planned to lead him into a conversation about Priscilla and just how well they knew each other. Once she was certain he was Priscilla's lover, she would go to Tanner with the information and demand a thorough investigation. She hoped the man would admit Cole wasn't the only one who might have had reason to want Priscilla dead. He might even acknowledge she had been telling the truth all along about Cole's whereabouts that fateful night.

A world of maybes. A universe of what-ifs. A galaxy of uncertainty.

A night breeze whispered through the rafters. The floorboards creaked and groaned. Every sound seemed magnified. Sinister. Claire found herself jumping at her own shadow. Then, after what seemed like hours but in actuality was only minutes, she heard muffled footfalls.

She whirled around just as a figure separated itself from the shadows and slowly advanced toward her.

Claire braced herself for her confrontation. She only hoped Nils had seen Lamont arrive and was close behind. As the shadowy form drew nearer, Claire gasped in surprise. It wasn't a man, but a woman wearing a long cloak.

"Sophie!" she cried as the hooded figure stepped from the darkness and into a patch of moonlight.

"I see you received my message."

Claire's hand flew to her chest. Still not recovered from her initial fright, Sophie's words failed to register at first. "You gave me quite a scare. What are you doing here?"

"James never received your note, I'm afraid. I decided to meet you instead."

Puzzled, Claire shook her head. "But why?"

"You've become a nuisance, dear Claire. And, as if Cole weren't enough for you, now you have designs on my husband."

Claire laughed. "Surely you can't be serious. I'm not interested in James. I only wanted to ask him a few questions."

Sophie's expression remained bland. "I don't believe you. Regardless, James *is* interested in you. I've seen how he looks at you when he thinks no one is watching. It's only a matter of time before he makes his intentions known. He assumes you and Cole were lovers. That makes you more intriguing than ever."

Claire felt increasingly uneasy. Though appearing outwardly calm, the woman's thinking was illogical. Claire suddenly wanted to get as far away from this dark, isolated building as possible. Knowing Nils was nearby helped keep a tight rein on her escalating fear. "Sophie, why don't we go somewhere and talk about this. Perhaps over a nice cup of hot tea?"

"Tea will have to wait until later," Sophie replied quietly. "First I have work that needs to be done. As I said before, you've become a nuisance. And I'm afraid as such you must be eliminated."

"Eliminated?" Claire felt as though all the oxygen had left her lungs.

"You're ruining all my plans," Sophie said, her voice calm. "I simply can't allow that to happen."

The woman was mad. Claire couldn't believe what she was hearing. Thank goodness she had had the foresight to ask Nils to accompany her. Where was he, anyway? She looked past Sophie's shoulder, expecting to see him appear at any moment.

Sophie bestowed a parody of a smile on Claire. "No use looking for your brother to come to your rescue."

"Why? What have you done to him?" Claire took an involuntary step forward, only to freeze when Sophie withdrew a small pistol from beneath her cloak and pointed it at her.

"Poor Nils." Sophie clucked her tongue sympathetically. "He's liable to have a horrible headache when he finally regains consciousness and finds you gone. No one will believe the ranting of a drunk if he tries to explain what happened."

"Nils hasn't been drinking," Claire contradicted with more conviction than she felt. "He'll make people listen."

"After I hit him over the head, I took the precaution of pouring some of his own whiskey over him. People will think he had too much to drink, fell, and struck his head. In his condition, it's no wonder he's not making sense. Now," Sophie motioned with the pistol, "I think we had best be on our way before he wakes up."

Claire made one last, desperate attempt to reason with her. "Sophie, if you're doing all this for James, it isn't necessary. If he was responsible for Priscilla's death, the authorities will take everything into account. He's a well-respected member of the community. I'm sure they're prepared to be lenient."

"James?" Sophie looked startled. "Why, James didn't kill Priscilla, dear. I did."

"Why not just admit you killed your wife, Garrett." Tanner shoved a sheet of paper across the desk. "Make a confession, then sign your name. Have it over and done with."

A muscle ticked in Cole's jaw as he stared at the blank page. A short time ago he had been escorted to the chief of police's office where his left wrist had been manacled to the arm of a chair. Tanner sat behind his desk, impeccably groomed, his thinning hair slicked to his scalp, his mustache neatly clipped. "You're wasting your breath, Tanner, if you think I'm going to confess to a crime I'm not guilty of."

"Nothing to gain by putting off the inevitable." Tanner played with the polished stone paperweight atop a stack of files. "Any court in the country will convict you on the basis of the evidence alone."

"Is that right?" Cole shifted in the uncomfortable wooden chair, causing the chain at his wrist to rattle. "How many times do I have to tell you? I have no idea how that peavey hook came to be in the shed below my office."

"A mystery, eh? Magic?"

"I didn't put it there."

"And someone else did, I suppose." Tanner's lean face could have been chiseled in granite. Hard, unyielding, implacable.

"That's the only explanation I can come up with. You're the expert. You make the deductions"

"Pretty flimsy explanation, in my opinion."

"Think about it, Tanner. Certainly it must have occurred to you that this so-called murder weapon was a little too easy to find. I'm not stupid. Don't you think if I had killed Priscilla, I would have been smart enough not to hide incriminating evidence on my own property?"

Tanner scowled, but remained silent.

"By the way, how *did* you know just where to look after all this time?"

"We got an anonymous note telling us where to look."

"And in your bold pursuit of justice, it had never dawned on you until then to search the shed near the spot Priscilla's body was found?"

"Of course we did," Tanner snapped irritably.

Cole pressed on. "Then why didn't you find it sooner?"

Tanner's mouth firmed into a hard line beneath his luxurious mustache. "We just didn't, is all. Must of been overlooked."

"Until a mysterious note told you where to find it?" Cole scoffed. "I'm no detective, but it seems to me that if you find the person who sent the note, you'll find the killer. But then, you're not really interested in justice, are you? All you want is to please the man who put you in office."

"Enough!" Tanner leapt to his feet, his face red.

A loud, irate voice penetrated the tension. "I don't give a tinker's damn what he's doing!"

A commotion in the hallway outside the office caused both men to turn toward the door just as Padraig Mulligan stormed through. The burly bar owner shook off Homer Bailey like a pesky fly.

"Told 'im you were busy, Chief." Bailey spoke his piece, then ducked out before Tanner could issue a reprimand.

"No one makes a fool of Padraig Mulligan. I'm here to press charges," he said, leaning close to Tanner's face. "If she can't show up for work like she promised, I'm taking her brother to task."

"You're not making sense, Mulligan. Who the devil are you talking about?"

"Claire Sorenson." Mulligan's ruddy face turned even ruddier. "If she's not here, then where the hell is she?"

Cole surged to his feet, only to be jerked back into his seat by the handcuff at his wrist. "What business is it of yours where she is?" he demanded, angry and frustrated. And more than a little anxious. *God, had something happened to Claire?*

Mulligan noticed Cole for the first time. "What business is it of mine? Because she works for me, is why," he said with more than a trace of belligerence. "She agreed to work off her brother's debt. I took her at her word. Now I'm a laughingstock. Figured she was probably down here, Garrett, holding your hand."

Cole lifted his chained wrist. "Well, Mulligan, as you can see, she's not."

"Hey, you can't just barge in . . ." Homer Bailey's protest was cut short.

Bleeding profusely from a gash on the head and reeking of cheap whiskey, Nils staggered into the room. "He took her. She's gone, and I don't know where."

Tanner's lip curled in disgust. "You're drunk as a skunk, Sorenson."

Nils leaned on the desk to steady himself. "You've got to listen to me."

"Go home, Sorenson. Sleep it off," Tanner advised.

"Claire's in trouble."

"Trouble!" Cole and Mulligan exclaimed in unison.

Cole's mouth went dry with fear. "What sort of trouble?"

"We've got to stop him," Nils insisted doggedly.

"Sit down man, before you fall down." Mulligan shoved a chair at him, and Nils sank into it gratefully. "Now suppose you tell us what happened."

"I'll ask the questions, if you don't mind." Tanner shot Mulligan a dismissive glance and took over. "All right, Sorenson. Tell us your tale, then get the hell out of my office."

Mulligan disregarded Tanner's edict. "What happened to your head, Nils?"

Nils winced as he touched the back of his head. "Someone crept up on me from behind, then tried to bash my skull in."

Tanner snorted in disbelief. "More likely you fell down drunk and hit your head. The blow scrambled your brain."

"I'm telling you my sister is in trouble," Nils insisted, his voice thready with panic. "We've got to find her. He'll kill her."

Cole strained against his fetter. "For the love of God, man, what are you talking about? Who's got Claire?"

Mulligan calmly handed Nils a handkerchief, which he

pressed against the bloody gash at the back of his head. "Take a breath, lad, then start at the beginning."

Nils drew a shaky breath and let it out. Fear swam in his eyes as he gazed into the faces of his audience. "Claire came up with this wild idea. I tried to talk her out of it, but she wouldn't listen. She sent a note to James Lamont asking him to meet with her. He wrote back, telling her to be at the sawmill promptly at nine o'clock."

"Lamont . . ." Cole breathed the name.

"Claire persuaded me into coming along for protection. She had a bunch of questions she needed answered. Wanted me as a witness in case he admitted killing Priscilla." Nils gave Tanner an accusing look. "She knew you'd never believe her, but you might believe me, knowing Garrett and I are at odds."

Tanner flushed and glanced away.

"Some protection I turned out to be." Nils gave a harsh laugh, then flinched and held a hand to his head. "I was waiting for Lamont behind a skid of lumber. Next thing I know, my head feels like it's been split in two, and there's no sign of Claire. She'd never go off and leave like that unless . . ." His voice cracked.

Cole leaned forward. He could barely think past the terror clawing at him. "Nils is right, Chief. We've got to find her."

Tanner studied Cole skeptically. "What's Lamont got to do with any of this?"

"Everything points to him as Priscilla's lover. Who else but a lover would she have been meeting the night she was killed? Think about it, Tanner. It wouldn't be the first time a lover's quarrel ended with one or the other dead."

Mulligan's meaty hands bunched into fists. "We're wastin' time. Let's go after the bastard."

Still Tanner hesitated.

Cole had reached the limits of his endurance. His fingers curled around the arms of the chair he was chained to, the knuckles white as they pressed into the wood. "If anything happens to Claire, Tanner, do you want it made public that it was because you were too much of a coward to stop it?"

Animosity crackled in the room. Finally, Tanner dropped his gaze. "Very well, Garrett. But when I bring her back all safe and sound, I expect your signed confession. Do we have a deal?"

"Deal," Cole returned, his voice clipped. "Take me with you. We might not have much time."

Tanner snorted. "I'd have to be crazy to release a prisoner for a wild-goose chase. This is a matter for the police."

Mulligan, Nils, and Cole watched as the police chief issued orders to the pair of policemen on duty. Bailey was to ride to the Sorensons' to see if Claire might have returned home. The second was dispatched to the Garrett house, where she used to work. Picking up his hat, Tanner himself set out to find James Lamont, all the while complaining about the likelihood he'd find him at the city council meeting.

A weighty silence engulfed the trio who remained behind. Mulligan shuffled his feet, then came to a conclusion. Reaching into his jacket, he pulled out a pocket knife and extracted a small gadget. Using the wirelike device, he unlocked the handcuff securing Cole's wrist. "A little trick I learned in Dublin," he muttered. "Tanner couldn't find a chamber pot in the dark."

The instant he was freed, Cole bounded from the chair. "Let's spread out and pray we find Claire before it's too late."

Mulligan and Nils didn't need further encouragement.

Sophie seemed in no particular hurry. Claire tried to engage her in conversation, stalling for time in the hope Nils would regain consciousness and sound the alarm about her disappearance. Although, she wondered bleakly, who would think to find her inside the darkened Lamont home? She and Sophie hadn't encountered a single person on their way from the sawmill. Once inside the house, Sophie had taken the precaution of not lighting a lamp. Instead she chose to rely on the moonlight filtering through the windows and her familiarity with her own home.

"Are you the one who made up that story about a murder weapon?" Claire asked, knowing her voice trembled and despising the fact.

"It was ridiculously simple." Sophie laughed, delighted at her own cleverness. "A little blood from last night's liver on one of those nasty hooks. Then a little note to Mr. Tanner. Child's play."

Claire kept her gaze trained on Sophie. The woman's eyes were flat and emotionless like those of a dead trout. "Why did you kill Priscilla?"

"'Kill' is such a strong word, isn't it?" Sophie smiled vacantly. "I never intended to hurt her. I prefer to think of her death as an unpleasant accident."

"Did you hate her that much?"

"Kill? Hate?" Sophie laughed. "There you go again, dear. Such a passionate choice of words."

"Did you?" Gazing into Sophie's eyes, Claire wondered how she had been fooled for so long. The woman who had befriended her was nothing more than an empty shell. Normal in every appearance on the outside, but completely void of conscience. The concept terrified her.

Sophie advanced a step, the pistol leveled at Claire. "Priscilla turned greedy. She wanted James to run away with her. I couldn't let that happen, you see."

"So you killed her?"

Sophie shrugged. "It was just a little shove. It wasn't my fault she fell backward onto one of those nasty hooks the lumberjacks use."

Claire shuddered at the thought of Priscilla's violent end.

"Of course," Sophie continued conversationally, "I

couldn't tell anyone what happened. I do have my social standing to consider. So when everyone assumed Cole was responsible, I simply let them go on thinking that. I wasn't about to go to prison for something that was really all Priscilla's fault."

"Why are you determined to kill me? I explained that I have no interest in your husband. It's Cole I love."

"Keep moving toward the stairs," Sophie directed. "That's good," she said as they crossed the foyer toward the winding staircase. "I noticed how you looked at Cole during the river drive. That just wouldn't do. You see, I planned that after Cole was sent to prison, I'd prevail upon James to adopt Daisy. We've been trying to have a baby for years, but without success. If you and Cole married, however, all my effort would have been in vain. I tried to show my displeasure when I gave you those eclairs. I made sure they had been left out in the sun where the custard filling would spoil."

"You brought them knowing they would make me deathly ill?" Claire was constantly being shocked by the cunningness of Sophie's mind.

"Of course. You needed to be punished for interfering. Now," she ordered, "all the way to the third floor."

Claire mounted the stairs, one slow step at a time. "You won't get away with this, Sophie."

"I beg to differ with you. I've thought this through quite carefully. Your death will look like a suicide. I'll explain how distraught you were about losing Cole. That you fled up the stairs, determined to hurl yourself out the window. I tried to stop you, reason with you, but," she giggled, "I was too late."

Upwards they climbed. The second floor, the third.

"Don't try to wrestle the gun away from me," Sophie warned, anticipating Claire's thoughts. "At this range, I couldn't possibly miss."

"How would you explain bullet wounds? Or bloodstains

on the carpet?" Claire asked with more bravado than she felt.

"I'll simply tell Chief Tanner that you came here making wild charges about James. When I professed disbelief, you became enraged and attacked me. I was forced to defend myself the only way I could. No one will doubt my word. I can be quite convincing."

Claire swallowed her fear. "Sophie, please, don't do this."

"This is your fault, Claire, not mine. After we first met, I intended to ask you to stay on as Daisy's nursemaid. That is, until James became more interested in you than he should. Besides, you kept asking questions about Priscilla. You just wouldn't let the matter rest. Once Cole was sent to prison, life would have gone on as it was meant to, and Daisy would have grown up with me as her mother. Once you're no longer stirring up trouble, everything will still work out exactly as I planned."

The thought of Sophie as Daisy's mother helped Claire push past the panic. They had reached the third floor, part servants' quarters, part attic. Bright moonlight poured through the window, illuminating the attic with a silvery glow. Claire frantically looked around for an object with which to defend herself. A hump-backed trunk, a sewing machine, a dressmaker's dummy, discarded furniture. Nothing she could readily use to launch a defense.

"It's a bit stuffy in here, don't you think? Open the window, dear."

Open the window? So she can push me out? Claire's blood roared in her ears. Her heart seemed to gallop.

"Do it!" Sophie commanded. "Now."

With the gun a mere foot away, Claire turned and did as Sophie asked. A wave of dizziness washed over her at the sight of the ground far below. She imagined she saw figures move stealthily around the back of the house, but couldn't be sure if they were real or the product of a desperate desire to be rescued from a madwoman.

"We'll be such a happy family," Sophie prattled on. "I think Daisy looks exactly like James, don't you? You can't blame a man for wanting to father a child—even though I should have been her mother. Not Priscilla."

Claire straightened and cautiously inched away from the yawning window. She moistened her dry lips with the tip of her tongue. "James isn't Daisy's father."

For the first time that evening, Sophie's composure slipped.

TWENTY-SEVEN

"James not Daisy's father? What are you talking about?" Sophie demanded. "Of course he is."

Claire had no way of knowing for sure who Daisy's real father was, but she seized the moment to plant doubt in Sophie's mind. In the distance, she imagined she heard someone pound on a door. A door she distinctly remembered Sophie locking. Hope rekindled that help had arrived. She prayed it wasn't too late. All she had to do was keep Sophie talking. Distract her. Just a little while longer. "Priscilla was seeing someone else just before she became pregnant . . . and it wasn't James."

"That's a lie!" Sophie's thin veneer of sanity cracked and splintered before Claire's eyes. "You're doing it again," she accused shrilly. "You're deliberately trying to ruin my plans."

Lunging sideways, Sophie picked up a heavy poker in her left hand from a set of fire irons propped against a bookcase. Still clutching the gun in her right, she brandished the poker in front of Claire. "I won't allow you to spoil everything for me."

The pounding from downstairs became more insistent.

"Help!" Claire screamed, hoping her voice would carry. "Help! She's insane."

Upon hearing this, Sophie flew into a frenzy. Letting the gun drop to the floor, she gripped the poker with both hands and made broad, slashing motions in an effort to strike Claire.

Knowing any attempt to bend down and grab the pistol would be foolhardy, Claire concentrated instead on dodging the blows from the poker. She held up her arms to protect her face. The poker whistled by her ear, narrowly missing her head.

Again and again, the poker came perilously close. Step by step, Claire retreated, hoping to escape Sophie's furious attack. One blow would render her senseless. And she had no doubt that Sophie wouldn't stop after one. The woman had turned into a rabid animal bent on vengeance. Claire could barely think beyond the pounding of blood in her head.

"Claire!"

Nils's shout sounded through the open attic window. Footsteps pounded on the stairs. Someone, somehow, had gained access to the house and was coming to help.

Sophie chose that moment to rush at her. Wielding the weapon like a sword, she brought it crashing down. Claire dodged the blow, but lost her balance. Sophie jabbed the poker against Claire's shoulder as hard as she could and shoved.

Screaming, Claire tumbled backwards out the open window.

Cole watched in horror from the ground below as Claire slid down the steep pitch of the roof. His heart caught in his throat as he saw her claw wildly at the shingles in an attempt to stop her mad plummet. Her fingers caught the narrow cornice at the edge of the roof. She hung there suspended, arms straining, three stories above the ground.

"Claire!" he called. "Hold tight. Don't let go."

"Oh my God," Nils whimpered at seeing his sister dangling by her fingertips.

Sophie leaned out the window, the poker still in her hand, expecting to find her victim sprawled unmoving on the drive below. Instead she saw Claire clinging to the edge of the roof. "Die, you bitch!" she screeched. "Can't you be like Priscilla and just *die?*"

In one final attempt to eliminate the woman she deemed responsible for her problems, she brought the cast-iron rod crashing down. This time she caught Claire on the head. Claire's grip on the cornice relaxed, and she plunged toward the ground.

As Cole instinctively moved forward to break her fall, Claire's petticoat snagged on the wood molding separating the first and second floors. For a heart-stopping moment she hung there, a marionette on a string. Cole watched, along with others who had been drawn by the sound of her screams. Homer Bailey, his partner, Padraig Mulligan, and neighbors from up and down the street. All eyes were trained on the figure dangling above their heads.

All of Cole's senses were riveted on Claire. The fabric of her petticoat slowly gave way with a loud ripping sound. With a prayer on his lips, Cole rushed forward and caught her as she slipped the remaining distance. He sank to the ground from the force of the fall, her unconscious body cradled in his arms. The witnesses to his feat broke into an excited babble of voices.

Cole's hands shook as he smoothed back strands of hair from a face as pale as alabaster. A red trickle flowed from a deep gash on her scalp.

Nils knelt beside him, furiously blinking back tears. "Oh God, Sis, please be all right."

Claire's eyelids fluttered, then opened. With eyes dazed and unfocused, she stared into Cole's face; then, with a sigh, she lapsed back into unconsciousness.

"She's alive," Cole marveled, hugging her against his chest. His steel-gray eyes were suspiciously moist. "She's alive."

"No thanks to you," Nils snarled. "My sister nearly lost her life trying to save your worthless hide. She's too good for the likes of you. You don't deserve her."

Cole couldn't dispute Nils's claim. Claire had risked

everything for him. She was brave, loyal, loving. And he hadn't even had the courage to tell her he loved her. She could have died never knowing how he really felt. Nils was right—he didn't deserve her.

He glanced up in time to see Sophie Lamont escorted from the house, her husband on one side, a grim-faced Edward Tanner on the other. "You understand, don't you, James?" he heard her say. "I never meant to kill Priscilla. It was an accident. Her fault, really. And as for Claire, this was all her doing. She needed to stop interfering with my plans."

James placed his arm around his wife's shoulders. "It's all right, dear. I think it's time you have a nice, long rest in the country. Never fear, I'll take care of everything."

Cole rose to his feet with Claire in his arms. Nils, his face set, dared him to interfere when he took his sister from him. "She needs a doctor. If you want what's best for her, Garrett, you'll keep your distance."

Mulligan, who hovered close by, stepped up. "Here, Sorenson, hand 'er over. It's easier for someone with two good legs—quicker as well."

Cole stood in the moonswept yard while Padraig Mulligan marched off with Claire. Nils limped alongside him, doing his best to keep up. Cole felt hollow inside. Empty-handed, empty-hearted.

Once more he was forced to agree with Nils. What Claire needed most at the moment was medical attention, not two grown men fighting over her. With a sigh of resignation, he followed them toward Doc Wetherbury's.

Where Cole was concerned, the following day had twice as many hours as usual. That morning he had been summoned to Edward Tanner's office and officially informed that all charges against him had been dropped. He had run into Leonard Brock just as he was leaving. While his former father-in-law didn't tender an apology, he was civil when he told Cole of his plans for an extended stay abroad.

The remainder of the day had been spent at the sawmill trying to get things back into operation. He had been gratified to find his workers trickling back, some with hang-dog expressions, others exuding genuine good will that his name had been cleared. Even so, his life seemed a far cry from normal. Still seemed empty. Meaningless.

My sister nearly lost her life trying to save your worthless hide. Nils's words hummed through Cole's mind like an unfinished melody. Cole admitted he might not deserve a woman like Claire. But that didn't stop him from loving her. Missing her. Wanting her so badly he ached.

It was evening now. Though long past Daisy's bedtime, she was still wide awake—much to the chagrin of her nursemaid, Mabel Holland. Cole didn't mind in the least. So what if the attention he showered on his daughter was construed as spoiling her? The baby provided a welcome distraction from his gloomy thoughts.

"I've been thinking, Peanut," he said to Daisy as he walked the hall with her, "maybe it's time I tell Claire how I feel. Let her, not Nils, be the judge of whether I'm worthy or not. What do you think?"

Daisy grabbed his ear and twisted.

"Ouch!" Cole took out his gold pocket watch and used it to amuse the baby. "Should I go to Claire and tell her I love her? Then ask her to share the rest of her life with us?"

"Ba-babba!" Daisy tried to stuff the entire watch in her drooling mouth.

"I'll assume that's an enthusiastic yes," Cole chuckled. "I know kittens are nice, but what do you say about having the entire house filled with playmates? A brother or two? Maybe a baby sister?"

Tired of her father's watch, she let it drop on its fob and sucked her thumb instead. The expression on her tiny face could only be described as thoughtful.

"Not so sure if you're ready to be a big sister, eh?" He pressed a kiss to her curls. "I think it's time for me to leave you in Mrs. Holland's capable hands. I've got some proposing to do."

After handing Daisy over to Mrs. Holland and informing the woman he was going out, he left the house. Too impatient to wait for Tim, he saddled his horse himself and rode out of town.

All the way to Claire's house, he rehearsed what he would say and how he would say it. Once he found her, he wouldn't take no for an answer. Even if it took all night. All night, every night. Spending his nights with Claire was what he wanted most in all the world. Making love to her, loving her, being loved in return. His mighty ambitions had boiled down to just one thing: Claire. She was his heart, his soul. What had he been thinking to stay away even for a day?

Cole felt a jab of disappointment at finding the house dark. It never occurred to him that she might not be at home. He fully expected to find her still recuperating from last night's ordeal. He had waited outside Doc's long enough to learn her injuries weren't serious. The wound on her head required several stitches, but should heal nicely.

Urging his horse around to the back of the house, he saw a solitary light shining from the kitchen. Dismounting, he knocked on the door and found himself face-to-face with Lud Sorenson.

Lud grunted, then returned to the kitchen table and sat down. He stared morosely into the near-empty glass of whiskey in front of him. "Whaddaya want?" he growled.

Cole studied Lud's slovenly state with distaste. He marveled that Claire had sprung from such an environment, a lovely rose growing in rocky soil. "I've come for Claire."

"She's not here." Lud emptied his glass, belched. "She's workin'."

"Working . . . ? Where?"

Lud regarded him through bleary eyes. "In town. At Mulligan's, same as Nils."

"Claire works at Mulligan's Bar?" Cole cursed his faulty memory. He should have known as much from the Irishman's comments the night before when he had charged into Tanner's office, ready to press charges. So much had happened in the interim that he had simply forgotten.

Without another word, Cole left Lud to his drink and headed back toward town. How like Claire, he thought, to insist on paying her brother's debt. Too honorable to renege on her word. Too proud to ask for help.

Mulligan's Bar swarmed with activity. It was noisy, smoky, and full of rough-looking characters. Not the type of place he envisioned for Claire. Cole stood just inside the entrance, surveying the crowd, but saw no sign of Claire. He threaded his way through the throng to the bar. When he got closer, he spied Mulligan tending bar in shirtsleeves, a stub of a cigar clamped between his teeth. Nils, too, was behind the bar, filling a mug with beer.

All traces of affability vanished from Mulligan's ruddy face at spotting Cole. "What are you doing in this part of town, Garrett? This isn't your usual watering hole."

Nils was even less friendly. "I thought I told you last night to leave my sister alone. Like I've been reminding her all day, she's better off without your kind."

Cole bit back his temper. "And exactly what is 'my kind,' Sorenson?"

"You're the sort who needs to prove to the world that he's got the best money can buy. The biggest, the fanciest, most expensive. Claire doesn't fit your picture."

Cole leaned against the bar and took a sip from the mug Nils had just filled. "You know, it's rare, Nils, that we agree on things, but you're absolutely right. I do want only the best—and the best happens to be your sister. That is, if she'll have me."

The bar had grown quiet enough to hear a pin drop.

"Oh, she'll have you, all right. But only on one condition," said a female voice.

Cole swung around to discover Claire standing behind him. A smile bloomed on her face, lit from within. The world seemed to stop spinning on its axis; his heart ceased to beat. His entire future hinged on the answer to a single question. "And that condition is?"

"That you love me as much as I love you."

The world began to spin again, this time at a dizzying, breakneck speed. His heart pounded so furiously he thought it would explode. "Yes!" he cried exuberantly. Sweeping Claire off her feet, he spun around in circles. "Yes! Yes, of course I love you."

Claire hung on, her arms wrapped around his neck, laughing and crying at the same time.

Finally, Cole set her back on her feet. Framing her face between his hands, he looked deep into eyes that shimmered like the lake on a summer's day. "Marry me, Claire. Be my wife, my lover, the mother of my children. Be my life's partner. Grow old with me."

She nodded, too choked to speak.

He claimed her mouth for a long, leisurely kiss. A kiss that promised, pledged, cherished. A joining of hearts. When at last they broke apart, both were smiling. Cole swept Claire up in his arms and triumphantly started through the crowd of interested spectators. Her cheeks a becoming pink, Claire buried her face in the curve of his neck.

Padraig Mulligan began to clap his hands. Others joined in the applause. Soon the barroom rang with cheers and well-wishes.

Even Nils relented upon seeing Claire's obvious joy. "Drinks are on me, fellas," he called out. "Looks like my little sister's getting married."

Cole nudged the door of the bar closed behind them. Overhead, stars sparkled like jewels in the night sky. The future glowed with promise. A peacefulness such as nothing he had ever experienced invaded his soul. And all because of the woman he held against his heart.

"I love you, Claire. I want your face to be the last thing I see every night before I fall asleep, and," he brushed a soft kiss across her mouth, "the first thing I see when I awake . . . just before daybreak."

DO YOU HAVE THE HOHL COLLECTION?

__Another Spring 0-8217-7155-8	$6.99US/$8.99CAN
__Compromises 0-8217-7154-X	$6.99US/$8.99CAN
__Ever After 0-8217-5660-5	$5.99US/$7.50CAN
__Something Special 0-8217-6725-9	$5.99US/$7.50CAN
__Maybe Tomorrow 0-8217-6054-8	$5.99US/$7.50CAN
__Never Say Never 0-8217-6379-2	$5.99US/$7.50CAN
__Silver Thunder 0-8217-6200-1	$5.99US/$7.50CAN

Call toll free **1-888-345-BOOK** to order by phone or use this coupon to order by mail. ALL BOOKS AVAILABLE DECEMBER 1, 2000.

Name_____
Address _____
City _____ State _____ Zip _____
Please send me the books I have checked above.
I am enclosing $_____
Plus postage and handling* $_____
Sales tax (in NY and TN) $_____
Total amount enclosed $_____
*Add $2.50 for the first book and $.50 for each additional book.
Send check or money order (no cash or CODs) to:
Kensington Publishing Corp., Dept. C.O., 850 Third Avenue, New York, NY 10022
Prices and numbers subject to change without notice. Valid only in the U.S.
All orders subject to availability. **NO ADVANCE ORDERS.**
Visit our web site at **www.kensingtonbooks.com**